EX LIBRIS

VINTAGE CLASSICS

ALMS FOR OBLIVION: VOLUME III

Simon Raven was perhaps known as much for his controversial behaviour as for his writing. Born on 28 December 1927, he grew up reading and studying the classics, translating them from Greek and Latin into English and vice-versa. He was expelled from Charterhouse School in 1945 for homosexual activities, having first been seduced at the age of nine by the games master (an experience he described as giving 'immediate and unalloyed pleasure') and went on to join the army. Following his National Service, Raven attended King's College, Cambridge to read English. Raven later returned to the army but was asked to resign rather than face a court-martial for 'conduct unbecoming'. It was at this point that he turned his focus to writing. The publisher Anthony Blond paid Raven to write and to move away from London to Deal, Kent. His works span a multitude of genres including fiction, drama, essays, memoirs and screenplays. Simon Raven died in May 2001, having written his own epitaph: 'He shared his bottle – and, when still young and appetising, his bed.'

OTHER WORKS BY SIMON RAVEN

Novels

The Feathers of Death
Brother Cain
Doctors Wear Scarlet
Close of Play
The Roses of Picardie
An Inch of Fortune
September Castle
The Troubadour

Alms for Oblivion sequence

The Rich Pay Late
Friends in Low Places
The Sabre Squadron
Fielding Gray
The Judas Boy
Places Where They Sing
Sound the Retreat
Come Like Shadows
Bring Forth the Body
The Survivors

Belles-Lettres

The English Gentleman
Boys Will Be Boys
The Fortunes of Fingel
The Old School

Plays

*Royal Foundation and
Other Plays*

Autobiography

Shadows on the Grass
The Old Gang
Bird of Ill Omen
Is There Anybody There?
Said the Traveller

First Born of Egypt sequence

Morning Star
The Face of the Waters
Before the Cock Crow
New Seed For Old
Blood of my Bone
In the Image of God

SIMON RAVEN

Alms For Oblivion

Volume III

Bring Forth the Body
The Survivors

VINTAGE BOOKS
London

Bring Forth the Body
First published in Great Britain by Blond & Briggs Ltd in 1974
Copyright © Simon Raven 1974

Places Where They Sing
First published in Great Britain by Blond & Briggs Ltd in 1976
Copyright © Simon Raven 1976

First published by Vintage 1999

Vintage
Random House, 20 Vauxhall Bridge Road,
London SW1V 2SA

www.vintage-classics.info

Addresses for companies within The Random House Group Limited
can be found at: www.randomhouse.co.uk/offices.htm

The Random House Group Limited Reg. No. 954009

A CIP catalogue record for this book
is available from the British Library

ISBN 9780099561347

The Random House Group Limited supports The Forest Stewardship
Council (FSC®), the leading international forest certification organisation.
Our books carrying the FSC label are printed on FSC® certified paper.
FSC is the only forest certification scheme endorsed by the leading
environmental organisations, including Greenpeace.
Our paper procurement policy can be found at:
www.randomhouse.co.uk/environment

MIX
Paper from
responsible sources
FSC® C016897

Printed and bound in Great Britain by Clays Ltd, St Ives Plc

Contents

PRINCIPAL CHARACTERS IN
ALMS FOR OBLIVION

The *Alms for Oblivion* sequence consists of ten novels. They are, in chronological order: *Fielding Gray* (FG), set in 1945; *Sound the Retreat* (SR), 1945–6; *The Sabre Squadron* (SS), 1952; *The Rich Pay Late* (RPL), 1955–6; *Friends in Low Places* (FLP), 1959; *The Judas Boy* (JB), 1962; *Places Where They Sing* (PWTS), 1967; *Come Like Shadows* (CLS), 1970; *Bring Forth the Body* (BFB), 1972; and *The Survivors* (TS), 1973.

What follows is an alphabetical list of the more important characters, showing in which of the novels they have each appeared and briefly suggesting their roles.

Albani, Euphemia: daughter of Fernando Albani *q.v.* (TS). Albani, Fernando: Venetial merchant of late 18th and early 19th centuries. Author of manuscripts researched by Fielding Gray *q.v.* in 1973 (TS).
Albani, Maria: wife to Femando (TS).
Albani, Piero: son of Fernando (TS). Not to be confused with the Piero *q.v.* of no known surname who lives with Lykiadopoulos in Venice in 1973 (TS).

Balliston, Hugh: an undergraduate of Lancaster College, Cambridge in 1967 (PWTS); retreats to a convent of Franciscan Friars near Venice, and is recognised in Venice by Daniel Mond in 1973 (TS).
Beatty, Miss: a secretary in the firm of Salinger & Holbrook (RPL). † 1956 (RPL).
Beck, Tony: a young Fellow of Lancaster College, well known as a literary critic (PWTS).
Beyfus, The Lord (life Peer): a social scientist, Fellow of Lancaster College (PWTS).
Blakeney, Balbo: a biochemist, Fellow of Lancaster College (PWTS); still a Fellow of Lancaster and present at Daniel Mond's funeral in 1973 (TS).

Blessington, Ivan: a school friend of Fielding Gray in 1945 (FG); later a regular officer in the 49th Earl Hamilton's Light Dragoons (Hamilton's Horse); ADC to his Divisional Commander in Germany in 1952 (SS); by 1955 an attaché at the British Embassy in Washington (RPL); by 1972 retired from the army and working at high level for a prominent merchant bank (BFB); pensioned off from the bank for indiscretion in 1973 (TS).

von Bremke, Herr Doktor Aeneas: a prominent mathematician at the University of Göttingen (SS).

Brockworthy, Lieutenant-Colonel: Commanding Officer of the 1st Battalion, the Wessex Fusiliers, at Berhampore in 1946 (SR).

Bunce, Basil: Squadron Sergeant-Major of the 10th Sabre Squadron of Earl Hamilton's Light Dragoons at Göttingen in 1952 (SS), and on Santa Kytherea in 1955 (FG); present at Daniel Mond's funeral in 1973 (TS).

Bungay, Piers: Subaltern officer of the 10th Sabre Squadron at Göttingen in 1952 (SS).

Buttock Mrs Tessie: owner of Buttock's Hotel in the Cromwell Road (RPL, FLP, JB, CLS), a convenient establishment much favoured by Tom Llewyllyn and Fielding Gray *q.v.*

Canteloupe, The Marchioness (Molly): wife of The Marquis Canteloupe (FLP, SR).

CANTELOUPE, The Most Honourable the Marquis: father of The Earl of Muscateer (SR); distant cousin of Captain Detterling *q.v.* and political associate of Somerset Lloyd-James *q.v.*; successful operator of his 'Stately Home' and in 1959 Parliamentary Secretary for the Development of British Recreational Resources (FLP); Minister of Public Relations and Popular Media in 1962 (JB); Shadow Minister of Commerce in 1967 (PWTS); Minister of Commerce in the Conservative Government of 1970 (CLS); still Minister in 1972, though under heavy pressure (BFB). † 1973 (TS).

Carnavon, Angus: leading, male star in Pandarus/Clytemnestra Film Production of *The Odyssey* on Corfu in 1970 (CLS).

Carnwath, Doctor: a Cambridge don and historian; an old friend of Provost Constable, and a member of the Lauderdale Committee; † early 1950s (BFB).

Chead, 'Corpy': Corporal-Major (i.e. Colour Sergeant) of the 10th Sabre Squadron at Göttingen (SS); present at Daniel Mond's funeral in 1973 (TS).

Clewes, The Reverend Oliver: Chaplain to Lancaster College (PWTS).

CONSTABLE, Robert Reculver (Major): demobilised with special priority in the summer of 1945 to take up appointment as Tutor of Lancaster College, Cambridge (FG); by 1955 Vice-Chancellor of the University of Salop, and *ex officio* member of the Board of *Strix* (RPL); elected Provost of Lancaster in 1959 (FLP); still Provost in 1962 (JB) and 1967 (PWTS) and 1972 (BFB); ennobled as Lord Constable of Reculver Castle in 1973 (TS).

Corrington, Mona: an anthropologist, Fellow of Girton College, Cambridge. Chum of Lord Beyfus *q.v.* (PWTS).

Cruxtable, Sergeant-Major: Company Sergeant-Major of Peter Morrison's Company at the O.T.S., Bangalore, in 1945–6 (SR); 'P.T. expert' at Canteloupe's physical fitness camp in the west country (FLP).

DETTERLING, Captain: distant cousin of Lord Canteloupe; regular officer of The 49th Earl Hamilton's Light Dragoons (Hamilton's Horse) from 1937; in charge of recruiting for the Cavalry in 1945 (FG); instructor at the O.T.S., Bangalore, from late 1945 to summer 1946 (SR); by 1952 has retired from Hamilton's Horse and become a Member of Parliament (SS); still M.P. in 1955 and a political supporter of Peter Morrison *q.v.* (RPL); still M.P. in 1959, when he joins Gregory Stern *q.v.* as a partner in Stern's publishing house (FLP); still M.P. and publisher in 1962 (JB) and 1970 (CLS), and 1972, at which time he gives important assistance to those enquiring into the death of Somerset Lloyd-James (BFB); inherits his distant cousin Canteloupe's marquisate by special remainder in 1973 (TS), and insists that the spelling of the title now be changed to 'marquess'.

Dexterside, Ashley: friend and employee of Donald Salinger (RPL).

Dharaparam, H.H. The Maharajah of: an Indian Prince; Patron of the Cricket Club of the O.T.S., Bangalore (SR).

Dilkes, Henry: Secretary to the Institute of Political and Economic Studies and a member of the Board of *Strix* (RPL, FLP).

Dixon , Alastair: Member of Parliament for safe Conservative seat in the west country; about to retire in 1959 (FLP), thus creating a vacancy coveted both by Peter Morrison and Somerset Lloyd-James *q.v.*

Dolly: maid of all work to Somerset Lloyd-James in his chambers in Albany (BFB).

Drew, Vanessa: *v.* Salinger, Donald.

Engineer, Margaret Rose: a Eurasian harlot who entertains Peter
Morrison *q.v.* in Bangalore (SR).

Fitzavon, Humbert: otherwise called Lord Rollesden-in-Silvis. The man
with whom the manuscripts of Fernando Albani *q.v.* are principally
concerned (TS).

de FREVILLE, Max: gambler and connoisseur of human affairs; runs big
chemin-de-fer games in the London of the fifties (RPL), maintaining a
private spy-ring for protection from possible welshers and also for the
sheer amusement of it (FLP); later goes abroad to Venice, Hydra,
Cyprus and Corfu, where he engages in various enterprises (PLP, JB,
CLS), often in partnership with Lykiadopoulos *q.v.* and usually
attended by Angela Tuck *q.v.* His Corfiot interests include a share
in the 1970 Pandarus/Clytemnestra production of *The Odyssey*
(CLS); still active in Corfu in 1972 (BFB); still in partnership with
Lykiadopoulos, whom he accompanies to Venice in the autumn of
1973 (TS).

Frith, Hetta: girl friend of Hugh Balliston *q.v.* (PWTS). † 1967 (PWTS).

Galahead, Foxe J. (Foxy): Producer for Pandarus and Clytemnestra
Films of *The Odyssey* on Corfu in 1970 (CLS).

Gamp, Jonathan: a not so young man about town (RPL, FLP, BFB).

Gilzai Khan, Captain: an Indian officer (Moslem) holding the King's
Commission; an instructor at the O.T.S., Bangalore, 1945–6; resigns
to become a political agitator (SR). † 1946 (SR).

Glastonbury, Major Giles: an old friend of Detterling *q.v.* and regular
officer of Hamilton's Horse; temporary Lieutenant-Colonel on Lord
Wavell's staff in India 1945–6 (SR); officer commanding the 10th
Sabre Squadron of Hamilton's Horse at Göttingen in 1952 (SS).

Grange, Lady Susan: marries Lord Philby (RPL).

Gray, John Aloysius (Jack): Fielding Gray's father (FG). † I 945.

Gray, Mrs: Fielding Gray's mother (FG). † *c.* 1948.

GRAY, Major Fielding: senior schoolboy in 1945 (FG) with Peter
Morrison and Somerset Lloyd-James *q.v.;* scholar elect of Lancaster
College, but tangles with the authorities, is deprived of his scholarship
before he can take it up (FG), and becomes a regular officer of Earl
Hamilton's Light Dragoons; 2 i/c and then O.C. the 10th Sabre
Squadron in Göttingen in 1952 (SS) and still commanding the
Squadron on Santa Kytherea in 1955 (FG); badly mutilated in Cyprus

in 1958 and leaves the Army to become critic and novelist with the help of Somerset Lloyd-James (FLP); achieves minor distinction, and in 1962 is sent out to Greece and Cyprus by Tom Llewyllyn *q.v.* to investigate Cypriot affairs, past and present, for BBC Television (JB); in Greece meets Harriet Ongley *q.v.*; by 1967 has won the Joseph Conrad Prize for Fiction (PWTS); goes to Corfu in 1970 to rewrite script for Pandarus/Clytemnestra's *The Odyssey* (CLS); in 1972 is engaged on a study of Joseph Conrad, which is to be published, as part of a new series, by Gregory Stem (BFB); derives considerable financial benefit from the Conrad book, and settles temporarily in Venice in the autumn of 1973 (TS). His researches into a by-water of Venetian history cause trouble among his friends and provide himself with the material for a new novel.

Grimes, Sasha: a talented young actress playing in Pandarus Clymnestra's *The Odyssey* on Corfu (CLS).

The Headmaster of Fielding Gray's School (FG): a man of conscience.

Helmutt, Jacquiz: historian; research student at Lancaster College in 1952 (SS); later Fellow of Lancaster (PWTS); still a Fellow of Lancaster and present at Daniel Mond's funeral in 1973 (TS).

Holbrook, Jude: partner of Donald Salinger *q.v.* 1949–56 (RPL); 'free-lance' in 1959 (FLP); reported by Burke Lawrence *q. v.* (CLS) as having gone to live in Hong Kong in the sixties; discovered to have retired, with his mother, to a villa in the Veneto 1973 (TS), having apparently enriched himself in Hong Kong.

Holbrook, Penelope: a model; wife of Jude Holbrook (RPL); by 1959, divorced from Jude and associated with Burke Lawrence (FLP); reported by Burke Lawrence (CLS) as still living in London and receiving alimony from Jude in Hong Kong.

Holeworthy, R.S.M.: Regimental Sergeant-Major of the Wessex Fusiliers at Göttingen in 1952 (SS).

Jacobson, Jules: old hand in the film world; Director of Pandarus/Clytemnestra's *The Odyssey* on Corfu in 1970 (CLS).

James, Cornet Julian: Cambridge friend of Daniel Mond *q. v.*; in 1952 a National Service officer of the 10th Sabre Squadron at Göttingen (SS).

Joe: groundsman at Detterling's old school (BFB).

Lamprey, Jack: a subaltern officer of the 10th Sabre Squadron(SS).

La Soeur, Doctor: a confidential practitioner, physician to Fielding Gray (FG, RPL, CLS).

Lawrence, Burke: 'film director' and advertising man (RPL); from *c.* 1956 to 1959 teams up with Penelope Holbrook *q.v.* in murky 'agency' (FLP); *c.* 1960 leaves England for Canada, and later becomes P.R.O. to Clytemnestra Films (CLS).

Lewson, Felicity: born Contessina Felicula Maria Monteverdi; educated largely in England; wife of Mark Lewson (though several years his senior) and his assistant in his profession (RPL). † 1959 (FLP).

Lewson, Mark: a con man (RPL, FLP). † 1959 (FLP).

Lichfield, Margaret: star actress playing Penelope in the Pandarus/ Clytemnestra production of *The Odyssey on* Corfu in 1970 (CLS).

LLEWYLLYN, Tom: a 'scholarship boy' of low Welsh origin but superior education; author, journalist and contributor to *Strix* (RPL); same but far more successful by 1959, when he marries Patricia Turbot *q.v.* (FLP); given important contract by BBC Television in 1962 to produce *Today is History,* and later that year appointed Napier Fellow of Lancaster College (JB); renewed as Napier Fellow in 1965 and still at Lancaster in 1967 (PWTS); later made a permanent Fellow of the College (CLS); employed by Pandarus and Clytemnestra Films as 'Literary and Historical Adviser' to their production of *The Odyssey* on Corfu in 1970 (CLS); still a don at Lancaster in 1972, when he is reported to be winning esteem for the first volume of his magnum opus (published by the Cambridge University Press) on the subject of Power (BFB); comes to Venice in the autumn of 1973 (TS), nominally to do research but in fact to care for Daniel Mond.

Llewyllyn, Tullia: always called and known as 'Baby'; Tom and Patricia's daughter, born in 1960 (JB, PWTS, CLS, BFB); on the removal from the scene of her mother, is sent away to school in the autumn of 1973 (TS). Becomes a close friend of Captain Detterling, now Marquess Canteloupe.

Lloyd-James, Mrs Peregrina: widowed mother of Somerset Lloyd-James (BFB).

LLOYD-JAMES, Somerset: a senior schoolboy and friend of Fielding Gray in 1945 (FG); by 1955, Editor of *Strix,* an independent economic journal (RPL); still editor of *Strix* in 1959 (FPL) and now seeking a seat in Parliament; still editor of *Strix* in 1962 (JB), but now also a Member of Parliament and unofficial adviser to Lord Canteloupe *q.v.*; still M.P. and close associate of Canteloupe in 1967 (PWTS), and by

1970 Canteloupe's official understrapper in the House of Commons (CLS), still so employed in 1972 (BFB), with title of Parliamentary Under-Secretary of State at the Ministry of Commerce; † 1972 (BFB).

Lykiadopoulos, Stratis: a Greek gentleman, or not far off it; professional gambler and a man of affairs (FLP) who has a brief liaison with Mark Lewson; friend and partner of Max de Freville *q.v.* (FLP), with whom he has business interests in Cyprus (JB) and later in Corfu (CLS); comes to Venice in the autumn of 1973 (TS) to run a Baccarat Bank and thus prop up his fortunes in Corfu, which are now rather shaky. Is accompanied by Max de Freville *q.v.* and a Sicilian boy called Piero *q.v.*

Maisie: a whore (RPL, FLP, JB) frequented with enthusiasm by Fielding Gray, Lord Canteloupe and Somerset Lloyd-James; apparently still going strong as late as 1967 (ref. PWTS) and even 1970 (ref. CLS), and 1972 (BFB).

Mayerston: a revolutionary (PWTS).

Mond, Daniel: a mathematician; research student of Lancaster College (SS) sent to Göttingen University in 1952 to follow up his line of research, which unexpectedly turns out to have a military potential; later Fellow of Lancaster and teacher of pure mathematics (PWTS). † in Venice in 1973 (TS).

Morrison, Helen: Peter Morrison's wife (RPL, FLP, BFB).

MORRISON, Peter: senior schoolboy with Fielding Gray and Somerset Lloyd-James *q.v.* in 1945 (FG); an officer cadet at the O.T.S., Bangalore, from late 1945 to summer 1946 (SR) and then commissioned as a Second Lieutenant in the Wessex Fusiliers, whom he joins at Berhampore; by 1952 has inherited substantial estates in East Anglia and by 1955 is a Member of Parliament (RPL) where he leads 'the Young England Group'; but in 1956 applies for Chiltern Hundreds (RPL); tries and fails to return to Parliament in 1959 (FLP); reported by Lord Canteloupe (CLS) as having finally got a seat again after a by-election in 1968 and as having retained it at the General Election in 1970; in 1972 appointed Parliamentary Under-Secretary of State at the Ministry of Commerce on the demise of Somerset Lloyd-James (BFB); appointed Minister of Commerce on death of Lord Canteloupe *q.v.* in 1973 (TS); soon after is in Venice to take a hand in industrial intrigues in Mestre.

Morrison, 'Squire': Peter's father (FG), owner of a fancied racehorse (Tiberius). † *c.* 1950.

Mortleman, Alister: an officer cadet at the O.T.S., Bangalore, 1945–6, later commissioned into the Wessex Fusiliers (SR).

Motley, Mick: Lieutenant of the R.A.M.C., attached to the Wessex Fusiliers at Göttingen in 1952 (SS).

Murphy, 'Wanker': an officer cadet at the O.T.S., Bangalore, 1945–6; later commissioned as Captain in the Education Corps, then promoted to be Major and Galloper to the Viceroy of India (SR). † 1946 (SR).

Muscateer, Earl of: son of Lord and Lady Canteloupe *q.v.*; an officer cadet at the O.T.S., Bangalore, 1945–6 (SR). † 1946 (SR).

Nicos: a Greek boy who picks up Fielding Gray (JB).

Ogden, The Reverend Andrew: Dean of the Chapel of Lancaster College (PWTS).

Ongley, Mrs Harriet: rich American widow; Fielding Gray's mistress and benefactress from 1962 onwards (JB, PWTS, CLS), but has left him by 1972 (BFB).

Pappenheim, Herr: German ex-officer of World War II; in 1952 about to rejoin new West German Army as a senior staff officer (SS).

Percival, Leonard: cloak-and-dagger man; in 1952 nominally a Lieutenant of the Wessex Fusiliers at Göttingen (SS), but by 1962 working strictly in plain clothes (JB); friend of Max de Freville, with whom he occasionally exchanges information to their mutual amusement (JB); transferred to a domestic department ('Jermyn Street') of the secret service and rated 'Home enquiries only', because of stomach ulcers in 1972, when he investigates, in association with Detterling, the death of Somerset Lloyd-James (BFB); joins Detterling (now Lord Canteloupe) in Venice in 1973 in order to investigate a 'threat' to Detterling (TS). Becomes Detterling's personal secretary and retires from 'Jermyn Street'.

Percival, Rupert: a small-town lawyer in the west country (FLP), prominent among local Conservatives and a friend of Alistair Dixon *q.v.*; Leonard Percival's uncle (JB).

Philby, The Lord: proprietor of *Strix* (RPL, FLP) which he has inherited along with his title from his father, 'old' Philby.

Piero: A Sicilian boy who accompanies Lykiadopoulos *q.v.* to Venice in 1973 (TS). Becomes friend of Daniel Mond. Not to be confused with Piero Albani *q.v.*

Pough (pronounced Pew), The Honourable Grantchester Fitz-Margrave: Senior Fellow of Lancaster College, Professor Emeritus of Oriental Geography, at one time celebrated as a mountaineer; a dietary fadist (PWTS).

Pulcher, Detective Sergeant: assistant to Detective Superintendent Stupples, *q.v.* (BFB).

Restarick, Earle: American cloak-and-dagger man; in 1952 apparently a student at Göttingen University (SS) but in fact taking an unwholesome interest in the mathematical researches of Daniel Mond *q.v.*; later active in Cyprus (JB) and in Greece (CLS); at Mestre in autumn of 1973 in order to assist with American schemes for the industrialisation of the area (TS); present at Daniel Mond's funeral.

Roland, Christopher: a special school friend of Fielding Gray (FG). † 1945 (FG).

Salinger, Donald: senior partner of Salinger & Holbrook, a printing firm (RPL); in 1956 marries Vanessa Drew (RPL); is deserted by Jude Holbrook *q.v.* in the summer of 1956 (RPL) but in 1959 is still printing (FLP), and still married to Vanessa; in 1972 is reported as having broken down mentally and retired to a private Nursing Home in consequence of Vanessa's death by drowning (BFB).

Schottgatt, Doctor Emile: of Montana University, Head of the 'Creative Authentication Committee' of the Oglander-Finckelstein Trust, which visits Corfu in 1970 (CLS) to assess the merits of the Pandarus/Clytemnestra production of *The Odyssey*.

Schroeder, Alfie: a reporter employed by the Billingsgate Press (RPL, FLP, SS); by 1967 promoted to columnist (PWTS); 'famous' as columnist by 1973, when he attends Daniel Mond's funeral (TS).

Sheath, Aloysius: a scholar on the staff of the American School of Greek Studies in Athens, but also assistant to Earle Restarick *q.v.* (JB, CLS).

Stern, Gregory: publisher (RPL), later in partnership with Captain Detterling *q.v.* (FLP); publishes Tom Llewellyn and Fielding Gray *q.v.* (RPL, FLP, JB, PWTS, CLS); married to Isobel Turbot (FLP). still publishing in 1973 (TS), by which time Isobel has persuaded him into vulgar and profitable projects.

Strange, Barry: an officer cadet at the O.T.S. Bangalore, 1945–6, later commissioned into the Wessex Fusiliers, with whom he has strong family connections (SR).

Stupples, Detective Superintendent: policeman initially responsible for enquiries into the death of Somerset Lloyd-James in 1972 (BFB).

Tuck: a tea-planter in India; marries Angela, the daughter of a disgraced officer, and brings her back to England in 1945 (FG); later disappears, but turns up as an official of the Control Commission in Germany in 1952 (SS). † 1956 (RPL).

TUCK, Mrs Angela: daughter of a Colonel in the Indian Army Pay Corps, with whom she lives in Southern India (JB, FLP) until early 1945, when her father is dismissed the Service for malversation; being then *in extremis* marries Tuck the tea-planter, and returns with him to England in the summer of 1945 (FG); briefly mistress to the adolescent Somerset Lloyd-James *q.v.*, and to 'Jack' Gray (Fielding's father); despite this a trusted friend of Fielding's mother (FG); by 1955 is long separated from Tuck and now mistress to Jude Holbrook (RPL); in 1956 inherits small fortune from the intestate Tuck, from whom she has never been actually divorced *pace* her bibulous and misleading soliloquies on the subject in the text (RPL); in 1959 living in Menton and occasional companion of Max de Freville *q.v.* (FLP); later Max's constant companion (JB, CLS). †1970 (CLS).

Turbot, The Right Honourable Sir Edwin, P.C., Kt: politician; in 1946 ex-Minister of wartime coalition accompanying all-party delegation of M.P.s to India (SR); by 1959 long since a Minister once more, and 'Grand Vizier' of the Conservative Party (FLP); father of Patricia, who marries Tom Llewyllyn (FLP), and of Isobel, who marries Gregory Stern (FLP); by 1962 reported as badly deteriorating and as having passed some of his fortune over to his daughters (JB). † by 1967 (PWTS), having left more money to his daughters.

Turbot, Isobel: *v*. Turbot, Sir Edwin, and Stern, Gregory.

Turbot, Patricia: *v*. Turbot, Sir Edwin, and Llewyllyn, Tom. Also *v*. Llewyllyn, Tullia. Has brief walk-out with Hugh Balliston *q.v.* (PWTS) and is disobliging to Tom about money (JB, PWTS, CLS). In 1972 is reported by Jonathan Gamp to be indulging curious if not criminal sexual preferences (BFB); as a result of these activities is finally overtaken by disaster and put away in an asylum in 1973 (TS), much to the benefit of her husband and daughter.

Weekes, James: bastard son of Somerset Lloyd-James, born in 1946 (BFB).

Weekes, Mrs Meriel: *quondam* and random associate of Somerset Lloyd-James, and mother of his bastard son (BFB).

Weir, Carton: Member of Parliament and political associate of Peter Morrison (RPL); later official aide to Lord Canteloupe (FLP, JB). P.P.S. to Canteloupe at Ministry of Commerce in 1972 (BFB); becomes P.P.S. to Peter Morrison *q.v.* when the latter takes over as Minister of Commerce on the death of Lord Canteloupe.

Winstanley, Ivor: a distinguished Latinist, Fellow of Lancaster College (PWTS).

'Young bastard': assistant groundsman at Detterling's old school (BFB).

Zaccharias: an officer cadet at the O.T.S., Bangalore, 1945–6; commissioned into a dowdy regiment of the line (SR).

BRING FORTH THE BODY

CONTENTS

TABLEAU

In the bathroom of Somerset Lloyd-James's chambers in Albany the bathwater gradually lost its temperature, from hot to warm to tepid to cool. By the time the early sun first reached the window the water was quite cold; cold, and deep orange in the busy sun, placid and rather scurfy, drawn up, like a blanket, under Somerset Lloyd-James's chin.

Later on some letters pattered on to the floor of the hall a few yards away; and a little while after that the telephone rang in the drawing-room, was silent, rang again (thirteen times) and then again desisted. But Somerset Lloyd-James, who had so often answered that telephone with eagerness, listened into it with anger or relish, and spoken down it in command or prohibition—Somerset Lloyd-James stayed quiet beneath the waters, recking naught of the filth and the chill; for no telephone could summon him to bustle now, nor any bright morning quicken his stiff shanks.

PART ONE

MATTER FOR A MAY MORNING

At 10.30 a.m. on Wednesday, May 10 1972, Captain Detterling, M.P., decided to pay a morning call on his old friend, Somerset Lloyd-James, M.P. As both men lived in chambers in Albany, Detterling had not very far to walk; but he took his time over it, thinking, as he went, of what he would say when he arrived.

The object of his visit was to check up on an item of political gossip about the Ministry of Commerce, in which Lloyd-James had been Parliamentary Under-Secretary of State since the Conservative Party had been returned to power in June 1970. It was whispered that the Minister, a distant cousin of Detterling called the Marquis Canteloupe, was showing signs of cracking, and Detterling was anxious to ascertain what Lloyd-James opined in the matter. Everyone knew that pressure of business had been mounting at the Ministry ever since Canteloupe had assumed office there nearly two years before, and that these pressures were by now very tough indeed. So was it true that Canteloupe was no longer capable of coping, as rumour had it, and if so was this due to his health, his years, or his liberal use of alcohol? In particular, Detterling wished to know whether Canteloupe had managed to make adequate arrangements for the representation of Great Britain at an important Trade Convention which was to take place at Strasbourg at the beginning of June. For wishing to know all this Detterling had two reasons: first, it was the sort of thing which he enjoyed knowing; and secondly, he wanted to receive ample warning in advance if, as he suspected, his ageing relative was about to make a public fool of himself.

But the immediate problem, as Detterling reminded himself

en route, was how to frame his questions. Somerset Lloyd-James did not give away information, even to old friends, for nothing. He would want his *quid pro quo* and, even if Detterling could meet him in this respect, he would also want to know the motives behind Detterling's enquiries. Mere curiosity he would certainly refuse to gratify, while a plea of family solicitude he would probably dismiss as irrelevant. For Detterling would not be enquiring into the health of his cousin Canteloupe (which he could perfectly well ask of elsewhere), he would in fact be enquiring into the competence of the Minister of Commerce, a very different and a very delicate matter, about which it would be naïf to expect candour.

And so what, thought Captain Detterling, am I to say to Somerset? Shall I try to provoke him? E.g., 'I hear the old boy's getting pissed too often', or, 'They say the P.M.'s very worried about the arrangements for Strasbourg'. But that kind of thing was too tentative; it would provoke Lloyd-James only to curt and simple denial, whereas what Detterling wanted was a full assessment of the factors *pro* and *con*. Well then : should he formulate a charge so definite and powerful that Lloyd-James would be bound to refute it in some detail? Such detail could then be checked, and would be almost as useful where found to be false as where found to be true; for falsehood detected would indicate those areas in which the Minister and the Ministry were vulnerable and, quite possibly, why. The only trouble with *this* plan, Detterling now thought, was that he had no really strong or definite charge which he could formulate—nothing that could not be dismissed in a dozen words at most.

By this time Detterling was standing in front of Somerset Lloyd-James's door, and was still no clearer how to proceed than he had been when he left his own. But he did not let this deter him. He knew of old that if one scripted one's conversation too carefully beforehand, if one prepared one's questions and effects too precisely, one was very easily put out of countenance : for one's opponent seldom spoke or behaved in accordance with the script, and this could be very awkward if one was too heavily committed to it. Far better to be flexible, as they used to say in the army, far better play it by ear and feel one's way gently in. Captain Detterling considered himself rather a hand a feeling his way in, and he had good hope, now, that either luck or instinct would tell him what questions to ask and when. He had known Lloyd-James for over twenty-five years (off and on); after all that time he really ought to be capable of judging his friend's mood and teasing out the information he wanted. He smiled in self-encouragement and pressed Somerset Lloyd-James's bell.

The bell was answered, after an unusually long time, by Somerset's woman-of-all-work, Dolly, who looked rather glum.

" 'Morning, Dolly," said Detterling. "Mr Somerset here? Or has he gone to the Ministry?"

"Mr Somerset is inside, sir," said Dolly. "Please to come in and see him."

When Dolly introduced Detterling to Lloyd-James's dead body in the bath (which she did in precisely the same manner as she would have used to show him into the drawing-room) Detterling's first reaction was one of disapproval (how very *infra dig.* of Somerset to let himself be found in such a state), his second reaction one of sorrow, and his third one of pleasurable curiosity. Somerset had sprung a few surprises in his day but this beat everything. For some three or four minutes Detterling looked down at Somerset's face, almost as if he hoped it might still be able to open its mouth and tell him something. Then he made a noise between a sigh and a whistle, and went to find Dolly, who had discreetly withdrawn to the kitchen.

"Have you sent for the police?" he said.

"No, sir."

"How long have you known about it?"

"Since I came."

"Since *seven*?" (Detterling knew all about Somerset's domestic routine.)

"Not quite then, sir. A while after—when I went to do the bathroom."

"But my dear Dolly, it's now getting on for eleven. What have you been doing all this time?"

"Sitting here in the kitchen," Dolly said.

"I see," said Detterling easily. "But you really ought to have sent for the police. They've got to come, Dolly."

"Not just yet. Once they've taken him away . . . that's it, isn't it?"

"He can't stay here, my dear."

"A little longer, sir?"

"Sorry. It's been far too long already. You'd like me to do the telephoning, I expect?"

"If you would, sir."

So Detterling rang up the police and then sat down by Dolly at the kitchen table to wait. As they sat there together, he let her hold his hand and listened to her quiet talk of her Mr Somerset, who had never forgotten her birthday in all the years.

"So to sum up, sir," said Detective Superintendent Stupples to Captain Detterling, "what we have is this : Mr Somerset Lloyd-James, identified by your good self, dead in the bath of his own uncurtained bathroom and naked except for his spectacles. His wrists have apparently been slashed, a safety razor blade has been found at the bottom of the bath, and the bathwater is coloured by a red substance which we may assume to be Mr Lloyd-James's blood. Nothing more can be said until the medical experts have examined the body and given us the results of all the appropriate tests. That's about it . . . eh, Sergeant Pulcher?"

"That's about it, sir," Sergeant Pulcher said.

Detective Superintendent Stupples was long, thin and fibrous, with a small oval head and very bright eyes which were protected by mathematically circular spectacles. Detective Sergeant Pulcher was round yet hard, like a jacketed barrel. Both men wore plain clothes, Pulcher a blue double-breasted suit, Stupples a tweed coat and mustard-coloured corduroy trousers.

"But tests or no tests," Stupples now continued, "there can only be one solution."

"Suicide," said Pulcher. "Stands to reason. No evidence of intruders, nothing been pinched or damaged—not if we're to believe the char, that is."

"Dolly," said Detterling, "is not 'the char'. She is a valued servant who enjoys Mr Lloyd-James's affection and trust. If she says nothing has been interfered with, then nothing has been interfered with."

"Except for Mr Lloyd-James," said Stupples, "who must have interfered with himself. Slit his veins in the bath. The old Roman way."

"Why?" said Detterling.

"You claim to be an old friend of his," said Stupples. "Why ask *us*?"

"I was asking myself, Superintendent."

"And what's the answer, sir?"

"That," said Captain Detterling, "I should very much like to know."

"Anything been troubling him lately?"

"Not that I heard of. He was always well off, and since his father died some years ago he's been rich. He's always had interesting work—and done it well—and recently he's been highly successful as a politician. He has . . . he had . . . a wide social acquaintance among the very best people in every sense of the expression. His relations with women . . ."

". . . He wasn't married?" put in Pulcher.

". . . And didn't miss it. His relations with women, as I was about to remark, were always . . . sensibly regulated."

Superintendent Stupples glinted through his spectacles at this information, while Sergeant Pulcher nodded with conscious sophistication

"In short," Detterling concluded, "so far from having reason to commit suicide, he had just about every reason not to."

"And yet," said Stupples, "suicide it must be."

"I suppose so," said Detterling, remembering the tableau in the bathroom.

"Beyond any possible doubt," corrected Stupples.

"Very rum," grunted Sergeant Pulcher.

"And even rummer," said Detterling, "as Mr Lloyd-James was a Catholic. They don't usually go in for that kind of thing."

"Perhaps he wasn't a very serious Catholic," Stupples said mildly.

"As to his private spiritual beliefs, it is hard to say. He was a worldly man, Superintendent, and not, on the face of it, much affected by religious or moral scruple. But he *did* set great store by formal and well-mannered deference to all recognised rules and ordinances . . . whether Catholic or other. That is not to say that he obeyed them, but it *is* to say that he would never willingly have allowed himself to be detected in their violation. It would have offended his sense of good order. But what more indecorous a violation could you have, *and what more certain of detection*, than an act of *felo de se*?"

"And such a very messy one too," said Superintendent Stupples. And then to Pulcher, "Get Dolly in here, would you, Sergeant? It's time we had a word with her."

"Do you mind if I stay?" said Detterling as Pulcher went out. "Dolly is an intelligent woman in her kind, but nervous of strangers. It might steady her to have someone she knew in the room."

"Very considerate of you, sir."

"Not really. As you may have gathered, I am rather curious about it all."

"And you think that Dolly will say something of interest?"

"Quite possibly. Dolly, like her master, set a high value on routine. She will have noticed even the tiniest departure. . . ."

". . . The last I seen of Mr Somerset—seen of him proper, I mean—was yesterday morning," Dolly said. "He was in his brown country suit and he said he was going out of London for the day. But he'd be back in the evening—after I'd gone, which is always five o'clock—and if anyone rang up I was to say so. He'll be back some time after five p.m., that's what I had to say."

"He didn't tell you where he was going . . . or why?" asked Superintendent Stupples.

"Oh no, sir, and of course I didn't enquire."

"When did he leave?"

"About eleven o'clock, sir. So then I went on with my cleaning work, and answered the telephone . . ."

". . . Did many people ring?"

"No, sir. His friends all know he's usually at the Ministry any time after eleven, so anyone who wanted him would have rung there."

"But you answered the telephone, you say, so *somebody* must have rung here."

"Yes, sir. Just the one time. It was Lord Canteloupe's secretary, Mr Carton Weir, from the Ministry. He knew Mr Somerset was away for the day, he said, because Mr Somerset had warned them he would be. But would I please tell Mr Somerset when he got back that the Minister particularly wanted to have dinner with him on Wednesday—meaning today, sir—and to cancel any other engagements he had, because there was going to be an important discussion about Strasbourg."

"About the Trade Convention in June?" put in Detterling.

"I suppose so, sir. I know Mr Somerset's been doing a lot of work getting ready for that, because he told me something about it. 'It's going to be make or break at Strasbourg, Dolly,' he said—about a week ago it was—'make or break at Strasbourg, I can tell you. The work's just about killing me.' But I knew he was enjoying it, really, because he had that look on his face."

"And that was all he said about it?"

"Oh yes, sir. He never told me much—why should he? But every now and then he'd tell me something, just a little . . . particularly if he was enjoying it himself . . . to make me feel part of it all."

"I see," said Stupples. "Let's get back to this telephone call. What time was it?"

"Around three o'clock, sir."

"And you were to tell Mr Lloyd-James that he must cancel any other appointment in order to dine with Lord Canteloupe the next day—*i.e.* today, Wednesday?"

"That's right, sir."

"But Mr Lloyd-James wouldn't be back until after you left at five. So what did you do about it?"

"I decided to tell him in the morning, sir. I could have left him a note, but he didn't care for that unless it was absolutely necessary. 'Notes give things away, Dolly,' he told me once: 'they're always apt to be lost—or read by the wrong people. I'd sooner trust to your memory, Dolly—it's never let me down yet.' So I thought to myself about this dinner, I'll tell him first thing in the morning, that'll leave time enough."

"And then?"

"And then I left at five like I always do and came back this morning at seven."

"And . . . then?"

"I followed my usual programme, sir. Mr Somerset always dined out, but I checked the dining-room, in case he'd had a late-night snack in there or something."

"And had he?"

"No, sir. So then I laid the breakfast things and went to call him. He liked to be called at a quarter past seven for breakfast at a quarter to eight—an early rising gentleman he was. So I'd call him at a quarter past seven, and he'd get shaved and that while I cooked his breakfast, which he never sat down to until he was all dressed and ready for the day. 'It doesn't feel right, Dolly,' he used to say, 'flopping about at the breakfast table in slippers and pyjamas'."

"But what happened when you called him this morning?"

"He didn't answer when I knocked nor even when I'd knocked twice, so I opened the bedroom door and went in. Bed not slept in. 'Oh dear,' I thought, 'he's decided to spend the night away after all. I hope he's coming back in time for me to tell him about this dinner.' But meanwhile there was nothing for it except to carry on as usual, so I went and had the cup of tea which I always had while I was cooking his breakfast, and then, when it was his breakfast time at a quarter to eight, I went like I always do to clean out the bathroom, being as how he's a clumsy shaver and makes spots on the mirror and blood on the towels. Poor gentleman . . . he suffers cruel from pimples, you see."

"And when you went into the bathroom," said Superintendent Stupples, "you found . . . what you found. Did you touch anything?"

"Oh no, sir." Although Dolly's face crumpled slightly, she remained in control of herself. "I said to myself, 'So *that's* where you've been instead of your bed. No point in telling you about that dinner until you're in a fit state to listen.' I didn't quite take it all in, you see, sir. I just went and sat in the kitchen . . . hoping that things would somehow come right again and we could just go on as usual without mentioning it. And there I sat until the letters came at nine . . . I heard the noise of the flap. But I didn't go for them, nor I didn't answer the telephone, though it rang soon after the letters, because it seemed to me that if I didn't do things for him he might pull himself together and start doing for himself. He was always very fierce about answering the telephone, so perhaps, when he heard it ringing, it might *make* him get out of that bath."

Dolly paused and shook her head slowly from side to side.

"Go on," said Stupples briskly.

"So there I sat, quite still in the kitchen. And as time went on, the telephone began to ring more and more, and still I didn't answer it, hoping for what I told you to happen. But nothing did. And at last, much later, the door-bell rang; and I thought, 'I'll give you one final chance, Mr Somerset. I'll leave you to answer that bell . . . a whole minute I'll give you. And if you still don't answer it, I'll have to go myself . . . and then whoever it is will have to know what you've been up to.' Well the, minute went by, and I went to the door myself . . . and it was Mr Somerset's friend, Captain Detterling. . . ."

". . . A routine-minded lady, as you said," remarked Stupples to Detterling, while Sergeant Pulcher was seeing Dolly into a

police car to be driven home. "The sort that's totally reliable
. . . until something out of the ordinary happens. *Very* weird,
the way she seems to have behaved over this." He removed
his glasses, blinked energetically, and then replaced them.
"Not," he said, "that it changes anything. Anything important,
I mean."

"Would it have helped if she'd called you in right away?"

"Not really . . . though of course she should have. The
doctor's rough estimate is that Lloyd-James had been dead
between ten and twelve hours. If we'd been called in earlier,
he might have been able to be more exact. But what difference
does it make whether Lloyd-James died at midnight or two
a.m.? Suicide it must be."

"I wonder where he went yesterday," Detterling said. "Out
of London for the day . . . He went off aboslutely calmly, it
seems, in one of his country suits; he gave Dolly some simple
instructions, and he'd warned them at the Ministry that he
wouldn't be coming in. All of it entirely sane and sensible,
nothing the least bit out of the way—*but then he comes back
and does this.*"

"It wasn't an official outing," said Stupples casually, as
if the matter were of little moment. "If it had been, he wouldn't
have needed to warn the Ministry about his absence. He must
have been taking a day off, for private business or pleasure."

"*What* business or pleasure? Where did he go and whom
did he see? It could explain everything."

"It could."

"You don't sound very interested."

Stupples shrugged. "Perhaps I am," Stupples said, "and
perhaps I'm not. Either way, I shan't follow it up officially."

"But damn it, man," said Detterling, "you *must*. You want
to know why he did it, and this outing of his—"

"—Ah," interrupted Stupples, " but *do* I want to know why
he did it?"

"Of course you do. The coroner will want to know and it's
your job to tell him."

"The coroner will be told . . . pressure of work," said

Stupples. "The work is killing him—as Dolly says he told her himself."

"But that was only humorous exaggeration—of the kind people make every day. Dolly said he was really enjoying his work, and from what I've seen of him lately I entirely agree with her."

"Nevertheless, his actual words refute you, sir. 'The work's just about killing he,' he said. The coroner and his jury needn't know he was joking . . . if we only take a little care with Dolly."

"In which case," said Detterling disingenuously, "you'd be deliberately serving up lies."

"Look, Captain Detterling. You've been a Member of Parliament for a very long time, and I have heard that you are a man of some experience in other fields. Do you really need me to spell it all out for you?"

"Yes, Superintendent. I wish to be sure that you've got your spelling correct."

"Very well," sighed Stupples. "Here is a top man in the Ministry of Commerce—a man second only to the Minister himself—who would have had an important role to play at the forthcoming Convention in Strasbourg. Right so far?"

"Right so far."

"Now, this man suddenly kills himself for no ostensible reason. That reason, when discovered, could be political dynamite. Still correct?"

"Yes, but you've given me an abbreviation. I want the spelling in full, please."

"As you like. In most suicides," Stupples pursued, "the motives are just squalid or pitiful; but what is just squalid or pitiful in an ordinary case can start a national scandal in a case like this. Rows about politicians' morals, public hysteria about security, God knows what. And so we, the humble police, not wishing to embarrass our betters, we play the whole thing down. We do not look behind locked doors, we pretend we can't find the key. We do not rip away the arras because we do not want to discover the rats there—or rather, we don't

want the Press and the public to discover them. What we do
instead is to settle as quietly as we can for the least disturbing
explanation : in this case for overwork, for temporary mental
unbalance due to strain—one of the few plausible reasons
which are also respectable. He was desperately tired and
anxious, we say in the Coroner's Court for everyone to hear, he
went for a day in the country to rest and calm himself down,
it didn't help, he returned as depressed as he set out, and then
he killed himself. So there we are; a verdict of suicide due to
strain and overwork; official enquiry closed; public indifference at such a boring conclusion; and a grateful sigh of relief
from our betters in Downing Street."

"Very good, Superintendent. And I suppose that takes care
of everything?"

"Except for the truth, sir. We still have to find that out.
It could be dangerous, you see, not to know it."

"Ah yes," said Detterling, "the truth. I'm glad we're getting
round to that."

"As soon as the official investigation is publicly completed
by the police," Stupples went on, "and as soon as the coroner
has recorded his tame and harmless verdict, the whole thing
goes underground along with the body. But unlike the body
it is still alive. I tell all I know to a little man in a scruffy
office in Jermyn Street, and then *his* men take over. *They* nose
through the dustbins and dig out all the dirt from the sewers.
They discover whether there has been a breach of security
or anything in that line to sort out. And at length the little
man in Jermyn Street composes a very secret report—"

"—Top Copy to the P.M.—"

"—From whom he asks permission to take the necessary
steps to repair any damage."

"Permission granted, I take it."

"As a rule, yes. And meanwhile Somerset Lloyd-James,
quondam Under-Secretary at the Ministry of Commerce, lies
in his grave, conveniently forgotten both by the newspapers
and their readers—"

"—Who know as little of this second *post-mortem* as he

does. A very ingenious system," Captain Detterling commented, "but not in the least original. Also expensive to operate and liable, I should have thought, to back-fire . . . particularly at the early stages when you, Superintendent, must deliberately falsify police enquiries."

"*Limit* police enquiries, sir. But you're right : the method does have its drawbacks, and . . . er . . . *they* . . . are often reluctant to employ it."

"Then why are you so sure that they'll instruct you to employ it here?"

"Because they already have instructed me, sir. You remember all those telephone calls Dolly talked of—the ones she didn't answer. Well, those—or most of 'em—were from the Ministry, it seems. Lord Canteloupe's secretary, Mr Carton Weir —"

"—Wanting to check up that Lloyd-James was all set for this dinner tonight?"

"I dare say. After he'd tried time after time and couldn't get through, Mr Weir got rattled. He knew Lloyd-James was due back in London last night and he knew that anyhow Dolly should have been here to answer. So at length he phoned our people, to ask us to come and check up just in case something was wrong here. As it happened, he came through to us just after your good self."

"So you were able to tell him there was indeed something wrong here—"

"—And exactly what it was. Mr Weir gave a screech like a night-owl, and within three minutes, sir, my superiors were instructed by telephone from No. 10 that this case was to be treated as Category Sigma—that is, on the system I've just been outlining to you."

"So clearly somebody regards it as being very sensitive. I'm much obliged to you, Superintendent, for telling me all this so frankly. I had not expected your account to be quite so . . . so comprehensive."

"It's not only to oblige you, sir. I expect you, in return, to oblige us."

"How can I do that?"

"By not ballsing us up, sir. As I've told you, we need an uncontroversial verdict from the coroner's inquest to douse the whole thing down before our friend in Jermyn Street can get properly started. Now, Dolly's evidence about Mr Lloyd-James telling her his work was killing him is going to be a god-send . . . and we can present it so that the jury will think he really meant it. In fact, Sergeant Pulcher's squaring Dolly about that now—telling her that it will be the best way to preserve 'Mr Somerset's' good reputation, all that kind of thing. But when it comes to you, sir . . ."

". . . I might not be so amenable a witness, you think. I might say that Lloyd-James was enjoying his job very much, and was right on top of it."

"And you being you, they'd listen. Which wouldn't suit us at all. Because then they'd start looking in other directions—"

"—Much more interesting directions, like the direction he took into the country on the day before he died. Which would suit *me* very well, Stupples. Because I, as I have told you, am curious about the truth. I'm in no mind to help you suppress it."

"It's your own party, sir—your own Ministers—who want it suppressed. Isn't it your duty to help them? Everyone else will go along with the theory that Mr Lloyd-James's suicide was due to overwork. Lord Canteloupe, Mr Weir—all of them. Why must you be so difficult?"

"Because I want to know what really happened."

Sergeant Pulcher came in. "Sorry I've been so long, sir," he said to Stupples, "but I thought I'd see Dolly right home."

"And she appreciated your kindness?"

"She did. She understands that we mean everything for the best—and she realises now that her poor gentleman *was* very tired these last weeks, and that's what she'll tell the coroner."

"It's not what she told us in here," said Detterling.

"No, sir," said Pulcher, poker-faced. "But she's remembered, you see, how kind and thoughtful her Mr Somerset was; and *now* she's sure that he meant what he said about his work killing him but was then suddenly afraid he might be upsetting her. So at the last moment, him being the gentleman he was, he tried to put on a cheerful face and turn it into a joke. She won't go into all that at the inquest, of course, because she agrees with me it might be rather muddling : she'll just say that he said it and he meant it."

"You see, sir?" said Stupples to Detterling. "Everyone else . . . on reflection . . . understands what will be the most fitting way to look at it all. Why do you want to spoil things?"

"I don't want to spoil anything. *I simply want to know what really happened.* For my own satisfaction."

"Ah," said Stupples, "for *your own* satisfaction? Not because you think there is a duty to inform the coroner . . . or the British people?"

"Be damned to the coroner and be damned to the people. I simply want to know for myself."

Superintendent Stupples lifted his arms to heaven and gazed on Detterling, with condescending and unctuous charity, like a member of a religious order in the act of welcoming a novice.

"In that case, sir," he intoned, "we can surely come to an accommodation. If you will respect our wishes and support our line at the inquest, I for my part will guarantee that you shall be subsequently informed, by the Jermyn Street men themselves, of everything which they turn up in their investigation."

"Why should they confide in me?"

"Because I shall ask them to. And because I shall tell them that you can be very helpful to them if they make themselves agreeable. In fact, sir, I'm going to propose you to them as a temporary assistant."

"With what qualifications?"

"As an expert on the subject in hand. On Lloyd-James' past and present—past and recent, I should say. They will listen to my recommendation, I promise you that. So do you accept my terms?"

There was a knock at the door, and a uniformed constable

appeared. Sergeant Pulcher went to him. There were whispers.

"The wagon's here, sir," called Pulcher, turning back to Stupples.

"Then tell them to take him away, and then follow the usual procedure about this apartment." Stupples turned to Detterling. "Your friend must leave his home now," he said, "and I must go after him where he is taken. So before I go, do you accept my terms?" He pursed his mouth plummily and almost ogled. "Your . . . discreet cooperation with us now," he purred, "in return for full enlightenment later?"

Detterling nodded briefly. "I accept," he said.

When Captain Detterling was back in his chambers, he thought at some length of the deal he had done with Stupples. Although he disliked the man, he did not resent the bargain (he was no stranger to such agreements) and he was inclined to think he could have done no better. In return for his silence while the police proposed to the coroner a false motive for Somerset's suicide, he, Detterling, would later be made privy to—indeed party to—the investigation which would seek out the truth (never mind what others might believe); and since it was to be elicited by the secret processes which were directed by 'the little man in Jermyn Street', his only hope of learning it was to be accepted as an ally in that quarter. This he would now be, if he could trust Stupples to perform the offices promised, and on the whole he did trust him : disagreeable though Stupples might be, there was no reason to doubt his word— quite the reverse, in fact; for if Stupples were to renegue on his part of the deal, Detterling, knowing what he did about the conduct of the case, would still be in a position to make trouble for him.

Very well then, thought Detterling : as soon as the second and secret enquiry begins, I shall be in on it. But it would not begin for a little while yet, not (or so Stupples had stated) until the inquest was safely done with. If Detterling himself wished to make an immediate start (which he did), he must depend, for the next few days, on his own sources of information and his own unaided wits. These might not take him very far; but at least, he told himself, he could do some useful homework. There were several pertinent questions which lay, so to speak, in his own area; to some one or two of these at least he could probably find answers fairly quickly, and he could thus have some useful information with which to impress the representatives from Jermyn Street when they came knocking on his door. Jermyn Street must be made to realise that it was in truth getting an assistant and not just a privileged spectator.

The first person whom Detterling intended to approach was his own cousin and Somerset's immediate political superior, the Most Honourable the Marquis Canteloupe, Minister of Commerce. Although the cousinhood lay at several removes, Canteloupe had always acknowledged it, and was on personal grounds well-disposed towards Detterling; they had been mixed up in several intrigues together over the years, and Detterling was in no doubt that his noble relative both could and would tell him a great deal that he wished to know about Somerset's recent activities on behalf of the Ministry. An evening with Canteloupe (for an evening Detterling was decided it should be, the old man being always more amenable after the fall of darkness) would also give him the opportunity to examine the Minister's physique with some care, to assess his consumption of drink, and to determine whether or not the rumours of his deterioration were well founded. It was to check on these rumours that Detterling had originally sought out Somerset that morning; he was still without satisfaction on the topic, and he now had an additional reason for pursuing it. While the motives behind his abortive morning call—family *pietàs* and sheer inquisitiveness—were still as pressing as ever, he now, moreover, had an interesting conjecture which he wished to test : if the Minister were indeed deteriorating, and if this were proving deleterious to the running of his Ministry, might there not have been some muddle or mistake or even disaster which, having impinged on Somerset as second-in-command, had some connexion, indicative if not causative, with his death ? It was, Detterling told himself, a long shot but just worth the cartridge; and if it went wide, well, there were other, nearer, and more definitive targets for his attention. For example, he was particularly anxious to learn from Canteloupe the nature and, if possible, the exact scope of the operations which Somerset was to have undertaken in three weeks' time at Strasbourg.

And so, after a restoring luncheon of gulls' eggs and stuffed quails, Detterling telephoned the Ministry of Commerce and was connected with the Minister's P.P.S., Carton Weir.

"Ghastly news about Somerset," said Weir. "I'm being tortured by the Press."

"Well, don't tell 'em I was in on it. I don't want 'em round here."

"But whatever *can* I tell them, my dear?"

"I thought the official line was quite clear. Suicide due to strain and overwork."

"But that's so *boring*."

"I gather it's meant to be."

"Oh yes, dear, and we'll stick to it all right, but you can't expect the Press to find it madly amusing, and they keep nagging away trying to make me say it was something else."

"Well, if it was, there's not the slightest clue anywhere, so you're batting on a pretty sound wicket."

"Stone-walling. It makes them so nasty and cross. Like vampires, my dear, who have spotted someone full of lovely blood, only to find themselves sucking a waxwork . . . Oh dear, there's more of them just arrived—panting with excitement, the doorman says. So what can I do for you before they tear me apart?"

"I gather my cousin is now free for dinner tonight?"

"That's right. It was to have been with poor, dear Somerset —not that I ever liked him much, he was a rotten, scheming old sod, but *de mortuis* and all that."

"Where were they going?"

"The Ritz. So nice and empty, you see, if there's anything shady to talk about."

"Had they got something shady to talk about?"

"I never knew them talk about anything that wasn't. And what with this great big conning match that's coming up at Strasbourg . . ."

"Well, look here, Carton. Tell Canteloupe that if he cares to dine with *me* at the Ritz tonight, I'll pay the bill."

"Oh, he'll love that. Being paid for is his very best thing. But you must be nice to him, Detterling, in other ways, I mean. He really is cut up about that old bitch Somerset—about poor, dear Somerset, that is—and he needs taking out of himself."

"How's his drinking form these days?"

"Same as ever. No less—but certainly no more. You mustn't listen to any of these tales about his boozing, Detterling. He's a lovely old darling, so he is, and in splendid shape all round. But he *is* sad about Somerset—though why he should bother about the stringy old cow is more than I can imagine—so you must be very sweet to him."

"All right, Carton. Tell him eight-thirty for a drink at the table. . . ."

This settled, Detterling decided on a little revision, to make quite sure he had the elementary background of his subject right. He took the latest volume of *Who's Who* from a shelf and turned to

LLOYD-JAMES, Somerset; MP (C) Bishop's Cross, Somersetshire, since Oct. 1959; Parliamentary Under-Secretary of State, Ministry of Commerce, since June, 1970 . . .

Funny, thought Detterling; it sometimes seems, when I look back, as though he's been in the House at least as long as I have; yet of course it was only in 1959 that he came in, at the General Election, nearly ten years after I did. But then he was up to his neck in politics long before he became a Member of Parliament, so I suppose that accounts for the illusion. It only goes to show the value of revision . . .

. . . *b* 11 Dec. 1927; *o s* of late Seamus Lloyd-James, and of Peregrina Lennox Lloyd-James (*neé* Forbes Eden), of Chantry Marquess, Near Bampton, Devonshire. . . .

Peregrina Lennox Lloyd-James, thought Detterling : the old mum. Still alive, it seems. I don't remember that he ever spoke of her to anyone (nor of his father, except to announce his death). I wonder how often he saw the old lady. Perhaps it was her he went to see on the last day of his life? Can one get to Devonshire and back inside the same day? Hardly, unless one turns round as soon as one gets there. Whether he went or not, however, old Peregrina may know something to the point. But she'll need very careful handling at her age; best leave her to the experts from Jermyn Street.

... *Educ* : St Peter's Court, Crediton ...

How very odd. Never before, thought Detterling, have I known anyone list his preparatory school in *Who's Who*. But of course Somerset was always a cracking snob, and St Peter's Court was once a very smart private school, much patronised by the Royal Family. Now surely, Detterling remembered, it was really situated at Broadstairs and was evacuated to Crediton (Devon) for the duration of the war. So that if, as this entry implies, Somerset attended it only when it was at Crediton, he cannot have gone to it before September of 1939, by which time he must have already been eleven years and nine months old. Either, then, the little Somerset was too delicate to go away to school until he was nearly twelve, or he attended another prep. school first—one which he doesn't deign to name here. Could he have been expelled from it? Or did Seamus and Peregrina merely transfer him to St Peter's when it arrived in their own vicinity? And if so, were their motives primarily snobbish or educational? No doubt, thought Detterling, Peregrina Lennox will know the answer to that question, if anyone thinks it worth asking; but the important point is, as regards the adult Somerset and his character, that he wished the world to know that he had been to a preparatory school held fit for little princes . . . and wished the world to know so imperatively that he risked making a fool of himself by ostentatiously recording it.

Compensation, thought Detterling, as he returned his eyes

to *Who's Who*: compensation for the next place he went to, which was a decent enough school but middle-class to say the least of it. For as Detterling well knew and as *Who's Who* now confirmed, Somerset had attended, between 1941 and 1946, the same public school, one of the first six in the kingdom but definitely low in the category, as Detterling himself had attended in the 1930s. It was there, indeed, in the summer of 1945, that Detterling remembered he had first met Somerset. Detterling, the returning old boy, had been gorgeously got up in a Service dress jacket and the cherry trousers of his regiment, the 49th Earl Hamilton's Light Dragoons; Somerset had been scrofulous, sickly and underfed, in appearance a more than usually seedy schoolboy even for that more than usually seedy period, and Detterling had instantly written him off as of no account whatever. Wrongly, of course; for even then Somerset had been a power in the land—or at least in the school—though of this Detterling was only to learn years later.

For after that summer's day in 1945, he had scarcely set eyes on Somerset for a whole ten years. While Somerset Lloyd-James (according to *Who's Who*) was winning a scolarship to Cambridge, taking firsts in the History Tripos and potting the Lauderdale Essay Prize, Captain Detterling had been moving round the world in the last stages of his somewhat desultory career as a regular soldier; while Somerset had been struggling to prove himself as an apprentice journalist on an economic daily, Detterling had been moving comfortably into a safe Conservative seat and making prudent dispositions for his ample inheritance. Detterling, the Member of Parliament and the Member of Lloyd's, was worlds removed from Somerset, the toiler in Grub Street; and even when, as occasionally happened, they were asked to the same party, Detterling, who by this time hardly even recognised Somerset, saw no reason at all for renewing so slight and unattractive an acquaintance.

Only when Somerset, his apprenticeship conscientiously and profitably concluded, emerged as the Editor of a new weekly called *Strix* ('A Journal of Industry and Commerce', as he

sub-titled it in *Who's Who*) and had made of it an organ powerful enough to win the attention of astute politicians, did Somerset and Detterling at last meet as equals. That would have been
in 1955, Detterling thought now, when *Strix* had started to
give valuable support to the so called 'Young England Group',
a crusading movement of young Conservative M.P.s (clean-up-
the-dirt-and-fling-wide-the-windows) to which Detterling himself had once briefly belonged. There had been a dinner party,
given by Peter Morrison, the leader of the group, which Detterling and Somerset Lloyd-James had both attended. The object
of the meeting had been to discuss unethical property deals,
against which the Young England Group wished to legislate
and on which Somerset was something of an expert. Even now,
nearly seventeen years later, Detterling remembered the fluent
and lucid exposition with which Somerset had both entertained
and instructed Morrison and himself; remembered, too, how
Somerset's pimples had flared as he warmed to his work and
how his tongue had come coiling out through his teeth in a
pronounced and slobbering lisp whenever he came to any
passage in his discourse which particularly excited him.
Nothing, of course, had come of the plans mooted at that
dinner, nor had any of those present (Detterling now thought)
really supposed that anything would; but for Detterling himself the evening had had a lasting importance, in that it had
brought him once more into contact with Somerset Lloyd-
James.

This time he did not make the mistake of writing Somerset
off. Although the Editor of *Strix*, with his spots, his lisp and
his shamble, bore a good deal of resemblance, in manner and
physique, to the distasteful hobbledehoy first encountered in
1945, Detterling recognised from the tone of Somerset's
exegesis that here was a man of good value—a man who might,
over the years, provide him in ample measure with just that
kind of corrupt and sophisticated amusement that was most
to his liking. He had no thought at first of making a close friend
of Somerset; he wanted him as a mere casual familiar whom
he could watch and relish, whose intrigues and antics he could

follow and annotate, upon whose sources of information he could occasionally draw. Somerset, he had told himself in 1955, was for enjoyment, not for intimacy. But as the years went on the enjoyment he derived from the connexion was of such quantity and quality that gratitude had brought him to regard Somerset with immense affection and at last almost with love.

But never with trust. The business of the Desmoulins letter, for example, which had led, in 1959, to Somerset's securing his seat in Parliament—no one who had observed *that* with any care, thought Detterling, could ever again look on Somerset with trust. For Somerset had always chosen the crooked way, even when the straight would have served as well and better. Possibly this was why his entry in *Who's Who*, while factually correct, was yet so unrepresentative of his career; all his most notable activities had been conducted in large part *sub rosa* (there was even a story that he had contrived to cheat in his Tripos examinations) and so it was impossible that *Who's Who* should convey the true flavour of the man and his achievements. 'Editor of *Strix*, A Journal of Industry and Commerce; personally edited the literary and artistic, etc., sections as well as the main text . . .' While this was accurate enough, it suggested nothing of the whoredoms and imbroglios, the tortures by financial racking, the literary jobberies and the professional assassinations which were the real stuff of his ten years odd of editorship. 'Resigned in 1964 to devote his full time to politics . . .' Who could conceive, from reading those few innocent words, that Somerset had in truth resigned to become political and social hatchet-man for Lord Canteloupe. Canteloupe and Somerset had taken to each other right back in the spring of 1959, when Canteloupe had first joined the Tory Government and while Somerset was still worming his way towards Parliament. From that time on Somerset had begun to help Canteloupe with shrewd unofficial advice (advice on one occasion at least not far short of murderous) and had continued to do so right up to the fall of the Conservatives in 1964. At this stage Canteloupe, seeing boundless scope for their iniquitous alliance during their forthcoming period in Opposition, suggested that

Somerset should now assist him in a full-time capacity. What, Somerset enquired, was in it for Somerset? What reward did Canteloupe propose for the dedicated dirty work which he was doubtless going to require? Office under Canteloupe when the Conservatives came back. And if Canteloupe was in no position to give such patronage when the time came? That was the gamble, Canteloupe had answered, which Somerset must take. In the end, the gamble had paid off handsomely in 1970, when Canteloupe had gone to the Ministry of Commerce and taken Somerset with him. But who, Detterling now reflected once more, could ever deduce even the possibility of such murky trading from the simple, almost idealistic words 'to devote his full time to politics' that covered the affair in *Who's Who*.

There was little more to read. No publications listed (too busy with the dagger, thought Detterling, to spare time for the pen); address given as care of his bank (Coutts & Co., Piccadilly); no telephone number. '*Clubs*: Whites'—membership of which he had only attained, so Detterling recalled, through blackmailing two committee-men.

Detterling was just trying to reconstruct in detail what he knew of the last little matter when the telephone rang.

"Mackeson here, sir," said the voice of the Head Porter of Albany. "There's a shower of journalists down here at the entrance. They want to know where your chambers are."

Bloody hell, thought Detterling: someone's told 'em I got a look at the body. Carton Weir? The police? Never mind; they always nosed these things out somehow, and they would probably have come after him in any case, knowing him to be a friend of the deceased.

"Keep 'em waiting another three minutes," he said to the Head Porter, "and I'll slip out through the coal hole."

"Very good, sir. . . ."

Lord's, thought Detterling, as he closed his front door behind him and headed fast for the boiler-room and the back entrance through which coal was delivered: always a good refuge at a time like this. The M.C.C. was playing Surrey, so his fixture list told him, and with luck the Australian touring side would

be practising at the nets. He would have a nice peaceful afternoon of cricket, and while it went by he would work out possible
(and flexible) methods of tackling Canteloupe at dinner that
evening . . . and also the best way of putting down that damned
rabble of reporters in case they caught up with him later on.

Lord Canteloupe, prompt to the second in his arrival at the
Ritz, stalked up to the table carrying an enormous glass of
something red.

"Bloody Mary," he announced to Detterling as he sat down.

"Ought you to have carried it in yourself?"

"Only way, dear boy. Servants drag their feet so these days.
But I made sure that they knew it was to go on your bill."

"How thoughtful of you. . . . You look very well, Canteloupe."

This was true. Canteloupe's multi-coloured face, shining
slightly from the effort of transporting his Bloody Mary, gave
an impression of sappy vigour; the smashed veins in the cheeks
somehow coalesced to simulate a pleasing tan, suggesting
years spent in mountaineering or exploring rather than in the
copious demolition of rich food and liquor. The Minister's
hair, short, crisp and curly, might have belonged to a subaltern
fresh off the polo ground. His eyes, despite the little pink worms
in them, were bright and cheerful. He's in good nick, thought
Detterling; but there's something . . . wary . . . about his mouth.
He's in good nick but he's got problems.

If so, the Minister was in no hurry to share them with his
cousin.

"Fresh Foie Gras," he boomed, looking down at the menu
in front of him. "Sole Florentine," he commanded, and emptied half his Bloody Mary down his throat. "Entrecôte Chas-
seur," he concluded, like a colonel bringing his battalion to
the 'Present Arms'.

"When the waiter comes I'll pass the order on," said Detterling mildly.

Canteloupe looked at him as if he expected him to double
away and fetch the food himself, and then partly relented.

"We'll need some decent wine," said Canteloupe, "to drink to Somerset Lloyd-James." His voice faltered slightly. "To give the poor bugger a send-off. A magnum of something, to show proper respect."

Detterling turned and beckoned. An elderly waiter hobbled over. Detterling repeated Canteloupe's order for food and added his own, which was only marginally more modest. He then tried to attract the wine-waiter, who, however, was busy snarling at a colleague. Canteloupe at once observed this failure and—

"—Sommelier," he bawled and then whistled like a practised doorman.

"No magnums," said Detterling, feeling it was time he asserted himself. "They're no good unless they're specially ordered first and there's plenty of time to prepare them."

"Magnums of champagne are all right whenever you order them," grouched Canteloupe.

"I don't much care for champagne these days. Those bubbles are so annoying, and I can't be bothered to use a swizzle-stick any more. A bottle of Montrachet '66," said Detterling to the wine-waiter, "and one of La Tâche '64."

"Hmm," said Canteloupe, mollified. "Not cheap, the La Tâche."

"As you say, Canteloupe, we must show proper respect to Somerset." Then, after an appropriate silence : "What do you suppose went wrong?"

"Ask me another."

"Anything to do with his work at the Ministry? Any trouble about that?"

"The only trouble about that is, who the hell's to do it now he's gone?"

"So he was on top of it all right?"

"Right on top."

"And what about Strasbourg? Was he happy about the arrangements for that?"

"Why do you ask about Strasbourg?"

Canteloupe's lips tightened, emphasising the look of wari-

ness which Detterling had already noticed about his mouth.
I mustn't go too fast, Detterling thought, let's get some food
and drink into us first.

"I ask about Strasbourg," he said reassuringly, "because
it's obviously going to be an important show, and I supposed
that Somerset would have had a lot to do with it."

"He certainly would. He couldn't have chosen a worse time
to drop off his hooks."

But no suggestion at all, Detterling thought, that anything
to do with Strasbourg had been the cause of his doing so.
Nevertheless, it would be very interesting, to say the least, to
know what Somerset and Canteloupe had been up to. Presumably they had been going to discuss it that very evening
at that very table. What were the chances that Canteloupe
might confide in him, Detterling, instead? Well, here was the
Foie Gras and the Montrachet: let them do their work.

When Canteloupe had wolfed his Foie Gras with silent and
reverential greed, and when he had drunk two large glasses
of wine, Detterling said:

"So Somerset was quite happy about what he had to do
at Strasbourg?"

"Quite happy. Right up the cunning sod's street. Just the
sort of thing he loved."

"Might one know what it was?"

Once again, Canteloupe's lips tightened. But then he took
a gulp of wine and relaxed. "In general terms, yes. He was
to push one of our products and depreciate everything in the
same line that came from ... from elsewhere."

What product, Detterling longed to ask, and how was he
to push it? And who were these rivals from 'elsewhere'? But
for the time being he felt it prudent to go along with Canteloupe 'in general terms'.

"Just push our product for what it was?" he said. "Or
crack it up for what it wasn't?"

"It's always hard to know where the first ends and the
second begins. Better *not* to know if you want to make a good
job of it."

"Somerset would have known. He always knew things like that."

"I suppose so. Well, let's say he was getting ready to make a few plausible exaggerations."

"To tell a few downright lies?"

"Don't be offensive, Detterling. You know the sort of thing which goes on in the world of commerce. If you don't shout your own wares, no one else is going to do it for you . . . Ah, that sole looks scrumptious. We need another bottle of Montrachet to go with it, my boy."

Detterling sent for a second bottle of Montrachet and once again left Canteloupe to eat in silence. Then, pouring his cousin his sixth glass of wine :

"So Somerset," he said, "was in charge of the . . . propaganda . . . for Strasbourg. An important job but not all *that* special. Why are you going to find it so hard to replace him?"

Canteloupe took a toothpick from his pocket and applied it messily.

"It isn't so much a question of boosting our own stuff," Canteloupe said at last and rather carefully; "I can get a lot of people who'd do that well enough. The really tricky bit . . . is blackening the competition effectively. Somerset had thought of a very smart plan for that . . . the sort of plan that needs Somerset to apply it."

"Sabotage?" said Detterling.

"Not quite that, dear boy. We're not vandals. Let's call it . . . industrial satire."

"Expand, please."

"Well," said Canteloupe, "suppose, just for the sake of example, that you're competing in the sale of motor cars. Now, if a rival car is blown to pieces while it's being exhibited, everyone bloody well knows that there's been a bomb put inside it, and the incident is simply discounted. But if a door falls out for no reason, or if a tyre goes flat while it's just standing there, your rival is made to look ridiculous. You follow the idea?"

"I do," said Detterling, "and I quite see that Somerset

would have been enjoying himself enormously. Nothing here
to make him commit suicide."

"Nothing."

"Unless someone had rumbled what he was up to and had
found some way of applying pressure."

"Not a chance," said Canteloupe: "he couldn't have been
rumbled because he hadn't even *begun* to do anything. It was
simply a promising plan which we were still discussing. No
one knew of it except him and me."

"I see . . . Here comes the La Tâche. Would you care for
a sorbet before you taste it?"

"No, I'll taste it when I've started on the beef. And meanwhile, I *think* I see another drop of Montrachet in the bottle."

So Canteloupe had the last of the Montrachet, then weighed
into his entrecôte, with lip-smacking intervals for bumpers
of La Tâche. God, thought Detterling, he's going to want a
second bottle of that too. What did Carton Weir mean by
saying he's not drinking more than usual? He must have been
referring only to *spirits*, I suppose—the consumption he sees
of the supplies in the office. And of course it's the spirits that
kill in the end, a few bottles of wine more or less can't make
any odds to a man like Canteloupe. But all the same, he's a
little old to be lapping up La Tâche as if it were water.

A second bottle of La Tâche was now ordered by Canteloupe
himself, without reference to his host. After it had arrived
and been approved, Canteloupe munched happily on to the end
of his entrecôte, wiped up the last of the sauce with his bread,
drained his glass yet again, and held it out for more while
Detterling filled it. This time it was Canteloupe who broke
the silence.

"You're inquisitive, aren't you?" he said.

"Yes."

"You must be *very* inquisitive—with this La Tâche at sixteen pounds a bottle."

"Very inquisitive."

"Well, there's a way you can find out more. Chapter and
verse."

"What way?"

"Take on the job yourself."

"You're offering me the job of Under-Secretary at your Ministry?"

"Why not? It's about time I did something for the family. And I reckon you could handle this Strasbourg business . . . if once you were told the details."

Detterling took a long steady drink (about thirty shillings' worth) of the La Tâche. He would indeed like to know the details he thought; but he scented danger here, or at least very considerable inconvenience. Clearly the plan which Canteloupe and Somerset had been getting up to 'blacken the opposition' at Strasbourg, though it might stop short of positive outrage, was not the sort of thing to be blithley undertaken. If the price of fuller knowledge of this plan was to be the responsibility of executing it, the price was too high. During Captain Detterling's career as a soldier, his first principle had always been at any cost to eschew the firing line; this principle he had carried with him into politics, and he did not see adequate reason to abandon it now.

"I am not an ambitious man," he said at length. "I don't think office would suit me—in your Ministry or any other."

"Cold feet, eh?"

"Yes. Have a savoury."

"Thank you : devils on horseback . . . I can't say I really blame you," said Canteloupe, when Detterling had given the order; "it's not a job to everyone's taste."

"Precisely so. And don't forget—a lot of my time is taken up with Gregory Stern and the publishing business. I can't go off to Strasbourg for weeks on end and do cloak and dagger stunts."

"It's much more sophisticated than cloak and dagger these days."

"Well, that finally rules me out," Detterling said. "I'm an old-fashioned man, and cloak and dagger are about my limit. I am not prepared to learn a new technology at my age."

Canteloupe's devils on horseback arrived, and Canteloupe took a furtive look at the nearly empty bottle of La Tâche.

"No," said Detterling firmly; "no more of that."

"Just as well," said Canteloupe. "I'm seeing Maisie later, so I oughn't to drink too much. . . . Now look here, young Detterling: I may not have told you any details, but I have given you a pretty fair notion of the kind of thing that's been going on. Now you owe me something in return."

"You're getting your dinner, aren't you?"

"That's of course. You owe me something more. I'm in a jam, young Detterling; I *must* have someone to do this job at Strasbourg. Somerset can't and you won't: who else is there?"

"Is it really as important as all that? Just a product to be advertised . . ."

"*And* the rival product to be done down, remember."

"All right. But does it really matter if you fail? One more of our products will flop—hardly the end of the world."

"No. But it could be the end of this Government. One concrete fact I will tell you: the product in question is a new light metal alloy, capable of standing up to higher stress than anything else on the market—"

"— So *you* say—"

"—And so I must bloody well get people to believe. Because if they believe me," said Canteloupe, ramming in the last devil and mashing it with one side of his mouth while still talking through the other, "then there will tens of millions of pounds' worth of export orders, and that will be fucking lovely. But if they *don't* believe me, then a major corporation, whose last fling this is, will go bankrupt, thousands of men and women will be thrown out of work, the shares will be a pig's breakfast, and it will be the Rolls-Royce affair all over again, with sodding great knobs on. Which would likely enough mean the end of our beloved Prime Minister, and would certainly mean the end of yours truly."

Detterling ordered coffee.

"Port or brandy?" he asked Canteloupe.

"Both."

"How *much* of both?"

"Just tell him to bring the decanter and the bottle."

Detterling did so, and the same time rather pointedly ordered a small Marc de Champagne for himself.

"You were saying . . . ?" he said to Canteloupe.

"In effect," said Canteloupe, "I was saying how urgent it is for me to find a capable chap to take over where Somerset left off; and I was asking you to suggest someone."

"Tell me," said Detterling thoughtfully, "how does one apply this . . . industrial satire of yours . . . to rival light metal alloys? The example you gave just now was motor cars, and I quite see how it might be made to work with them. But with light metal alloy—sheets of it, or strips of it, or whatever— how does one set about making *those* look ridiculous."

"That was Somerset's secret and mine. But you can surely imagine the sort of man I need."

"I suppose so. A sort of Somerset. They don't grow on bushes, you know."

"But for God's sake, dear boy, you must be able to think of *somebody.*"

"All right," said Detterling : "Peter Morrison."

"Morrison?"

"He's been back in the House since '68, and it's time the party did something for him. He's had rotten luck lately— his elder son's been wrecked for good by meningitis—and he'll be glad of interesting work to take his mind off it."

"I always thought Morrison was . . . rather mealy."

"That's what a lot of people think. You just try him."

"But he's supposed to be a pattern of integrity and all the rest of it."

"He is supposed to be, and he likes being supposed to be. But he has a remarkable knack of reconciling his supposed integrity with the more awkward demands of practical necessity. He is good at touching pitch an*d not* being defiled. Let me tell you a tale, Canteloupe. While Morrison was a subaltern in India in 1946, he won the Viceroy's Commendation—"

"—That's just what I mean. The kind of chap that's won a Viceroy's Commendation won't take kindly to shifting the shit in Strasbourg."

"Just listen, Canteloupe. Peter won his scroll of Commendation because during some riots he apprehended a key Indian— the rioters' leader, no less. What wasn't mentioned quite so emphatically was that this Indian was subsequently killed while trying to escape."

"Killed by Morrison?"

"Oh no. Morrison was too wily to be the man that puts the boot in. But Morrison was behind it. He rigged the whole thing up, Canteloupe, acting under secret orders from some *very* important people who wanted that riot-leader dead."

*"Why did they want him dead?"

"For one thing, he was an ex-officer of the Indian Army and so was making a troublesome precedent. But there's no need to go into details. Just take my word for it—"

"—Why should I?"

"Because at that time, as you may remember, I was on H.E. the Viceroy's Military Staff. I was in on all of this from the beginning, Canteloupe, and *you can take my word for it* that we wanted this Indian dead. This we had told Morrison, who knew the man by sight, and when Morrison got the chance, he fixed it for us. Even then it was no easy thing to kill a rioter without all hell being let loose by the politicians both in England and India; but so neatly did Morrison arrange it that although quite a few people were suspicious there was nothing they could do about it—except scowl at the Gazette which announced his Viceregal Commendation. Now, does it not occur to you that a chap who managed *that* little piece of business might be fully capable of shifting your shit for you in Strasbourg?"

"I don't quite like the sound of it. You say that the Indian who was killed had been an officer, and that Morrison had known him?"

* See *Sound the Retreat*, passim.

"More or less."

"They'd met while the dead man was still serving?"

"Something of the kind."

"So Morrison killed . . . or engineered the killing . . . of a man who had been his comrade?"

"But was now an enemy of the Crown. You're not getting fastidious, Canteloupe?"

"I can't afford to be. But I still don't like the smell of this story."

"To me it smells about the same as Strasbourg."

"Point taken," said Canteloupe. He had finished a second glass of port and poured some cognac. "Do you think Morrison will take it on?"

"I think he'll take on Strasbourg if offered the Under-Secretaryship," said Detterling, "provided he's carefully prepared. There's a certain idiom you have to use when proposing villainy to Peter: phrases like 'concealed moral duty', or 'beneficent violence', that kind of thing, to help him keep his ethical self-respect."

"Are you well versed in the idiom?"

"Tolerably."

"Then you can sound him out and send him on to me if he agrees?"

"I'd be glad to. He's a very old chum of mine and, as I say, he should have work."

"So that's settled." Canteloupe looked at his watch. "Thank you for a very passable dinner," he said, "but now you must excuse me. Maisie's expecting me."

"So you said earlier. You still find it worth going there?"

"I may have one leg in the grave, Detterling, but it's not the middle one."

"I'm glad to hear it. I hope you'll be worthy of the La Tâche."

"I hope I shall be worthy of Canteloupe," said Canteloupe. He drained his brandy glass and rose. "See Morrison as soon as possible," he said, "and pass him on to me at once. No time to lose."

"I'll get hold of him tomorrow, if I can," said Detterling, and himself rose and then waved as the old man marched from the dining-room, as straight as a halberd.

Well, thought Detterling, as he settled down again to finish his Marc de Champagne, he's still a strong old man and no mistake. Putting down his dinner like that and then hacking off to his whore. I wonder how . . . effective . . . he will be when he gets there. . . . From what Canteloupe had let slip at one time or another Detterling knew that Canteloupe had more or less retired from the field of love years ago—until, in 1962, he had been introduced to Maisie by Somerset. (*Memorandum*: perhaps Maisie, whom Somerset had been visiting since the middle 1950s, might just happen to know something or other that was pertinent to his death.) According to Canteloupe, his first encounter with Maisie had been almost miraculously rejuvenating, and he had been going to see her two or three times a week, without a single disappointment, ever since. Maisie, it appeared, was exceedingly versatile and full of invention; so that it was quite reasonable to suppose, as Canteloupe himself clearly supposed, that this evening's tryst would be a success. All the same, Detterling thought, his cousin couldn't go on like this much longer. Maisie, and the gargantuan eating and drinking, and all his worries at the Ministry—between the lot of them any old man, however tough for his age, must surely begin to buckle.

But he hadn't buckled yet. In so far, Detterling reflected, as the object of that evening's dinner had been to determine Canteloupe's state of health, the occasion had been highly reassuring. As to the question of Canteloupe's Ministerial competence, once again the verdict was in his favour: he was concerned about the difficult situation in which he was landed by Somerset's death, but he showed no signs of panicking, he had been modest enough to seek advice, and although surprised and perhaps offended by the form which it had taken, he had been sensible enough to sift and then approve it, at least on a provisional basis. If Peter Morrison was his man, and if Morrison was willing, then Canteloupe was not going to pass him up on the grounds of his own personal distaste.

For the rest, by the time Detterling had called for and then paid his formidable bill, he had come to two conclusions. First, that he was as far as ever from finding the motive for Somerset's suicide. On the available evidence (Canteloupe's) Somerset's death had no connexion whatever with his activities at the Ministry or with the plans that he had been making with Canteloupe for Strasbourg. These latter he had positively been relishing; and since no one except Canteloupe and Somerset knew anything about them, there was no possibility that he had been in any way 'got at' on their account, let alone compelled to take his life, by malevolent industrial competitors.

As for Detterling's second conclusion, he reached it somewhat as follows :

He, Detterling, was now charged by Canteloupe to recruit Peter Morrison in Somerset's place. It was quite possible that Peter would subsequently show his gratitude to Detterling by informing him, far more fully than Canteloupe had done, of what was afoot in Strasbourg, and this would be very amusing. But any such revelation must lie in the future. The *immediate* point about Peter Morrison was that he had known Somerset Lloyd-James even longer than Detterling had and might well be familiar with aspects of Somerset's life and character of which Detterling was ignorant. Morrison, therefore, might be able to see into the suicide more clearly than Detterling and suggest an entirely new range of possible motives. So Detterling's next step was quite plain to him : he would go to Morrison, as he had promised Canteloupe; he would use his best endeavours to persuade Morrison to take up the post on offer and the task that went with it; and then he would pick at Morrison's memories of Somerset and see whether anything in them could help to explain why, some time very early that May morning, Somerset should have decided to leave the world, and all that he had in it, in exchange for his coffin.

PART TWO

KNIGHTS ERRANT

The priest flapped a kind of fly-whisk and drops of water pattered on to the coffin. A few stray drops fell, to Detterling's annoyance, on his shining black shoes. Automatically he took out a handkerchief and started to bend down to wipe them off, but then he remembered where he was, and that the water was presumably holy. He straightened up again, and tempered his irritation with the priest and his clumsiness by counting the other people present. Not very many, he thought. But then Somerset's friends had not been the sort that were given to going to funerals. They would all have more pressing engagements. They would come, of course, to the memorial service later in the summer, for the occasion would be fashionable and the attendance recorded; but meanwhile—let the dead bury their dead. Apart from the undertaker's men, the priest and his acolytes, there were only fifteen persons assembled by the grave to bury Somerset, none of them known to Detterling, though he was almost certain that a plump old lady, who was wearing a very long black bonnet reminiscent of the 'Waterloo' style and was accompanied by a tall, scraggy female of upper servant's demeanour (probably her housekeeper), must be Peregrina Lennox Lloyd-James, Somerset's mother.

The bereaved woman appeared to regard the affair neutrally. Her face was composed rather than grave, her eyes tired rather than sorrowful. In so far as she displayed anything other than indifference to the proceedings, it was spasmodic disapproval, indicated, every thirty seconds or so, by a cross twitch of the mouth. Perhaps, thought Detterling, as a Roman Catholic she deprecates Somerset's suicide; but then again the inquest (at which the old lady had not been present but the findings of which must by now have been conveyed to her notice) must surely have dispelled any cause which she might have thought she had for censure.

For the inquest had gone off in accordance with the highest hopes of Detective Superintendent Stupples. Somerset had emerged from it with credit that at times seemed to approach beatification. Dolly, on whom Sergeant Pulcher had evidently done a very good job indeed, had stated with absolute conviction that her employer had been working himself, quite literally, to death and that he had confided this to her in so many words. Detterling and Carton Weir had supported Dolly's evidence, though in more sophisticated terms; Carton, for example, had referred most impressively to Somerset's increasing '*accidie*' or despair of spirit. Canteloupe had spoken of Somerset's 'inhuman task, at once massive and labyrinthine', and when asked by the coroner to say what it was had pleaded national security. Had there been, then, any particular *incident* which might have triggered off Somerset's suicide? Not so far as the Minister knew. Then thank you most kindly, Lord Canteloupe, and the coroner was very much obliged to him. . . .

Potentially awkward enquiries about Somerset's day out in the country, which had immediately preceded his death, were firmly blocked by Stupples himself, who insisted that the police were satisfied that nothing relevant to Somerset's death had occurred during the outing. The jury had seemed anxious to know why, 'in this day and age', Somerset should have chosen such a cumbrous method of killing himself; but they had been content with Detterling's volunteered statement that his friend had been much obsessed with the customs of antiquity and might well have reverted to them at this moment of stress. In the end the coroner had spoken in lapidary commendation of Somerset's devotion to his duty and his country, and had concluded that he killed himself after his mind had been broken by his labours.

(The undertaker's men now began to lower the coffin. It tilted slightly, causing the sun to flash off the brass plate at its head and into Peregrina's face. The housekeeper (or whatever she was) made a protective gesture, but Peregrina poked her hard in the midriff with one elbow.)

Only after the inquest was over had Detterling realised that the coroner had been a party to the charade. While the Court was in session, he had appeared to find every smallest opportunity to ask awkward questions and knock on embarrassing doors. In truth, however, while making a great banging and clattering, he had never really tried to get through any of them; he had merely poked his head round them, nodded, and then withdrawn with a knowing expression, as though thoroughly satisfied that all was well on the other side. In short, the coroner had been fixed by someone as surely as had the witnesses; it would have been interesting to see what he would have done if any of the latter had departed from the official line.

(Peregrina threw a trowelful of earth on to the coffin, and twitched emphatically. The housekeeper followed. Others formed a queue for the privilege.)

But if everything had gone according to plan at the inquest, this was not the case in other areas. When Detterling had telephoned Peter Morrison's London house, the morning after his dinner with Canteloupe, a rather rattled Mrs Morrison had said that her husband was away. She clearly did not wish to say any more, but when Detterling, using his right as an old friend of the family, had gone on to press the matter, Helen Morrison had admitted that Peter was in Switzerland, at a clinic where a last-ditch cure was being tried out on Nickie, their meningitic elder son. Helen herself had not had the heart to go because she knew the whole thing was useless. But Peter still had hopes, she said, and was prepared to back them with absurdly large sums of money; she only wished he would stop listening to these crooked mid-European quacks. When would he be back? In three or four days. Any chance of getting him back earlier, for something of importance? To Peter, Helen had said, Nickie, poor imbecilic Nickie, was the only thing of importance just then, and futile though his mission was, she did not think it would be either right or kind to try to interrupt it.

With this Detterling was compelled to agree, though privately he thought that the sooner Peter had some sense shaken into him the better; Peter needed distraction from Nickie's plight before he became totally obsessed with it and beggared himself in desperate pilgrimages from sanatorium to sanatorium. But however that might be, the immediate point was that there must be substantial delay before he could talk to Peter. He could not fly out to Switzerland to see him, even had he felt so inclined, because Helen, quite simply, refused to give the address of Nickie's clinic. This meant frustration and annoyance for Detterling, and perhaps rather more serious consequences for Canteloupe, who would be very short of time in which to make final arrangements for Peter to take over the work in Strasbourg, even if Peter, as was by no means certain, immediately consented to do so.

But Canteloupe had put a good face on it ('We can worry till our balls drop off, it won't help anything') and what with the inquest and now the funeral the interval was passing quick enough. According to Helen, Peter would now be back that very evening, together with Nickie, upon whom, as she had predicted, the cure had had no effect. Just how much easier or harder this would make it to persuade Peter to accept Canteloupe's offer remained to be seen.

Detterling, at the end of the queue, finally came to his turn with the trowel. Try as he might, he could think of no other valediction for Somerset than a Greek epigram which went:

The nettles which flourish on Mopsus his grave
Are more poisonous far than a hornet:
I pissed on them once, and the sting that they gave
Shot right up my stream to the cornet.

Ah well, he thought, Somerset would have enjoyed both the sentiment and the obscenity. Here's luck, old fellow. . . . Having finished with the trowel he was just about to give it back to the priest, when there was a tap on his right shoulder-blade. He turned, and saw that someone else had come up behind him. Someone who had not been present before; but someone, at last, that he knew or at least recognised: a man who had a face like Mr Punch's, with a chin that curved up almost far enough to meet the nose that jabbed fiercely down at it.

"Leonard Percival," said the man softly; "my turn to pay my respects."

Leonard Percival. The name Detterling had forgotten, though the face was unforgettable. Where had he met him?

Percival threw earth with the trowel, handed it to the priest and followed Detterling, who returned to his former position at the other end of the grave. They stood there together as the last words were said. Then the little congregation, led by the priest, moved away towards the gate of the churchyard. Since they were all strangers, Detterling decided to stay where he was for a little, and Percival stayed with him. Both of them watched as the woman in the long black bonnet (Peregrina it now must be, Detterling thought) took up her station by the gate and started to shake hands with the people that filed past her.

"We mustn't keep the old lady waiting," said Percival, at last breaking the silence between them.

The pair of them left the grave-side and walked towards the diminishing file at the gate.

"No," said Percival, as if reading Detterling's thoughts, "we don't tackle her today. We shan't have a proper chance anyhow. I gather she's not giving a lunch or anything?"

"No."

"So much the better. We can just disappear and come back to her later . . . after the lawyers have sorted out the will and the money and everything. By that time she might have something interesting to say. Though I very much doubt if we're going to need her. She wasn't in his life at all—the part of it that mattered to him. So what would she know of his death?"

By the time they came to the gate, there were only two people in front of them, a soft, balding, middle-aged man and a frumpish woman.

"I'm afraid this must have been a shock, Peregrina," said the man.

But Peregrina merely twitched, as she had by the grave, and said nothing. The man and the woman both shook her hand and passed through the gate without speaking further.

"Captain Detterling," said Detterling, offering his hand; "an old friend of Somerset's."

"He spoke of you once. It was kind of you to come, Captain Detterling."

She twitched dismissively, and Percival took Detterling's place.

"Leonard Percival," said Percival, without explanation.

"Mr Percival. . . ."

Peregrina nodded her long bonnet, then turned. A car started up a little way down the street and moved forward to the gate, a small Morris shooting brake, driven by the housekeeper. Peregrina, taking no further notice of Detterling or Percival, or of the priest who was hovering some yards away, climbed neatly into the front seat and twitched at the housekeeper, who drove off, in the direction that led out of London, rather fast.

Detterling and Percival surveyed the empty suburban street. The mourners and the undertaker's men had all disappeared. Two little boys in jeans and jerseys (the disrobed acolytes) ran silently but violently past the priest and through the gate, and fled in the direction opposite to that which Peregrina's car had taken.

"They shouldn't have children at funerals," said Percival.

"They shouldn't have funerals at all."

"Disposal service, eh? I agree. Just ring up for the man to come and collect. Less depressing that way. None of this hanging about."

"My car should be here in a minute," Detterling said. "You are from Jermyn Street, aren't you?"

"That's one way of putting it. Rather a tactful one."

"Then you'd like a lift?"

"Please. I came by train. They're very mean about minor expenses."

"I wondered when someone would be coming. It was promised, you see."

"Here am I," said Percival; "take me."

"We've met before," Detterling said.

"I hoped you'd remember. Hydra 1962. I was staying with your old chum, Max de Freville."

"He's in Corfu now."

"So I hear. Very much on my beat at one time, all that part of the world."

"What brought you back home?"

"Ulcers," said Percival : "too much of a risk in the field."

"Not very handy anywhere."

"Oh, I'm fit enough for standard domestic jobs, like this one. But I wish that car of yours would come. I don't like standing for too long."

"Then you shouldn't have come to this funeral."

"I had to make contact with you, according to my instructions."

"You didn't need to come here in order to make contact."

"No, but I like to get the feel of the thing. If you see the body being put away with your own eyes, it gives you a personal interest. And shaking hands with his old mother—that was a help too. It makes you feel part of the family, in a way."

"I don't think Mrs Lloyd-James quite thought of you as that."

"No. But now I've got a face to keep in mind. I can look at that face, mentally, and I can ask myself 'Could this woman's son have done so-and-so or such-and-such?' "

"Very well. Ask yourself 'Could this woman's son have killed himself?' "

"From what I hear, he must have done."

"Then try asking yourself 'Why?' "

"Let's not rush things, Captain Detterling. This your car?"

"Yes."

A large, deep red Mercedes, driven by a uniformed chauffeur, drew up by the churchyard gate.

"And your chauffeur?"

"My manservant."

The manservant got out of the car, revealing grey breeches and leather gaiters, and saluted in military fashion. Detterling raised his bowler in acknowledgement.

"You're late, Corporal."

"Sir."

"Why? It's not far from here to Mr Morrison's house in Putney."

"No, sir. But just as I was delivering that note of yours—I was giving it to Mrs Morrison at the door—Mr Morrison turned up in a taxi . . . with that son of his, Mr Nicholas. It seemed they'd driven from the airport, and Mr Morrison was disappointed because Mrs Morrison hadn't met them with a proper car and the nurse. *She* said she wasn't expecting him till the evening plane at 5.30, and *he* said he'd sent a telegram changing that, and *she* said she hadn't had it, and in the middle of this Mr Nicholas—well, sir, he forgot himself in the taxi. You know how they are when they're like that. So the taxi-driver took on something fierce about the puddle on the seat, and there was words all round, and I had to help get Mr Nicholas inside and find the nurse, and then Mrs Morrison had to get a bucket of water and a floor-cloth for the puddle in the taxi, and I had to help her, and the taxi-driver just stood there griping, the rotten sod, and—"

"—Oh God," said Detterling. "That'll do, Corporal. I understand."

"But one good thing, sir. In the middle of all this Mr Morrison somehow found time to read your note—he must have known it was urgent, me being there to deliver it—and he says he'll be able to come and talk to you this evening, as you suggest."

"Does anyone mind," said Percival, "if I get in and sit down?"

"Sorry," said Detterling. "Corporal . . ."

"Sir . . ."

The manservant opened the near-side back door and helped Percival in.

"Rug, sir?"

"Rug?"

"For your knees."

"No, thanks. It's my belly bothers me."

Percival moved along the seat and Detterling (having waved politely to the priest, who was still hovering) joined him in the back of the car. When Detterling too had been offered and declined a rug, they set off towards Barnes Common, for Hammersmith Bridge.

"Why was he buried round here?" said Percival. "You'd have thought it would have been somewhere grand in London or else down in Devon."

"Expensive, either way. Mrs Lloyd-James doesn't look the sort to spend money on inessentials."

"Or even on her own kit. That bonnet must have come out of the Ark. . . . Who's this Mr Morrison your man was talking about?"

"Corporal," Detterling said.

The manservant pressed a button on the dashboard; and a glass screen rose from the back of the bench-seat on which he sat and slotted itself into the roof. Detterling then told Percival at some length exactly who Peter Morrison was and what business he, and by extension Percival, now had with him.

"You'd better handle him alone," said Percival when he had heard Detterling out; "at any rate when he comes tonight. I'd be *de trop*. You reckon he'll take this job of Lord Cante-loupe's?"

"He's wanted a post for a long while now."

"Well, as to this affair in Strasbourg," said Percival, "I hope he'll have proper professional assistance. We don't like amateurs playing games in that kind of area."

"*Your* area, I suppose."

"Not any more. We in Jermyn Street are separate from the crowd which goes in for *that* kind of thing—though as it happens I myself used to belong to it, before my stomach started to play up. We in Jermyn Street," said Percival, "handle affairs here at home: internal security. Our particular concern is to keep our eye on politicians and important public servants."

"To protect them? Or to catch them out when they're naughty?"

"To protect them, and to catch them out *before* they can be naughty. Much more decorous that : no mess on the carpet, so to speak."

"And if the mess is made before you can stop it?"

"We clean up quickly without banging the mop about."

"Which is what you aim to do here?"

"That depends," said Percival, "on whether there really is anything to clean up. One politician who's committed suicide is nothing. The vital thing, as of course you know, is *why*. The *why* could lead us to lots of nasty messes hidden behind the curtains, in which case we mop up *pronto*. Or it could lead us to people who are just about to make other nasty messes, in which case we hold their heads over a basin. Or it could turn out not to interest us at all. But the all-important thing, the thing that has to be found out before we can take— or even contemplate—any action whatever is why Lloyd-James went and did it."

"Agreed. But just now, when I asked you that very question, you told me not to rush matters."

"Yes. You were premature, you see, like all amateurs. The 'why' behind this suicide is absolutely crucial and we must never for a moment forget it, but there are many other questions to be asked and answered first."

"Such as?"

"For a start, why do you suppose that I have been sent to make myself known to you?"

"Because Superintendent Stupples promised that I should be brought in on this enquiry, and he has told your chief that I might be helpful."

"Correct. But why have they chosen *me* to contact you?"

"Because we know each other—or at least we've met before."

"Correct again. But far more important is where we met before—in Max de Freville's house on Hydra."

"What's Hydra got to do with it?"

"Nothing. But Max might have a great deal. He knew Lloyd-James quite well, and he knows both of us. Which means that Max, you and I—three men who know and trust each other—might come on something very useful when we combine our efforts."

"I've never really trusted Max," Detterling said, "and I've no particular reason to trust you."

"Then let's say, three men who know and understand each other . . ."

"We could certainly have an interesting talk about Somerset," Detterling conceded. "Max has always been a collector of information."

"I know. I used to provide a lot of it—in order to augment my official stipend. In this case, perhaps Max can inform me for a change."

"The only trouble is, Max may not be very up-to-date. He's been a long time on Corfu, and he hasn't seen Somerset since he had him out there for Christmas in 1970."

"It's what Max may know of Lloyd-James's past that interests me. I look to you for the up-to-date stuff."

Percival adjusted his wire spectacles and gazed placidly at Detterling, as if waiting for him to issue 'up-to-date stuff' as a ticker-tape machine beats out racing results.

"I've been trying to sort it all out these last few days," said Detterling.

"And what have you got?"

"All that about Canteloupe and the Ministry which I told you."

"Leading nowhere."

"Leading to Peter Morrison, who may help."

"*May*. What other lines have you thought of?"

"This whole business of the day Somerset spent out of London just before he died. What I call his 'Last Day Out in the Country'. That could explain a lot."

"Only no one knows where he went."

"You can surely find out."

"How?"

"He may have been noticed. He may have had an appointment."

"Noticed by whom? Appointment with whom?"

"Well . . . anybody."

"Exactly. Anybody at all. So we'd have to make a song and a dance in order to find out who, thus advertising far and wide our continuing interest in the affair just when it's meant to be finished with for good. I wholly agree with you," granted Percival, "that the details of Lloyd-James's 'Last Day Out in the Country' could be very enlightening, but we'll have to trust to time and chance to bring us information about that. Meanwhile, what else had you thought of?"

"His mother. But her you want to leave till later, you say."

"Right. What else?"

"There's a tart he's been visiting for God knows how long. Maisie, she's called."

"Maisie what?"

"Search me. But Canteloupe will know where to find her."

"I see. And what else?" said Percival, persistent and almost aggressive.

"His friends. Max, as you suggest—though it'll probably mean going to Corfu. Then the rest of them if we're still getting nowhere."

"Not bad," said Percival, his tone turning suddenly to approbation; "all quite obvious, of course, but at least you haven't made the amateur's mistake of trying to think up brilliant short cuts . . . which in this game lead only to short circuits. And here we are at your place, if I'm not mistaken."

The Mercedes drew up outside Albany. The manservant turned to look through the glass screen, awaiting orders.

"Want to come in?" said Detterling.

"No thanks. You drop me off here—nice and handy for Jermyn Street. So," said Percival, summarising: "you'll see Peter Morrison tonight and do your stuff with him. Then we'll get on with the rest of them—his whore, his chums and his old mother if we need her. And that's the only way of it."

Percival started to leave the car. The manservant had anticipated him and was there to open the door. Detterling too climbed out on to the pavement.

"That's all, Corporal," he said. "Garage and maintenance."

"Sir."

The manservant saluted, turned to the right, dismissed himself back into the car, and drove away.

"Useful fellow, that," said Percival.

"He was in my regiment."

"And hasn't forgotten it, I can see." Percival tilted his face and caught the sun with his wired spectacles, flashing them in Detterling's face. "I'll come tomorrow," he said, "to hear about Morrison."

"What time?"

"Expect me when you see me. No need to sit at home though. I'll find you all right."

Percival bent almost double, gave a quick, sly imitation of a sleuth tracking footprints with a magnifying glass, and darted away through the traffic.

Peter Morrison arrived at Detterling's chambers at ten in the evening in time to be offered coffee and brandy.

"Sorry I couldn't ask you to dinner," said Detterling; "my man's evening off."

"I had to dine at home anyway," said Morrison. "My first evening back from Switzerland."

"Could they do anything for Nickie there?"

Morrison's mouth trembled.

"No," he said at last. "No one can. I know that now."

"What are you going to do with him?"

"He can live down on the farm at Whereham. He might be able to learn to do something in the fields. Either Helen or I will be there most of the time. We can't make much difference, but I think he still knows us . . . in a way."

Morrison closed his mouth very tightly. Then:

"But you haven't asked me here to talk about Nickie," he

said. "That note your man brought—it implied something pressing. Otherwise I shouldn't have come. My first evening back; Helen wasn't pleased."

Why, wondered Detterling, does he talk as if he'd been away a year instead of just a few days? Perhaps it seemed like a year to him, while he waited in some ante-room at the clinic, waited for the nurse to summon him into the office, where the doctor rose behind the desk, smiling an antiseptic smile and already beginning to shake his head. . . .

Aloud he said to Morrison : "It is pressing, Peter. There's a job for you. To replace Somerset as Under-Secretary in Canteloupe's Ministry."

"Job," said Morrison, pursing his lips to make the short word linger. "That would make a change, certainly. But why are *you* telling me about it ?"

"Because there are two conditions, and Canteloupe thought you might like to discuss them with me first."

"Again, why with you, Detterling ?"

"Canteloupe is too shy to mention such matters to you until I have prepared the way. He is overawed by your moral reputation."

"Whereas you are not ?" said Morrison, and smiled bland forgiveness.

"I've known you a very long time, Peter, and I understand —I have done ever since that business in India—that your moral code has a lot of notes in small print written underneath it."

"Well, talking of notes in small print, let's hear these conditions."

"The first is that you've got to say 'yes' or 'no' tonight. If 'yes', Canteloupe will want you to start tomorrow."

"Straightforward, if rather flustering. And the second ?"

"You've got to be prepared to undertake . . . a very special role . . . at this Trade Convention in Strasbourg."

Morrison sighed. "I might have known it," he said. "Some unfinished affair of Somerset's ?"

"Yes." Detterling started to explain, emphasising the benefits which it was hoped the new light metal alloy would confer on the country's economy. "So you see," he concluded, "how important it is to the Government, and to Canteloupe within the Government."

"So important," said Morrison, "that he is prepared to use almost any means to do down our rivals."

"Not 'any means', Peter. He merely wants to make fools of 'em. No doubt they're playing the same kind of game against us. It's just like an old-fashioned Horse Fair. A certain amount of . . . minor foul play . . . is part of the custom."

"Minor foul play?"

"Just tampering. Nothing crude or violent. Sabotage is out, Canteloupe said."

"I'm delighted to hear it. But does one . . . just tamper . . . with rival light metal alloys?"

"Canteloupe wouldn't tell me, but he said Somerset had thought of a way. You'll be told quick enough if you take this on."

"No doubt." Morrison passed his right index finger along his upper lip and rested it against the side of his nose. "Why did Somerset kill himself?" he said.

"That's what I was going to ask you?"

"How should I know?"

"I thought you might have some sort of a clue. Something out of the past. . . ."

"Nothing out of the past," Morrison said. "When I first read about it, in a day-old *Times* in a waiting-room at Nickie's clinic, I just could not believe it. I had plenty of time to kill, so I thought right back, as far as I could, to see if there had ever been anything, however slight, which could have indicated that one day Somerset might do this. There was nothing, Detterling. I thought of the years at school during the war—we were in different houses but I knew him well even then—and I could remember him only as totally equable and competent, never in doubt what he wanted and seldom failing to get it."

"A bit sickly, wasn't he?"

"Yes, but it never seemed to depress him. He used it very

cleverly. He was the average sort of age when he came, getting on for fourteen, but because his build was very slight he looked much younger, hardly twelve. So from his first day there he managed to get it generally accepted, by masters and matrons and anyone who counted, that Somerset Lloyd-James was rather delicate and special and must be allowed time off to rest when he felt like it. In fact he always felt like it when anything dull or difficult was going to happen, a Field Day or a compulsory run, but no one ever resented him for it. In those days we all had to spend one afternoon a week cutting down trees or doing something to help the war effort; never once, that I heard of, did Somerset spend five minutes helping the war effort, far less a whole afternoon, and yet it was never commented on, it was never even noticed. It was just assumed by everyone that such things were not for Somerset. 'Lloyd-James not here?' some beak would say at an early morning lesson. 'Oh no, sir, it's raining and he's got a cold coming on, so he decided to stay in bed.' 'Oh, I see,' the beak would say. And then later the same day, when the sun had come out and some sort of pleasure was in train, there was Somerset in the middle of it, chatting away to the very same beak whose class he'd cut that morning—and never a single cross word. No, Detterling; there's no clue to be found in Somerset's ill health . . . which, incidentally, disappeared fast enough when it was no longer necessary to ensure his comfort. He last used it in 1946 in order to evade National Service; he flannelled the Medical Board just as he flannelled his House matron. From that day on not a word has been heard of it. For the last twenty-five years and more Somerset has had far too many interests to allow time for illness."

"But there must have been other troubles. Couldn't you think of *anything* in his past that might have contained the seed of his suicide?"

"Nothing. Oh, he's had his disappointments from time to time. I remember, when he was Editor of *Strix* and I was on the Board with him for a while, he came badly unstuck over several little schemes he had going. But something always came along to make up. In Somerset's life, things have always, on the whole, got steadily better and better. Better money, better positions, better arrangements about sex; first repute, then influence, then real power. Everything improving for him all the time—right up to the day he killed himself. So the only conclusion I could come to—sitting there thinking in Switzerland—was that his suicide must have been connected with something very recent, perhaps his most recent job . . . the one which I am being offered now. Not that I knew—then —what was going on behind the scenes. Now that you've told me how—er—questionable some of it was, I'm even more inclined to think that I could have been right."

"Well you weren't, Peter. The same idea occurred to me. So I went into it, and I've satisfied myself that Somerset's suicide had nothing to do with the plans for Strasbourg or any other aspect of his job."

"How did you satisfy yourself?"

"I questioned Canteloupe."

"He could be hiding something."

"No. I know when Canteloupe's hiding things.'

"So whatever motive Somerset had, it was quite unconnected with the Ministry?"

"I'd swear to it. You don't want to be put off by what happened to Somerset."

"I'm still not sure I want to step into a dead man's shoes."

"They're the best pair you'll get, Peter. If you refuse this, you may wait a very long time before you're offered anything else even half as good."

"The Under-Secretaryship, that's all right, very much all right. But this business in Strasbourg . . ."

"What about it?"

"Well, it may not have caused Somerset's suicide—"

"—It didn't—"

"—But it still doesn't seem very wholesome."

"By which you mean it's not safe," said Detterling, remembering his own thoughts on the matter.

"I mean it's not straight."

"That's why Canteloupe wants you. You, my dear Peter, have a way of dealing with what's crooked and somehow making it look straight . . . to yourself as well as others."

"Maybe. It's not an exercise I care for. It's very demanding of one's mental resources."

"But if the service of your country requires it?"

"Does it?"

"Yes. The country's going broke, you know that. We've little enough dignity left, and if we go broke we lose even that. And when we lose our dignity, we lose our influence, which is still just reckonable and operates, by and large, on the side of decency in an indecent world."

"Something in that, I suppose. The sale of this metal alloy —will it stop us going broke?"

"No. But it will delay the process."

"And keep Canteloupe in his Ministry. Canteloupe: is he an influence on the side of decency, Detterling?"

"There are worse men than Canteloupe. You might do a lot with him—and for him—if you become his lieutenant."

"You're telling me it's my duty to take the job."

"So it is. You're a talented man, and it's time you were using your talents."

"You're very tempting. I'd like to take this offer, but I wish I could be clear about my own motive. Do I want it for the public good or for my own aggrandisement?"

"Who the hell cares about that?" snapped Detterling. "You're simply indulging yourself in moral doubt as other people indulge themselves in fake grief or fake indignation. Will you take the bloody job or won't you?"

"I'll take it," said Morrison, looking slightly surprised, though whether at his own decision, at Detterling's outburst of ill temper, or at the accuracy of Detterling's diagnosis, Detterling was unable to determine.

"Then ring up Canteloupe straight away," said Detterling. "You can use my telephone. He may even want to see you tonight before you go back to Putney."

"So that was all settled as my cousin Canteloupe would have it," said Captain Detterling to Leonard Percival, "but there wasn't much said to help us."

They were walking in St James's Park at 11.30 on the morning after Detterling had had his discussion with Peter Morrison. Detterling had gone out for a breath of air, and Percival, true to his promise, had encountered him without warning or ceremony.

"Tell me," said Percival now, "is Lord Canteloupe certain that the Prime Minister will ratify the appointment? He seems to be going it pretty much alone."

"That's Canteloupe's affair," Detterling said. "I've done my bit. And much good I've got of it. Not a thing did Peter tell me that could even begin to explain Somerset's suicide."

"No. But some of it was interesting for all that. What he said about Lloyd-James malingering at school—how he managed them all so cleverly. And that remark of Morrison's about how everything got better and better for Lloyd-James all the time—including his 'arrangements for sex'. That was the phrase, I think?"

"It was. And now I come to think of it, it was rather a surprising remark—coming from Peter, I mean. He seldom refers to that side of life unless he's forced into it. And again, the offhand attitude towards sex which the phrase implies— that's not Peter's usual style at all."

"But from what you've said to me, the phrase is very appropriate. There's a tart called Maisie, you said, whom Lloyd-James has been visiting for God knows how long. There's an 'arrangement' if ever there was."

"Yes. . . . Maisie next stop, I suppose?"

"I think so," said Percival: "she must have got to know *something* about him by now."

"Well, I'll ring up Canteloupe. He knows her address."

"No need. I've got it here."

Percival gave the number of a flat in Artillery Mansions.

"How did you find out?" said Detterling crossly. "You don't even know her surname."

"*You* don't know her surname," emended Percival. "We've had her on the books for a donkey's age. She has a distinguished clientele, you see . . . with one of whom I was very much involved about ten years ago."

"I thought you operated abroad then. Before your ulcers."

"I operated wherever the trail led me. This trail came back to London, at one stage, and right through Maisie's bedroom."

"You're sure *your* Maisie is the same as Somerset's?"

"Certain. The name rang a bell as soon as you mentioned it yesterday. So I looked *my* Maisie up in the files—her surname is Malcolm, by the way—and it all checked. She used to live in Shepherd Market, where she regularly entertained, among others, two Oxbridge dons, three novelists, a nuclear physicist, and a selection of politicians, which included Lord Canteloupe, as one of course you know, and our dead friend, Lloyd-James."

"Quite an Aspasia."

"I can't answer for her intellect, but it seems she's good-natured and honest—*and* an expert impresario of male fantasies. All of which explains why she has retained her appeal despite being rather long in the tooth by now. In fact during the last five or six years she's been more in demand than ever, which is presumably why she left Shepherd Market for Artillery Mansions. A less embarrassing address for her silver-haired gentlemen to give to taxi-drivers and a more commodious arena for romping in."

"You talk as if she ran a gymnasium," grumbled Detterling.

"Some people's fantasies take up quite a lot of space and effort. Why are you so huffy this morning?"

"Because *I* was the one who was going to find Maisie for us, and now you've gone and spoilt it for me. And I don't like unnecessary surprises. Why can't you meet a man at an agreed time and place instead of popping out from behind bushes in the Park?"

"Because you want waking up." Percival took Detterling's arm, steered him through a left wheel and set them both on course for Birdcage Walk. "You're altogether too comfortable, Captain Detterling. You need a little early morning P.T., so to speak. You need to change a few car wheels in the rain, instead of having an ex-corporal to do it for you."

"I know of nothing in our connexion which entitles you to moralise at me."

"I dare say not. But you won't resent a little practical instruction? I'm sure you want to be a credit to our partnership."

"What kind of practical instruction?"

"A simple training exercise, for a start. Here we are in Birdcage Walk. I've told you Maisie Malcolm's address. I'll bet you a fiver that ulcers and all I'm the first of us to ring on her doorbell in Artillery Mansions."

Percival sauntered away towards the Buckingham Palace end of Birdcage Walk, and thus had his back turned on an empty taxi which had now appeared from the Whitehall end and was at once hailed by Detterling.

"Have a nice walk," Detterling called through the taxi window as he sailed past Percival. "I hope you can get that fiver on expenses."

Percival grinned and sketched a military salute with his left hand. Detterling sighed happily and sat back in his seat. Although he was a very rich man, he always enjoyed winning a wager. . . .

. . . So that he was rather put out, having rung Maisie's bell and been admitted, to find Percival already sitting on Maisie's leather sofa.

"You see?" said Percival. "You need livening up. You didn't remember that it was just on twelve o'clock and that your taxi would be badly held up by the Changing of the Guard at the Palace."

"It was only for a minute or two."

"Long enough for me to slip down Petty France and take a short cut through that new hotel—in at the front and out through the kitchens—while you were driving round in a ruddy great circle at a cost of twenty-seven new pence. Or to be more precise, at a cost of five pounds and twenty-seven new pence."

Detterling handed over a fiver.

"Would one of you mind telling me," said the plump and jolly-looking woman who had let Detterling in, "what all this is about?"

"This gentleman," said Percival, "is Captain Detterling. He is an old friend of the late Somerset Lloyd-James, and he is helping me with my confidential enquiries into Mr Lloyd-James's suicide." He turned to Detterling. "Meet Miss Maisie Malcolm," he said.

"How d'ye do?" said Detterling, shaking hands.

"Not too badly, dear," said Maisie. "So you've come about poor old Somerset? You don't want a nice dirty, either of you?"

"A nice dirty?"

"You know—a nice old, dirty old time. We can all three do it together if that's what you fancy."

"Madam," said Percival, "it is not yet one o'clock."

"Lots of my people come and do it in the morning. Gives 'em an appetite for their lunch."

"Tell me," said Detterling, who could not resist the question, "does Lord Canteloupe ever come and do it in the morning?"

"Loopy Canteloupe? Friend of yours?"

"Distant cousin."

"He comes any old time, Loopy does."

"More to our immediate purpose," said Percival, "did Mr Lloyd-James ever come and do it in the morning?"

"Not as a rule. He was an afternoon man—lately at any rate. But there was one bit of kinkiness he used to like in the morning. He sometimes had this bit about being a little boy who can't do his motions, see, and I have to be his nanny and stand in the lav. and scold him while he sits there straining. Then when he still can't go I have to bend him over the bowl and smack his bare bottom. He always prefers *that* in the morning," said Maisie, "because he says it's the natural time for it. Half-past eight he comes round, right after his break-fast—and a bloody bore it is, 'specially as I have to get myself up in striped gingham with white cross-belts and starched cuffs and cap. A very particular gentleman is Mr Lloyd-James, as well as being inventive. But I can't think why I'm telling you all this."

"Because I asked you," said Percival.

"So you did. But I shouldn't be telling about my clients."

"Mr Lloyd-James won't mind," Percival said.

"I suppose not. I was forgetting he was dead. Why did he do it?"

"That's what we want to know," said Detterling. "We thought you might be able to help us."

"Haven't a clue, duckie. He's been coming to me for ever so long—1955, I think it was first—and he's always enjoyed himself, in one way or another, and then just gone off till the next time."

"When was the *last* time?"

"About a week ago."

"He seemed his usual self?"

"Very much so. We had the oils out, I remember."

"Had the oils out?"

"For massage, dear. I had to pretend I was a lady doctor giving him osteopathic therapy. And then suddenly I had to start shaking all over, and lifting my skirt and dropping my knickers, and doing it to myself with the neck of the oil bottle and begging him to let me climb on top. 'Oh, you've got a lovely one,' I had to say, 'it's so lovely I can't wait to sit on it'."

"I see," said Percival. "And was all this a success?"

"Oh yes. He went off with a bang like a bathroom geezer. And when he left he gave me three quid extra instead of asking for ten per cent off, which is what he usually does because he's such an old customer."

"Nothing suicidal about all that," Detterling said. "Did he tell you when he'd be coming again?"

"No. But that wasn't surprising. He usually rang up a few hours before. 'I can feel it beginning to bubble, Maisie,' he used to say on the telephone, 'and I'll be with you this afternoon at four o'clock' or whatever."

"How often has he been coming lately?" asked Percival. "Not as often as when he was younger?"

"Not quite, but often enough. Three times a fortnight, let's say."

"And his performance when he does come?"

"Well, I told you about the last time. It isn't always as good as that, mind, but he's never dried up on me, and he sometimes stays for a second helping."

"We should stick firmly to the past tense," Detterling said. "Let us conclude that when Somerset died he was sexually in excellent trim."

"But was he?" said Percival. "Perhaps he felt guilty or inferior because he was compelled—forgive me, Miss Malcolm —to hire someone. Perhaps he was ashamed of being ugly and repulsive."

"Ugly he certainly was," said Maisie, "but not repulsive. He had a kind of attraction, you know, just because he *was* so odd to look at."

"Did he realise this?" asked Percival.

"He'd made quite a few girls in his day," said Detterling; "smart ones at that. He must have known there was something about him. It's always been my belief that he came to Miss Malcolm only for the convenience of it—to save time and trouble."

"I wouldn't wonder if you were right," said Maisie. "He didn't need to pay for his onions, not unless it suited. Lots of women would have liked old Somerset, because he had a way of surprising you. Not only with all the things he made up— nannies and doctors and the rest of it—but with the sheer strength and vigour of him. He was all so white and weedy that you never expected him to show himself so horny. And when he did, it was exciting. Not that I can afford to get excited about my clients or it'd be the death of me, but when I saw those pale, scraggy thighs, and then saw what power he was pumping up between them . . . well, it was very sexy. It was as though all the strength which should have been in the rest of his body had come together in his cock."

"Priapic," said Detterling, "like a satyr. Satyrs were often ugly too. Half men, half goats."

"So that when you had to say 'Oh, you've got a lovely one'," said Percival to Maisie, "you really meant it?"

"No," said Maisie. "It wasn't lovely, it was too bloated, too demanding, you might say, for that. But it was certainly nothing for any man to be ashamed of, and it more than made up for the rest of him."

". . . Which is all very interesting to know," remarked Detterling as he walked back with Percival across St James's Park, "but takes us no further at all. No clues in Artillery Mansions."

"You said something in there," said Percival, "about the girls whom Lloyd-James had made in his day. *Smart* girls, you said. What did you mean by that?"

"I'll give you a good example: Lady Susan Grange as was, now married to Lord Philby. She'd been mine for a bit, then Somerset took her on. Or rather, she took him on."

"Why did she swop over—if it's not an embarrassing question?"

"Not after sixteen years. She was bored with me. The way she put it was that she wanted to try some really bad wine for a change. And then, to her surprise, it turned out to be rather stimulating."

"Meaning more or less what Maisie said—that Lloyd-James had some unexpected shots in his locker?"

"I suppose so."

"How long did it last?"

"Nobody lasted very long with Susan in those days. But Somerset went a fair distance—and was only dropped when she got engaged to Philby. Somewhat to his relief, he always said: she was a damned difficult girl and very expensive to feed."

"So that Maisie came cheaper as well as much more handy."

"Yes. All of which only confirms what both Maisie and I were saying: Somerset preferred whores because they were in every sense more economical and didn't interfere with the rest of his life. The preference did nothing to make him feel inadequate—far less suicidal."

They paused by the bank of the lake. It was a blue day but sharp, without much hint of summer. Detterling watched the ducks as they went briskly about their aquatic affairs, and waited for Percival to tell him what they must do next.

"Max de Freville," mused Percival, "is in Corfu."

"Indeed."

"Fancy a day or two there?"

"Certainly."

"What about the House of Commons."

"It won't collapse without me," said Detterling. "But what about your boss in Jermyn Street? You say he's mean about expenses."

"Mean about taxis, because he has to open the petty cash box. Aeroplanes are all right, because he can get tickets on an invoice. It's not the cost he minds, it's dishing out ready money. Civil Service mentality, you see."

"What about a hotel when we get there?"

"Why don't we stay with Max?"

"Why don't we?" said Detterling. "It's a very comfortable house. Let's go and telephone him. I've got the Corfu number."

"No," said Percival, "let's give him a surprise."

"Bad manners."

"Good tactics. If you warn someone you're coming, he has time to think of reasons for not telling you things . . . or for telling you the wrong things."

"Why should Max want to do that to us?"

"Because knowledge is power. When you share it with others, you depreciate it. Max of all people knows that."

"I still think this mania of yours for surprising people is both childish and tiresome. Suppose Max isn't there? Or suppose the house is full?"

"He's there," said Percival, "and apart from him and his servants the house is empty."

"More checking up behind my back?"

"Why not? You wouldn't know how to go about it yourself. And if you did no one would tell you anything."

"Let's get on, if you don't mind." Detterling moved along the bank towards the iron bridge. "I'm sick of these bloody quacking ducks."

"Not one quack," said Percival, "but has a definite purpose to summon, alert, encourage or command."

"Who told you that?"

"I read it in the *Reader's Digest*. Not your kind of thing, I know, but full of tidily compressed information for those of us who haven't much leisure. Did you know why penguins can't fly? Or the true meaning of the expression a 'swan-song'?"

"No, I didn't."

"There you are, you see. You shouldn't despise the *Reader's Digest*."

"All right. Why *can't* a penguin fly?"

"Because its wings are too short," said Percival triumphantly, "and incidentally, there is no such thing as a 'swan-song'. It's a poetic fiction."

When they reached the Mall, cars were whizzing along both ways. Percival dodged neatly in and out of them, and waited patiently on the other side for Detterling, who took nearly three minutes to get himself across.

"You must learn not to waste time," said Percival, "in ordinary everyday procedures, like crossing roads. It is simply a matter of having a sound method and using one's will-power to apply it."

"We're not pressed for a few minutes."

> "If you can fill the unforgiving minute,
>   With sixty seconds' worth of distance run,
> Yours is the Earth and everything that's in it . . ."

said Percival as though he really believed it. "For example, and here is another practical test, how would *you* propose to reach Corfu as quickly as possible?"

"Plane to Athens," said Detterling, "and an internal flight on to the island. That's how I did it last time I went to see Max—the only way, they said."

Percival clicked his tongue. "It hasn't occurred to you," he said as they walked towards St James's Palace, "that things might have changed since then. These days, Detterling, and at this time of the year, there are direct flights to Corfu."

"If you say so. Let's get one tomorrow."

"There are also night flights. We shall go tonight, joining Olympic Airways Flight 807 at 2130 hours at the Cromwell Road Terminal or 2200 hours at London Airport. And arriving in Corfu at 0300 hours, local time."

"And knocking on Max's door at four in the morning, I suppose, to give him a bigger and better surprise. Thank you very much, but I'll fly tomorrow."

"You'd better fly with me," said Percival lightly; "tonight."

Although both the tone and the phrasing were civil, Detterling was too old a hand not to recognise the disciplinary menace behind this remark. 'You'll do as I say,' Percival was telling him, 'or I'm finished with you.' Detterling did not wish to be finished with, and now tendered his compliance, though he made it as cool as he could.

"So be it then," he said. "Since you're arranging it all, you can get the tickets."

"Bureaucratic difficulties there," Percival giggled. "My ticket will be procured through Jermyn Street. They won't pay for yours."

"Why not? I'm helping them."

"At your own pressing request."

"All right. You ask 'em to get two tickets, and I'll write them a cheque for mine."

"That," said Percival, "would lead to complications in the accounts. We have to be very discreet, you see. I must ask you to get your ticket yourself."

"Very well," said Detterling, who now saw his chance to take a mild revenge on Percival for so stubbornly subjecting him to inconvenience. "I'll go to my travel agent this afternoon."

"Yes," said Percival, "that's what I should do."

He stopped at the newspaper stand near Prunier and bought

a midday edition of the *Evening Standard*. After a quick look at the front page, "You could learn something from your cousin Canteloupe," Percival said. "He doesn't waste any time."

He pointed to a paragraph at the bottom of one column. 'Mr Peter Morrison to be Under-Secretary,' Detterling read.

"That means," said Percival, "that he's already got the Prime Minister's official agreement. No grass growing under Canteloupe's feet."

"I dare say not. If you'll excuse me," said Detterling, pointing to Prunier's door, "I'll just turn in here for a spot of lunch. I rather fancy some fish."

"Won't your ex-corporal be expecting you at home?"

"There isn't any fish there."

"He doesn't know you suddenly want fish. He'll be cooking for you by now."

"He's very flexible. We taught them to be in our regiment."

"All the same, rather bad manners to let him down."

"I'll get a waiter to ring him up," said Detterling in a brittle voice, wondering why he was bothering to justify his arrangements to Leonard Percival.

"You do as you please," said Percival, flashing his spectacles in the sun. "It's no skin off my snout. But remember: 2130 at the Terminal or 2200 at Heathrow."

"I'll be there . . . ticket and all."

Detterling walked into Prunier's Restaurant, meditating the little surprise he had in store for Percival that evening. Percival needed putting in his place, and Detterling, thought Detterling gleefully, was just the man to see to that.

Captain Detterling had himself driven to London Airport by his manservant and arrived there at 2155 hours. When he had checked himself in on Olympic Airways Flight 807, he went through the passport barrier and found Leonard Percival, who was blinking up through his glasses at a television screen which announced imminent departures. In their case, it appeared, not so imminent.

"Flight's delayed by half an hour," Percival said.

"Oh dear. That makes thirty unforgiving minutes in which we shall *not* get sixty seconds' worth of distance run. Let us have a drink instead."

"Just a moment," said Percival. "What's that?"

He pointed to Detterling's boarding card, which was sticking out of his breast pocket.

"It's pink," said Percival in evident dismay : "first-class."

"What else?" said Detterling smugly. "Drink?"

"I won't be long," said Percival. "Please order me a light ale."

He swallowed slightly, then scurried away towards the passport barrier, spoke quietly to one of the officials, and passed back into the outer world. Detterling ordered a light ale and a double whisky at the bar, and sat down at a table with satisfaction. Percival, as he had hoped, was clearly discomforted by the assertion of independence implicit in the purchase of a first-class ticket. He had been reminded that Detterling had his own style of doing things, and that this style was, and always would be, superior to anything which Percival could deploy. Percival, in short had been put down. But where had he gone? If he wanted to report to Jermyn Street, about Detterling's behaviour or anything else, there was a telephone inside the passport barrier.

And then suddenly Percival was back again, with a pink first-class boarding card sticking out of his breast pocket.

"Well, well," said Detterling, "so you've had yourself upgraded. Jermyn Street won't like that. It will lead to complications in the accounts."

"No, it won't," said Percival. "They'd never allow it. I've had to pay the difference myself."

"Oh," said Detterling. "Why did you trouble to do that?"

"Because we're travelling together. Or that's what I thought." Percival raised his light ale. "Cheers," he said. "Just as well our flight has been delayed, or I'd never have had time to get my ticket changed." He took a sip of beer and set down his glass. "Why did you want to go first-class, Detterling?" he said.

"Better supper, better service, more room."

Percival nodded pleasantly, as though entirely satisfied by this.

"No," said Detterling, who in the last two minutes had begun to hate himself. "I did it to surprise you. To *spite* you. To show off. I'm very sorry."

"It's good of you to say so. We're not used to apologies in our line of work. But don't worry. I shall be interested to see what it's like going first-class, for once, and I dare say I shall be getting my own back before very long."

Although supper on the flight to Corfu was indifferent, Detterling rendered it passable by washing it down with four quarter bottles of Olympic Airways claret and topping off the lot with two double brandies. Percival, by his side, muttered something about his ulcers, ate only cheese and salad, and drank water, there being no milk. However, he watched Detterling's progress with interest and talked in a friendly way of the refreshments, some nice but most of them nasty, which he had consumed on various kinds of public transport during his former journeys round Europe. Dining-cars on German trains seemed for some reason to have pleased and even to have obsessed him; and it was while he was giving the details of a luncheon which he and an acquaintance had once eaten between Munich and the Austrian border that Detterling, having finished his second brandy, fell asleep.

"Detterling, Detterling, Detterling," said a small, persistent voice, whether hours or seconds after he'd dropped off Detterling could not tell. But he was still flying, that he knew, because the cabin of the plane was tilted back at an angle of almost forty-five degrees. Detterling did not care for the implications of this and closed his eyes again to return to the refuge of sleep.

"Wake up, wake up," said Percival, ramming his elbow into Detterling's side. "It's bloody bad manners to go to sleep when somebody's talking to you."

"Sorry," said Detterling. His mouth felt like pumice stone and the aeroplane started to buck about like a toy.

"No self-control, that's your trouble," Percival said. "No concentration. You can't carry anything through."

The aeroplane lifted like a kite and shuddered all over.

"I should have thought it was jolly sensible to sleep through this."

"Not when you're travelling with someone who's talking to you. Particularly when he's paid extra for the privilege. No stamina, Detterling."

"If you don't mind, I shall try to go to sleep again."

"No stamina," said Percival, shoving his face close to Detterling's. "You couldn't even carry through that mean little trick of getting a first-class ticket to annoy me. You thought I was hurt, so you just buckled up and apologised. No endurance, no guts. In *my* regiment we set a lot of value on guts."

"What was your regiment?" asked Detterling faintly.

"The Wessex Fusiliers. No, don't nod off. I'm telling you you've got to be tougher. In this game you don't apologise just because you've hurt somebody's feelings—not that you *had* hurt my feelings, because of course I'm much too tough. I was just pretending to be hurt to see what you'd do. If you want to be sick, there's a paper bag in there with those maps."

"I don't want to be sick. I want to go to the lavatory."

"Number one or number two?"

"Number two."

"Well, you can't go in any case because the sign up there says you've got to keep your seat belt fastened."

"Who's stopping me?"

"I am," said Percival, who occupied the outside seat. "I'm not going to let you endanger all our lives by walking about when you're meant to stay in your seat. If you only wanted to do number one, I dare say you could use that bag in an emergency. But not for number two. The air-hostesses wouldn't like it."

The plane dropped a long way like a very fast lift and made a noise as if all the engines had exploded.

"I can't wait much longer," said Detterling. "How long before we arrive?"

"At least forty minutes."

"Oh dear *God* . . ."

The plane dropped again, tilted left then right then left, dropped farther and faster, hit something, bounced violently, gave a great roar of rage, and then proceeded smoothly up the runway.

"You must have known we were landing. Why did you tell me there was another forty minutes?"

"To teach you not to play silly jokes on me," said Percival, looking at his watch. "0345 hours, local time. Not bad, since we started half an hour late."

"Well, I'll just go back to the lavatory. Let me past, there's a good chap."

"You're not allowed to move until the plane stops taxi-ing," said Percival, sitting firm, "and then you won't be able to get back because all the people at the back will be rushing forward to the exit. There may be a loo this side of the customs barrier, but I rather think you'll have to wait till we've been cleared. . . ."

By the time they had cleared their bags and Detterling had cleared his bowels, it was 0430 hours.

"What now?" said Detterling.

"A walk in the light of dawn. There's something I want to show you. We can leave our luggage here."

They walked 200 yards from the front of the airport up to the main road, turned left along it, and then, very soon afterwards, wheeled about 130 degrees right on to a subsidiary road which (Detterling thought) must be one of several possible routes into the town of Corfu. For ten minutes they walked past new houses, the roofs of which were flat, the designs distressing, and the colours still mercifully invisible except as light or dark. The wind was high but warm, the clouds low.

"I fear we shan't see the sunrise in this weather," Percival said, "but I promise you the walk will be worth it."

Once more they turned well over ninety degrees to the right, and walked down a lane, on the left of which stood an oddly handsome wedge-shaped house adjoined by a six-foot wall. A few yards along the wall was an iron gate; beyond the gate a grass walk, lined by cypress trees and high-arching shrubs.

"The British Cemetery," Percival said.

"I can't see any gravestones."

"You will."

Percival tried the gate. Locked. He then rang a bell, fiercely. After a few minutes someone shuffled up and grumbled obstructively out of the half-dark. Percival jabbed back a couple of sentences in demotic Greek. The gate opened very quickly, whereupon Percival led Detterling past a gaping man in vest and braces, and then up the grass walk between the shrubs and the cypress trees.

"What did you say to him?" Detterling asked.

"I said that we've come to see the grave of our cousin, whose name-day it is. Since we suspect this cousin of being a vampire, I said, it would be as well for anyone who lives in this neighbourhood to keep in with the family."

"I didn't know they had vampires in Greece."

"Not the blood-sucking Transylvanian kind. Greek vampires just get out of their graves and smash people up." Percival took a turn to the right, down a narrower walk with well-spaced tombs, separated by rough grass and casual flowers, on either side of it. "They're very stong, Greek vampires," Percival was saying, "and not wholly malignant. They often cart sacks and things round for members of their families. In fact they're very family-minded, which is what made my threat such a potent one. If we had got a cousin here who was a vampire, then he'd certainly have it in for anyone who kept us out."

Although there was still no sign of the sun, the light was improving with every second. The larger inscriptions on the graves were quite clear now.

"Nicest cemetery in the Ionian Islands, this," Percival said. "There's an amusing one for the British on Zante, but it's too crowded. And though some of the Jewish ones are good, they're apt to be used as hen-runs. *This* place is a model of proportion and propriety—except, I'm afraid, for what we've come to see. *There*."

Percival pulled up, and there, at the end of the walk, in an alcove set into a thick hedge of yew, was a real horror. Under a cupola, which was supported by four pillars but nevertheless contrived to look like a beach umbrella, reclined a lightly draped Rubenesque lady whose grinning face was propped on one elbow, in ghastly parody of the Etruscan manner. With her free hand she was reaching out to grasp a wine cup, which was being proffered on a platter by a group of four lanky and long-haired adolescents (after Beardsley) each of whom had one hand under the platter and the other three inches in front of his crutch. Inspection from any of several angles would indeed have given sight of their genitalia, but since these were supposedly concealed they had not been carved. Their absence lent the final touch of obscenity which turned the ensemble from a curiosity into an abomination.

"Recognise anybody?" said Percival.

"I can't say I do."

"Then look here."

Percival pointed to a small carven scroll, which lay on the platter by the wine cup, rather as though it was a bill for the refreshment. After some craning, *ANGELA TUCK*, read Detterling on the scroll, *1924 to 1970.*

"Angela Tuck," announced Percival superfluously. "Who was Max de Freville's mistress," he added with a mixture of malice and unction.

"You don't need to remind me of that. I suppose there is a certain grotesque resemblance. That mouth. . . . Had you seen this frightfulness before?"

"No. But I'd heard it was here. Since early this year."

"Let's see," said Detterling, trying to keep a grip on himself. "Angela died not long before I last saw Max, which was at the end of 1970. When I saw him, he obviously missed her, but he showed no sign of breaking out like this. I mean, I suppose Max *is* responsible for it?"

"Oh yes. Who else?"

"Then what got into him? Angela would have laughed herself sick."

"Perhaps that's the idea," said Percival. "Perhaps it's a joke to entertain her ghost. Anyway, he went to great trouble to get it set up. The authorities said it was unsuitable, but Max insisted, and since he's very important on this island, with his investment in tourism and the rest of it, they let him have his way . . . in return for a large contribution to the upkeep of the cemetery."

There was a spluttering noise behind them. The caretaker, now wearing a cardigan over his braces, was spitting out Greek.

"Oh dear," said Percival. "I'm afraid there's been a misunderstanding. He now thinks Angela Tuck is the cousin I spoke of and he's asking if she's really a vampire."

"Tell him 'yes'," said Detterling : "in some ways she was."

"*Nai, nai*," said Percival, pointing at the reclining Angela; "*afti.*"

The caretaker backed off, looking solemn, then turned and retreated rather fast.

"I'm afraid that was naughty," Percival said. "If Max hears he'll be very cross."

"If he put this up for a joke, as you suggested then he won't mind another one. Nor would Anglea. Why did you bring me here, Percival?"

"Joke or no joke, I thought it would interest you. For in either case," said Percival, "having seen this thing, we may expect to find that Max has has turned rather odd since you and I last met him. *Flighty* is perhaps the word."

"Then can we trust him to make some sense about Somerset?"

"I think we must be prepared for his approach to be somewhat eccentric." Percival leant forward and smacked Angela's huge uppermost flank. "No one who has done this . . . in fun or otherwise . . . is likely to be entirely straightforward on any topic. Back to the airport for some kind of brekker, I think, and then we'll trundle out to see Max. . . ."

"Not what one would have expected," Max de Freville said. He wrinkled his nose, thereby deepening the two purple clefts which ran from his nostrils to either end of his mouth. "I could hardly believe it when I saw it in the paper. In his bath. . . ."

Max had received Detterling and Percival, when they arrived at his villa at eight in the morning, without surprise, annoyance or pleasure. He had offered them breakfast, which they declined (having just eaten it at the airport), and the use of two bedrooms, which they accepted. At his suggestion they had spent the morning resting, while Max himself went into the town 'on business', and at his summons they had roused themselves for lunch, which the three of them were now eating in a furnished arbour on one side of Max's lawn.

"Mind you," said Max, in a tone that showed (Detterling thought) a lack of interest, "this sort of thing does have precedent. It is by no means unheard of for people to commit suicide even when everything's going well for them, as it was for Somerset. I once knew a chap—Darblay, he was called—a distinguished poet with a rich wife and a beautiful son, his own publishing business to play about with, smart friends and a gorgeous mistress thrown in—he had the lot, you'd have said. But one morning he woke up and just couldn't bear it. He was bored with it all, on the one hand, because it had come so easy, and terrified, on the other, lest it should all disappear like fairy gold. He didn't actually commit suicide, this one, but it came to much the same; he just lay in bed staring at the ceiling and wouldn't move. In the end they carted him off to a bin, and only got him going again with electric shocks."

"Somerset," observed Detterling, "is now beyond being revived by electric shocks."

"But you see what I mean? There could a parallel here."

"No," said Detterling. "Unlike your man Darblay, Somerset was neither bored nor terrified. He'd worked hard to get as far as he had and he was still working hard to get further. He was fascinated by what he was doing, and though there were certainly risks in it, he regarded them not with fear but with relish—as a professional challenge."

"If you say so. . . ."

"Canteloupe says so, and he was pretty close to him."

"Well," said Max, "I'll believe it. I remember when Somerset used to play in those chemmy games I ran in the '50s. He never got scared, though in those days he hadn't much money to lose, because he was always in control of his play. He used to bet just a little more than he could conveniently afford, to give the thing an edge of excitement, but never more than he could pay. I suppose that's how he played at politics; he'd balance his book so that he stood to make a very pretty win if things went smooth but not get skinned if the cards showed up with the wrong number?"

"That's about it, I'd say."

"Well then. . . ."

Max paused and looked rather blankly down his lawn towards the sea. He's not really with us, thought Detterling; he's got something else on his mind, and it's only through politeness he's making himself discuss our subject.

"Have you considered the possibility," said Max with a visible effort, "that someone might have been putting the screws on him?"

"We have," said Percival. "No dice so far. I'd hoped that you might be helpful in that area."

"I live too far away to hear about these things now," said Max with tired dismissal, "and I've seen very little of Somerset in these last years."

"We were hoping you might remember something from the more distant past. I have a hunch," said Percival, "that whatever caused this suicide goes back a long way. Can you remember any kind of quarrel or disagreement, anything of that sort, which happened a long time ago but might just have kept a strong enough spark going to cause a blaze later."

"Somerset," said Max, "was always very careful to extinguish sparks. He always tidied up, Leonard, because he was particularly aware of the kind of danger you refer to. Somerset never scotched his snakes, he killed them. And he did the same to the worms, just in case."

"Even so," said Detterling, "there could have been something that escaped. Some little maggot which crawled away and hid itself . . . and then grew, over the years, until it was strong enough to come out again, with poison in its fangs."

"It's always possible, of course. But I don't think you quite realise how incredibly careful Somerset could be."

Max shook his head and licked his lips. He looked intently at Percival and Detterling, as though making an important decision which had to do with their welfare. His gaze then shifted to a statue on the other side of the lawn : a long-eared faun with flute. The faun returned Max's gaze with a leer, his mouth curving softly over the flute. All at once Max brightened; for the first time he was willing, even eager, to talk.

"I'll give you an example," he said, "of Somerset at work. You both remember Angela, my Angela?"

"Of course."

"Well, years ago, in the summer of 1945 it was, Angela was living with her husband on the Norfolk coast. And there she met Somerset, who was seventeen at the time and staying with a school-friend. Came a night when her husband was away, and Angela asked Somerset and his friend over to her house, meaning to weigh up the form and take her pick of them." Max chortled at the notion, like an elderly clubman preparing his listeners for the climax of a smoking-room joke. "She often used to tell me the story, it was one of my favourite, and apparently what happened was this . . ."

'. . . I got us all drunk and playing strip poker,' Angela used to tell Max before she died, 'and in no time at all, as luck would have it, Somerset was bare except for his shoes and socks, and I had my bra off. But the other boy, Somerset's friend, was still fully dressed, and there was my problem, because he was a pretty boy and I badly wanted to look at him—in fact it was quite definitely him I'd meant to have when I started the whole thing going. And of course poor old Somerset was a real fright in those days, all shag-spots and yellow teeth, so you may wonder why I asked him to come along in the first place. The answer is that he had a way of looking at you, disapproving yet somehow collusive, accusing and excusing at the same time, rather like my father, who used to spank me with one hand and tickle me with the other—very exciting, I can tell you. So all in all, I felt Somerset was worth his seat in the house, and it might be fun to watch him pulling himself while I had it off with the pretty one.

'But it didn't work out like that. There I was with my tits wagging about—and bloody lovely they were then—and Somerset sitting there nude, as pale and damp as a dishcloth, and the pretty one as randy as a monkey under his trousers, and all I had to do, really, was chuck away the cards, undress him and get off the mark. But somehow I was too pissed to see it clear, I kept thinking I'd got to stick to the rules of the game; so I dealt another hand, hoping like hell I'd win a forfeit from prettikins and have the pants off him—and lo and behold, I won forfeits from both of them, my Ace over their Kings, so in any case I could now line 'em up any way I wanted. So I looked at 'em both, and worked out just what I was going to order—pretty boy under me on the sofa, with Somerset standing over us— and I opened my mouth to say the word. . . .

'. . . And then I saw something I'd missed. Somehow I'd cut myself earlier on, and some of my blood had got on to Somerset, smeared over his leg, it was, a lovely red stain on his skinny white calf; and there was Somerset looking at me as if to say, "I know you, you dirty bitch, you're longing to lick it off". So what with that blood on Somerset's leg and that look on Somerset's face, I suddenly found that prettikins didn't matter any more; he was just one more pink little boy, who'd come running along with a stiff tool any time I whistled, and probably shoot his load in five seconds flat. But Somerset, scrofulous, scrawny, *unwholesome* Somerset . . . who understood what went on in one's mind and one's cunt . . . he was something *rare*.

'So I turned prettikins out of the house, poor lamb, and I leant Somerset back in a chair, and I started to lick that blood.

Now, for all that look in Somerset's eye, I thought I'd have to do it all myself, that here was a virgin who'd have to be taught step by step. Boy oh boy, oh Somerset, was I wrong about that. I wasn't licking up blood for long, I was banging my arse on the floor and screaming for more and more of him and more and more of him I got, more and more, but never quite enough, he saw to that. I kept on sort of going off at half-cock, time after time after time, and when I did come at last it seemed to go on for ever, so that long after he'd taken his prick out I was still jerking about on the floor, shivering and shaking and blubbering and squealing, and then begging him—it's a thing I've asked of nobody else—to piss on me as hard as he could. . . .'

". . . In which particular," said Max de Freville, "he obliged most manfully and put Angela clean out for a count of twenty—or so she estimated later."

"All very entertaining," said Captain Detterling, "but I thought this story was intended to exemplify the wariness in Somerset's nature, not the wantonness in Angela's."

"And so it does if you'll listen to what happened next. It appears that Somerset and his chum went away somewhere very soon after, as had been previously arranged. A few days later Angela had a letter from him, in which Somerset thanked her politely for a pleasant evening and said he hoped they might meet again some time. As things fell out, they weren't to meet again for ten years or more, but that's by the way. What fascinated Angela was this: there wasn't the slightest overt mention, anywhere in the letter, of what had occurred between them; yet if you were in the know, as of course she was, the whole page was heaving with suggestion and invitation. To Angela, as she read it, it was one of the sexiest letters she'd ever had, making her want another steaming session on the spot; but it was so phrased that anyone else who saw it would have imagined he was thanking her for a couple of sedate drinks and expressing a vague hope that he would be able to return her hospitality. For a boy of seventeen, it was a masterly piece of prevarication: he had managed to put his message across hot and strong and yet to write down *nothing* that could possibly be held or used against him, by her or her husband or anyone else in the world who might just get hold of that letter."

"If he'd been really careful, he wouldn't have written at all."

"He had to. He wanted her to know where he could be found. He wanted the thing to go on."

"You said, just now, that it didn't go on."

"Only through bad luck. He had some engagements he couldn't break, and she had a doting husband to cope with— and before there was any opportunity of a repeat performance, the husband took her of to India. But the real point is this : here was Somerset doing his level best to have things the exact way he wanted them but also making absolutely certain that he took the barest conceivable minimum of chances consistent with his object. Of course he had to take *some* degree of risk, or his life would have been a total blank : what I'm saying is that both here and hereafter he used enormous labour and ingenuity to reduce that degree to near infinitesimal."

"Hardly as low as that," said Detterling. "What about this friend he was staying with ? He might easily have opened his mouth and done a bit of damage."

"Somerset had the whip hand of him." Max hesitated. His face went suddenly sombre. The gaiety induced in him by his memoir of Angela had somehow been spoilt. "You know who he was," said Max in tones at once portentous and peevish, "that friend ?"

"No. How should we ?"

"Fielding Gray. Angela always kept a soft spot for him, because he looked so disappointed when she turned him out that night. Pity, a sad pity," said Max heavily. "It would have been far better if she'd never seen him again."

"Why ?" said Percival. "What harm did he ever do her ?"

"He helped to kill her. It happened when he was here with a film company back in 1970. Writing the script, he was. So Angela saw quite a bit of him, and one day . . . well, he got her over-excited, and then she collapsed."

Max looked away towards the faun with the flute. This time he found no comfort there. He's looking old, thought Detterling; his clothes are hanging off him and he's scraggy round the neck; and yet he must be younger than I am, fifty to my fifty-five. Perhaps I look like that to others. They say you never see it in yourself.

"In what way . . . did Gray over-excite her?" Percival asked Max.

"We needn't go into it. It wasn't even his fault really, I see that now. She'd been ill for some time, and she'd have gone soon in any case. But it was . . . what he did . . . that killed her, so I can't forgive him. I'm so lonely without her, you see. I told you both, this morning, that I had business in the town. But that wasn't true; my partner, Lykiadopoulos, takes care of all that now. The reason I went out this morning was to go to her grave. I've had a statue put up, and I spend a lot of time there. Most days, I go. It's peaceful there, and I can look at the statue and think of her . . . as she was when we first met, not when she got so ill towards the end. She was so vital, always laughing and drinking, full of stories like the one I've just told you, warm, unashamed . . . I never slept with her, you know, or rather, we often shared a bed but nothing ever happened. I just wanted her to be there, and now all that's there is that statue. I must take you to see it, it's rather beautiful. At first they didn't want to put it up, it's a bit *risqué* for a cemetery, and even now they resent it. When I was there this morning the caretaker kept buzzing about and pointing at it and jabbering away in Greek. He seemed angry or frightened or something . . . as if a statue could do any harm. Well, all I can say is they'd better not try to move my Angela." He raised his head and his eyes blazed. "By God, they'd better not try, by God, if I find—"

"—No one's going to move her," said Detterling, and touched Max's arm.

"No, of course not. I'm imagining things. I get upset very easily these days—that Greek fellow upset me, yittering on and on like that, but of course it didn't mean anything, just some silly fuss about nothing. Anyway, I've given them a lot of money, so they won't want to annoy me. Angela would have been pleased about the money, she always wanted it to be used like that—to make things more beautiful. She hated what Lyki and I were doing to this island, all these hotels and camping sites, so now I'm doing what I can to make up. I'm trying to stop any more horrors being built, but it isn't easy and Lyki's no help at all. He's my front man, you see, I had to have a Greek, so what he says goes, and what he says is more and more hotels, because he thinks they bring foreigners here and make his people richer. He can't understand that it's making them rich in the wrong way, that in a few years they'll be just like everyone else in Spain and Italy and so on, all motor cars and television sets and not a tree or a blade of grass in sight. That's what Angela always said, but I didn't heed her then, when she was alive, only now, but I know she's glad I've understood even if it is so late, I hear her voice telling me when I look at her statue. . . . But I don't know," said Max, heaving his whole body in order to collect himself, "why I'm boring you with all this. I'm sorry."

"No need to be," said Detterling.

"You came here to ask about Somerset, and all I've done is talk about Angela. I wonder . . . is there anything else I can tell you about Somerset?"

"I think not," said Percival quietly. "I think we must go back to London and get on with our search there."

Max did not seem anxious to detain them.

"You can take the evening plane," he said. "I'll come and wave you off—and we can all look in to see Angela on the way."

PART THREE

KNIGHTS VAGRANT

"It's clear that poor old Max is going quietly barmy," said Percival on the day after Detterling and he had returned from Corfu, "but he did make one very important point with that tale of Lloyd-James and Angela Tuck."

"For God's sake, run up," called Detterling, on whose insistence they were watching cricket at Lord's. "*What* point did Max make?"

"That Lloyd-James was a master at covering up . . . at eliminating or suppressing anything which might have led to trouble later—*or, by the same token, might have been helpful to our enquiries now.*"

"Perhaps," said Detterling. "But you must remember this : a man can only eliminate something which may lead to trouble if he knows that it is there. He can only prevent the future results of his misdeeds if he knows what misdeeds he has committed."

"We all know when we've done something which may lead to trouble."

"Cross-bat stroke," said Detterling, looking sorrowfully down from the pavilion balcony in which they sat. "Very ugly. I don't know what these young pros are coming to. But the point is, Percival, that he doesn't know any better. He's been badly taught and he doesn't know what he's doing wrong. He doesn't even know that he *is* doing wrong."

"What's that got to do with it?"

"He's a perfect instance of someone who, unknowingly, is doing something that may get him into trouble at any second. He cannot prevent that trouble because he does not know that he's inviting it."

"If I'd known you were going to be so portentous about this

idiotic game, I'd never have agreed to come here."

"For someone who's been doing what you have all your life,"
said Detterling, "you are in some ways remarkably unsubtle.
We all of us resemble that young cricketer. We are all of us
apt to do things, every day of our lives, which come so natural
to us that we hardly notice we're doing them, but which, if
we only knew it, could lead to horrible trouble later on. So now
consider Somerset. He knew very well that what he was up to
with Angela could certainly lead to trouble, and so he took
careful and ingenious steps to prevent this. But suppose that
he had done something dangerous—like that batsman down
there—without any notion that it *was* dangerous, indeed hardly
knowing that he'd done it?"

"What sort of thing?" said Percival, in a more tolerant but
still sceptical voice. "Give me a concrete example."

"Very well. From my own experience."

There were only three other spectators up in the balcony,
and these were at the other end of it. Nevertheless, Detterling
now lowered his voice as if he were about to pronounce something positively treasonous.

"It was early in the war," he said, "summer of '41 and I'd
just been made a temporary captain and second-in-command
of a sabre squadron."

"By which you mean a fighting squadron of cavalry. But
I suppose that by this time they'd taken your horses away?"

"Alas, yes. We'd changed over to beastly tanks in 1939. And
they were the start of my trouble, as you'll see in a few
minutes. . . . But as I was saying, there I was, second-in-command of this squadron, which was guarding part of the Suez
Canal. Regimental Headquarters were in Port Said, which
wasn't too bad in a filthy sort of way, but all four sabre
squadrons were out on detachment, each looking after its own
section of the canal—and that, my dear Percival, was absolutely
bloody. It meant camping in the desert, in acute discomfort,
with nothing, but nothing, to look at, except this dreary canal,
along which we had to patrol night and day in case somebody
tried to fuck it up."

"Who was going to do that?"

"Dissident Gypos. Enemy agents. Desert tribes on the Axis pay-roll. German patrols in depth, trying a thousand to one long shot. . . . Not that *we* bothered about the theory of it. As far as we were concerned, we were there because we were there, and wishing to God that we weren't. If only there'd been a few more ships to watch it might have been a bit jollier; but even those were in short supply, because by that time the Mediterranean was so damn dangerous that everything which could was going round by the Cape. The only thing most of us had to look forward to was being called back to R.H.Q. for some reason or other and having a binge in Port Said.

"But I was one one of the lucky ones. (There you are, you see, that cross-bat artist has been bowled neck and crop, and doesn't begin to know what's hit him.) Yes, I was quite lucky, because as squadron second-in-command I was responsible for all rations and supplies and this meant that I had to take a small convoy, once a week, to rendezvous with the regimental supply column which brought up all our stuff from Port Said. All the other squadron second-in-commands would gather at the same rendezvous, which was usually a town called Qantara, and after a time we got a small hotel there to put up quite a decent meal on the days we came in, so that we could have a bit of a party. Later on the owner even produced some girls, and we sometimes fixed it so that we could spend the night and go back to our respective squadrons the next morning. So although I seldom got to Port Said itself, I did have these weekly outings in Qantara, getting pissed and hearing all the gossip from R.H.Q. and the other squadrons, which made me a damned sight better off than most people."

"Trust you to be," said Percival.

"No need to be offensive, old man. I just took what I could get, as we all did in those days. Of course, we were riding for bad trouble. The hotel in Qantara was out of bounds to all British troops, the girls might well have been poxed, and officers oughtn't to be drunk when responsible for securing and transporting their squadron's weekly rations. However, it is just the point of this little tale that trouble, when it came, did not come from any of the obvious sources. They were so obvious, you see, that we took precautions. We hired a local doctor to examine the girls just before we had them. We persuaded the local Provost Marshal, whom we found a good-natured chap considering his office, to put the hotel in bounds for 'personnel in transit'. We let the N.C.O.s and men who came with us have a bit of a fling to keep *them* happy. And in the end I worked out a system with my Corporal-Major (our equivalent of Colour-Sergeant) whereby one of us was always sober enough to see we drew the right kit and got back to the squadron without losing it. So all the obvious dangers were dealt with and everything went as merry as a marriage—until one day I made a tiny but absolutely fatal slip without even noticing, at the time, what I was doing."

Detterling paused and gave a melancholy smile.

"And even if I had noticed," he said, "I wouldn't have worried. What I did was—well—routine. *Anyone* in my situation would have done it. I couldn't *not* do it. Let me explain."

Below them the cricketers moved into the pavilion for tea. The three other spectators on the balcony departed. It was so quiet where Detterling and Percival sat that they might have been the last two people left in the world.

"As I've told you," said Detterling, almost in a whisper now, "it was tanks, bloody tanks, that started it all off. At least indirectly. You see, one of our Troop Leaders needed a particularly rare and difficult spare for an immobilised tank of his. We sent an indent through to the farrier at R.H.Q. . . . ."

"The *farrier*?"

"Yes. That's what we used to call the chap who took care of the horses, so we used the same title for the chap in charge of servicing the tanks. Why bother to change? Anyway, we sent in this indent, and as usual in such cases nothing happened. After a bit we sent in a second one marked 'urgent', and the next time I got to Qantara a note was handed to me from the farrier, who said that the spare part needed was not available in Port Said, and would I go, in person, to an Armoured

Corps depot at a place called Zagazig (yes, Zagazig) and ask there. When I looked at the map, I saw that this was quite a sensible suggestion. Zagazig was about fifty miles west by south of Qantara, and though it wouldn't be much fun getting there along the desert road, it would clearly be much quicker and easier for me to go myself than for our farrier in Port Said to make a formal application through the correct channels, et cetera, et cetera.

"Well, there didn't seem to be any problems about it. This was one of the occasions when I'd fixed it for us to spend the night in Qantara; so the ration trucks could stay there with the Corporal-Major while I drove on to Zagazig in my armoured scout car. If my journey took too long for me to get back back to Qantara that evening, or if there was trouble negotiating for this precious spare part, then I could spend the night at Zagazig and pick up the rest of my convoy the next day for the return to our squadron camp.

"And so it all worked out . . . and even better than I'd hoped. The journey to Zagazig was a sod, so I did have to spend the night there; but they made no fuss about letting me have this spare part, in fact they gave me five of it for luck, which I knew would please the Squadron Leader; and I was up and away early in the morning and back to Qantara well before lunch, with the whole afternoon to roll back to the squadron camp, where we were due at any time before sundown.

"But in Qantara I found snags. The Corporal-Major, whose turn it was to get drunk, had seen no reason to forgo the privilege. I'd forgotten to warn him that he'd best not overdo it in my absence, so he'd got himself absolutely *arseholed* in our 'transit' hotel, and had then proceeded to beat up his girl, who was threatening to complain to the police. I had to pay through the nose to persuade her to hold her tongue—or it'd have been all up forever with our cosy little arrangements, to say nothing of the Corporal-Major, who by this time was rather a chum.

"The next snag was fuel. My driver, a pleasant old sweat called Tom Chead, said we'd used so much getting to Zagazig and back that we needed a fill to take the scout car on to the squadron. So I applied to the Provost Marshal for help . . . only to find him turn up sticky. This was all Armoured Corps business, he said, I should have got more fuel from the depot at Zagazig; he had his own show to run, and he couldn't serve up juice for scout cars to swan all over Egypt. But he was a good-natured fellow, as I've told you, and eventually he relented. He dug out some regulation which made it okay for him to supply vehicles in cases of geniune emergency. There was the usual sort of business with some form I had to sign, and then he sent Tom Chead off to the pump while he gave me a last little lecture on what he called logistic anticipation. He quoted Wellington, I remember : 'a prudent officer empties his bowels and fills his belly whenever he has the opportunity'. Well, amen to that, I said, and I'd try not to bother him again. Not to worry, he said : 'to err is human, to forgive divine'. Full of tags he was; I dare say he got them from the *Reader's Digest*.

"And after that all was well. The Corporal-Major was still shaking a bit, but he'd got the wagons loaded up all right; and so off we all went, after a sustaining lunch at the hotel. Home in good time; the Squadron Leader all over me for having had the sense to follow up the farrier's lead and go out to Zagazig; a good mark for Detterling, that promising young temporary Captain; in a word, journey's end—or so it seemed."

Percival sat looking puzzled and slightly peeved. "But somewhere you'd made a slip—a fatal slip, you said."

"Yes. You're pretty sharp; you tell me where."

"Bribing that whore to keep quiet about the Corporal-Major?"

"No, Leonard. I've told you. It was none of the obvious things."

"Those spare parts—you drew them without proper forms of requisition?"

"I'd certainly cut a lot of red tape, but the suggestion had come from my Regimental H.Q., so I could hardly be blamed. Anyway there was never any more heard about that."

"No official authorisation for the extra journey to Zagazig?"

"As a captain and second-in-command of a squadron I was fully entitled to authorise it myself."

Percival licked his lips. "That Provost Marshall reported you for negligence? For failing to refuel at the depot in Zagazig?"

"He didn't report me. Anyway, I'd already told my Squadron Leader what had happened, and he'd just laughed it off."

"Food poisoning from the hotel?"

"Leonard, you're just guessing."

"All right; you tell me."

"Very well," said Captain Detterling.

Somewhere below them a bell tinkled.

"The umpires will be out again in a minute. Good."

"Please get on with your story and never mind this absurd game."

"As it happens," said Detterling, "it is a cricket match at which the next scene takes place. Three, four months have passed. My regiment has been moved to commodious pre-war barracks in the environs of Alexandria, to recuperate and dust itself down. The desert by the canal is only a memory, disagreeable but fading fast; and although more active service is certainly coming, it will not come just yet. And so here we are, amusing ourselves with this cricket match, between Hamilton's Horse and the Second Battalion of the Prince Consort's Own Regiment of Foot. Matting wicket, of course, but reasonable turf for an outfield, and an elegant marquee, full of brave men, fair women and expensive refreshments. Into the marquee steps Captain Detterling (a substantive captain by now) having just made seventy-six runs for Hamilton's Horse and being about to consume a huge beaker of champagne.

"Among Detterling's circle of admirers is his own Commanding Officer—who, when the excitement has subsided, moves Detterling quietly on to one side and tells him to take himself back to barracks a bit smartish, as there are two gentlemen from the Special Investigations Branch waiting to talk to him there. Never mind the rest of the cricket match; the Colonel will explain Detterling's defection. Just let Detterling get his pads off quietly and slink out through the back, where a car is waiting with one of Detterling's brother officers inside it to hold his hand on the way home. But what the devil is all this about? The Colonel knows no details; only that it is something to do with Detterling's conduct in a place called Qantara."

Detterling paused and gravely applauded a late cut to the boundary.

"And of course," he said to Percival, "I instantly imagined that it had all come out about those women at the hotel and so on, and I fully expected to find all the other chaps concerned queuing up to be interviewed too. Not a bit of it. I was taken to my own quarters, and left alone there with a smooth-faced lieutenant in General Service uniform and a bulky Sergeant-Major of the Military Police. The subaltern asked a series of polite questions to confirm that I'd made those regular trips to Qantara, and then got out a large sheet of notes and examined them in silence for several minutes. Here we go, I thought : that's a list of the girls and now he's coming in with the knife. I was as taut as a tent rope by now, and I can still remember the conversation which followed, almost word for word. . . .'

'. . . Now, Captain Detterling. You've already told me'—at last looking up from the sheet of notes—'that it was your practice, from time to time, to stay overnight at Qantara.'

'Yes. With my Squadron Leader's approval.'

'Of course, sir. Now, please tell me about one such night— Wednesday, March 15.'

Long pause.

'March the *fifteenth*?'

'Yes, sir.'

'Well . . . that was the time I went to Zagazig to collect some spare parts from the Armoured Corps depot there.'

'So we understand. You spent the night at Zagazig instead of Qantara, and returned to Qantara the next morning.'

'Yes. What about it?'

'Nothing, sir. But what happened when you got back to Qantara?'

'I had some lunch and took my convoy back to the squadron camp in the desert.'

And bribed a whore on behalf of the Corporal-Major. Going, going, gone.

'Indeed? You still had enough fuel in your scout car to get to your squadron camp?'

Fuel?

'Sorry, I forgot. I *was* short of fuel by then, so I asked the town Provost Marshal to give me some.'

'How much did he give you?'

'I've no idea. My driver took the scout car to the pump.'

'But *you* countersigned the AF(ME)2224X.'

'The what?'

The Army Form (Middle East) which has to be completed in such emergencies. The issuing officer states to whom the fuel was issued and why, and the recipient, in this case yourself, signs for the amount received.'

'All right. I signed for the amount received.'

'How much was it?'

'I can't remember. Whatever we needed, I suppose.'

'And how much *did* you need?'

'How should I know? The drivers and the Corporal-Major always take care of that kind of thing.'

'Very well, sir. Your driver, Trooper Chead, states that, allowing for the fuel still in his engine he needed ten gallons to get back to your squadron camp over desert country, and that he actually drew fifteen from the pump "in order to be on the safe side".'

'You're not blaming him for that?'

'No. He behaved very prudently. Unlike yourself, sir, who signed for twenty-five gallons. . . .'

". . . And so there it was," said Detterling to Percival. "Exactly how it was worked, I don't know. I imagine the amount was still blank when I signed the form. Perhaps I noticed and perhaps I didn't. If I did, I probably assumed that the Provost Marshal would check up with whoever had actually pumped the stuff out and fill in the correct amount later. But the point is that I wasn't really thinking along those lines at all. Here was a man doing me a good turn, and it never occurred to me to start haggling about pieces of paper.

"But you see what it meant? It meant that the Provost Marshal had issued fifteen gallons and accounted for twenty-five; so he had ten left over to flog on the black market. And of course this was his little vice. Very hard to spot; indeed he might never have been spotted, only he offered some juice to a Gypo who, by a thousand to one chance, was one of our agents and loyal at that. So then the S.I.B. went into the Provost Marshal's affairs, starting with his tickets—and here was one signed by yours truly, name, rank and unit. If they'd come to me first, I might have been able to fob them off; but I was playing cricket, so they asked to see my driver, and Chead loused everything up by being too bloody accurate. Fifteen gallons he'd had, and fifteen gallons he said. 'You're sure it wasn't more, Trooper Chead? Twenty-five, perhaps?' 'Quite sure, sir. It was an emergency issue, see, and they were that tight they tried to make me only take ten.' That kind of thing. And by that time he'd landed me slap in the shit without knowing it, and there was nothing he could do to pull me out.

"And I mean *shit*, Leonard. You see, these policemen thought, or purported to think, that I'd connived at the fraud or even that I'd taken a cut on the profit. For Christ's sake, I told them : I had a private income which amounted to three times my pay; what the hell did I want with half the profit on ten gallons of fuel? Very well, they said, or rather, the smooth-faced lieutenant said : even if he believed me about that, and he wasn't saying he did, at the very best I'd been negligent, criminally negligent. Did I realise that the war was at crisis-point, that the allies were hard-pressed on every front, that oil derivatives were like so much liquid gold? And here was I, so casual, so incompetent—if not positively fraudulent—that I'd signed away ten gallons of our life's blood.

"And they were right. There'd been a great deal of that sort of thing going on. Wastage caused by rackets or mere carelessness had been enormous; and they were minded to make a stern example, as many stern examples as they could. They were busy rounding up all those with whom this Provost Marshal had had similar dealings, and they intended to stage a series of court martials and cashierings the fame of which would ring round Egypt. And although I, with my ten gallons, wasn't exactly the star name on the list. I would do very well to swell out the scene. So there I was, placed under open arrest pending further enquiries, threatened with possible charges that ranged from gross negligence up to conspiracy against the realm and all because I'd signed an army form when asked to by my superior officer."

"Come, come," said Percival. "Surely a substantive captain of Lord Hamilton's Horse wasn't going to take this lying down?"

"I can't say I did very much about it myself. I was winded, you see. But the regiment came to my assistance. Chead, the driver, now tried to say that I'd told him to draw twenty-five gallons and he'd forgotten to tell me he'd only been given fifteen; but in the light of what I'd told the S.I.B. myself, that didn't help very much—and nearly got Chead into a nasty spot of bother. At a higher level, the Adjutant saw to it that I was not made to suffer the usual humiliations of being under arrest; in return for my parole, I was allowed to dress and go about the place like anybody else. As for the Colonel, he was a common-sense fellow who set about fixing the whole thing in a common-sense fashion. It was absolutely clear to him that this was just a piece of bad luck or at worst of venial slackness, and so he said to the divisional general, who was an old chum of his. But the S.I.B. wasn't easy to fob off; they wanted a full pound of flesh, and it was only with great difficulty that they were got to settle for a few ounces: the charge was adjusted so that I need not, indeed submit myself to court-martial—but I had to go in front of the General to receive a severe reprimand."

"So that was all right. A severe reprimand never broke a man's bones."

"It can break a man's career though. From that time on

there was a big black mark against my name in the book. I
was, quite simply, a man not to be trusted. Not to be trusted
by the Army Council—'the fellow who fiddled the fuel'—and
so never allowed promotion. Not even to be trusted by my
own regiment : because although they'd been decent and helped
me what they could, they now saw me as a squalid little
nuisance. I'd drawn attention to them, you see. My regiment
liked to keep itself to itself; and now here were detectives
prying all over the bloody place, and rumours all over Alex,
and it was all my fault. As the Adjutant remarked one day,
it was rather as though I'd farted on parade : by my miserable
petty ineptitude I'd turned my regimentals to motley and made
the rest of them look like a parcel of clowns as well. They didn't
much care what I'd done, or whether or not I'd really done
it, but what they couldn't forgive me, and didn't forgive me for
years, was being found out."

"But surely . . . you were given some quite respectable
appointments later on?"

"*Much* later on. And even then, although the jobs seemed
respectable, if you examined them you found they were jokes.
I was made, after the war, recruiting officer for the cavalry,
which sounds important until you remember that recruiting
officers are figures out of low comedy who seduce sluts and can't
pay their battels. And in any case I didn't last long at that;
someone in the War Office opined that a spiv (you remember
the word?) wasn't much of an advertisement. After that I was
sent to teach at the Officers' Training School at Bangalore : a
very responsible assignment—except that the School, as they
very well knew, was about to be turned into a cut-price cram-
mer for low-grade native Cadets. Thence to the Viceroy's staff
in Delhi—"

"—Now there at least was distinction—"

"—As a kind of doorman and cloakroom-attendant for
social occasions—and chucker-out if one was needed. Luckily
I had an old friend there, one of the few who *did* trust me,
and he found me some interesting work in Intelligence. I was
the chap who chose and briefed the thugs for any dirty work

we had in hand. Even my friend, you see, thought I'd be best employed on something shady."

"But all this was much later, as you say. What did you do immediately after the trouble in Egypt?"

"I was sent on courses. As soon as I came back from one, they sent me on another. P.T., catering, fire precautions, education, religion, welfare. On and on and on. Detterling, the man we can't trust; get him out of the way; send him off on another course where he can't do any damage."

"A very comfortable existence."

"And safe. I was delighted to be sitting quietly in Cairo or Alexandria, learning how to interest the men of my regiment in hobbies like raffia-work or kite-flying, while the men themselves were in the Western Desert being shot at. Oh yes, I was very relieved. But in another way I was very angry. Angry because I had become a man of no account, because I had been so shabbily exposed when I had done nothing to be ashamed of. It was the unfairness of it all, Leonard. I had committed a tiny misdemeanour which wasn't really even that. All I'd done was to trust another officer and sign a paper without looking at it—something which everyone in the army did fifty times a day; but as a result the earth had suddenly turned to quicksand underneath me, long after I'd forgotten the whole trivial little affair. It made me feel that the world was made of water; all things in flux, as Heraclitus said. It made me feel foully injured and quite desperate . . . that some kind of Fury must have been pursuing me. It made me feel, at one time, nearly suicidal."

"But you're here to tell the tale thirty years later."

"To tell it and now to ponder it. If something like this could happen to me, something like it could have happened to poor Somerset. Some small mistake which he neither noticed nor remembered . . . something which anyone might have done in total innocence . . . and then, years later perhaps, this tiny piece of loose detritus, which he left lying because he never even saw it, is shifted by a chance wind and starts an avalanche which overwhelms him."

"An ingenious theory, my dear. But there's been no sign of the avalanche."

"A private avalanche, Leonard. Something in his mind. We never saw it, but we could picture what it might have been like for him, if only we could discover where and how it began."

"Which means finding this . . . 'tiny piece of loose detritus' . . . which on your theory began it. Not easy. The area of search is large. And surely, it is the essence of the kind of mistake, which you are positing, to be unnoticeable."

"To the person who makes it. Not necessarily to others. I spotted what was wrong with that cross-bat player although he himself never could."

"Spare me him again . . . though the point is taken. And that's enough of theory," said Leonard Percival: "time for more action."

"What next?"

"Devonshire," said Percival, "and Somerset's old mother, Peregrina."

Chantry Marquess, near Bampton in the County of Devon, the seat of the family of Lloyd-James, proved to be neat and pretty if in no way imposing. It stood about a hundred yards back from a minor road, being separated from the road by a pleasant and well-kept lawn, on the right-hand side of which a drive ran between two rows of elm trees up to a small stone courtyard. This lay off what should have been the west wing of the house but was in fact its front, since the wall that faced over the lawn and towards the road turned out, on inspection, to be only a side wall, blank except for a few first-storey windows. The mild eccentricity of this arrangement had an undoubted charm, thought Detterling as his manservant drove the Mercedes carefully through an arch into the courtyard; for the white Georgian west front, under which the car stopped, had a shy and almost shifty look about it, as if it knew it should be facing another way and was not sure whether it was shunning the road out of modesty or out of cowardice.

"Very lonely," remarked Percival as Detterling pulled the

bell chain; "not another house in miles. I suppose their kind likes that."

"Wouldn't you Leonard?"

"If you have stomach ulcers, it's as well to have neighbours."

The door was opened by the housekeeper-type woman whom they had seen with Mrs Lloyd-James at the funeral. Since Percival had agreed, contrary to his general principle, that an unexpected arrival would be discourteous to an old lady, Detterling had rung up on the evening after their conversation at Lord's and applied for an interview. They had been invited to afternoon tea on the following day and now, precisely at 4.30 as bidden, they announced their names to the housekeeper, who looked them up and down as if to make sure they were fit to appear on parade and then, without a word, led them across a wide stone-flagged hall and through an open doorway into a study.

Peregrina Lloyd-James, who was sitting with her legs straddled in front of a generous wood fire, did not get up to greet them. She smiled civilly at Detterling, nodded at Percival, and pointed to a table on which stood, not tea, but a decanter of what looked like Marsala. A moment later the housekeeper reappeared carrying a seed cake, which she placed on the table. She looked at the fire and then at her mistress, who shook her head. The housekeeper bowed hers very slightly, took two steps backwards, turned about and left them, closing the door. Detterling and Percival cut themselves slices of cake and poured themselves glasses of wine, in Percival's case a very small one. At last,

"May we sit down, ma'am?" said Detterling, speaking the first words that anyone had uttered since they entered the house.

"If you please, gentlemen."

Detterling and Percival sat. Peregrina Lloyd-James spread her hands in front of the fire. Something rustled (rats, thought Detterling, surely not?) behind a row of shiny leather-backed books, a ten-volume economic history of Europe by an author of whom Detterling had never heard. A clock on the mantel tinkled primly, prematurely announcing a quarter to five.

"What can I tell you?" asked the old woman, rubbing her left hand on the cheek just below the right ear.

"First," said Percival bluntly, "did your son come here on the day before he died? All that day he was away somewhere before going home and killing himself very late at night. We would very much like to know where he went."

"He didn't come here, Mr Percival. He hasn't been near here for three months."

"You've no idea where he did go?"

"How should I have? But surely . . . you have special methods you can use to find out?"

"Yes, but that would entail drawing some attention to the matter. The whole object of our enquiries is to ensure that from now on it shall receive none at all."

"I see. You are investigating my son's death in order to suppress any scandal that might lie behind it. In the interest of the Government to which he belonged."

"Very shrewdly summed up," said Detterling.

"Shrewdly? The whole thing is perfectly obvious. You, Captain Detterling, his old friend and yourself a Conservative Member. And this other gentleman with the—forgive me, sir —very shady air about him."

"Shady?" said Percival reproachfully.

"Not exactly that. Surreptitious. I once went, years ago, to a dog race meeting. When they paraded the animals before each race, there was a man who crept along behind them with a brush and pan, ready to clear up their stools. You remind me of that man, Mr Percival. You have the demeanour of someone whose working life is spent sweeping up dog-stools and who very much hopes (like that wretched fellow at the races) that he will not be noticed."

"Well, let's just say," said Detterling, "that Percival's aim is to prevent trouble."

"Yours too, Captain Detterling?"

"It's a bit more personal with me. Having known Somerset for a quarter of a century and more, I am naturally . . . concerned . . . to find out why he should have done such a terrible thing to himself."

"Concerned? Or curious?"

"Both, to be honest. So now you know what we're here for, Mrs Lloyd-James, will you help us?"

Peregrina Lloyd-James leant forward and kicked a log hard with her heel.

"I," she said, "have been a lifelong Socialist. Why should I help the Conservative Party bury its scandals?"

"The scandal would also be your family's—if there is a scandal, and if it ever came out."

"There is no family. Only me now."

"There is your son's good name," said Percival.

"My son is dead. He was a poor thing at best, and now he is gone for good. No need to protect him."

"Look," said Percival, " it *could* be a question of national security. Your son, when he died, was working in a very sensitive area. If his death is in any way connected with his work for the Ministry of Commerce, then in the national interest we must know why and how."

"National Interest. Ministry of Commerce. Why should an old woman . . . an old Socialist . . . care for either?"

"If you were going to take that attitude, why did you let us come?"

"Idleness. Boredom. To find out what you were going to ask."

"But not intending to answer?"

"I can't," said the old lady, and grinned merrily. "My son never spoke to me about his work for the Government, so I can't tell you anything about that. In any case, as I told you, he hasn't been near me for months. He hardly ever came. Twice a year at most, to make sure that the house and the grounds were in good order. They belonged to him, you see, after his father died. I was his pensioner, and so he regarded me. Important politicians do not tell their secrets—political *or* personal—to their pensioners."

"Look, Mrs Lloyd-James," said Detterling gently. "We have

an idea, or at least I have, that Somerset's death may be connected with something which lies a long way back. Would you
care to talk about the past?"

"Not much. There's too much of it—and almost all of it
boring. Still," said Peregrina, frowning at Detterling, "you
were his friend, as we all keep saying, and you have come a
long way from London. If you have any specific question. I
will try to answer it."

"Very well," said Detterling, shooting at a venture. "According to *Who's Who*, Somerset was sent to a preparatory school
called St Peter's Court. It's a pretty odd thing, to record one's
prep school in *Who's Who*. Why do you think he did it?"

Percival looked at Detterling as if he thought him suddenly
deranged. This did not surprise Detterling. What did surprise
him was the vicious look of rage with which Peregrina received
the question.

"That horrible school," she said, with a malevolence that
brought out goose-pimples on Detterling's skin. "It destroyed
him. Peverted him for life."

"Oh, come, Mrs Lloyd-James. Somerset was entirely normal.
I mean," said Detterling, recalling Maisie's revelations, "he
was incontestably heterosexual."

Somerset's mother gave a yapping little laugh.

"I didn't mean *that*," she said. "It didn't turn him queer,
or not in the sense you took me. But it changed him in a far
worse way. You see, until he went there we educated my son
here at home. Or rather, I educated him. I was a proficient
blue-stocking, and he learned all the usual lessons very thoroughly. Latin, Greek, Mathematics, History, French, and a bit of
German and Italian thrown in. He also learned . . . how to
interpret what he was taught. In the light of Socialist principle.
Not Marxism, I was never a Marxist. But with due regard
to justice and equality—fair play, as I conceived it and still
do. He accepted what I told him; he thrived on it. He also
accepted my word that the family religion was so much
bunkum. His father was quite a keen Catholic, but not keen
enough to insist on Somerset's being indoctrinated, or he

wouldn't have married a woman like me. There was a nasty row with the priests, but my husband let me have my way with Somerset—on pain of not having his own way with me in bed. So what with one thing and another, by the age of eleven Somerset had been thoroughly grounded in conventional knowledge and also in correct political and philosophical principle—"

"—*Your* political and philosophical principle," put in Percival.

"I tell you, he thrived on it. We were close," she murmured, "oh, very close in those days, Somerset and I." She lifted her head high and started to talk loud and fast. "Then the war came. My husband went off with his Yeomanry—and for the first time in my life I was suddenly very ill. So back came my husband, who'd hardly been gone a week, and packed Somerset off to that loathsome school while I was lying in hospital. Nine months later, when I came home to convalesce, I found I'd lost my son. He'd been taught by them, somehow persuaded, that it wasn't very clever or smart to be a Socialist, or an atheist either. He made a friend, little Lord Somebody or Other, who asked him to stay in the holidays while I was ill. The family was High Church and High Tory, and in no time at all they charmed Somerset back into the fold. Privilege and paternalism, *noblesse oblige*, upper-class responsibility—he just loved it all when they ladled it out, nicely cooked in a rich, bland sauce and served on the family silver. As for religion, when he realised that the Lloyd-Jameses had been quite famous as recusants, he couldn't go back to Catholicism fast enough. It was the word 'Recusant' that did it; it was almost as good as 'Cavalier'."

Peregrina paused and positively bared her teeth.

"But of course it all started with his being sent to that school—*St Peter's Court* forsooth. He wanted to go on to Eton. I managed to put a stop to *that*, and soon afterwards little Lord Footleroy went and died on him, but by then the damage was done. In the end he went to a middle-class public school— yours, Captain Detterling, I understand—but they weren't going to cure him there, quite the reverse, and I was still too ill to try. I'd lost him anyway. He'd been taken from me just too early and too long. After that I never had a chance."

"So now we know," said Percival lightly, "why he mentioned St Peter's in *Who's Who*. After all, it had provided him with a very memorable educational experience. It had switched his whole conception of life—and of death, come to that. Tell me, Mrs Lloyd-James : was he *sincere* as a Roman Catholic?"

Peregrina shrugged.

"How should I know? I couldn't understand that kind of sincerity even if I saw it. Anyhow, he never told me anything. He'd been poisoned against me, and for the rest of his life he never spoke to me of anything that mattered to him. Except once, when he spoke of money. After his father was dead he told me what he was going to allow me. He got it almost all, you see. I'd come to the family with very little—it was a love match, believe it or not—and so what was settled on me was tiny. If I'd had to make do with my own when my husband died, I'd have had about 300 a year. But of course Somerset was too good a Catholic to turn me out of the house, and too good a Conservative to let me live in an unbecoming style. So he made me an allowance. 'Twenty-five hundred a year, mama,' he said; 'and I'll pay all household expenses, including Mrs Strange'—that's my companion-housekeeper. 'I'll review the arrangement every year,' he said, 'in respect of current monetary values.' Pompous little pig."

"Nevertheless, he was doing the right thing," said Detterling, "and doing it quite generously. I hope he did the same in his will."

"Didn't I tell you?" said Percival. "He died intestate."

"So it's all come to me at the last." Peregrina snickered. "I'm the queen of the castle—because there's nobody left of the whole fine recusant family of Lloyd-James of Chantry Marquess, except me. And to whom shall *I* leave it when I die?"

"Who were all those people at the funeral?"

"A few locals who came to support me. And some of my own blood relations."

"Ah. You were a Forbes Eden, I think. Why not leave it to them?"

"They hate me. For being an atheist, for marrying a Catholic. Puce Peregrina, they call me."

"How unkind of them," said Percival. "Perhaps some Socialist cause would be a grateful beneficiary."

Peregrina wrinkled her nose.

"They're a rotten lot now," she said. "All greed and envy. They never give a thought to the real poor—those still in England, all those in the rest of the world."

"Then sell all you have," said Detterling slyly, "and give to the real poor yourself."

"Charity's no answer. It's a proper way of life they need. Anyhow," said Peregrina, quite unabashed, "I think I shall leave the house and the estate to Mrs Strange."

"Your housekeeper?"

"Yes. She's a thoroughly common woman, and it will annoy the landed gentry when she sets up as one of them."

Detterling rose to his feet. He glanced at Percival, who pursed his lips but then rose also.

"All this talk of wills," said Detterling, "reminds me that Lord Canteloupe is getting up a memorial dinner for your son."

"A memorial *dinner*?"

"Yes. There was going to be a service, but few of Somerset's friends are of a church-going persuasion and the Catholic thing might have made it tiresome. So Canteloupe's proposed a dinner. If you'd like to come, Mrs Lloyd-James, I know he'll be happy to send you a card."

"I think it impertinent of Lord Canteloupe to take the office on himself."

"Why? Were you going to?" asked Percival.

"He should certainly have asked my intentions first. No," said Peregrina, "I shall not attend this dinner. I doubt whether the sight of my son's friends assembled would give me much pleasure, and you must be aware by now that I get none from remembering him."

"We could have given her a little longer, I suppose?" said Detterling in the Mercedes on the way back to London.

"No point. She made it quite plain that they'd steered clear of each other ever since 1939."

"That's what I thought. But I saw you hesitate when I got up to leave."

"I was in two minds for just a moment. But then I took a look at her face, Detterling, and I realised, quite finally, that we'd never get anything useful out of Mrs Lloyd-James. You see she wasn't talking about her son at all. She was talking and thinking—and cursing—about someone who'd never existed. Even on the rare occasions she *had* seen him over the years, it wasn't him she saw. It was some . . . chimera . . . of her own imagining, which moved and acted only in accordance with her conception of it. She wouldn't even have noticed anything about him that you and I might want to know."

"I don't quite follow you, old chap. Anyway, how did you realise this just by looking at her face?"

"Because it reminded me of my own on a comparable occasion. She was obsessed; totally convinced that she and she alone was right, that she and she alone saw clear and understood. Not to be reasoned with; not caring about any other opinion or interpretation or aspect; frozen as hard as ice in the truth as she saw it. And then I remembered a time, years ago, when I myself had been in the same condition—and had seen the same kind of face looking at me out of the mirror."

"My dear Leonard . . . no doubt you are as opinionated as the next man, but I cannot see you as the bigot you're describing."

"Well, once I was. Luckily I was taught a very sharp lesson. Unlike that old woman, who will never realise what has happened to her, I was woken up, so to speak, and made to snap out of it. It all occurred on the first assignment I ever had—but I won't bore you with that."

"You will not be boring me, Leonard. I promise you."

"All right. You've got yourself to thank." Percival joined his hands over his breast and rested his long pointed chin on them. "I was originally got into this game," he said "by an uncle of mine, Rupert Percival, who was a country lawyer in a place called Bishop's Cross—not far from here, as it happens, in Somerset. Uncle Rupert had a lot of pull in various quarters, but he didn't find it very easy to fix this for me because I'd had an abominable record at school. I was what these days they'd call a late developer, only just scraping through School Cert. at the age of seventeen—a real muggins. Not the kind of thing they wanted in this profession. But I was dead set on it, always had been, and after one hell of a struggle Uncle Rupert got them to take me on probation. So you see, it was very important that my first job should go off well."

Percival produced a large wallet from which he took a tattered picture postcard in black and white.

"Recognise that?" he asked, passing it over to Detterling.

"Biarritz?"

"Right. I keep this picture to remind me of the disaster which nearly happened there. Whenever I find myself becoming too dogmatic in my theories, too certain that I must be right about somebody or something, I get out this picture and tell myself, 'Leonard, remember Biarritz'."

Percival put away the postcard with reverential care, as if laying up a relic.

"Biarritz, summer of 1950," he said. "My first assignment. An easy one, but very lowering, in almost every sense. You remember that in those days the Government was very strict about foreign currency—fifty pounds was all you could take abroad with you. Well, I was one of a number of agents employed to detect people who were cheating. I used to hang about in bars and casinos and whatever, and if I saw an Englishman who was spending suspiciously large amounts I'd try to follow up and discover where and how he came by the money. But of course it wasn't easy actually to pin anything on anyone, so I was instructed, among other things, to act as *agent provocateur*. For example, if I saw a rich-looking type lose a packet at roulette, I'd go up and offer to cash him a cheque, at a heavy discount, drawn on his English bank—I had a special fund of francs for that. If he said yes, then I took his cheque, which had to be made payable to cash or bearer, and sent it off to our H.Q. in London, who made life most unpleasant for him when he got home; because passing a cheque abroad at that time wasn't far off being treason."

"What a mean trick, Leonard. Like those games the police get up to in public lavatories."

"I said it was a lowering business. But then, one day, I found a real interest—something which, for a number of reasons, I much enjoyed investigating. There was a girl of about twenty-nine or thirty, attractive, very smartly but plainly dressed, reserved, even haughty, in manner, whom I'd seen come into the 'Casino du Palais'—the grandest one—some three or four times the same week and play chemin-de-fer. Now it's not very often you see a *young* woman alone at the chemmy table, and of course the stakes were comparatively high, so this little spectacle would have been interesting whoever the girl was. But very soon I learnt that although she spoke excellent French, she was in fact English—I heard her, one night, dressing down an Englishman who was drunk at the table. And then, of course, I was more intrigued with her than ever. How did she manage it? She always played carefully, but at any one time she'd be winning or losing the equivalent of seventy or eighty pounds, and that's a lot of money for a girl with a travel allowance of fifty. Where did she get it to play with? I'd already tried my old cheque routine on her—one evening when she'd lost—but she hadn't taken the bait. Which meant she had a source of her own."

"A source which could have been quite legitimate, at least from your point of view. Suppose she was whoring, for example. The Treasury had no rule against *that*."

"Whoring was what I thought it was—at first. And I even wondered whether I might not use some of my special fund to buy myself a treat with her. But she just didn't fit the part. You can always tell whores in casinos. As soon as they lose, they sit about showing a lot of thigh and start drumming up custom. The second night I saw my girl lose, she just got up, marched out like a queen, and sailed off in a taxi."

"A rich protector somewhere?"

"Another theory of mine—but only one out of dozens. By this time, you see, she had me really fascinated and determined to find out what kept her propellor running. And quite apart from being exceedingly curious to know what was going on, I also had hopes that it might lead to really important charges, if not for currency offences then perhaps for something even more serious and exciting. *Then* London would know what a good man they'd got—and how proud Uncle Rupert would be.

"So here was my own heaven-sent mystery woman, and I, Leonard Percival, was going to rumble her. Perhaps she was working a con-game of some kind; or involved in some criminal racket like drugs; or perhaps she was a beautiful spy—one of ours, why not?—who was blowing Government funds at the tables; or a double agent who was in French pay as well as British. She might have been almost anything; but the great point was, as I saw it, that she just had to be something shady —something wicked, or immoral, or secret, and with any luck all three. A pretty young woman who came out by herself to play chemmy . . . who would sit down in her place as cool as mint with two hundred quids' worth of chips piled under her dainty knockers . . . she couldn't but be more or less bent.

"And then Detterling, I got an important clue—or so I thought. I'd taken a day trip to San Sebastian, just over the Spanish border, to do some cheap shopping. Shirts and things like that, which were still more or less rationed in England and very expensive in France, were going two a penny in Spain. And whom should I see, while carting my haul of haberdashery towards the bus-station, but my own gorgeous chemmy girl—stepping into a car the size of a cathedral, with the assistance of a character who had a face like Fu Manchu and was got up like flash Harry. A crook if ever I saw one. Whatever madam was mixed up with, part of it happened in Spain. When I saw her the night after, at chemmy again in Biarritz, she had a much larger stack of chips than usual in front of her. Obviously, when I'd seen her in San Sebastian, she'd been at some stage of a mission—which had paid off very sweetly, thank you."

"But you were still no nearer to discovering what she was at?"

"No. And the problem was, how to go about it. I thought of several schemes; like following her home, then burgling the place when she went out to see what I could find. But eventually I decided that the safest way would be to buttonhole her in the Casino in my role of dubious character (already established by my offer to cash her cheque), to pretend that I knew what she had been up to in San Sebastian, and then ask for a large sum to keep my mouth shut. That should elicit *some* response, should make *something* happen, and if I kept my wits about me I should learn a lot about her, particularly if I could make her lose her temper."

"A rather . . . tenuous scheme?"

"In those days I was still an apprentice—as indeed I was about to be very forcibly reminded. When I appeared at the gaming-rooms that evening, I found the entrance barred to me by a round and doleful Frenchman, whom I had often seen standing gloomily about the place but whom I did not know, so ignorant I still was of the world, to be the casino detective. He took me away to an office, where he said that I had been observed pestering the customers, that I had in general the look of a shabby and undesirable nuisance, and whatever my business was would I kindly take it elsewhere and cease to pollute the air in the 'Casino du Palais'. I then told him what my business in fact was and satisfactorily identified myself, whereupon we enjoyed a hearty laugh as being, in a sense, colleagues; but I was told that nevertheless the ban against me must stand, as it was no part of the policy of the Société des Bains de Mer de Biarritz to assist the British Government in catching currency offenders, and I had already caused grave offence to clients. To which clients? To the young English lady, who had complained that I had impertinently offered to discount her English cheques at an exorbitant rate—as if totally ignorant of her character and standing, and offensively

assuming that she was short of ready money. All right, I said :
I knew a lot—if none of it very exact—about *her* character and
standing and goings-on, and if they were going to make a fuss
on *her* account—*What* did I know of her? the casino detective interrupted. That she was a thoroughly bad lot, I said,
who was up to something highly suspicious just across the
border. I followed up with a detail or two and told him how
I'd planned to unmask her.

"At this my friend (for such he was to prove) gave a long
sad sigh, and informed me that the young English lady
(*Madame la jeune Anglaise*, as she was locally known) was a
hero of the wartime resistance, who had been parachuted into
France in 1943, had figured in many brave adventures, and had
married, at the end of the war, her comrade in arms, M. le
Comte de St Jean de Luz, whose château she now adorned,
being all but worshipped for forty miles around as the friend
of France and the pride of the Province. Her independence of
demeanour, which had doubtless misled me, was due to her
military experience; her companion in San Sebastian was a
retired bull-fighter gone to seed but generously maintained
at the château by M. le Comte, a great aficionado;
and her fondness for chemin-de-fer was a foible which
she could well afford and indulged but moderately if
one considered the amplitude of M. le Comte's finances.
In short, such was the lady's position that if I had
accosted her that evening in the manner I had intended, I
should, said the casino detective, have been languishing in a
French prison for many months to come.

"It was at this moment I caught my face in a mirror on the
office wall. I remember the letters in gilt at the top of it—
S.B.M. de Biarritz; and underneath them my face, scowling,
incredulous, absolutely set in its brutal and irrational insistence,
knowing that it was right and that this fat fool had somehow
or other been deluded by the young woman into believing the
tale he'd just told me. When I blurted out something of the
kind, he grabbed my shoulders very tightly, shook me for half
a minute like a pup who'd peed on his chair, and then showed

me a photo of Mme la Comtesse, with her name underneath it, in the local paper. 'Evidence,' he shouted in English : 'where is yours?'

"And at these four words my sanity was restored. I saw that I'd been the victim of a colossal delusion which, out of loneliness, discontent, sexual fancy and an overheated imagination, I had manufactured solely by myself and for myself. So I apologised most humbly. After which the good fellow patted me on the head (literally) and mumbled something about in youth is folly and in age is death; I must haunt no more casinos, he told me, but if I promised to be a 'sage garçon', he would give me a letter to a friend of his who was hotel detective in the 'Maurice' at Cap Breton, just up the coast. This friend would give me a tip or two about likely currency offenders in exchange for a tip or two in currency."

"How did that work out?" Detterling asked.

"Very well, as it happened. I netted one rather big fish whom they were very pleased to put in the pan. With the result that my appointment was made permanent and I have become what you see today, an ulcerous and washed-up nosy parker, who will retire on a pension of peanuts. But you take the point of my tale?"

"I'm not sure that I do."

"Well, instead of looking at what was under my eyes and simply asking who the girl was—a question that could have been answered by almost anyone in the streets of Biarritz—I wilfully and perversely preconceived and elaborated a ridiculous myth, and then allowed it to enslave me. Now, Peregrina Lloyd-James has done rather the same. Her myth is of a promising young Socialist intellectual, who weakly let himself be duped and flattered into betraying the ideals she had taught him, and thereafter spent a worthless and frivolous life in his own worldy advancement. But of course that's not the truth at all. Somerset just found a rig he liked better, changed his mind as all children will, and threw in his lot with the Old Gang, because pound for pound and penny for penny he thought they offered quite as much in value achieved and value forthcoming as Peregrina and her levellers. Somerset may or may not have been right in his decision, but the decision itself is entirely understandable—to everyone except that old fanatic in Chantry Marquess, who was so jealous and angry, so incapable of mental flexibility, that she ceased to see her son as a human being at all."

"How does that help us?"

"It doesn't," said Percival: "the whole point of this conversation is that she never could have helped us and can now be written off entirely. As far as Somerset is concerned, she has not properly *seen* him since he was twelve. Just as I failed to *see* that card-playing countess and saw something I'd dreamed up instead."

"All of which has made for an interesting philosophic lesson —and for an entirely fruitless day. What now?"

"More of his friends." Percival took out a notebook. "Quite a list, with some impressive names. I thought we might start, tomorrow afternoon, with Provost Constable of Lancaster College, Cambridge. There we shall also find another old acquaintance of Somerset's, Tom Llewellyn, the historian."

"We could go on, quite easily," suggested Detterling, "to Broughton Staithe on the Norfolk coast. Fielding Gray still lives there."

"Yes. Fielding Gray, the novelist. . . . You're a publisher. Is he well regarded these days?"

"I'm *his* publisher. So-so, I'd say. He's spent most of the last two years or so working on a book about Conrad for us. A lot depends on that."

"So he's done no novels just lately?"

"No."

"Good. I do not want him in the fictitious vein when we talk to him. . . . By and large, an interesting old lot to talk to," said Percival, considering the list. "I'm looking forward to the next two or three days. And to spending them with you," he said.

"Thank you, Leonard," said Detterling: "ditto."

PART FOUR

THE PUNDITS

"No," said Provost Constable; "I hardly knew Lloyd-James when he was up. It was later that I became well acquainted with him."

"We'll be coming to that," said Detterling. "But first—did you know *nothing* of him while he was here?"

"Very little. Except . . . I do remember clearly that he won the Lauderdale in 1948."

"The Lauderdale?" said Leonard Percival.

"A University prize for an historical essay. . . ."

Provost Constable had received Detterling and Percival in his study in the Provost's Lodge of Lancaster College. Detterling, with whom he had some very slight previous acquaintance, he recognised with bleak civility; Percival, who was a stranger to him, he greeted with a suspicion which almost amounted to open distaste. The same old Constable, thought Detterling, as cold as a cod and as close as a crab; but at least he will tell us absolutely nothing which is not the unqualified truth—even if he may wrap it up in layers of donnish allusion.

". . . The essay must not be less than 30,000 words in length," Constable was saying now, "and the prize is open to all resident members of the University beneath the degree of Doctor. Since Lloyd-James was still an undergraduate when he won it, it was a somewhat notable performance on his part."

The word 'notable', to Detterling's ears at least, was not kindly uttered.

"So he must have been quite a figure about the place," said Percival.

"I dare say. He and I did not frequent the same circles. Even so long ago I was already Tutor of this College, and so considerably his senior in every way."

"But you did know him by sight?"

"Yes. Just."

"Did you ever hear any gossip about him?" Percival persisted.

"I don't listen to gossip, Mr Percival."

"Then what did you hear about him in a *serious* way? For praise or blame?"

"For praise, that he was a diligent student who achieved outstanding results. For blame, that he was . . . more interested in awards than in studies."

Here's my cue, thought Detterling.

"You never," he put in, "heard any hint that he might have been given to cheating? In his exams, for example?"

Constable looked silently at Detterling and then at Percival.

"What makes you ask that?" he said at last.

"I have heard it mooted—admittedly with no proof at all and only in the thinnest of whispers—that he might have cheated in his Tripos."

"I told you : I do not listen to gossip."

"But *we* have to," said Detterling. "As you know, we are looking for a clue to the true cause of Somerset's suicide. We cannot afford to overlook anything that might give us this clue. No matter how long ago it happened, no matter how remote from his death it might seem. You see, if Somerset *had* cheated in his exams, and somebody else had proof, then it is just conceivable that this proof was used to blackmail him on threat of humiliating exposure."

Constable nodded reluctantly. "Just conceivable," he said. "But what is not conceivable is that anyone should cheat in his Tripos examinations. They are far too closely invigilated, and the papers are far too closely guarded beforehand."

"If you say so. . . ."

"So much for your whispers. I can, however, offer you in exchange for them . . . a piece of informed speculation." Constable glared at Detterling and Percival with extreme severity, as though they were a pair of delinquent undergraduates whom he was about to expel for ever. "So long," he continued, "as it is firmly understood by both of you that I am speaking only in order to assist you as servants of the State, and that you will in no case use the information to entertain your acquaintance."

"*Is* it entertaining then?" Percival asked.

"Some might find it so. As I say," said Constable, "there can be no suggestion that Lloyd-James cheated in his examinations. But I once heard it . . . convincingly argued . . . that the essay with which he won the Lauderdale contained a very culpable element of plagiarism."

"Surely, the judges would have spotted that straight away?"

"Not if the material which he exploited had not yet been published."

"You mean," said Percival, "that he filched some stuff from someone else's work in progress?"

"Not exactly, no. Let us begin at the beginning. The subject set for the Lauderdale Essay Prize in 1948 was 'Eighteenth Century Concepts of Monarchical Function'. Lloyd-James's prize essay proposed the theory (a totally original one, or so it seemed to the judges at the time) that after the English Crown passed to the House of Hanover, the outlook and mentality of successive monarchs was that of petty German princes more fit to rule over a province than a great kingdom—"

"—Nothing original in that—"

"—And that this outlook so far qualified their sense of function that they were incapable of acting as independent sovereigns and *became, in effect, the vassals of their own nobility.*"

"But surely, they were very much at odds with their own nobility?"

"*Not* a valid objection, Captain Detterling. Vassals are usually at odds with their overlords. They remain, none the less, vassals."

Constable raised his square jaw as if deprecating the insolence of Detterling's interruption. For a well-known Socialist, Detterling thought, the man had an outrageously aristocratic manner. But then of course the Constables were indeed aristo-

crats : hereditary castellans of Reculver Castle from some time
way back in the Middle Ages. But he, Detterling, was damned
if he was going to be put down so easily.

"Isn't this theory just an elaborate way of saying that the
Hanoverians did what they were told—and not only told by
the nobility? Walpole and Pitt were very powerful as com-
moners."

"You have misunderstood my statement. Lloyd-James was
positing a definitely *feudal* relationship, with all the special
conditions of service, protection, duty and privilege. But whereas in properly feudal times the nobility gave service and duty
to the king in return for tenure of their lands, in this case
the king gave service and duty to the nobility in return for
tenure of his kingdom."

"Or in plain words," said Detterling obstinately, "he was
told to toe the line or get out. The relationship was no more
feudal than me and my aunt Fanny."

Oh God, he thought, I'm beginning to talk like Leonard.

"Of your relationship with the lady you mention," said
Constable, "I do not presume to speak. But it is quite irrelevant whether or not you or I agree with Lloyd-James's
approach; I am simply telling you what it was—or trying to.
What you must also understand is that in the opinion of the
judges, back in 1948, this was an original thesis urged with
style and argued with ingenuity. So they gave Lloyd-James
the prize—a cheque for two hundred pounds and a small gold
medal—and that, one might have thought, was that."

"Only it wasn't?" said Percival with relish.

"It would have been," said Constable, "but for a very
curious accident. A good four years after the prize had been
awarded, a close friend of mine, an historian called Carnwath,
had the task, as Vice-Master of his College, of writing an
obituary for the Annual College Report of a recently deceased
Fellow called Pennington. The task was delicate, because Pennington's private affairs had caused substantial and enduring
scandal as a result of which he had for many years resided
away from Cambridge—though still retaining his Fellowship,

which was for some technical reason inalienable. But however all that might be, appearances had to be upheld. As a Fellow of the College, Pennington must have a minimum of two and a half pages in the Annual Report, and none of this must be less that cordial. My friend Carnwath therefore eschewed much mention of his personality and concentrated on his published work. Unfortunately there was very little of this, and that little mostly indifferent and entirely forgotten. At last, in some despair, Carnwath visited his College library and extracted the typescript of the Dissertation on the strength of which Pennington had first been awarded his Fellowship in 1925. The College, though small, was not undistinguished, and there must have been *some* quality about the dissertation—so my friend told himself—for it to have led to Pennington's election. With any luck the typescript might provide material for a page or more's discussion in the obituary of Pennington's 'early promise', after which some charitable reason might be assigned for its sad lack of fulfilment.

"Pennington's dissertation turned out to be an analysis of the moral and religious ideas which informed the Feudal System. There was also a long passage about the survival of such notions and their influence on later politics. Carnwath found it quite enlivening by comparison with Pennington's published work, but he was puzzled because one chapter had an oddly familiar flavour. He knew he had read something like it before. . . ."

"And of course," said Detterling in a blasé manner, "he'd read it in Somerset's prize essay ?"

"Nothing as crude as that, Captain Detterling. Carnwath had indeed been one of the judges of the Lauderdale in 1948, and it was indeed Lloyd-James's essay of which Pennington's work reminded him. But whereas Lloyd-James had applied the 'inverted feudalism' theory to the relationship between the British nobility and the Hanoverian kings, Pennington had applied it to the relationship between the populace and the monarchy in modern Scandinavian countries."

"A pretty embracing sort of theory," observed Detterling.

"And what's more," said Constable icily, "Lloyd-James's supporting arguments were of a totally different kind, and there was no idiomatic or stylistic resemblance between the two pieces of work. Only the basic theme did they apparently have in common."

"Then it must have been a coincidence," said Percival, looking disappointed.

"So my friend thought—and would have gone on thinking had it not been for one more thing. Pennington had two or three times perpetrated what Carnwath thought was a solecism but was in fact an archaism : he had used the word 'baronage', not in the accepted modern sense of 'the barons collectively', but in the sense of 'barony', *i.e.* the dignity, rank, estate or domain of a baron. When he checked in the dictionary, Carnwath found that the latter usage was very rare but in theory just permissible—and then suddenly recalled that he had gone through exactly the same experience while perusing Lloyd-James's essay four years before. Lloyd-James, discussing the legal powers and privileges of peers in the eighteenth century, had at one stage written : 'One Scottish peer, the Lord Kilmarnock, could still preside over his own private court and could even hand down sentence of death; but the privilege was peculiar to the baronage.' Now if 'baronage' there is taken in its usual meaning of 'the barons collectively', the passage is slovenly nonsense . . . so on that occasion too, Carnwath now recalled, he had gone to the dictionary, and, after noting the archaic usage, had been able to construe the clause as meaning that this murderous privilege was peculiar to the estate and domain of the Barons Kilmarnock."

"There are said to have been good reasons for it," Detterling began.

"Good or bad, they are nothing to our purpose. What concerns us," said Constable, "is that my friend Carnwath was convinced that their similar and eccentric misuse of the same term established a connexion between Pennington's work and Lloyd-James's. Perhaps Lloyd-James had repeated Pennington's error without noticing it, or perhaps he had simply assumed (being a tyro) that Pennington's use of 'baronage' was correct, that a successful Fellowship dissertation could not contain error in such matters. But no matter exactly how it had happened, Carnwath was convinced that in one way or another Lloyd-James had caught the usage from Pennington. In which case he had also caught his basic idea from Pennington, stolen it, in fact, from a thesis that had never been published and survived, as far as was known, only in one typed copy which was locked away in the back room of a small college library."

"Rather thin—the evidence," Percival said.

"Ah. There was more to come. 'Baronage' began it; more concrete things followed."

"But surely," said Detterling, "Pennington was still alive when Somerset wrote his essay. Wouldn't Somerset have been afraid that Pennington would spot the stolen idea even if no one else did?"

"Pennington, as I have already indicated, was a discredited scholar of dissolute habit, who lived at the other end of the country. He no longer concerned himself with academic affairs —or certainly not to the extent of procuring and reading a prize essay. Lloyd-James need not have been deterred by any fears on the score of Pennington. A far greater objection to Carnwath's hypothesis was this : how could Lloyd-James ever have had access to Pennington's dissertation? When I say it was locked away in a back room, that is the literal truth—and what is more, the College in question wasn't even Lloyd-James's. If it comes to that," intoned Constable sternly, "how had Lloyd-James ever known such a work existed and might be of use to him? But my friend Carnwath was a determined man, who trusted his instincts. 'Baronage' and the resemblance of ideas had convinced him. He began to enquire further. . . ."

There was a noise of girlish laughter from outside. Constable went to the open window, looked out of it and down, and brooded like Jupiter.

"All these wretched women here for May Week," he said, more to himself than his guests. "These days they even think they're entitled to walk on our lawns. How can you keep a lawn in good order with hundreds of people trampling on it— even if half of those young trollops do go barefoot?" He turned heavily away from the window and now spoke directly to Percival. "How would *you* have gone about Carnwath's enquiries?" he asked.

"I'd have started with the librarian and his assistants. Although the dissertation was locked up, Lloyd-James might have applied to see it; and since, as you say, it wasn't his College, such an odd request would certainly have been remembered, even four years later.'

"Neither the librarian nor his assistants could recall that anyone had ever asked for Pennington's thesis except Carnwath himself when he was working on the obituary. No one else had had it since they'd been there—and they'd all been there for over ten years."

"Did they never have vacations?"

"Never all at the same time. At least one of them was in that library, in term and out of term, every day of the year except Christmas Day, when the place was locked up as tight as the Bank of England."

"In which case," said Percival, "I should have asked whether there was not another copy in existence which Lloyd-James might have seen somewhere else."

"Very good. But *whom* would you have asked?"

"Typing agencies who might have typed the thing originally."

"Their records did not go back to the mid-twenties."

"Pennington's colleagues and contemporaries."

"None of them could recall having seen a second copy. Few of them even knew about the first."

"Then I should have asked a question of myself—whether the game was still worth the candle."

"It was to Carnwath. He was morally certain that Lloyd-James had stolen another man's ideas—a cardinal crime in our circles, Mr Percival—and he wanted proof in order to be able to exact justice. So he asked himself this question : if there *were* other copies of the thesis, where would they be?"

"Among Pennington's own papers?"

"Not according to his executors."

"He might have presented someone with a copy?"

"Too vague. Presented whom with a copy?"

"You tell me," said Leonard Percival.

"His old school—or so Carnwath reckoned. In 1925, when Pennington won his Fellowship, he had still been young, hopeful and proud of his achievement . . . his *first* achievement. What more natural than that he should have sent a copy of his dissertation to his old school—like a child bringing its prize to show to his mother? So to Pennington's old school Carnwath went; and there in the school library, in a special section for the books of old boys, was what Carnwath was hoping for— another typescript copy of Pennington's thesis, with a rather touching inscription of gratitude to 'the friends and tutors of my boyhood at the best school of all'. There was a prominent notice saying that no books from this section could be removed in any circumstance; but the shelves were open, and anyone at all could examine any of the books in them. So there it was. A second copy of Pennington's thesis, which had been readily available ever since 1925, at Pennington's old school."

"Which was also Somerset Lloyd-James's?"

"No," said Constable. "*Not* Somerset Lloyd-James's. Very different. A grammar school."

"Well," said Percival, "that was a bit of a damper."

"Not at all. A grammar school but a prominent one—in the West Country. Sir Thomas Martock's School for Boys, founded in Yeovil in 1727 and later removed, in 1789, to one of the Martock properties near a town called Bampton in Devon. It had a Governing Body largely made up of local magnates—one of whom was Seamus Lloyd-James, of Chantry Marquess in the County of Devon, Esquire. The father of Somerset Lloyd-James. The latter no longer came into the neighbourhood very often, as Carnwath now learned, but had quite often been there, during his school holidays and university vacations, as a boy. A studious and responsible boy, who needed a good library and was granted, at the request of his father on the Governing Body, the freedom of the library at Sir Thomas Martock's. Even when Martock's closed for its holidays, the caretaker had instructions to open up the library for Mr Somerset Lloyd-James. Who was very grateful for the privilege; who, it was rumoured, was on uneasy terms with his mother and therefore particularly glad to slip away from home and work at Martock's . . . where he was most appreciative of the fine selection of historical volumes bequeathed by the late Sir George Martock, Baronet . . ."

". . . And where," said Detterling, "he one day examined, in a mood of idle curiosity, the section devoted to the books that had been written by the school's *alumni*. . . ."

". . . And was surprised to see," put in Percival, "that one of them was in fact unpublished. The typescript of a Fellowship Dissertation. Rather a rarity. . . ."

". . . So he took it down and read a few pages, was perhaps favourably impressed. . . ."

". . . And some time later, when deciding to enter for the Lauderdale Prize in 1948. . . ."

". . . Remembered that there was a passage in this unpublished thesis back at Martock's that might be helpful. So on his next visit to Chantry Marquess," Detterling pursued, "he went over to Martock's in the depth of the vacation, was admitted to the library by a deferential cartetaker, spent some hours reading the Pennington thesis and making notes on it, then returned it to its shelf and went his way, as usual leaving everything just as he found it but taking with him the seminal idea—someone else's—which was to win him, before the year was out, a cheque for two hundred pounds and a small gold medal. *Quod erat demonstrandum*."

"But it was very far," said Constable, "from being demonstrated. To Carnwath it was now clear what had happened: something, by and large, of the sort you've just suggested. But was his case strong enough for him to take action? It was at this stage he first consulted another person, an old friend, myself. He told me the entire story, as I have told it to you, and then

asked me to give an opinion . . . not as an historian, for I am
in fact an economist, but as a man, he was kind enough to say,
of balanced and logical judgement. In four words : would the
charge stick?"

"And your answer?"

"In one word : no. There were extremely strong grounds
for suspicion, but absolute proof was not possible. If Lloyd-
James had transcribed whole sentences, or even some important phrases, of Pennington's, that would have been proof. But
the echo of an idea and the similar misuse of the word 'baronage' were not enough. There was no *proof* that Lloyd-James
had read and exploited Pennington's material, even though
we knew that this material had been available to him. Mind
you, I thought Carnwath was almost certainly right; but Lloyd-
James's plagiary had been too cleverly and cautiously carried
out for anyone to make an official accusation; and indeed if
anyone did make such an accusation, he would be laying
himself open to an action for libel or slander. With some reluctance, Carnwath agreed. But did I not think, he asked as a
man eager for the academic honour and purity of Cambridge
University, that something ought to be done? And indeed I
did so think."

"But what?" said Detterling. "What could either you or
Carnwath possibly do?"

"We could do nothing official. We could make no open
accusation, and even in private it would be unwise, the only
evidence being what it was, to speak explicitly. But by *unofficial*
action, by *implicit* accusation, we could exact a punishment
to fit the crime. We could let Lloyd-James know that we knew;
and we could so far discredit him by indirect means that he
would never again be recognised by his College or his University—except with contempt. All this we could and must do,
as we told each other, so delicately that Lloyd-James would
never be able to make legal charges of malice against us—
just as he had plagiarised so delicately that we would never
be able to make official charges of cheating against him. We
were determined, in short, to spike him on his own weapons."

"But I dare say," said Detterling, "that you found him, even at that age, quite a formidable opponent."

Constable gave a low grunt of assent. Once more he looked fiercely out of the window, as though wishing (like the Emperor Nero, Detterling thought) that the May Week mob had one throat only which he might cut. Then he moved nearer his two guests, seated himself on a hard chair, and leant forward to resume his tale.

"First," he said, "Carnwath took Pennington's thesis from his college library and had another three copies made, two of which he deposited in his bank. The third copy Carnwath sent to Lloyd-James, who was at that time working for a well-known financial newspaper in London. Carnwath marked the passages from which Lloyd-James had pillaged his key idea, and enclosed a letter saying that he had been much interested by the obvious influence which Pennington's early and unpublished work had had on Mr Lloyd-James's prize essay for the Lauderdale in 1948. Since Pennington was now dead, and since very few people were acquainted with his work at all, let alone his dissertation of 1925, Dr Carnwath would be most grateful if Mr Lloyd-James would prepare a paper for *The Historical Quarterly* (which he, Dr Carnwath, edited) on Pennington's contribution to historical scholarship. This would be of great interest to subscribers to the *Quarterly* and also a graceful gesture towards the neglected scholar to whom Mr Lloyd-James clearly owed so much.

"A week later Carnwath received the reply he expected. Mr Lloyd-James thanked Dr Carnwath for his interest in Mr Lloyd-James's work and for his invitation to contribute to *The Historical Quarterly*; but Mr Lloyd-James had never heard of a scholar called Pennington and in any case was far too busy at that time to prepare historical papers. However, he was grateful to Dr Carnwath for letting him see Pennington's thesis, which he had now sent back to Cambridge under separate cover, by the parcel post."

"Love-fifteen in Somerset's favour," grinned Detterling. "Next service, please. . . ."

"Carnwath then wrote again, expressing his disappointment at Mr Lloyd-James's refusal. However, Mr Lloyd-James might be interested to know that Dr Carnwath himself now proposed to write the paper in question. It would take the form of a comparative study between Pennington's theories on latter-day manifestations of feudal attitudes and Mr Lloyd-James's equally stimulating theories on the same subject as expressed in his prize essay. Such notice of Mr Lloyd-James's essay was clearly called for in the *Quarterly*, since the Administrators of the Lauderdale, recognising the essay's importance, had now decided to subsidise its publication by The Cambridge University Press under the terms of the Lauderdale benefaction. Normally, wrote Carnwath, this decision would have been made at the time the prize was awarded, in 1948; but at that time paper and printing materials had been very scarce, so a final decision had been deferred. Now, however, publication of the essay could be readily undertaken by the C.U.P., and Mr Lloyd-James might expect to receive the galley-proofs very shortly. Would Mr Lloyd-James accept Dr Carnwath's congratulations . . . and rest assured that Dr Carnwath, in his forthcoming paper for *The Historical Quarterly*, would do ample justice to Mr Lloyd-James's essay on the happy occasion of its public appearance."

"How much of this was bluff?" asked Percival.

"None of it. The Lauderdale Committee were indeed empowered to pay for Lloyd-James's essay to be published, albeit it was now rather late in the day, and Carnwath had persuaded them to do so. As for the paper, Carnwath could certainly have written a piece for the *Quarterly* which purported to be a comparison between the original work of two men but in fact made it plain, without ever saying so straight out, that one had pilfered from the other."

"And of course Carnwath as editor could easily arrange for his piece in the *Quarterly* to coincide with the C.U.P.'s publication of Somerset's essay."

"Precisely. Carnwath intended, you see, to award Lloyd-James a minor academic triumph, which would then be subtly transformed, under the very eye of the spectators, into academic disgrace."

"And although there would not be many spectators," mused Detterling, "there would be quite enough to pass the word around—and pass it as far as Somerset's employers in London."

"As to London, we were more or less indifferent. Our primary object was to discredit Lloyd-James here in Cambridge, where it really mattered."

"I see, Provost. And how did Somerset get *this one* back over the net?"

"He never had to. He enjoyed what is sometimes known," said Constable wryly, "as Bentley's luck."

"Bentley's luck?" Percival said.

"Richard Bentley was appointed Master of Trinity College in 1699," said Constable didactically. "He so scandalised and outraged his Fellows that they summoned the College Visitor to enquire into his conduct. The night before the enquiry the Visitor passed in the best guest-room—where he was found dead the following morning."

"Of natural causes, I trust?"

"Indisputably. The enquiry was of course postponed *sine die*. Bentley's luck. Something rather similar," said Constable with a quick twist of malice over his usually mamoreal face, "occurred quite recently in a senior College at Oxford."

"What and where?" said Detterling.

Constable's face resumed its state of stern repose.

"It does not concern us," he said shortly. "What does concern us is that before Carnwath could bring his plan into action he fell dead of a stroke. Bentley's luck for Lloyd-James, and sorrow for myself. Carnwath was perhaps my oldest friend. Despite our disagreements over politics—Carnwath was High Tory in his views, while I, as you may know, am a Socialist— we had been very close to each other since we were boys. We had served together in the Gurkhas during the war; in Burma, under Wingate."

Constable fastened his eyes close on Detterling's and then went on: "Carnwath's death was undoubtedly hastened by the appalling physical hardships which he had endured in the jungle."

There was a cool innuendo conveyed by this statement (when did *you* ever serve in the jungle?) which Detterling did not consider to be justified.

"You at least seem to have survived in very sound health," he said.

"Yes," said Constable neutrally. "I survived. And I decided that I owed it to my friend to continue his work of justice for him. Lloyd-James must still have his lesson. But how to give it to him? I was not an historian; I could not write Carnwath's piece for the *Quarterly*, and I had no influence with the Administrators of the Lauderdale, who, now that Carnwath was dead, quietly cancelled the publication of Lloyd-James's essay on the grounds of expense. Clearly, Carnwath's plan was in the coffin with Carnwath, and I must think of another. But I did not share the Machiavellian talents of my friend, and a whole year and more later I was still thinking, not to much purpose. Then two things happened. I was appointed Professor of Economics at the University of Salop, and some fifteen months afterwards Somerset Lloyd-James was appointed editor of *Strix*. The Professor of Economics at Salop is, *ex officio*, a member of the Board of *Strix*. Thus time and chance had at last brought Lloyd-James and myself face to face.

"It was at this time that my personal acquaintance with Lloyd-James commenced. When he was up here at Cambridge, I had known him, as I told you, very barely by sight and by repute. After he left, while I'd heard a great deal of him from Carnwath in the Lauderdale connexion, I had still neither met nor corresponded with him myself. But now . . . now we were sitting round the same table, discussing the policies and fortunes of *Strix*. Now if ever I must find a way of carrying out my old friend's intentions—or else devise a new set that would serve as well."

"Your original intention—yours and Carnwath's—had been to expose him in Cambridge," Percival remarked. "You didn't mind about London, you said. But by now I suppose the emphasis had shifted a bit?"

"Let's say . . . that I felt he must be shown up for what he had done before one or more people who mattered to him and by whom the meaness and fraudulence of his act would be fully appreciated. I no longer cared much whether these people were in London or in Cambridge. But since it was clear to me soon after he came to *Strix* that he now regarded Cambridge as long since behind him, I inclined to think that he should be discomforted before one of his London circle."

"I never heard that he was discomforted before anybody," Detterling said.

"I dare say, Captain Detterling, that even you do not hear everything. Now, at that time a regular and prominent contributor to *Strix* was a young man called Tom Llewyllyn. Although I did not know Llewellyn, indeed never met him until several years afterwards, I had a high regard for the personality revealed by his writing. His articles were honest and accurate, and showed a genuine concern, informed but never sentimental, over social issues. He was known to be less than reputable in his private life, but as far as I could gather he was not a vicious man, only a cheerful and Chaucerian sinner. And however that might be, I knew that Lloyd-James valued him both as a friend and a writer, and that this regard very much increased (as did everyone else's) on the publication, in 1956, of Llewyllyn's book *The Bear's Embrace*, which was, in its kind, a minor classic. I imagine you've both read it?"

"I was abroad in 1956," said Percival shiftily.

"And I myself can hardly think of it," said Detterling, "as a minor classic. Too many gimmicks. But I can tell you this. It was published by Gregory Stern, whose partner I later became, and even now we find it still goes on selling. Not enough to keep Tom in caviar, but enough to tickle his vanity."

"Well," said Constable, who clearly deprecated the terms of Detterling's assessment, "it certainly brought him substantial and enduring esteem, and of course this was at its height in

1956—both with the public and with Lloyd-James, who constantly reminded the Board of *Strix* what a privilege it was to have Llewyllyn writing for us and how clever it had been of Lloyd-James to secure his services. So it occurred to me that Llewyllyn was the man before whom Lloyd-James must be exposed. In this way Lloyd-James would be much chagrined and incommoded, and what was more, gentlemen, the information would have gone to a man who knew how to make just and effective use of it. For both just and effective, on the evidence of his writing, I took Llewyllyn to be."

"So you told Tom Llewyllyn, did you?" said Detterling. "What on earth did he say?"

"I didn't *tell* him anything. As I've told you, I never met Llewyllyn until some years later. I merely . . . put him in the way of finding out what had happened."

"Ah," said Percival : "more tricks?"

"Stratagems, let us say." Rather unexpectedly, Constable gave Percival a thin, apologetic smile. "I did not want to involve myself directly," he went on in a careful and meditative tone. "After all, this was Carnwath's affair more than mine. I was only so to speak his executor."

"And of course," said Percival, "it was wiser to keep your distance, Mr Provost, in case the thing back-fired?"

"Yes," said Constable flatly.

"Well then, tricks, stratagems, call 'em what you like," said Percival with a grin of enjoyment, "how did you set them going?"

"If you'll both excuse me," Detterling said. "Before you tell us that, Provost, I'd like to have one thing clear. Was it your intention, or any part of your intention, to get Lloyd-James removed from the editorship of *Strix*?"

"It was my intention," said Constable, "to expose the unscrupulous piece of plagiarism, of which Lloyd-James had been guilty in 1948, to a fair-minded man of Lloyd-James's close acquaintance. What followed would not be in my hands. All I was concerned with was the revelation which justice required."

"But you've admitted that you hoped he would be 'discomforted' and 'incommoded'?"

"Yes. Justice certainly required that."

"Yet you had no *specific* result in mind?"

"No. The only *specific* result I had ever desired from all this was that Lloyd-James should be prevented from returning to Cambridge in an academic capacity. With his ostensible record, you see, he might well have been invited to. But now that it was plain to me that he would never wish to return to Academe, my interest had become almost abstract. Justice required that he be shown up and take the consequences, and that was all. With what those consequences might be, I could not concern myself."

"So there was no element of personal spite in this?"

"None."

"And you had no axe to grind with regard to *Strix*?"

"Speaking for myself," said Constable patiently, "I despised Lloyd-James as a cynical self-seeker and I rather admired him as an efficient and perspicacious editor. But all that was quite beside my purpose at that present—which was only that the truth about the Lauderdale should be made known to someone with whom it would count for what it was."

"Even though by this time the Lauderdale incident was nearly ten years in the past."

"That could not signify. There is no . . . statute of limitations . . . for fraudulence of the kind which Lloyd-James had practised. Scholarship must not be mocked."

"Agreed," said Percival. "We cannot allow people to cook the Books of Truth and get away with it. So now back to the nitty-gritty, Mr Provost. You wanted to let this man Tom Llewyllyn know what Somerset had done but you were not prepared to commit yourself to a direct assertion : so how did you work it?"

"I asked myself how Carnwath would have set about it, and then proceeded as follows. I sent a copy of Lloyd-James's prize essay to Llewyllyn's publisher, Gregory Stern, and explained in my accompanying letter that I was an executor of the late Dr Carnwath, who had been very interested in this essay and had hoped to achieve its publication. Unfortunately, I went on, the C.U.P. had now dropped the idea of printing it, but I thought it might be worth Mr Stern's attention; for I knew he sometimes took on historical work with a modern application, such, for example, as Mr Tom Llewyllyn's distinguished book *The Bear's Embrace*. Perhaps, indeed, he might ask Mr Llewyllyn to read Lloyd-James's essay and give an opinion?

"A little later I heard from Stern that he had passed the essay to Llewyllyn, as I had hoped he would. I myself then sent a copy of Pennington's dissertation direct to Llewyllyn. Might I presume, I wrote, as a member of the Board of *Strix*, to congratulate him on his articles—and to ask a favour? My late friend, Dr Carnwath, had been very concerned to promote interest in the ideas of the historian Pennington, whose Fellowship dissertation of 1925 I begged to leave to enclose. If Mr Llewyllyn could find in it the substance of an article for *Strix* or any other journal for which he wrote, such an article would afford me pleasure and earn my gratitude on behalf of Pennington and Carnwath."

"I see," said Detterling. "So now Tom would be reading Pennington's thesis within only a day or two of reading Somerset's copy-cat essay. Or so you hoped. You didn't suggest he should compare them?"

"Oh no. I didn't nudge him in any way. In accordance with my policy of non-involvement, I was responsible only for contriving that Llewyllyn should have both pieces of work on his desk at the same time. The rest I left to him. It was, you see, in part a test of the evidence: if Llewyllyn, unprompted, drew the same conclusion as Carnwath and myself, then clearly we had been right."

"And if Llewyllyn did not draw that conclusion?"

"Then we might have been wrong, and Lloyd-James would, quite correctly, receive the benefit of the doubt—for nothing would then be done about it."

"So in effect," said Percival, "you were dumping the entire

onus both of judgement and action on Llewyllyn?"

"I believed him to have strong shoulders," said Constable, with the air of a man well-pleased with his own skills in delegation.

"So you have told us. What happened?"

"Lloyd-James's essay was not published by Stern and Pennigton's thesis was not used as material for an article by Llewyllyn. But Llewyllyn wrote me a line or two when he returned the thesis. The exact phrasing is perhaps worth your attention. 'Thank you for sending me Pennington's work,' he wrote, 'but my order book is full and I haven't the time to give it the care it doubtless deserves. As for Lloyd-James's essay, which is also, I gather, under your sponsorship, what sort of care *it* deserves is rather a tricky problem.' And that was all."

"So the penny had dropped in the slot?" said Percival.

"Perhaps. And then again, perhaps not. Perhaps he was simply referring to the problem of whether or not the essay should be published. All I could ever be certain of was that my part was done. I had sent Llewyllyn the evidence, without any prejudicial comment, so that he might make of it what he would and then act as he saw fit. My duty was discharged."

"But this was the *crunch*, Mr Provost. Did nothing further come of it?"

"Nothing . . . that I know of." Constable smiled blandly at Percival's evident exasperation. "Some five years later I came to know Llewyllyn quite well. Early in the sixties he was awarded a Research Fellowship at this college, and he was later given a permanent appointment. But in all the time since he's been here, he has never once referred to this affair, and I cannot remember that the name of 'Lloyd-James' has ever passed his lips in my presence."

There was a knock on the door, and a thin white female face snaked into the room on a long, scraggy neck.

"They're here for lunch," the face said.

"Very well, Elvira."

"You've got to come and talk to them. They're too clever for me."

"Two minutes, my dear."

The face withdrew.

"My wife," said Constable with well-bred contempt. "She has rather a nervous disposition. So if you'll excuse me, gentlemen. . . ."

They all rose. Detterling felt like a schoolboy who had worked through some huge equation, only to find, after five pages of wrangling, that 'x' equals 'x'. But whenever that happened, he told himself, it always turned out that one had made a mistake. There must be some positive value in Constable's story; otherwise he would not have wasted the time to tell it.

"Provost," he said. "You've told us all this because you felt it might help us. But how? You say that nothing at all came of it."

"I said no such thing." Constable preceded them to the door. "I said nothing came of it that I myself knew of . . . nothing *overt*." He seized the door-handle and opened the door wide with one long circular sweep of his arm, like a state janitor in a palace. "Let me wish you, gentlemen, a very good afternoon."

"He certainly made us work for it," said Percival, "but it's pretty plain what he meant."

"Not to me," said Detterling.

They were walking together in Lancaster College Chapel, Percival having opined that they might as well take a squint at it while it was handy.

"Ah," said Percival, "a tomb. I like a good tomb."

He led the way through an elaborate screen of stone tracery and into a little chantry, much of which was occupied by a high box tomb.

"Really grand," said Percival. "The sort of thing that Provost Constable ought to be lying in. With his effigy in armour on top."

"Funny you should say that. He comes of a fighting family.

A line of knights and captains going back to the Plantagenets. It's a wonder they've never been ennobled."

"Too grand to bother with it, I expect. I was impressed by Provost Constable."

"You looked pretty annoyed with him once or twice."

"Because I found him perverse. But later on I began to understand his technique and respect it."

"Then for heaven's sake, Leonard, tell me what he was getting at."

"He was saying," said Percival, "that it was about even money that Llewyllyn got the message."

"I gathered that much."

"He was also saying that he neither knew nor wanted to know what happened then, but that if anything *did* happen it might be very much to our purpose to find out what. Because as he kept reminding us, this Llewyllyn is a capable man —that's why Constable picked him. Is Llewyllyn capable, Detterling?"

"Yes. And perservering. A Socialist like Constable. Despite his dissolute youth he takes very tough moral views."

"Exactly. So the very fact that whatever action he took was *not overt*—a point which Constable stressed for us—makes it sound all the more formidable. When perservering men of tough moral views take covert action, it's time to fall to one's prayers."

"We don't know that Llewyllyn took any action at all."

"It's my bet that it's Constable's bet that he did."

"And if he did . . . it might have led, all these years later, to Somerset's suicide?"

"It entirely depends," said Percival, "on how and when Llewyllyn used his knowledge. The question is, will he tell us?" He stooped down to examine a Maltese Cross which was carved near the base of one end of the tomb. "That Head Porter chappie said he had rooms in college but would be staying away from the place during the May Week celebrations. Why May Week," he said crossly, "when we're well into June?"

"Academic perversity—like Constable's. They're so keen to avoid being obvious that they end up by being obscure."

"Will Llewyllyn be obscure?"

"I don't think so. He wasn't bred up as a don, you see, and I think he's too rugged to have been infected since he got here. Did the Head Porter say where we could find him?"

"At a house he has in Grantchester."

"God," groaned Detterling. "That wife of his will be there. A real pain in the neck."

"Then I'll buy you a nice lunch before we go out there, said Percival, "to give you strength."

The front door of Tom's house in Grantchester was opened by a very pretty little girl of about twelve (Detterling guessed) who was wearing white knee-socks and a very short tartan dress.

"Professor Llewyllyn's residence," she said, rubbing her silky bare thighs together.

"I didn't know he was a Professor."

"He's not," said a tired voice. "How are you, Detterling?"

He looks very much older, Detterling thought as Tom Llewyllyn stepped up behind the girl in the doorway; nearer sixty than his real forty-odd. It must be his wife. Everything else has gone well for him; he's respected at Lancaster, it seems, and that last book of his was a success, in academic circles at least. No great problems about money—or there shouldn't be, not now. Yes; it must be his wife.

"Hullo, Tom," he said. "I suppose this is Baby?"

"Yes," simpered the girl deliciously, "I'm Baby Llewyllyn, I am."

Detterling offered his hand to her. She clutched two of his fingers in her left hand and two plus his thumb in her right, stared up into his face with adoration, and went on rubbing her thighs together.

Dear God, thought Detterling, as he introduced Percival to Tom and Baby, wait till she sprouts tits and then watch the balloon fly. Even while being introduced to Percival, Baby continued to hang on to Detterling's hand with both of hers, and indeed she was now kneading his palm against the woollen jersey which she wore above the tartan skirt.

"How's Patricia?" Detterling said to Tom, pretending not to notice Baby's advances.

"Well enough," said Llewyllyn. "She's gone to London for the day."

"To the dentist," volunteered Baby. "Mummy was mean. She wouldn't take me with her." She looked spitefully at her father. "I think Mummy'th got a *man* in London," she lisped, "or why else wouldn't she take me? It wath the thame last week—when she went to have her new cothtume fitted."

Tom Llewyllyn heard this speech out calmly, then took firm hold of both of Baby's wrists and detached her hands from Detterling's.

"I shan't be a moment," he said.

Baby opened her mouth very wide, whether to howl or to perpetrate some further obscene conjecture Detterling never knew, as Tom now clapped a palm across her face and whisked her into the house. For about three minutes, while Detterling and Percival waited by the front door, there was absolute silence within. Then Tom Llewyllyn reappeared alone.

"Sorry about all that," he said. "Let's take a turn by the river."

"Will Baby be all right by herself?" said Detterling, prompted by curiosity rather than concern.

"She's not by herself." Llewyllyn hesitated slightly. "There's a governess," he said, "and it's her time to take over. That's why I told you on the phone to come now."

He led the way round the house, down a long and ill-kept garden, and out through a gate into a meadow which sloped down to the river.

"Baby doesn't go to school," he said abruptly, "and Patricia has to be away a lot. Hence the . . . the governess."

"Well, give my regards to Patricia when she gets back this evening," said Detterling easily.

"I'll do that. When she gets back from London." To judge from Llewyllyn's tone, she might (or might not) have been coming back from the South Pole. "Now, what did you want to talk about?"

"Somerset Lloyd-James," said Percival.

"Poor old Somerset. God alone knows what got into him."

"We're trying to find out," said Detterling, and explained why.

Tom Llewyllyn listened carefully. Then,

"I doubt whether I can help you," he said. "I haven't seen him in years."

"But you knew him well once?" said Percival.

"Intimately."

"In the old days of *Strix*," said Detterling.

"I did a lot of work for him when he was Editor there."

"But you *didn't* write an article on an historian called Pennington?"

Llewyllyn's face went quite blank. Either he doesn't remember, thought Detterling, or he doesn't want to.

"Constable wrote to you about him," Percival prompted, "some time in 1956 or '57. He sent you a dissertation which Pennington had written."

"I didn't know Constable. Not then."

"But Constable was on the Board of *Strix*. He wrote to congratulate you on the standard of your work. . . ."

"Yes," said Llewyllyn slowly. "Ye-es." He paused. "He sent me somebody's thesis which I didn't have time to read. I remember now. I was too busy, because Gregory Stern had just sent me something of Somerset's which he wanted an opinion on. So I read this thing of Somerset's, but then, when the *other* thing arrived from Constable—from a man I'd never even spoken to—I got fed up. So I let a decent interval pass, and then I sent it back with a polite note."

"And that's all."

"That's all."

"Well," said Percival heavily, "you *did* read Lloyd-James's essay. What did you do about that?"

"In the end I told Gregory not to publish it. You see, there was something wrong about it."

"You knew that," said Detterling, puzzled, "just from reading it . . . and that alone?"

"More or less."

"But surely, you say you didn't read the Pennington thesis, so how did you know there was something wrong with Somerset's essay?"

"What the hell has Pennington got to do with it?" said Llewyllyn.

Detterling opened his mouth to attempt an explanation but Percival held up his hand like a policeman.

"Halt," he said very firmly. "Let us not get ourselves confused." And then to Llewyllyn, "*What* did you find wrong with Somerset's prize essay?"

"It was a long time ago. Let me try to get it straight."

Llewyllyn stopped walking and started to examine a clump of river-reeds as though they had been rare orchids.

"Somerset's essay," he said at last, "was about the function of the monarchy in the eighteenth century. Some of it was quite brilliant; there was one long passage, about the survival and perversion of feudal practices, in which Somerset put forward a striking new theory. But the trouble was that in the rest of the essay a lot of the material was faked."

"You mean stolen?"

"No; faked. And very ingeniously. For example : Somerset opened his essay with character sketches of the first three Georges. Now, if he'd just lifed these clean out of some well-known work—Thackeray's *The Four Georges*, let's say—and tried to pass them off as his own, it would at once have been spotted. But what he'd done was entirely different and far more subtle. He'd taken passages from Thackeray and elsewhere, and quoted them with full and precise acknowledgment; but every now and then he'd altered the text very slightly, or even inserted a phrase or two of his own, so as to slant everything which he'd quoted in such a way as to make it consistent with the theories (especially the one about feudal survivals) which he was later going to propound. He was manufacturing support for himself, and lending this support prestige by falsely attributing it to prestigious men. And yet his alterations were so neat, his insertions so plausible and brief, that it was a hundred to one against anyone's getting suspicious and going to check with the original."

"Then how did you come to spot that he was cheating?"

"Ironically enough, through a piece of my *own* cheating. One of Somerset's quotations was a sentence from Edmund Burke's *Address to the King*. Now, as it happened, I'd just been sent a new edition of Burke's speeches to review for *The Observer*. I was pressed for time, and not very anxious to grind my way through Burke, so I decided I'd fudge up an article just from reading the introduction to the book and a few selected passages. Since I'd been rather impressed by the sentence which Somerset quoted in his essay, I thought I'd look the passage out in the book, in case it might suit me to quote it at greater length (which would help fill out my review) or in case there were any more useful gobbets in the adjacent text. This had to do with the attitudes which Burke thought George III ought to adopt towards the American Colonies and the disastrous nature of the advice which the King had received from his Privy Council—or so I gathered from Somerset's transcription in his essay. But when I turned to Burke himself, I found that in fact he was excoriating, not the Privy Council, but Parliament as a whole. What Somerset had done was to substitute the phrase 'Privy Council' for the single word 'Parliament', thus giving the impression that the King was in the hands of a small group of aristocrats who determined his every act for him—an impression very much in line with the theory he would later produce about the neo-feudal dominance held *over* the king *by* the aristocracy."

"It could have been a slip of Somerset's."

"It could indeed. But I knew my Somerset; so I checked on the rest of his quotations, and found that he'd played very much the same kind of trick with passages from Macaulay, Froude, Thackeray and Trevelyan, to name only a few. The thing was quite clear : Somerset had been fiddling the evidence, but in such a way that he would never have been found out but for the pure chance of my being up to a similar fiddle over my review of Edmund Burke."

"At least *you* weren't out to falsify."

"Only to save myself trouble. But it often comes to the same thing."

"Did you disapprove of what Somerset had done?"

"Very deeply. Just as I disapproved of the way in which I myself had meant to treat Burke. So then I did two things. I set about reading Burke fully and properly, in order to write a pukka review and purge myself, so to speak, of my intended treachery to letters. And secondly, I went to see Somerset and told him I'd rumbled his prize essay."

"How did he react?"

"He was very put out. He hadn't known Gregory was thinking of publishing it—he thought, as well he might, that it was safely buried in the past. And now here was I, telling him I could prove it was a fraud, and that it was my duty to expose him to Gregory to make sure Gregory didn't publish. When the story got round, and Gregory would see to that if I didn't, Somerset was going to look exceedingly silly to say the least of it. I had him strapped over a barrel, buttocks spread for a whipping."

"But you never," said Detterling thoughtfully, "handed that whipping out. Did you keep it hanging over him? Did you remind him, from time to time over the years, that you could make him a public laughing-stock whenever you wanted? How did you *use* your knowledge, Tom?"

Tom laughed softly, still looking at the river-reeds.

"You're not suggesting," he said, "that *I* drove Somerset to suicide? All because of a crooked essay?"

"You had the power," said Percival, "up to the day he died *you had the power*, to humiliate him cruelly. And the higher he went, the crueller the humiliation."

"I dare say," said Tom; "but I am not vindictive, and Somerset was an old familiar. Besides, I wanted him at *Strix*, where he could help me, not grovelling about in a crap-heap— then or ever. So what I did was to put up a deal."

"Money, I imagine," said Detterling with weary disappointment.

"Money, but not in the way you think. Some time before my book *The Bear's Embrace* was published—indeed before it was even finished—Somerset had lent me five hundred pounds, which I desperately needed, on condition that I paid him half of every cheque I received for rights or royalties after the book was ready.* He'd got it all on paper, all sealed and signed, in case I tried to rat. Fair enough, I suppose, remembering the sort of chap I was then."

At last Tom turned away from the river-reeds. He smiled at Detterling and Percival and gave a modest shrug.

"Well, in the event," he said, "*The Bear's Embrace* did much better than anyone had hoped, and by the time we're talking of, what with American rights and all, Somerset had already received well over £3000—and jolly good luck to Somerset, because he'd taken a long shot with his five hundred quid and done me a good turn when it counted. But by now I reckoned he'd had enough. So I told him that his secret would be safe with me, and that I would tell Gregory to send the essay back where it came from as being unsuitable, merely on general grounds, for publication; but that all this must be on the strict understanding that Somerset would no longer invoke his piece of paper to demand any share of the money which might still accrue from *The Bear's Embrace*. He could keep the paper as a guarantee that I would keep the secret; but let him ever again try to enforce that paper, and I would shout the story of his Lauderdale Prize from the rooftops."

"He agreed?"

"Of course. So that was how the contract stood between us and it remained unbroken on either side. Other little differences we had from time to time, and Somerset at least did not always observe the Queensberry Rules. But when it came to our Lauderdale agreement—well, he always needed my silence and I always needed my royalties. The bargain was kept as firm as a rock by both of us . . . until today, when poor

* See *The Rich Pay Late.*

old Somerset has ceased to care about the Lauderdale or any
other of the earthly prizes for which he fought so dirtily. So
dirtily, and yet"—Tom smiled, almost with love—"with so
much sheer bloody guts as well, and bless his rotten heart for
it."

"An interesting old day," said Detterling, as the Mercedes
carried them through the loitering fenland afternoon towards
the Norfolk coast and Broughton Staithe.

"Yes. . . . What in God's name was the matter with that
child of Llewyllyn's?"

"Perhaps it saw something in the woodshed."

"That generally frightens them off it," said Percival. "This
one couldn't wait to start. And why did she say her father was
a professor?"

"Infantile paranoia."

"But what brought that on? She's got nothing to complain
of—as pretty as paint she is."

"Something to do with her mother may have upset her.
Patricia Llewyllyn has been behaving very oddly of late. There's
some tale that she got keen on an undergraduate a few years
back, and ever since then she's wanted them younger and
younger."

"Is she a good looker, this Patricia?"

"Frumpish. But she's got a lot of good firm flesh and a warm
motherly way with it. So if you were a healthy growing boy
with nothing to do on a summer's afternoon, you might be
rather glad of Patricia to teach you a trick or two. Anyway,
she finds plenty that are."

"Where does she get 'em?"

"According to Jonathan Gamp—"

"—Jonathan Gamp?—"

"—An old London friend of Tom's, the original Madame
Tattle. According to Jonathan, who's often acurate, Patricia
picks up her little friends in public swimming-baths. Not in
Cambridge, Tom's put his foot down about that—"

"—But while visiting her dentist in London?"

"That's it, I suppose. Jonathan says she spots out the talent while she's in the pool, then makes her pick and asks him to a flat she's got for tea—"

"—And serves it up with hot buttered crumpet. No harm in that so long as he's over sixteen. Nothing illegal."

"The trouble is, so Jonathan says, she's getting greedy. It's not just tea for two any longer, it's bring all your friends."

"Now that," said Percival, "could be naughty. It's still just all right provided they form an orderly queue outside the bedroom door. But if she once gets party games going and the word slips out, somebody's mummy might turn up very nasty."

"God knows what goes on. Even Jonathan Gamp doesn't claim to know the details."

"But it doesn't sound as if she's giving poetry readings."

"No. So what with all that, and what with Baby shaping up as a teenage vampire, it's small wonder that Tom looks about a hundred. He probably thinks it's all his fault. He has a comprehensive conscience."

"Well," said Percival after a pause, "at least he hasn't got Somerset Lloyd-James on his conscience. If we believe his story that is. And we do believe it, Detterling, because if he had anything to hide he wouldn't have admitted that he ever knew that essay was faked."

"I agree. No clue to Somerset's suicide here. But we have learnt," said Detterling, "something of great interest about Somerset. Think of the incredible pains he went to in order to pass off that fraud on the judges."

"We always knew he was painstaking."

"But the point is, Leonard, that it took him almost more pains to write that essay crookedly than it would have done, given his knowledge and abilities, to write it honestly. It's as if he didn't want to win that prize honestly, which he might well have done if he'd tried, but was determined to win, if at all, by cheating. You see, Leonard . . . *it gave him more pleasure that way.* That must be it. He enjoyed deceiving people, enjoyed getting away with it. On the face of it, no one was more concerned to uphold moral and social systems—but that was because, if the systems hadn't been there, Somerset would not have had the pleasure of finessing and defrauding them. I suppose that's what Tom meant by saying he had a lot of guts : he preferred to do things the dangerous way."

"It's the same with some people about sex. They do it better if there's a risk of someone coming in and catching them at it. The extra excitement caused by anxiety stimulates their performance."

"But what happens to such people if they *are* actually caught? What would Somerset have done if he really had been exposed?"

"He was. He was rumbled both by Carnwath and by Llewyllyn."

"But only by them. One of them died, and he did a deal with the other. Constable knew too, of course; but he was on the side line; he couldn't take any action by himself because he just wasn't qualified, which Somerset knew as well as he did. No, Leonard, what I meant was, suppose Somerset had been subjected to full public exposure. How would he have behaved then?"

"Interesting question. But nothing to our purpose now."

"More to our purpose than you might think, Leonard. The line I'm following is this. On the one hand, we have reason to suppose that Somerset enjoyed playing things dirty more than he enjoyed playing them straight. On the other hand, as we have often told each other, he took immense care to cover his tracks. But he must have known that there was always a risk, however careful he was, of his being caught out. And therefore, simply because he was indeed so careful, he must have had contingency plans in case he *were* caught out. All right so far?"

"Yes. . . ."

"Now. Somerset being what he was—full of sheer bloody guts, to quote Tom Llewyllyn—it's my bet that his contingency plans would have been pretty strong ones. They would not have included surrender; they would have been plans for carrying on the fight."

"I dare say. And so what of it?"

"Well, several times today we have assumed the possibility that the threat of exposure over this Lauderdale business *might* have led to Somerset's suicide. We now know that there was never any real such threat and therefore that this didn't happen. But my point is that even if the threat of exposure had been a thousand times stronger, even if Somerset had actually been exposed—whether over the Lauderdale or anything else—he still would not have committed suicide, because he would have had these contingency plans ready to cope with the situation."

"But when all this is said, Detterling, we know that he *did* commit suicide."

"Exactly so. And therefore whatever drove him to it must have been something *for which he had no contingency plan.* Whatever the threat or the danger or the sorrow, it was something which, with all his care and foresight, Somerset had never anticipated. Something totally devastating that came right out of the blue. Which brings me back to the proposition which I formulated that afternoon at Lord's: I'm sure that the train of events which led to Somerset's suicide originated in some action of Somerset's so natural to him and so commonplace that he didn't notice it at the time and never even thought of it again."

"And hence the lack of contingency plans in that area?"

"Right, Leonard. And it is particularly important that we should remember that proposition just now."

"Why just now?"

"Because we are on our way to see Fielding Gray."

The Mercedes cornered sharply, passed a derelict pub, and mounted a narrow bridge.

"The Ouse," said Detterling.

The car descended a steep gradient off the bridge and took a left turn of ninety degrees. On the left of the road was a grassy dyke between the road and the river; while on the right an apparently unsown expanse of dark brown earth lay absolutely flat to the horizon, hedgeless, treeless, lifeless, unbroken by anything whatever except a line of telegraph poles which carried a single wire only from nowhere to nowhere else across the mud.

"Hell," said Percival. "That's what hell will be like. That mud, with you all alone in the middle of it. Only 'middle' won't have any meaning because the mud goes on for ever. Why," he said, "is your proposition—which, by the way, I had not for one moment forgotten—so particuarly to be remembered now that we're going to see Fielding Gray?"

"Well . . . what do you know of Fielding?"

"I knew him twenty years ago when he was still in the army and I was on a job in Germany.* And I had quite a lot to do with him ten years later, when he was doing an enquiry for the B.B.C. in Cyprus.† My department was trying to turn that enquiry to its own ends."

"I remember."

"He made a botch of the thing," said Percival. "He didn't stick to it. He let himself . . . be distracted."

"It wasn't his kind of work," said Detterling; "he should never have taken it on. There's only one thing he does passably well, and that's write books. Have you ever read any of them?"

"No," said Percival flatly.

"One of the early ones, a novel called *Love's Jest Book*, is largely autobiographical. It's about the time when Fielding was a boy at school. One of the characters is based on Somerset Lloyd-James."

"So where does that get us?"

"It gets us right back to 1945 . . . and the earliest known instance of foul play by Somerset. The book is a blow-by-blow account of how—among other things—the boy Somerset did the dirty on the boy Fielding."

"Who resented it, I suppose?"

"Not overmuch. According to the novel, Fielding seems simply to have observed and accepted it. For one of the points

* See *The Sabre Squadron*, passim.
† See *The Judas Boy*, passim.

made by the story is that the young Fielding thoroughly
deserved everything he got, including Somerset's knife between
his shoulders."

"How did Somerset react when the novel came out?'

"He shrugged it off. Only those few who remembered him
as a boy would have recognised his portrait; and nobody holds
his schoolboy antics against an adult. It couldn't do Somerset
any damage worth talking of."

"Then if Somerset wasn't injured by the book, and if Fielding
had more or less forgiven him the deeds recorded there, surely
nothing more ever came of it?"

"Nothing."

"So for Christ's sake, what help is this bloody book to us?"

"It's of no direct help to us, Leonard, but it shows us how
Fielding himself might be. The young Somerset in that book
is very subtly observed. Fielding really knew his Somerset. And
so Fielding, if anyone, will understand my theory about Somerset's suicide. He will know just what I mean when I postulate
some action which came so naturally to Somerset that Somerset would hardly have noticed it. He will know exactly the
kind of thing Somerset might have done in this way, and where
it might have led without Somerset's being aware of it until
too late. Indeed, with any luck, he may have seen what Somerset did, and taken note of it where Somerset had failed to."

"All right," said Percival. "I'll buy that—on appro. But
now another thing. He was living with some widow woman,
or so I was told—"

"—Harriet Ongley. She scraped him out of the mess he got
himself into in '62, over that Cyprus enquiry; and then they
set up together."

"Is she still with him?"

"Not as far as I know. She was a possessive woman, and after
a time—quite a long time, to be fair to both of them—he got
fed up. There was some kind of crisis nearly two years back,
and to my belief she's not been near him since."

"So he lives down in Broughton by himself. Lonely for him.
Perhaps we should have asked ourselves to stay."

"We'll be more comfortable at the hotel. I do not see Fielding Gray in the role of responsible housekeeper."

Nor did Fielding Gray, it appeared. For when, later that evening, Detterling and Percival entered the dining-room of the L'Estrange Arms Hotel in Broughton Staithe, they immediately spotted Gray, who was alone at a small table in one corner. As they crossed the room, Gray raised the one little eye in his shining pink face, rose from his seat, gestured quickly to the Head Waiter, and steered Detterling and Percival to a larger table, at which he sat down with them.

"We didn't expect to see you till tomorrow morning," said Detterling.

"I should have told you on the phone : I always dine here, so we were almost bound to meet tonight."

The Head Waiter gave menus to Detterling and Percival and a wine list to Detterling.

"It's absurdly expensive for the rubbish they dish up," said Gray, in a voice audible to the hovering Head Waiter, "but they know me, and I get some kind of service. Anyway, I've no patience for cooking my own food at home."

Detterling and Percival ordered their meal. Gray took the wine list from Detterling and closed it firmly. "You'd better have what they keep for me," he said. And to the Head Waiter, "A bottle of Les Pucelles, Charles, and one of Cent Vignes. I'll have coffee and brandy here, while these gentlemen eat."

"Yes, Major Gray," said the Head Waiter, whose tone and manner (Detterling thought) showed the kind of wary affection that a zoo-keeper might bestow on a man-eating animal which had been many years in his charge and was now, supposedly, tamed. "The Hine as usual, sir ?"

"The Hine," said Gray : "my measure."

"Well, old fellow," said Detterling as the Head Waiter left them, "it's nice to see you. And how's the book on Conrad coming along ? Gregory's getting very excited."

"The final draft will be with you by the agreed date," said Gray : "please ask Gregory to be equally prompt with his cheque. He was two days late with the last one." He turned his eye from Detterling to Percival. "Leonard," he said; "long time no see. I trust you've been having happy hunting."

"My hunting days are over," Percival said: "I'm only a scavenger now, sniffing after dead meat."

"Somerset Lloyd-James's meat. Or so Detterling said on the telephone. I should have thought it would have had a very distinctive smell."

"On the contrary, there's been no smell at all. That's our trouble."

The wine arrived.

"I should have told you," said Percival to Gray; "I can't take my juice any more. A glass at most."

"Then I'll drink some of this before my coffee. Another glass, please, Charles—two glasses, one for each bottle. And some Cheddar to go with it."

"Yes, Major Gray. And still *your* measure of Hine, sir?"

"Of course," said Gray dully. And to Percival, "What's the matter, Leonard? Ulcers?"

"That's it. Caused by worry and irregular meals. Occupational hazard."

"Will they increase your pension?"

"Will they fuck. They'll try to cut it down, because from now till I finish it's home duties only."

"But so much nicer, Leonard, than mixing with all those beastly foreigners. You know how you hated them . . . especially the Greeks."

"Something in that," said Percival.

"And this time at least you've got someone to help you. Detterling here." Gray's face changed from ironic concern with Percival's affairs to ironic puzzlement. "But Detterling's strictly an amateur, Leonard. Is this wise, we ask ourselves? I should have thought you'd be leery of amateurs—after the way I buggered you up over Cyprus."

"Captain Detterling is a volunteer. You were conscribed by us. Anyway, this is very different from Cyprus."

"Is it?" Fielding Gray giggled and drank off a glass of wine.

"It seems to me very much the same. The only difference is that in Cyprus you were looking for dirt which you could throw at someone else, whereas here you're looking for dirt which someone else might throw at you—or rather, at the Government —if you don't find it first and have it disposed of. But either way, your problem is the same : *cherchez la merde*."

Gray giggled again, then nibbled at a fragment of cheese. Detterling looked suspiciously at his 'Fresh Caught Local Plaice'. Percival sipped his wine and smiled gloomily at its forbidden excellence.

"You were *always* a scavenger," Gray went on. "Even in your hunting days, Leonard, all you hunted was shit."

"All right," said Percival calmly; "and that was why I tried to use you in '62. Because you had a natural nose for it "

"And Detterling? Has he got a natural nose for it?"

"His nose has twitched once or twice. But I told you : there's been no real scent."

"And what makes you think I can find it for you?"

"You knew Lloyd-James, at one time, better than anyone. We think you might show us new places to start sniffing. Detterling will explain to you."

Percival looked across at Detterling, who started, very deliberately, to explain his theory.

"My word," said Gray when Detterling had finished, "what's he gone and done to you, Leonard? Do you *believe* all this nonsense?"

"I think there could be a good deal in what Detterling says."

"You—gritty old grimy old Leonard, charmed by an amateur into believing that load of ghoulies? You of all people? So there was a teeny weeny mistake which Somerset didn't even notice, was there? And this was the spark—was it, Leonard?— which set a hidden fuse-train slowly burning down the corridors of time? And then at last the long-delayed and fateful explosion? In a pig's arsehole. Jesus Christ, Leonard, he's talking like a fucking novelist."

Fielding Gray laughed, painfully stretching his thin little mouth as he did so, and then uneasily inspected the enormous cognac which the Head Waiter had just set before him (at least a quadruple, Detterling estimated) as though fearful lest he might have received short measure.

"Poor old Leonard," he said : "no wonder they'll try to cut your pension."

"I don't ask you to accept my theory," said Detterling to Gray, part-angered at the unexpected rejection and part-humble in the face of it : "I do ask you to help us in our efforts to apply it." He leant forward and almost whispered to Gray : "*Res unius, res omnium*. Remember, Fielding?"

"What's that?" said Percival.

"Our old regimental motto," said Detterling blandly. "It recommends us to assist one another."

They both looked at Fielding Gray, whose face had now ceased to mock and had become, very suddenly, very sad.

"Of course," he said, lifting his cognac. "If you're going to put it like that. . . . But how can I help you?"

"We want you," said Percival, "to think over all the time you knew Somerset Lloyd-James, right back to the beginning, and tell us in what areas he might have made errors of conduct or judgement or sentiment, and what such errors, if any, you ever observed him make."

"You don't want much, do you? Only the wisdom of Socrates and the memory of a bloody computer."

"Try, Fielding. Try."

"All right," said Fielding Gray. "*Res unius, res omnium.* I'll try." His eye blinked, and he passed a finger under his collar. "God, it's hot in here," He took a long, avid drink of his cognac, as though hoping this might cool him. "Finish your dinner and let's get out. Then I'll try."

"The trouble is," said Gray, as they walked along the beach in the dying mid-summer evening, "that whatever Somerset did, he behaved at the time with such an air of righteousness and authority that it was impossible to think he might be wrong. Either tactically or morally wrong. It was only a confidence trick, but a very effective one. Years after I'd first learnt how crooked he could be, I would still be made to feel, when Somerset came up with some new scheme or suggestion, an overwhelming sense of Somerset's rectitude, though intellectually I knew jolly well that he was almost certainly up to something rotten. He diffused a mixture of self-confidence and sweet reason that anaesthetised one's faculties of judgement."

"But only for the time being," said Detterling. "Sooner or later one always woke up to the reality."

"Usually later; just as the guillotine was coming down on one's neck. And even then one couldn't exactly blame Somerset. Even then one felt that what was happening was somehow inevitable, that he was the executioner appointed by a superior court against which there was no appeal."

"Concrete instance, please," said Percival.

"Very well. Somerset was largely responsible for getting me sacked from school.* He leaked certain information to certain people—and I was out. He wanted me out because he was afraid that they might make me Head of the School later on, and he coveted the post for himself. But although I knew that was his motive, I still found it difficult to feel angry with him. It was all done in such a way that it seemed to be entirely justifiable—as from many points of view it was. Somerset had simply seen to it that I got my proper deserts."

Fielding led the way off the beach and in among the sand dunes. The spiky grasses, which sprouted from the sand in clumps, swayed in the seaward breeze, giving off a low hiss.

"He came to stay with me here in the summer of '45, not long before it all happened. We went for walks, just where we are walking now; and Somerset talked of school. It was obvious then that he was getting ready to do me down. But even so I was . . . paralysed into acceptance. I couldn't resist or resent it; I was his creature and must obey his will. Somerset's will be done.

"Now, you're interested in his mistakes—'errors of conduct

* See *Fielding Gray*, passim.

or judgement,' you said. But how could I ever have spotted such errors if, in all my dealings with him, my own powers of judgement were suspended? You see, it wasn't as if he only served me bad turns. I was all the more under his spell because he also did me kindnesses—with the same monumental air of righteousness and with great efficiency. When I came out of the army with this"—Fielding pointed up at his face—"Somerset found me work as a writer, although I was completely untried, and set me on the road to being quite successful. Or again, less than two years ago he came with you and Canteloupe, Detterling, and rescued me from those brutes at Vassae."*

Detterling nodded and held up a hand to silence Percival, who was clearly about to investigate this last remark.

"Nothing there for us, Leonard. Let him get on. Yes, Fielding?"

"There's been a pattern. Somerset trampling all over me, going away for years, and then reappearing to help me to my feet. So whenever he turned up, I knew he was going either to harm me or to help me, depending on what fate had in store for me at the time, almost as if Somerset himself *were* fate . . . or at any rate the agent or executive—even, as I said just now, the executioner—that fate had appointed. Impartial, carrying out his orders."

"But of course he was no such thing," said Detterling firmly. "Whenever he came across you, Somerset just dealt with you as happened to suit his own plans at the time. It suited him to get you sacked from school; it suited him, or did not unsuit him, to help you when you left the army. He must have known very well that you had potential talents as a writer, and he could use these for *Strix*."

"Yes; I did a lot of work for *Strix* at one time."

"And also, of course, other things being strictly equal, he would have been glad to earn your gratitude. Rest assured, Fielding: Somerset was no emissary of God's will, he was

* See *Come Like Shadows*, passim.

simply concerned to check you or to exploit you as might best conform with his own projects."

"Oh, I always knew that at bottom. Nevertheless . . . he always gave this impression of having some absolute or divine warrant. In his presence I became totally unable either to defend myself or to criticise him. Even if I did try to act or fight back, I did it so feebly and ineptly that I would only deliver myself further into his hands."

They passed a rubble of brick and concrete which was fenced round by rusty barbed wire.

"Whatever's that?" said Percival.

"Gun emplacement. One of six left over from the war. You'd think they would have shifted them by now," said Fielding, "but instead they've fenced them off so that people can't go inside to copulate. Somerset used to like them when we came on our walks here. That was a very long time ago, of course, but even then they looked almost as forlorn as they do now—as if they'd died on the day the soldiers left them. 'It's remarkable,' Somerset said, 'what decay can do for a building. However commonplace or functional the design, as soon as a building falls into ruin it attains to romance. These rotting gun-sites have a melancholy appeal quite as powerful as the stones of the Acropolis.' 'Have you ever been to the Acropolis?' I said—this was in 1945, remember, and no one had travelled for years. 'Yes,' he said : 'in spirit.' That was the sort of thing I was always letting him get away with."

"Which brings us back to the point," said Detterling. "Although you let him get away with things like that, you came to realise, in the end, what he was getting away with. So despite this mental and moral paralysis from which you say you suffered in his presence, you would have realised—if only much later—when he was making mistakes, the sort of mistakes we wish to hear of."

" 'Errors of conduct,' you said, 'or of judgement or sentiment'." Fielding shook his head and raised a hand to his eye, as if some long effort of reading or writing had tired it.

"Let's put it even more simply," Detterling said : "you must, at some time or another, have seen Somerset when he was caught on the wrong foot or in some way looking silly."

For answer Fielding only shook his head once more, still holding his hand over his eye.

"You said you'd try," prompted Percival.

"I am. Be patient. I know there's something. Something."

They were now walking along the fairway of a golf course. Though it was very nearly dark, Detterling knew by the smell that they were approaching the salt-marshes.

"My house is just by here," said Fielding abruptly. "You'd better come in for a drink."

As he spoke they came to the end of the golf course. There was a lonely green, slightly raised, the sandy banks being held in place by vertical planks of heavy wood; beyond this stockaded outpost, the no man's land of the salt-marshes. Fielding led them along a path, through a gate in the hedge, across a lawn, and up stone steps to a verandah, from which a glass door led into a living-room. Fielding switched on a light. Detterling saw a large desk at a window which looked towards the sea, two comfortable armchairs, a scruffy but expensive carpet, some Norwich School landscapes on the walls, and a table which bore the remains of a meal.

"My breakfast," said Fielding, in tones of explanation, not apology. "I can't go out for every meal, so a woman comes in to tidy up and cook breakfast. She's meant to clear it up before she goes, but she usually forgets."

He fetched three glasses.

"Whisky?" he said.

"Milk," said Leonard Percival.

"Poor old Leonard."

Fielding went out of the room and returned with a pint of milk.

"It's cold and fresh," he said; "I drink a lot of it myself. But not at this time of the day."

He poured very stiff whiskies for himself and Detterling.

"Where were we?"

"You were trying to remember," said Percival. "You think there is something that might help us . . . some occasion on which Lloyd-James made a fool of himself. . . ."

"It couldn't," said Detterling, "be anything to do with that time you and Somerset played strip-poker with Angela Tuck? We've heard about that."

"No," said Fielding. "He made no mistakes there. Although he was so ugly and weedy, he kept his head and won that game hands down. I was the one who was sent packing."

"So we heard. But he might have slipped up somewhere?"

"Not from what I saw. She was all over him."

"Later? Something might have gone wrong later?"

"Not that I ever heard. Anyway, it wasn't that I was thinking of. I'm sure it wasn't."

"Then what was it?"

"It'll come. I'm sure there was *one* time when Somerset stepped out of line . . . did something ill-judged or incongruous. Just talk about anything. It'll come. Go on, talk."

"All right," Detterling said. "You've finished with Harriet Ongley?"

"She's finished with me. She lit out of here just before I got back from scripting that film. She wrote later, saying I could keep the house—she paid for most of it—and anything of hers still inside it."

"Generous."

"Yes. Provided she doesn't use it as an excuse for coming back."

"You think she might?"

"If she's short of someone to mother."

"Could be a good thing." Detterling glanced at the greasy remnants of breakfast. "You need a proper servant."

"She was an admirable housekeeper, I grant you. The trouble was, she also thought of herself as a wife."

"You must have got used to that. You lived with her for eight years."

"Only because she wouldn't bloody well go sooner."

"But you found her money handy?"

"Yes."

"And you might again."

"I can do without it. I've got some money in Switzerland if things get really rough—stashed away from that film. Meanwhile, Gregory's advances on Conrad are enough to keep me in liquor."

"*Good* advances. Which means that it'll be some time before they're recovered and you start receiving a royalty. Don't rely on Conrad too much, Fielding, or you'll be drinking pretty cheap liquor."

"That's it."

"That's what?"

"Cheap liquor. Somerset's one little mistake. The only time I've seen him commit an error."

"Explain."

"You'll probably laugh at me. It *can't* have had anything to do with his suicide. But it's the only thing I have for you. The only little thing of the sort you seem to want."

"*Then explain.*"

"All right." Fielding took a very long drink and then liberally subsidised his glass. "Back to summer 1945 again. Back to school. The end of the Summer Quarter—a few weeks before Somerset came to stay with me down here. The very last night of the Quarter, of the whole school year. Party night. Fashionable boys give little parties in their studies and groups of us roam from House to House joining in. It is the done thing. The Headmaster distrusts the custom but tolerates it, indeed could not stop if he tried. And now observe: one such party going full swing, given by Somerset."

"A mistake on his part?" put in Percival. "After all, Somerset wanted to be Head of the School, or so you said just now. Silly of him to annoy the Headmaster by giving one of these parties."

"Not really, no. Anybody who was anybody either gave or attended such a party, and Somerset was definitely somebody. The Headmaster knew all that. He would have preferred Somerset not to give a party, but he would not hold it against him if he did. And then the school was a big place, Somerset was not in the Headmaster's house, probably the Headmaster never knew. No mistake there, Leonard; not yet."

"Ah," breathed Percival.

"So. Four or five of us come over from my House to Somerset's, 'to take a glass of wine with him', as he had so elegantly put it when inviting us. And there is Somerset at his desk, dispensing Woodbine cigarettes and cocktails from a bottle. Gimlets, if I remember : a kind of ready-mix gin and lime. *Not* very elegant, even given the war-time shortage of decent drink, and not at all the thing for ten o'clock in the evening. Where was this wine Somerset had promised? Somerset explains : he had asked for a case of fine hock from home, but it was never sent because his father said it would be pilfered *en route* by railway workers. A very common thing at that time. All allow this to be a plausible excuse, and happily get on with the Gimlets."

"Who was there?" said Detterling lightly.

"Peter Morrison, for one. I remember walking over with him. Under the moon. There was a very big bright moon that night."

"Who else was there?" asked Detterling.

"No one else you'd know. Does it matter?"

"It might."

"Several boys from Somerset's House whose names I've forgotten. Ivan Blessington from my own House."

"I know *him*," said Detterling. "He came into the regiment while I was still in the army. Had quite a good career—always being chosen as an attaché, that kind of thing. He's out now, though; with some merchant bank."

"Shall we get on with the story?" said Percival.

"In a minute," said Detterling. "Who *else*?" he said to Fielding.

"Christopher Roland," said Fielding shiftily.

"Thank you," said Detterling with the air of someone who has made an interesting private point.

"Who was he?" asked Percival.

"A particular friend of Fielding's. Long since dead, as it happens."

"He's no real part of this story," blurted Fielding, and drank savagely at his whisky.

"But he *was* just there at the party," said Detterling with quiet satisfaction.

"Drinking Gimlets with everyone else," said Percival. "What happened then?"

"We had a few toasts," said Fielding, clearly grateful (Detterling noted with further satisfaction) to be done with Roland and resume his narrative; "toasts to departing friends and happy holidays and next year and the captain of cricket and the Headmaster ('wish he was with us') and the school tart ('wish *he* was with us'), and by this time, as you can tell from the tone, the Gimlets were doing their work. More people came, and Somerset told them what a pity it was the hock had run out before they arrived, but would they like a Gimlet, but oh dear the Gimlets were all gone, but Somerset thought there was some sherry. Which, to do him justice, there was. So we all poured ourselves some sherry, and then Peter Morrison, who was leaving that quarter, said he wanted to propose a toast: THE SCHOOL."

"The School," said Detterling, raising his glass. "I hope you all did it with dignity."

"Peter Morrison burst into tears," said Fielding, "and while we were comforting him, Somerset Lloyd-James was sick all over his desk."

Percival laughed and Detterling looked cross.

"Somerset passed out," said Fielding, "with his head in his own mess. The sherry, as Ivan Blessington observed, had been a mistake."

There was a long silence.

"Well, go on," said Detterling.

"That's the end of it. We all went home to bed, leaving Somerset sleeping it off with his head on his desk. Best not to disturb him, we thought. I didn't see Somerset again until he came down here to stay about four weeks later. He did not say anything about his party, then or ever."

"I'm rather surprised that you have now," said Detterling. "What good can this sordid little anecdote possibly be to me and Leonard?"

"It's the kind of thing you said you wanted to know. Some mistake, you said, some small mistake, something so common-place that he wouldn't even have noticed it himself."

"He'd have noticed this one all right," said Percival, "when he woke up surrounded by sick."

"Yes. But it was hardly anything very serious. We were all inexperienced, and on the rare occasions when we were allowed to drink, something of this kind usually happened. When it did, it was good for a coarse laugh, and there an end of it. Peter and I discussed it on the way back to our House that night. I said Somerset had made an exhibition of himself, but Peter just wouldn't have it. 'Five bob to a skivvy to clear up the mess,' he said, 'and tomorrow is a new day'."

"Exactly," said Detterling. "So why tell us about it?"

"Because," persisted Fielding irritably, "it's the kind of thing you asked me to tell you. Some little mistake, in this case a crapula brought on by inferior sherry, that appeared at the time to be almost a matter of routine, but might conceivably, on your theory, have started a train of events which led to crisis and disaster much later."

"But what train of events could *this* conceivably have started?"

"That's for you to find out. It's *your theory*. I told you it was balls, but you begged me to help you, to think of any little incident I could from which Somerset came off badly. So now I *have* helped you"—Fielding poured himself whisky—"I've told you of the only time I remember when Somerset lost control of himself, and it's no good blaming me if you can't make any-thing of it."

"It was so very long ago," said Percival mildly, and sipped his milk. "Tell me: why was Detterling so interested, just now, in establishing the presence of that friend of yours—what was his name, the one that's dead—Christopher Roland?"

"You ask Detterling," said Fielding miserably. He looked at his glass, raised it, but then retched slightly and set it down. "You'd better go now, both of you. I've got to work on Conrad in the morning."

"Well, thank you for trying," said Detterling in a disappointed voice.

Fielding shrugged and led the way through a hall to his front door.

"Straight down the lane," he said; "don't stray on to the salt-marshes, or you'll be in trouble. And don't forget, Detterling : tell Gregory to be prompt with my next cheque."

"Well," said Percival to Detterling the next morning, as the Mercedes headed towards London, "why *were* you so persistent about Chistopher Roland? It obviously made Fielding unhappy."

"Christopher Roland," said Detterling, "was Fielding's favourite. There was a scandal about it some time later. Somerset got the scandal going."

"I see. And that's what Fielding meant by saying that Somerset leaked information which got him sacked?"

"Yes. Now, when Fielding started to tell us about this party, it occurred to me that Roland might well have been there. I wanted to know, Leonard. You see, if, as turned out, Roland was there, it made the scene so much more entertaining. Woodbines and Gimlets on the last night of the school year. Somerset, shambling, grubby and pustular, telling lies about hock. But also a huge and beautiful moon, looking through Somerset's study window on a pair of pretty schoolboys in love. A delicious mixture of the squalid and the romantic—particularly piquant since the scene was being re-created for us by one of the erstwhile lovers, now a paunchy middle-aged drunk with one eye and a face made of surgical plastic."

"So . . . you tortured Fielding into telling about Roland just for your personal enjoyment. Solely in order that you might indulge your fancy with a few amusing ironies."

"Yes, Leonard. And serve Fielding right. He behaved very

badly to Roland later on, and he deserves to be punished now and then. And if I need any other excuse—well, the Roland thing might have been relevant."

"Only it wasn't. There's nothing in all that for us. All Somerset did, in that connexion, was shop Fielding for buggery or whatever and get him sacked. As Fielding himself admits, this action of Somerset's can be readily justified, and anyway Fielding has long forgiven Somerset, who did him many kindnesses afterwards, one of them as recently as 1970. Nothing in any of that can help us to explain Somerset's suicide. So I suggest we pass to the real point of Fielding's story—which is that Somerset got pissed at the party, and passed out publicly after being horribly sick."

"Nothing for us there either. It was a lovely little scene, that party, but there's nothing there for us from beginning to end of it, and that's why I was so sour with Fielding when he'd finished."

"He did his best, and he was quite right when he said that this was just the sort of incident we were asking for. That's why you were so sour, Detterling. There was nothing the matter with Fielding's story. It was your theory that came unstuck, or at least didn't rise to the occasion."

"The occasion was *wrong*," said Detterling crossly. "It all came to an end too abruptly. If only Somerset had done *anything* rather than be sick and pass out, there might have been a line we could follow. But as it is . . . nothing."

"Ah well," said Percival kindly, "bettter luck next time."

"What's your plan now?'

"First, you go to that Memorial Dinner which Lord Canteloupe is getting up. See if you can find out anything new there. Someone may come up with something better than Fielding Gray did.'

"Yes. . . . I'm sorry I can't get you asked to that dinner, Leonard."

"Why should I be asked. It's for Somerset's old friends. No place there for me . . . though I'm beginning to know him quite well.

"And after the dinner? If I find nothing for us there?"

"There are still some more people we could talk to." Percival produced his list. "Donald Salinger and Jude Holbrook. They owned some printing firm which tried to buy *Strix* while Somerset was Editor. There could be something there."

"Jude Holbrook disappeared years ago. He's said to be in Hong Kong ... though no one has an address."

"Salinger?"

"In a home somewhere."

"A home?"

"His wife was drowned by accident five years back. He loved her, although she was a slut, and after that he just fell to pieces."

"Holbrook of no fixed address in Hong Kong, then, and Salinger in a nut house. Not very helpful." Percival looked at his list. "Lord Philby," he said: "proprietor of *Strix* when Somerset was Editor. Anything there?"

"Could be, I suppose." Detterling twitched slightly in embarrassment. "His wife ... Susan. Somerset had a brief affair with her before she married Philby. The trouble is, I was the chap before Somerset. Philby's never said anything, but I really wouldn't relish talking about the old days with *him*. Or her."

"I see. So all in all," said Percival, "we very much hope that we shan't have to concern ourselves with Messrs Holbrook, Salinger or Philby. But I'm afraid we shall have to, my friend, unless you can find us another lead at that dinner."

Detterling looked as glum as he felt.

"I'm beginning to think there is no lead," he said. "or none that we'll ever find. All this time—and all anyone's really told us is that they can't begin to imagine how Somerset could possibly have done it."

"He did it," said Percival. "There must be a reason somewhere. If we are patient we shall find it. Your theory is as good as any, because in practice it means we just go on talking to everyone we can, which is the only thing we could have done anyway. So fettle yourself up for this dinner, Detterling, and be of good cheer, and when you arrive there just get them all talking and listen. Sooner or later someone will tell us what we want to hear. Listen and wait. Theories come and go, good, bad and indifferent, but in the end there's only one way to do this work, my friend—listen and wait."

PART FIVE

THE ENVOYS

Captain Detterling was in a taxi on his way to the Memorial Dinner for the late Somerset Lloyd-James, for which occasion Lord Canteloupe had hired Annabel's Club in Berkeley Square. Since this was only a few hundred yards from Albany, Detterling would normally have walked; but Lord Canteloupe had ordained 'Evening Dress with Trousers and Decorations', and Detterling did not fancy parading himself through the streets in a white tie and tails. He was, indeed, very annoyed with Canteloupe for insisting on such formality, not because he objected to formality in itself, but because his medals, which commemorated survival rather than gallantry, always made him feel a fool. 'Here's Detterling in his NAAFI Gongs,' Canteloupe would undoubtedly say, fingering his own *Croix de Guerre.* The fact that this had been awarded to Canteloupe in return for his procuring a much needed issue of British Army Sheaths Rubber for De Gaule's Free French Troops was no help whatever. For if Detterling brought it up, Canteloupe would merely admit it and roar with laughter, whereas Detterling's cheap ribands and tinny discs weren't even good for a giggle.

But never mind that, Detterling now told himself firmly. I have more important things to think of. Leonard and I need a new line, and here, if anywhere, I should be able to find it. The trouble is, shall I know it if I see it? For about one thing I am right, I must be right: whatever caused Somerset's suicide must have been something for which he was totally unprepared; otherwise, being Somerset, he would have had tough plans ready to meet it. But if it was something for which he, of all people, was unprepared, it must have been something the origin of which went unnoticed. Whatever incident or action started it all off was so commonplace that Somerset ignored it. But I might hear of any number of such incidents or actions this evening, and how shall I possibly know which to follow up? Come to that, how *could* I follow them up? That is why I have found no use for this tale of Fielding Gray's; even if the incident had led on to something else (and why should it have done?) there is now no way of picking up the trail in order to follow it. The whole thing just appeared to come to a dead stop. But something of that kind it must be; something more open-ended, no doubt, and probably much more recent, but nevertheless something of that order. How am I to spot it? How am I to come at the trail that leads on from it? Only by luck, thought Detterling as he paid off his taxi : as Leonard says, I can only listen and wait—and at least Annabel's will put up a damn good dinner while I do it.

"Here's Detterling in his NAAFI Gongs," said Lord Canteloupe.

"Don't be so childish, Canteloupe."

"Hoity-toity. Remember I'm your host."

"Then where can I get a drink?"

"At the bar, where else?" Canteloupe pointed to it. "Dinner in twenty minutes," he said; "seating plan on the wall."

He walked away to welcome another arrival. Detterling went to the bar, where he was given a generous tumbler of Mimosa, and then turned to study the assembly.

This, he now realised, was much smaller than he had expected. Tom Llewyllyn, who gave him a smile and a wave, was talking to Gregory Stern. Canteloupe, attended by Carton Weir, was now greeting Peter Morrison, And that, so far, was all . . . except for Jonathan Gamp, who came prancing out of a doorway opposite the bar and crossed the room to join Detterling. He was wearing a miniature M.C. and one of his campaign ribands carried an oak-leaf.

"I've just been inspecting the dinner table," Jonathan said : "*very* tasteful arrangements."

"Where is everybody, Jonathan?"

"This is everybody, sweetie. Except for just one more."
Jonathan pointed to the seating plan, which was hanging on
the wall, framed and glazed like a minor masterpiece. "Only
eight of us. It was to have been ten, Canteloupe told me, only
Fielding Gray wouldn't come up from Norfolk, and Max de
Freville was tied up in Corfu."

"No wives?"

"Oh, dear me, no. It's going to cost Canteloupe a small fortune as it is. You wait till you see what's in that dining-room."

"But isn't it rather pointed? No wives, I mean?"

"Did any of them know Somerset? Not really, when you
come down to it."

"It's going to look jolly odd in *The Times*. 'A dinner was
given by the Most Honourable the Marquis Canteloupe in
memory of the late Mr Somerset Lloyd-James' . . . and not a
single woman on the list."

"Correction, duckie. One woman."

Who was now arriving : Maisie.

"Is this Canteloupe's idea of a joke?" said Detterling. "Getting us to come here in full rig and clanking with medals, to
meet Miss Maisie Malcolm."

"Don't be such an old snob, dear. Canteloupe's idea was to
invite only those who really appreciated Somerset or whom
Somerset really appreciated. On that reckoning, from what I
hear, Maisie Malcolm has earned her place with the best of us."

"Just as well the old mother wouldn't come."

"Ah well, if she'd accepted it might have been different. It
was when Canteloupe heard she'd refused that he hit on the
idea of doing it like this. Just a few people who understood
what Somerset was all about. So much better than having rows
of civil servants and their middle-class women. Besides, it
wouldn't have been physically possible to lay on what Canteloupe's laid on for more than a very small number."

"What has he laid on?"

"A little surprise. You'll see. Here comes naughty Tom to
talk to us, with poor old Gregory. *Comè va, Gregorio mio?*

Detterling's just been saying that he wants you both to publish
Maisie Malcolm's memoirs."

"What nonsense is this, Detterling? I never heard of the
lady until she walked in here just now. I forbid you to take on
her memoirs."

"I think Jonathan's pulling your leg, Gregory."

Gregory Stern tapped his decorations with his fingernails.
Less impressive than Gamp's, they were nevertheless more reputable than Detterling's. My only consolation, thought Detterling, is that Tom Llewyllyn has none at all.

"People are always pulling my leg," said Gregory Stern with
huffy amiability. "Isobel my wife does nothing else. Her latest
joke," he said with pride, "is to pretend I wish to be knighted
like George Weidenfeld. 'Poor Gregory,' she says, 'you will
never win your spurs until you publish lots of books with glossy
pictures, just like George's. The Queen likes only picture books,
and that is why she has made Georgie a knight.' 'Pictures are
expensive,' I tell her : 'Detterling and I cannot afford them.'
'Never mind,' she says, 'to me you are always my own true
Yiddisher knight, my shining Hebrew horseman, my Jewish
jouster with the peerless lance'."

"Was Isobel cross at not being asked to this?" said Detterling.

"No. 'You have your night out with the boys,' she said, 'and
don't mind about me. Englishmen are all queer really, even
you, my lovely Levantine, which is why they are always having
parties for the boys.' She did not know, you see, that this Miss
Maisie was coming. I think," he said, looking at Maisie, who
was deep in conversation with Canteloupe, "that she is a tart."

"Darling Gregory," said Jonathan Gamp.

"But we shall not talk of that. We shall talk of Somerset
our friend whom we are here to remember. Ai-yai," he smiled
wistfully at Tom, "it seems only yesterday that we were young,
and you were writing *The Bear's Embrace*, and our friend
Somerset was in Gower Street, Editor of *Strix*."

"We are not so very old now," said Tom.

"And yet already Somerset is gone. We shall not look upon

his like again," said Gregory, "and just as well, perhaps. But he is a loss, Somerset our friend. Come, Tom, Detterling, Jonathan, a toast to our old friend. To Somerset, sailing over Acheron."

As they drank they were interrupted by Carton Weir.

"Canteloupe says it's time to go in," he told them in his fussiest A.D.C. manner; "please don't hang about."

He shepherded them all towards the door which led to the dining-room. Peter Morrison was just disappearing through this, while Canteloupe, with Maisie, was standing to the left of it.

"Your hostess, Miss Maisie Malcolm," said Canteloupe.

Maisie smiled like a princess, and held out her hand to each of them as they filed past her and into a short corridor.

"What's all that about?" whispered Detterling to Weir. "Our hostess?"

"Don't ask me. It's the way he wants the thing done. He's planned it all very particularly from beginning to end. Now go on in."

Detterling stepped from the corridor into what he supposed was the dining-room, looked about him, and then shuddered with delight.

For he had not entered a room; he had passed, as it seemed, out into the open air, into a little grove of trees, which must surely be high up in the mountains, because the view from where he stood was of a re-entrant that descended almost sheer from the far end of the grove, and then slowly widened and levelled until, thousands of feet below, it ran into a broad plain which was traversed by noble aqueducts and bounded by the distant sea. On either side of Detterling, he now saw, peaks towered into a gentle early-evening sky; a stream cascaded from rocks just behind his left shoulder, ran across the grove at his feet, and descended with the re-entrant into the plain, where it became a broad river on which barges and caiques rode slowly between fields and townships, to and from a harbour at the river's mouth. On the right of the grove was a wall of rock and in the wall the mouth of a cave; set on the grass between this and the stream was a table of marble, crowded with wine-jars and cornucopias and birds of brilliant plumage. In a circle round the table stood young boys and girls, ready to serve, dressed in dainty white tunics which ended just above the knee; and in a larger circle, a few feet outside the ring of pretty little servants, were the couches on which the guests would recline, each couch being shaded from the evening sun (which was sinking towards the sea) by a small tree of holm-oak or lady-birch.

The seating plan had shown eight names but nine places; and on the ninth couch, which was set before the mouth of the cave, was a skeleton caparisoned in ermine, which lay open to show the bones beneath.

"Very quaint," whispered Jonathan Gamp to Detterling. "It was Canteloupe's idea, but I helped him work it all out. We got Oliver Messel to do the décor and the *trompe*."

But Detterling hardly heard him. He and the other guests stood speechless, now looking on the reclining skeleton (whose skull was propped by the hand of one splintery arm), now gazing out over the plain towards the sea. At last the silence was broken by Maisie :

"Loopy dear, how he'd have loved it," she said, and kissed Canteloupe wetly on the lips.

Canteloupe looked gratified.

"Places, please," he said in a gruff voice.

Canteloupe and Maisie went to their couches, Canteloupe's to the left of the skeleton, Maisie's to its right. On Maisie's right was Tom Llewyllyn, on his Peter Morrison, and on his again Captain Detterling; Weir, Stern and Gamp completed the circle to Canteloupe. As they settled, there was a sound of flutes among the trees, and the cupbearers came forward from the table to serve each guest with a beaker of wine.

"To our Guest of Honour," called Canteloupe : "a bumper to Old Death;" and all the revellers raised their winecups while the servants stretched out their arms before their faces and bowed to the ground.

It is not easy to recline comfortably in evening dress with medals, and before long all the guests (except Old Death) were in fact sitting on their couches, bending forward to feed themselves from the little tables on which each course was served to them. As the second course (a soup of écrevisses) was being cleared, the diners joined each other, two to a couch, the better to converse. Tom Llewyllyn joined Maisie, and Detterling joined Peter Morrison. In the grove behind them nymphs and satyrs rustled and flitted and tittered; and against the tree which overshadowed the couch just vacated by Detterling a cross-legged faun now leaned, piping a ditty of thin, spiteful tone.

"What do you make of all this?" said Peter Morrison.

"Unexpected imaginitive—for Canteloupe."

"He has more imagination than you might think. I've learnt that since I've been working for him. Canteloupe, Detterling, is a romantic."

"And your work for him . . . is that romantic?"

"The conception behind it is. Or at any rate the conception that is behind our activity in Strasbourg—which is the main part of our work at the moment."

"From what Canteloupe told me some weeks back, it seemed essentially a matter of common sense. Whoever went to this Convention at Strasbourg, he said, must discredit rival products on exhibition at the Trade Fair there. Our great hope, I remember, is some new light metal alloy; so I suppose you spend your days running down other people's light metal alloys. Not very romantic, Peter."

"Yes, very," Morrison insisted. "That's why I'm back in London at the moment and able to come to this dinner. The romance is coming to a crisis, and I have to consult very urgently with Canteloupe."

"Well, I'd be glad to know how you squeeze romance out of light metal alloys."

"It all starts with Somerset. You remember that before he died he'd interested Canteloupe in a special plan for Strasbourg?"

The sun sank close to the sea below them and lights began to appear in the towns along the river. Somerset's plan for Strasbourg, Detterling thought : there could be something here. Although Canteloupe had denied that Somerset's operations for the Ministry had anything to do with his death, that might (just might) have been policy on the part of the Minister.

"Yes, I remember," he said to Peter Morrison. "So you've inherited Somerset's plan—and romance along with it?"

"Yes. I'm afraid I can't go into details."

"But you can tell me the general principle?"

"If you like. . . ."

The third course was served to them, quails' eggs in aspic. A nymph ran out of the cave and started, reverently but fiercely, to make love to the skeleton. Grinning satyrs capered with delight as she unrobed and embraced it.

"That," said Morrison, pointing at the spectacle, "that is the general principle behind the plan which Somerset left to us."

"Be plainer, my dear."

"Assume that skeleton is the rival product you wish to discredit. You start by paying someone to show interest in it and evince mounting pleasure, just as that poor girl is doing. The pleasure rises until it approaches climax; the audience looks on breathless; the girl has her orgasm and very nearly faints with delight. But of course everyone really knows that the whole thing has been faked. Cleverly faked, no doubt," said Peter, as the girl swooned to the ground and was carted off by the satyrs, "but nevertheless faked. Now, consider : if, as I say, the skeleton equals the product to be done down, and the girl equals the agent you have hired to simulate enthusiasm, what have you achieved?"

"I've achieved nothing. Indeed, I've helped my rivals. I've advertised their product by getting up a public demonstration of how desirable it is."

"Except," said Peter, "that the public realises the desire was *faked*. So you then start a rumour that the agent was in fact employed by the makers of the product, in a bid to achieve false prestige for it. What a pity for them, you say scornfully, that they couldn't afford a better actor, that the final orgasm over their product clearly wasn't genuine. Are you with me, Detterling?"

"Not entirely, old man."

"Well then, in real terms. We have set up what appears to be an international consortium (I'm sorry, but I mustn't name it to you) which wishes to buy light metal alloys. This consortium shows interest and then intense pleasure in the product of our rival, whom we shall call 'X'. The affair culminates in a dramatic deal—so dramatic that there is something suspect about it, we see to that. And then we spread a highly circumstantial rumour, to the effect that the 'international consortium' is in fact a phony which 'X' himself has rigged up to advertise his product by feigning enthusiasm for it. What a pity for 'X' we tell everyone with a sneer, that the enthusiasm was so evidently theatrical; no one will be taken in by *that*. Thus 'X' and his product are discredited by the charade; and the audience comes flocking to buy our metal alloys instead."

"Suppose," said Detterling, "that the news gets round that it was really your phony consortium and a charade of your making?"

"We should be in trouble," said Peter Morrison; "but at the moment all is well over that. Our problem just now is that although we are approaching the fake climax on schedule, it promises, for various reasons, to look very much too genuine. There has not been enough spurious ecstasy. If we are not careful, we shall wind up with a performance so realistically played that people will actually believe in it and we shall have provided, *gratis*, a valuable advertisement for 'X' instead of making him look silly."

"I see. And hence the necessity to consult with Canteloupe?"

"Yes. You understand what I mean by calling the stratagem romantic?"

"I do. It is not the first time that 'romantic' has been used as a euphemism for dishonest."

"Let's call it . . . an exercise in sleight of hand. Other people

over there are being much nastier, Detterling. Our rivals use
violence, blackmail, political pressure. Compared with theirs,
our methods are positively decent . . . as well as being rather
witty, as Somerset might have said."

The old Morrison, thought Detterling: always ready with
the right reason for doing the wrong thing. In telling Canteloupe to appoint him, I certainly gave good advice. Aloud he
said:

"One thing, Peter. It's important I should know. Is there
the remotest chance that the preparations for producing this
illusion could have laid Somerset open to something—this
blackmail you talk of, perhaps—that might have led to his
suicide?"

"None whatever," said Morrison flatly. "At the time Somerset died, the thing was only an idea, and known only to him
and to Canteloupe."

Another dud trail, Detterling thought. A pity; but then I
never had much hope of it. I must start somebody else off talking. Will Peter be offended if I move to another couch?

As Detterling wondered how to shift his place without giving
offence, the sun slipped into the sea and the evening star
appeared high over the nearest peak. The table and the circle
of couches were now lit by torches of pine; a little breeze
shivered in the leaves above them; and as the boys and girls
cleared the third course, the music of flutes began again in the
heart of the grove. Then sudden silence. Then the sound of
crying, the flutes once more, thin wails of anguish both from
human throats and from the instruments. A figure in white
cap-à-pé, pointing up at the evening star. A sweet, pure
voice:

> "Weep no more, woeful shepherds, weep no more,
> For Lycidas, your sorrow, is not dead,
> Sunk though he be beneath the wat'ry floor;
> So sinks the day-star in the ocean bed,
> And yet anon repairs his drooping head. . . ."

I can't move while this is going on, thought Detterling. A

silly poem, I always considered. Yet the old man at school used to say that this passage was the most musical in all English poetry.

> "So Lycidas sunk low, but mounted high,
> Through the dear might of him that walked the waves,
> Where, other groves and other streams along,
> With nectar pure his oozy locks he laves,
> And hears the unexpressive nuptial song
> In the blest kingdom meek of joy and love."

Ridiculous, thought Detterling. Imagine the old twister risen up to the 'blest kingdom meek' and listening to the 'unexpressive nuptial song'. Clothed all in white, like this fellow who's reciting. Too absurd. And yet . . . the lines soared on in irresistible triumph; and now the stars were coming out, one by one, and gathering round the evening star, that was Hesperus . . . Lycidas . . . Somerset. . . .

> "There entertain him all the saints above,
> In solemn troops and sweet societies
> That sing, and singing in their glory move,
> And wipe the tears for ever from his eyes.
> Now, Lycidas, the shepherds weep no more;
> Henceforth thou art the Genius of the shore."

But Detterling was still weeping and so was Peter Morrison, tears and snot dribbling down his face and off his chin. I can't leave him just yet, Detterling thought, I'd better sit here and get control of myself. Say something; we can't sit here blubbering like a pair of schoolgirls; say something to get a normal conversation going again.

"If only we knew," he said off the top of his head, "where he went to on his last day."

"What was that?" snivelled Peter.

"I've been trying to find out," said Detterling, "why he did it. There has been absolutely no clue."

"What was that you said about 'his last day'?"

"The last day of his life. Before he came home and killed

himself. His servant said he went somewhere; out of London, she said. Nobody knows where."

The boys and girls were distributing the next course: tiny chickens stuffed with truffles and foie gras.

"Listen," said Peter to Detterling after they had been served: "you know Ivan Blessington, don't you? He was in your regiment."

"Yes," said Detterling. We might as well talk about him as anyone, he thought, though God knows what made Peter think of him. "Yes. He's a lot younger than me, of course, but he joined some time before I resigned. I never knew him well, but I kept in touch, for a time at least. I used to hear interesting things from him when he was military attaché in Washington."

"He's out of the army now."

"Working for a merchant bank, I believe."

"Yes. The Corcyran. Off-shoot of the Corinthian. He's been in Strasbourg—at this Convention."

"Don't tell me he's anything to do with this fake consortium of yours."

"As a matter of fact he is. But that's not the point."

"What is the point, Peter?"

"Somerset's last day."

"What's that got to do with Ivan Blessington?"

"He told me something. It might help you."

"What could he possibly know about it?"

"Listen. Listen."

A beat of drums, very low, very slow, was coming from the centre of the grove.

"Drums," said Detterling.

"No. Listen to *me*, Detterling." Peter leaned close to his companion and started to talk fast and earnestly. "A few days ago I met Ivan Blessington in Strasbourg. After we'd discussed our . . . our business, I mentioned that I was coming to London, and to this dinner for Somerset. Now, Detterling, listen very carefully . . ."

'. . . Pity about old Somerset,' Ivan Blessington had said to Peter Morrison in Strasbourg.

'Yes.'

'I saw him only a day or so before he died. I was at the Ministry of Commerce for something, so I popped in on him to say "Hallo". He seemed in very good nick. Top of the world. Very pleased with himself about something.'

'Pleased with himself?' Peter Morrison had said. 'Only a day or so before he died?'

'Yes. So pleased that it rather got on my nerves. Made me feel quite ill-natured, you know how it is. So just to give him a prick, I reminded him of that party he threw years ago—you remember, on the last night of the Summer Quarter in '45. When he was sick all over the place.'

'I remember. Fielding Gray was there. And Christopher Roland.'

Silence for a moment. Then,

'I didn't make anything of that,' Ivan Blessington said; 'I just ribbed him about how he was sick. You know, to pull him down a peg or two. But it didn't. He seemed more pleased with himself than ever. "That party," he said; "thereby hangs a tale." Which he told me there and then. So tickled he was, he couldn't keep it to himself. Not at all the usual canny old Somerset—he was just bubbling at the seams with it.'

'What did he tell you?'

'Well, you remember we all left him, clean out, with his head on his desk. It seems he woke up about three hours later, was sick again before he could stop himself, but this time was strong enough to get off to bed. And before he went he pulled himself together and wrote a note of apology for the boys' skivvy, who'd have to clean up the mess in the morning, and with the note he left her half a crown for her trouble.'

'It should have been five bob. Five bob was the going rate for sick.'

'Ah. When he woke up in the morning he found the boys' skivvy standing over his bed and saying just that. In a loud voice. "Five bob, Mr Lloyd-James," she said, waving his note in the air : "it's five bob for cleaning up filth like you left, and so I've come up here to tell you." So Somerset blinked and sat up, and then he realised it must be quite late, because the two other senior boys, who shared his dormitory with him, had already gone. "What time is it?" he said. "Time for me to get my five bob," said the boys' skivvy, "that's what time it is. And time for you to get up and go home like the rest of 'em. The whole place is empty," she said, "except for you and the cat." And then Somerset looked at the boys' skivvy, and saw a well set up young woman with a red round face, an angry face just then but underneath the anger a pleasant one. And the boys' skivvy looked at Somerset, and saw an acne'd adolescent with a hangover, but also saw something else which women, I'm told, often seemed to see in Somerset, a kind of elemental libido pushing up under the shagspots. And so they both looked at each other, and all around them was the strange, eerie silence which the boys had left behind them, the sort of silence which says you've got no business to be where you are, but since you *are* there you can do anything you want to, because you're in a place which isn't real at a time which doesn't count. "Empty?" said Somerset. "Empty," said the boys' skivvy, not angry any more, standing over the bed . . . bending over the bed and slowly pulling back the bedclothes and very pleased with what she saw—there's nothing like a hangover to bring you on in the morning—and starting, there and then, on a nice healthy piece of mid-morning exercise.'

'Rather odd,' Peter Morrison said to Ivan Blessington, 'that Somerset was so pleased with himself just because he'd had the boys' skivvy one morning long ago.'

'That wasn't the end of it—though Somerset thought it was at the time. A few weeks later, before the next quarter began, he had a letter from the skivvy (addressed c/o the school and forwarded by the porter) which said she was going off to be married and leaving her job at the school, so ta-ta for good, but hadn't it been jolly? Yes it had, thought Somerset, but just as well she'd be out of the way when he got back in September. And out of the way she remained for twenty-seven years. Until a few days before Somerset and I were having this conversation. And then he'd had another letter from her. Did he remember that morning long ago, after the boys had gone? She'd left the school to get married, as she'd written at the time; and then she'd had a child. Not her husband's, Somerset's. But she'd passed the boy off on her husband all right, and indeed she would never have told Somerset at all, only her husband was just dead, leaving her and her son, who was unmarried and still lived with her, really rather poor. Since Somerset was really rather rich (or so she gathered from the newspapers) would he care to help? She was aware she had no legal claim, and she wouldn't dream of making a fuss—*couldn't*, after all this time, as she very well knew—but all the same she would be most grateful, et cetera, et cetera. And if Somerset wanted to be sure the boy was his, would he care to come and meet him? He'd be certain the moment he saw him.

'And that's why Somerset was so excited. He'd never been a father, he said, and he was intrigued by the idea. There could be no danger of scandal—it was all too long ago, and the tone of the woman's letter had been very agreeable. She couldn't and wouldn't make trouble. So he was going to help her, see what he could do for her and the boy; it would be great fun, helping him on in the world, like an eighteenth century grandee and his bastard, like Chesterfield and Stanhope. He was looking forward very much to meeting his son—and he was going down to the country to do so the very next morning. . . .'

". . . And that," said Peter to Detterling, as the drum beats from the centre of the grove began to quicken, "was what Ivan Blessington told me in Strasbourg. But you see what I'm getting at? According to Ivan, he'd heard all this from Somerset 'a day or so before he died', and Somerset was going down to the country to see his newly discovered son 'on the very next morning'. . . ."

"So *that* must have been what Somerset was doing on the day before the night he killed himself."

"Exactly," said Peter. "Somerset's last day . . . about which you could find out nothing. . . ."

". . . Until now. He went into the country, as Dolly the

servant told us . . . saw his son and the mother . . . came back
. . . and committed suicide. *Why*, Peter?"

"How should I know?"

A golden glow was now spreading like a halo behind the
tallest of the peaks that rose above them. The drums quickened
still more.

"As Somerset told Ivan, there was no fear of scandal. On
the contrary, there was the promise of pleasure and amusement, and plenty of money to make the very most of the situation. So Somerset was pleased, tickled pink, before he went.
And yet, when he came back . . . where did he go, Peter? Where
did this woman live?"

"I asked that, *and* the woman's name; but Ivan didn't
know because Somerset hadn't told him, and it hadn't occurred
to Ivan to ask. It would have been most impolite."

"Oh, bloody hell," said Detterling. "There must be some
connexion between that journey and Somerset's suicide. Somerset wasn't afraid of scandal or blackmail, nothing like that, but
some connexion between all this and Somerset's death there
just must be. If we could find that woman . . ."

"I've told you all I know, Detterling. You might find out
about her from Somerset's old House at school. After all, she
was employed there."

"Yes," grouched Detterling; "in 1945, twenty-seven years
ago. How can I possibly hope that she'll still be re—"

He broke off to give a long, deep sigh of pleasure. For the
golden glow behind the peak had suddenly turned into a full
round moon, which now sailed out to illumine the plain below
and the re-entrant which led from it to the grove. Up the re-
entrant a procession was coming, in single file along the right-
hand bank of the stream. The procession was still distant;
but a faint beat of drums could be heard from it, which was
now answered by the drums in the grove. After three or four
tattoos had been given and answered in this way, the members
of the procession began to chant; and as they came closer,
Detterling could distinguish the words:

"Dies irae, dies illa,
Solvet saeclum in favilla
Teste David cum Sibylla. . . .

A stripling boy set large glasses of cognac before Detterling
and Peter; he was followed by a girl, who placed wreaths of
rose petals on their heads.

"Day of wrath and doom impending,
David's word with Sibyl's blending,
Heaven and earth in ashes ending. . . ."

The procession was much nearer now. By the light of the
torches which some of its members carried Detterling began
to make them out more plainly; they wore white cowls and their
faces were bowed and invisible in their hoods.

"Quantus tremor est futurus
Quando Judex est venturus
Cuncta stricte discussurus. . . ."

The procession wound out of sight as the re-entrant narrowed
and turned steeper. They'll be in the dead ground beneath
the lip of the grove, thought Detterling, making the final ascent
up here. The sound of their voices is nearer every second. But
these are only shadows on a wall, he thought: they can never
reach us. Wrong. Over the brow of the hill they came, flesh
and blood, still chanting:

"The dead are risen from the tomb,
Lo at last the Judge is come,
To unseal the Book of Doom."

Then silence, absolute silence.

As the single file of white monks threaded its way through
the grove, the nymphs and satyrs rose up out of the nooks and
bushes to greet them. Swiftly the two parties paired off, one
nymph or satyr to each monk, and two by two they advanced
towards the diners, then swung right or left to pass round them,
then took up stations in front of the cave-mouth and

behind the couch on which the skeleton reclined. Still an un-broken silence except for the slight swish of the monks' habits.

"What now?" whispered Peter to Detterling in a troubled voice.

Several of the monks were carrying the drums which had been heard beating down in the valley. One of these now played a brief roll, and then, after a pause, gave a single sharp beat. As at a signal all the monks raised their bowed heads. Another beat, and they swept back their hoods.

"Oh, Christ," said Peter.

The faces were representative of disease. There was the chalk-white and wasted face of tuberculosis, the drooping mouth and wall eye of the incurable stroke, and the wild, slobbering grin of sheer idiocy; there were cheekbones laid raw by leprosy, noses flattened by the pox, and chins so eaten with cancer that they appeared to have been freshly carded by nails. There were lolling tongues, black buboes, and huge wet open ulcers where there should have been lips; there were goitres hanging like bunches of grapes and eyes running with puss.

"Christ," Peter said again.

But the nymphs and satyrs raised a howl of happy laughter. They pranced and capered with glee, nudging each other and pointing to particularly succulent deformities, running hither and thither to relish each exhibit, pressing their bodies up against the monks to peer even more closely at their sores and carbuncles. A lively tune sprang up, and they began to dance.

"Hey nonny no," they sang, "hey nonny nonny no."

Round and round the monks they danced.

> "It's a splendid thing to laugh and sing
> When the bells of death do ring
> And turn upon the toe
> And cry 'Hey nonny no,
> Hey nonny nonny no'."

And the monks began to dance with the nymphs and satyrs. At first reluctantly, then faster and more warmly, then lewdly. As they danced they sang and laughed and gibbered. As before, the two parties paired off, one monk to each nymph or satyr. The little servants, the boys and girls, danced too. Some of them partnered each other, some of them attached themselves as satellites to adult couples, some of them danced singly, leaping up and down for the joy of it. The dance spread, came swirling among the couches. Bottles and dainties were seized from the marble table; bumpers were drunk, food torn and gobbled.

"Hey nonny no; hey nonny nonny no."

The monks ripped away their habits, revealing petticoats and pantaloons of tainted linen, and bodies as deformed and festering as were their faces. The nymphs and satyrs laughed the louder and sang and danced the faster.

> "Oh-ho-ho, a splendid thing
> When the bells of death do ring
> To dance and drink
> And laugh and stink
> And turn upon the toe
> And cry 'Hey nonny no'."

And couple by couple, group by group, child by child, they danced past Death, saluting him, as they went, with blown kisses or arms outstretched in gratitude, and away into the cave. One by one the stars began to go out, and the moon failed. Pitch darkness. And from the cave, wild, piercing laughter; unquenchable; peal after peal; the laughter of those who are about to sink, madly, foully, irreclaimably, into an oblivion of lust.

"Lights," called the Marquis Canteloupe: "LIGHTS."

The laughter stopped as if it had been switched off. Some bright bare bulbs lit up round walls which had been daubed with crude patches of paint and hung about with pieces of gauze and sacking and tissue paper. There was a gutter where the stream had been; gaps between squares of turf; pots showing through the paper foliage at the base of the trees. Here and there Detterling saw half-hidden projectors which were trained on to some part of the wall. At the end of the grove the top

of a step-ladder protruded above a slab of green cardboard.
Four or five tired and middle-aged midgets, their faces running
with grease paint, came out of a nasty gash in one wall and
started to help themselves to the broken meats on the table,
wiping their fingers, from time to time, on knee-length smocks
of coarse and grubby cotton.

"Though it was only a cardboard moon," sang Jonathan
Gamp,

> Sailing over a painted sea,
> Though it was only make-believe
> It was paradise to me.

Congratulations, Canteloupe. A very pretty show. I only
hope Oliver doesn't charge too much."

"Very animated," observed Peter Morrison, "but what did
it all add up to?"

"Easy," said Maisie : "old Somerset rises up out of his watery
grave and becomes the Genius of the Shore, like the poet says.
This bit of shore"—she waved towards where the sea had been
—"and so he lives in this wood in the mountains overlooking
it. Right?"

"Right," said Detterling.

"But of course anywhere old Somerset lives there's bound to
be goings-on, and so this is where all the monks and that sort
come up for a nice secret dirty."

"But why such horrible monks?" said Carton Weir. "Dropping to bits they were."

"White monks," said Gregory Stern tentatively : "White
Friars. They once had a monastery in Fleet Street and gave
their name to the district. Diseased White Friars from Fleet
Street equal journalists—the corrupt and filthy priests of our
own age who also parade themselves in shining white. Somerset, himself once a journalist and later an editor, becomes the
patron saint of the whole rabble. Am I right?" he said to Canteloupe.

"Ingenious," said Canteloupe, "but a bit too specialised. You
could say those whited monks were the entire modern establish-

ment, the whole rotten, greedy, envious, trendy mob, not only of journalists, but of politicians and lawyers and dons and businessmen—the lot. And there's one thing more. Those nymphs and whatever. They were the creatures of Somerset's grove, and they were prepared to give those filthy old monks a good time, taking great pleasure, as you saw, in what they were doing and without any apparent fear that they themselves might be infected. What does that suggest to you?"

There was a long silence.

"That Somerset enjoyed playing with dirt?" said Detterling at last.

"And also that he was immune from it. It never stuck to him long enough," said Canteloupe, "to get under his skin. Or you might say he was like a scientist—examining all kinds of disgusting microbes but never getting bitten. His was the pure spirit of investigation."

"He certainly knew how to investigate," said Maisie fondly.

"But something got him in the end," said Detterling. "One of those microbes got through his rubber gloves. You're sure," he said aside to Peter, "that Ivan didn't know that woman's name? Or where she lives with the boy?"

"Quite sure."

"Because if only we could find them . . ."

"I've told you. Try his old House at school. They may have records of their employees."

"What's all this muttering?" said Canteloupe.

"Peter has been telling me about the very last investigation which Somerset undertook. It could be the one that proved fatal."

"Ah well," said Canteloupe softly, "even *his* luck had to run out some time. 'Weep no more, woeful shepherds, weep no more.' He had a fucking good ride for his money."

"Such goings-on," said Percival the next morning, after Detterling had rendered an account of the dinner. "And one big dividend. Now we know where he went on his last day."

"Correction. We know his errand. We do not know where it

took him, and we do not know the name of the people he went
to see."

"Well, Morrison was quite right about that : we must go to
Somerset's House at your old school. They have long memories
in places like that."

"The Housemaster will have changed at least twice since
that woman left in 1945," said Detterling; "and the man that
had the House in Somerset's time is dead."

"Never mind. There'll be others who could remember. Let's
be off, Detterling."

Detterling rang a bell.

"I keep asking myself," he said, "what could have happened
on that journey to make Somerset do what he did. He was
pleased with the woman's letter, he was reassured by the
manner of her approach, he was looking forward to his visit . . ."

"The journey may have nothing to do with his death," said
Percival. "We are not entitled to make any assumptions. We
just follow where the arrow points—and at the moment it
points to your old school. Going to wear the tie, are you?"

"No," said Detterling crossly; "it looks like the flag of a
banana republic. I shall wear the one I have on. Hamilton's
Horse."

"Yes, I remember the crest," said Percival, looking at it
closely : "the skull and coronet. Really rather appropriate—
in our present line of business as well. But someone did tell
me once that crested ties were common."

"That depends on the crest. Corporal," said Detterling to
his manservant, who was now standing to attention in answer
the bell, "please have the car round in ten minutes."

"Order of dress, sir?"

"Summer order : light tunic and overall trousers."

"Sir," said the manservant.

"Do you go back to the old place often?" said Percival, as
the Mercedes ran past Virginia Water.

"About once a year. Usually to watch the Eleven in the
summer."

"Were you happy there?"

"I suppose so. I managed to be quite important towards the end of my time. Senior cricket colour next to the Captain, second Monitor in my House. But it wasn't a very good school, you know, not in the '30s, when I was there. Narrow, with a priggish Headmaster. Mind you, a good man took over in 1935—but that was after I'd left. There was only one of the beaks I had any time for—the Senior Usher, 'the old man', as we called him. He taught the Sixth Classical."

"But I suppose you were in the army class?"

"No. That was run by a little brute called Morris. I read the classics, and punched up enough stuff for Sandhurst on the side. You couldn't fail Sandhurst in those days unless your head was made of teak."

"Why did you go into the army, Detterling? Family tradition?"

"No. My family don't run to traditions. We're just money, Leonard—very old money by now, so we pass as belonging to the old gang, but in fact we don't because none of us has ever served the country. We've just taken and spent."

"You served in the army."

"You should have a fair idea after what I've told you, Leonard, of the quality of my service."

"Well . . . let's just say, I don't think that *au fond* you were suited to the army. Which brings me back to my question : what sent you to Sandhurst in the first place?"

"I *wanted* to serve, Leonard. I wanted to be unlike my family and serve my King and country as a gentleman should. The trouble was . . . I just couldn't." Detterling winced. "But by the time I found that out, it was too late. I couldn't resign because the war was coming. There I was, stuck with my regular commission."

"But you quite enjoyed the life, and you liked your regiment?"

"Oh, yes."

"Then why couldn't you serve it?"

"Because they took our horses away. That was one thing.

Up till 1939 we had horses, and I liked what I was doing, and I understood it, and I valued it. But then . . . tanks." Detterling shuddered. "But it wasn't just that, Leonard. It wasn't just the tanks that turned me into such a putrid soldier. It was something inside myself—something that's always been inside us Detterlings—a kind of rock-hard egotism that dictates, always and everywhere, *Detterling first*; Detterling before honour, before service, before friends, before love, before truth; Detterling before his regiment—before his sovereign, his country or his God. Although one side of me longed to serve faithfully, to be a loyal officer and lead my men with courage and skill, something else in me, the Detterling curse you might call it, dictated that if ever my life or my body, or even just my comfort, was at risk, I should immediately place my convenience before my obligations and contrive to bilk my duty in order to preserve my skin. Since I did this very cleverly, very plausibly, I was never finally disgraced; not even in my own eyes, because the Detterling curse carries complacency along with it."

"It's on record," said Percival, "that you rejoined your regiment for the Suez expedition in '56—though you'd resigned some years previously. That seems very quixotic behaviour and refutes what you say of yourself."

"I had to go, as far as I remember. Even though I'd resigned, I had to stay on the Reserve for a time. RARO Class I. They called us back for the Suez rumpus, and that was that."

"You could have excused yourself as an M.P."

"I dare say. I suppose," said Detterling, "that the chivalrous side of me was strong enough to make me answer the trumpet. But the Detterling strain saw to it that I never got within range of a bullet. Graceful and ingenious shirking—that's what we Detterlings are bred to."

"You're a distant cousin of Canteloupe's. Would you say the same kind of thing about him?"

"No. The Sarums—that's his family name—the Sarums, like the Detterlings, started as money. But they got beyond it. They have served. Canteloupe himself has served. If you ask him what he did in the war, he'll tell you he liaised with the Free French, and set up a chain of brothels for the allied troops during the invasion of Europe. What he might also tell you, but won't, is that he led the remnants of a smashed battalion clean through the German lines and into Dunkirk in time to get a ship out. He should have had at least a D.S.O. for it, but the Army Council wasn't in a very giving frame of mind just then."

"Come to that, Canteloupe still serves, as a Minister of the Crown. And so do you, Detterling, as a member of Parliament."

"Thank you for trying to defend me, Leonard, but I'm bogus on that count too. My seat in Parliament is like my commission in Hamilton's Horse; I wanted it and so it was got for me. But neither before or afterwards did I do anything to earn or deserve it. Whereas Canteloupe, in his maverick way, is quite genuine: he deserves his place, Leonard; he believes in what he's doing and he does it with all his might."

"Well, at least you've done one thing: you've helped me— and I mean *helped*, Detterling—in a necessary and perhaps important enquiry."

"Thank you, Leonard. But even here my motives are private: curiosity about an old friend. Detterlings do not serve. It might be our family motto."

For some time the Mercedes had been climbing a steep hill. Now the car took a very sharp turn to the right, and after a hundred yards turned right again, over a bridge that crossed the road by which they had ascended. At the far end of the bridge was a gatehouse, of modern but not unseemly design, having a broad arch at its centre through which they presently passed. On their left were now lawns and a somewhat officious twentieth-century chapel; while in front of them and to their right was a messy sprawl of late Victorian buildings, from among which protuded several capped and rebarbative towers. Yet the whole was not displeasing. The buildings, ugly in themselves, had settled down together in their place; they knew their business here.

"*Alma mater*," said Detterling in a mocking voice, "and welcome to it."

But even as he spoke he felt his eyes prick, as they always did when he came back.

"Well, well, well," said Percival, his glasses glinting in the sun. "So this is where you all grew up. You, and then Somerset and Morrison . . . and Fielding Gray. Can you see your own ghost?"

"Yes," said Detterling. He pointed to some trees that stood beyond the far end of the chapel, and to a green field which lay on the other side of them. "On that field," he said; "batting in the middle of it."

"We must go and meet him later. But first," said Percival, "we have work to do. Where do we begin?"

They began with the Housemaster of Somerset's old House. He and his wife had been there since 1967. There were no records of domestic staff, they said, which went back further than 1965. The House Matron, who had been there since 1964, deposed that the House Butler, who went back to 1955, might be able to help. The House Butler remarked, irrelevantly, that the office of Boys' Maid had been abolished in 1960, in accordance with the social scruples of the egalitarian Housemaster then incumbent. However, the gentlemen might be interested to know that lists of all employees together with their personal particulars were sent in by every House, once a year, to the Comptroller of the School Burse, or Bursar for short, who was responsible for making a statistical return to the Ministry of Labour. It was at least possible that this system had its origins in war-time regulations and therefore that the woman they sought would be on record in the Bursar's office.

Indeed she should be, the Bursar agreed . . . if his secretary could only find the back records. If they would care to come back that afternoon . . . no, it was his secretary's half-day off . . . tomorrow . . . no, he himself had to be in London for a Committee meeting . . . the next day, perhaps? At this stage Leonard Percival rose to his feet, went to a shelf and took down a box-file which was clearly labelled *Menial Employees: 1942–47*. The Bursar, deprived of the pleasures of obstruction, went puce with self-righteous fury, began to say something about 'presumption', was silenced by a quick look from Percival (a look which Detterling hadn't seen before and hoped not to see again), and consented to turn up the year 1945.

The returning date had been March 1; and the Boys' Maid in Somerset's House at that time had been 'ATWELL, Mrs Albert (Enid Silvia), of 22 Blixom Cottages, Nashley, Nr Guildford, age 63 yrs and 7 mns.' A pencilled note beneath the entry stated that Mrs Atwell had died suddenly the following April, and that notification would be received when her successor was appointed; as indeed it had been—but not until September 20 of 1945, against which date a new Boys' Maid was listed as 'TOMPKINS, Mrs Ethel (widow)' etc., etc. In short, the woman who had done the job during the Summer Quarter, Somerset's woman, had slipped through the system unnoticed.

"Bloody hell," said Detterling.

"What?" said the Bursar.

"Shit," hissed Detterling.

"Come on, old man," said Percival; and then insincerely to the Bursar, "Thank you, sir, for being so helpful."

When Detterling had calmed down a bit, Leonard Percival suggested a soothing walk on the cricket field which his friend had earlier pointed out. On the way there they passed groups of boys who had just been released from their class-rooms, and Detterling started once more to be angry. The boys mostly had longish hair, which, he explained, he could tolerate, but several of them had taken their ties off and, worst of all, one wore sandals.

Detterling gave this one a particularly fierce look, and was grinned at in return.

"All right," the boy said, "I don't like you either."

But luckily the cricket field was now in sight. They walked along a broad terrace, then down some steps and on to the grass.

"Ah," said Detterling; "there's Joe. We'll go and have a word."

"Who's Joe?"

"The groundsman. Mowing the square in the middle."

"He looks rather old to be mowing."

"Groundsmen live to a great age . . . as long as they're allowed to go on being groundsmen. 'Morning, Joe," called Detterling.

" 'Morning, Mr Detterling," said Joe. "Getting any runs this season?"

"I've given up, Joe."

"Pity. It was a handy 200 you made some years back.'

"Nearly forty years back, Joe."

"As long as that, is it? Ah well. This here's the only lad," said Joe to Percival, "who's made a double century in a school match. I doubt you'd get as many just now," he said to Detterling. "I was off poorly this April, and young bastard rolled bugger wrong. Didn't listen to what I told him. Knew best, young bastard did. Two balls in three go flying round their lug-holes and the third slips through flat as an adder. Who's he then?" said Joe, pointing to Percival as if now seeing him for the first time.

"Friend of mine. Mr Percival."

"Bat does he, or bowl?"

"Neither. But he's all right."

"If you say so, Mr Detterling. . . ."

Joe extended a hand to Percival.

"How do you do," said Percival as he shook it.

"Not so fine." Joe turned back to Detterling. "Retiring next year," he said.

"Surely not."

"They say it's time for young bastard to take over."

"Well, perhaps you could do with a rest."

"I'll be resting for good soon enough. Young bastard. So idle he is he won't push mower. Has to have one with a motor, dripping petrol all over bloody wicket. Here he comes now for a gossip, lazy young sod."

A venerable gentlemen perhaps five years younger than Joe was walking across to them.

"How do, Mr Detterling? How do, Mr D's friend? You've heard what happened to the wicket then? Joe put down soot last autumn, thinking it were the new weed-killer. Whole thing's full of clinkers."

"Clinkers my arse."

"I dare say, Joe. Now Mr D," said young bastard, "what about Mr Lloyd-James, now, doing away with himself? He was here well after you was, I reckon, but you must have known him, being in Parliament along with him."

"Never played cricket so's you'd notice," said Joe; "used to watch a lot, though."

"Did to the end," said Detterling.

"Played other games," said young bastard, and winked.

"Let's have respect," said Joe, "respect for a dead man even if he weren't a cricketer. He did watch to the end, Mr Detterling said."

"Oh, I respect him all right, dead or alive. Best of luck to him. Head of the School he was, so I remember. And the best of luck."

"Then stop making insinuendos."

"We know what we know, Joe."

"We only know what Meriel told us."

"She never told lies. A straight girl, Meriel."

"Straight enough."

"What is all this?" said Detterling.

"Just a summer's tale, Mr D. Can't matter if you hear it. Not now. Eh, Joe?"

"Suppose not," said Joe. "Not now."

"What did Meriel tell you? Who was she?"

"Nice girl," said Joe, rather gruffly. "They were mostly old hags with gristly tits and legs like bean-poles—because that was in the war, see, or not long after, and all the young ones were off wagging their butts about in uniform. But there was this Meriel, nice, young girl, had something wrong with her feet, so was excused any war service. Here only a few months

O

she was, and used to come down to The Chequers of an evening. Boys' skiv, in one of the Houses.''

"Mr Lloyd-James's House," said young bastard. "It was the summer the war ended. They had some plan for doing up the insides of the Houses, which they hadn't been allowed before, because of the war regulations. So they kept Meriel on through August, after the boys had gone, to help with the rough; she was glad of the extra money, she said. And most nights that August she'd be down at The Chequers, never overdid it, not really—till one night she got good and plastered, with the drink running out of her eyeballs. 'Bloody hell,' she said, 'do you know what? I've gone and got a bun in the oven'.''

" 'Gone and got myself lumbered,' " took up Joe. " 'Who was it?' we asked her. 'One of the boys.' 'Go on with you.' 'One of the bleeding boys, I tell you. That Mr Lloyd-James,' she says, 'with the fancy Christian name. I got hot for him one morning when there was nobody about, and I was that excited I never put a rubber on his john. Lovely job we did,' she said; 'I come off like a cartload of crackers, I'm telling you that. But now you see what's come of it. Up the spout.' "

"So I says," said the young bastard, pushing himself forward again, "that Mr Lloyd-James's people are well-to-do and perhaps they'd see to it all if she told them."

"Nosy, interfering bugger like you always was, knowing everything," said Joe. "But she says no, that'd get him into trouble with his parents and probably with the School as well, and she'd heard he's to be Head Boy some time next year, and she wouldn't want to spoil it for him. 'Not after that bit of fun we had together,' she says; 'it makes me wet to think of it, and I'll not do the dirty on him now. It was my fault; I should have put a rubber on his john.' Kind girl she was, you see; generous."

"So then I says," insisted young bastard, "that there's Jim Weekes over in the public, what's always liked her. 'He's a bit soft,' I says, 'that's why they wouldn't have him for a soldier, but he's good-hearted and hard-working. If you go and offer him a bit, he'll grab it, and then you can tell him it's his baby on the way, and he's so soft he'll believe it and marry you.' "

"Interfering bugger," said Joe.

" 'Well,' she says, 'I wouldn't mind settling down, and that's the truth, but it seems a bit of a mean trick to play on poor Jim.' Generous girl, even if Joe did say it first. 'Go on,' I says; 'he'd marry you anyway for twopence.' 'Maybe he would. But palming him off with Lloyd-James's get,' she says, 'it's a bit of a mean trick.' 'Well, it's now or never,' I tells her : 'you leave it too long, and even Jim Weekes will know it can't be his, what's cooking.' And there and then she's off and into the public, and the next thing we hear, Jim Weekes has up and married her."

"Where did they live, Mr and Mrs Weekes?" said Detterling.

"I saw her just after the marriage," said Joe. " 'I'm off,' she tells me. 'Weekes and me are going to live the other side of Guildford.' "

"Where?"

" 'I mean to make him a good husband,' she tells me, 'to make up for you know what, and if we stayed round here, I'd be hanging about that school all day, hoping Lloyd-James would come out for a turn in the bushes. No good for me, now I'm married, and none for him either. So Weekes and me are going off the other side of Guildford.' "

"WHERE ?"

" 'I don't want Lloyd-James to have no trouble,' she said, 'so you keep your mouth shut. It might have been your brat or young bastard's,' she said, 'though I know it's not because of when I started missing, and if it had of been, you wouldn't have wanted no trouble with the school any more than he does. So for the sake of the good times we've all had together—' '—Say no more,' I says, 'not a word shall pass these lips.' Nor it has, nor young bastard's either. You can rely on him for some things, I'll say that. But now, well, since the poor gentleman's gone and there's no harm talking of it, it's fun to remember. A summer's tale, like young bastard says, and there won't come another summer like it."

"Joe. It is very important that Mr Percival and I should know where the Weekeses went to."

"Why?"

"We want to help Mrs Weekes. Her husband is dead."

"So you knew the whole story?" said young bastard.

"Yes. No. From another angle. I can't explain just now. The thing is, we must know where to find Mrs Weekes."

"To see her right?"

"Yes."

"Sorry Jim Weekes has gone. I never knew. Soft, but you couldn't help liking him. What happened to him, Mr Detterling?"

"I don't know. Only that he's dead. Please, Joe: where did they go to live?"

"Sorry, Mr Detterling. I've been out of touch with them since they left. It's a long way, the other side of Guildford. Like I say, I didn't even hear that Jim was dead."

" 'The other side of Guildford. . . .' Surely she must have said where?"

But both Joe and young bastard shook their heads.

"She didn't mean we should meet again. She was going off to start fresh. And now, Mr D and friend, it's time for Joe and me to have our lunch; so if you'll be so kind as to excuse us . . ."

Both old gentlemen removed their caps, sweeping them down to their navels. Then they replaced them, turned together, and walked slowly away across the grass.

"Never mind," said Percival. "We know the name: Weekes. Somerset House—how appropriate—will have a birth certificate for the child. The certificate will carry the parents' address at the time of the child's birth."

"There could be thousands of Weekeses."

"But not all of them born round-about—let's see—April to May of 1946. Anyway, my department is entitled to special assistance in finding such documents. They'll turn it up for us quick enough."

" 'Signature, description and residence of informant,' " read Percival from the birth certificate : " 'Meriel Weekes, mother. 134 Long Lane, Engelfield Green, Surrey.' That's it."

"If she still lives there," said Detterling. "What did they call the child?"

"Born on May 1, 1946. . . . 'Name, if any'," read Percival : " 'James'."

"After the putative father, Jim Weekes. But also, unknown to Weekes, commemorating the real father."

"No doubt. And now at last," said Percival, "it is time to call on Mrs Weekes and James Weekes, junior."

And once again the deep red Mercedes was summoned, to carry them out of London, through Staines and Egham, to Engelfield Green.

Long Lane was a narrow street, mainly but not entirely residential, winding down a hill. No. 134 was a toy shop, a small old-fashioned toy shop, with a magic lantern in the window and a display of slides, these being arranged in front of a row of torch bulbs and showing, in rich primary colours, knights and princes on horseback, as they rode through deep forests in which lurked ogres and magicians. As Detterling and Percival went through the door, a little bell sounded. A stooping middle-aged woman came through a curtain of raffia and stood behind the counter. Detterling took a deep breath.

"Mrs Meriel Weekes?" he said.

"The same, sir."

Detterling breathed out again.

"My name is Captain Detterling," he said, "and this is my friend, Mr Percival. Let me now try to explain why we've come. I'll suggest, if I may, that unless you have an assistant it might be as well to close the shop. We don't want to be interrupted."

"Don't you worry, sir. No one else will come."

"Then perhaps we can go through?"

Detterling indicated the raffia curtain.

"We'll stay in here."

"Very well." And Detterling, standing on one side of the counter, started to explain himself to the woman on the other, while Percival examined a row of hand-made dolls and a model railway engine that had been built to run on steam.

"So you think," said Meriel Weekes when Detterling had finished, "that Mr Lloyd-James's suicide might have to do with something that happened when he came here?"

"All we know," said Detterling, "is that he left London, apparently in good spirits, in order to come here; that he returned to London; and that late that night he killed himself."

"So can you help us," said Percival, turning from the model railway engine, "to fill in the gap?"

"He came here all right," said Meriel Weekes.

"And of course you were expecting him?"

"Yes. He'd written some days before."

"Mrs Weekes . . . what happened while he was here?"

"He stood there, where you're standing. And I told him."

"Told him what?"

"Everything that had happened since . . . since we last met. About this shop, for a start. How it belonged to an uncle of Weekes's who took him on in 1945. He heard we wanted to move from where we were, and he invited us to come and live here. Weekes was good with his hands, see, and his uncle was getting too old to make things. His sight was going. So he taught Weekes." She pointed to one of the shelves. "Those wooden soldiers there : the ones in kilts were made by Weekes's uncle. But the ones in the middle, on horses, were made by Weekes. He took to it. He was . . . a simple man, Weekes, but very clever with his fingers."

"I can see that," said Detterling, looking up at the beautifully carved and appointed horsemen. "One of them is from my regiment. I should rather like to buy it, if I may."

"So time went on," said Mrs Weekes, ignoring Detterling's request; "little Jim was born; and Weekes's uncle died three years later, leaving us the shop and four thousand pounds in

savings. It was a good time, that, though we were sad when
the old man died. There was a decent living in the shop, then,
because the people who lived round about were interested.
Rich people, who liked the fine and pretty things that Weekes
could make. But now all the big houses have gone, and they've
built rows of bungalows over the fields, all the way to Runny-
mede. Another sort has come here now. . . .

"But then . . . then was a good time. Little Jim was growing
up nicely, and though we couldn't have no more we didn't
mind very much, as long as we had Jim. Weekes never dreamt
that Jim wasn't his own, so he was happy; and I was happy if
he was, because he was a good, kind husband, and he deserved
to be. So we all three lived behind the shop, and good money
came in, and everything was as it should be. It wasn't till 1960,
even later, that we started to go wrong."

She paused, went to the raffia curtain, peered through it,
and then returned to the counter.

"And all this," she said, "I told to Mr Lloyd-James when
he came here that day, just as I'm telling you. And then I
told him how we went wrong. Like this it was. Little Jim left
school in 1961, when he was fifteen, and Weekes wanted him
to learn the trade and help him make things to sell in the shop.
But little Jim had other ideas. To begin with, he wasn't much
use with his hands, having taken after his real father in that.
And then he could see, as could I, that already this neighbourhood was changing, and there wasn't the trade which there had
been. Even as long ago as that, we were starting to nibble at
Weekes's uncle's savings which we'd been left. Not much, not
just yet, but nibbling we were. So little Jim said, and I supported him, that the days for this kind of thing"—she jerked her
head at the shelves—"were coming to an end, and that he'd
sooner learn some other trade. He fancied something in business or commerce. So the end of it was he got himself a job
as an office boy in London, and went up and down every
day."

"Nothing so bad in any of that," said Percival.

"Not at first, no. Only he'd hurt his father—hurt Weekes,

I mean. Weekes had hoped for them to carry on together, father and son (as he thought), and it hurt him that little Jim thought himself too good for the shop. 'Don't be silly,' I used to tell Weekes, 'it isn't that. It's just that he wants something different. And anyway,' I said, 'it's no bad thing, just now, to have his extra money coming in.' But Weekes wouldn't see it. He was a simple man, as I've said, and he didn't realise what was happening in the shop. As long as he could go on modelling soldiers or making dolls, he was happy—or would have been, if he'd had little Jim doing it along of him. So about this time there was feeling between the two of them : Weekes being hurt with Jim and Jim thinking that Weekes wanted to tie him down to the shop and spoil his chances. And things got worse, because little Jim started feeling his oats and took to going with girls—London girls he met at his office. He was still only young, sixteen or so, but like his father he had a way with him. Although he was ugly, the dead spit of Somerset, he had a better skin and a fresher look, and since he put that same sexy feel into the air that Somerset used to, he had no trouble getting girls. But he had to treat them and so on, and he started getting late with the money he paid me for his board. I didn't tell Weekes that, but Weekes was angry just the same, because little Jim would stay up in London till late at night, and Weekes thought a boy's place was back at home in the evenings and he liked us all three to be together.

"And then, one night, little Jim didn't come home at all. We were worried. We went down the road to the telephone box and rang up the local police. "How old is he?" they said. 'Sixteen, nearly seventeen.' 'We can't chase after sixteen-year-olds who stay out late.' 'But something may have happened. You see, he always comes home, even if it's a late train. But now there'll be no more trains tonight. He's never done this before.' 'There has to be a first time for everything, madam; he'll turn up.' And so he did; in a London police court the next morning; charged with breaking and entering. He'd needed the money, he said, to take out one of those girls; he'd promised her a week-end in a posh hotel.

"In the end they put him away for six months. So that was
the end of his job, and it made it almost impossible for him to
get another when he came out—except as a common labourer,
and he didn't fancy that. So now he had to work at home here
with Weekes. And hated it. And hated us for it, though it wasn't
our fault. Miserable we all were together. The shop was doing
worse and worse, there was no extra money coming in from
Jim's job any more, Weekes's uncle's savings were going faster
and faster, and Jim and Weekes were quarrelling all day long.
'Sell the shop,' said Jim. 'Where would we go?' said Weekes.
'Australia, where no one knows about me being put away.' 'A
man's place is in his own country.' 'Some bloody country.'
And so on.

"And all this time Jim was still going with girls. Local ones,
but not nice ones, they wouldn't have anything to do with
him; low girls from Staines, whores more or less, they fancied
him, you see, they gave him some of the money they made. So
now he took to spending the day away from the shop, in pubs
and cafés, pimping for these girls, or befriending them as he
tried to call it when the police came. We hadn't known about it,
not really, till then : only when the police came and charged
him with living off immoral earnings did we realise what he'd
been up to. I thought it would have killed Weekes. This time
it was two years before we saw Jim again."

"I don't supose," said Percival, "that Somerset much enjoyed
hearing all this about his son."

"He was quite calm. Calm and quiet, Somerset was. 'Go on,'
he said to me : 'what happened when Jim came out again?'
Well, by then it was 1967, and Jim was twenty-one. Weekes
suggested the army—it was the only thing he could think of—
but of course Jim wouldn't go. He'd learnt a trick worth five
of that, he said, this last time in prison. He was going to be a
courier. 'A what?' we asked. A courier, a man who delivered
messages, and other things. Easy money, lots of money. He'd
met a bloke inside who'd fix him up as soon as he came out
himself. And in no time at all this man had come out and
my Jim was working for him—pushing drugs. The deadly

P

ones. Heroin, that sort. Not that I knew till later, but that's what it was."

"How did Somerset react when he heard that?" said Detterling.

"He looked very uncomfortable. 'Don't you worry,' I said; 'that's all over. He'll never push drugs again now.' Because what happened was, the police got on to him and there was a car chase. Jim's car crashed and caught fire, but the police pulled him out just in time. And the shock of all that made a good man of Jim. It reformed him. He knows now that honesty's the best policy, he's sorry for all he's done, he's going straight for the rest of his life, I can promise you that. Pure too. No more of those filthy girls. He lives here, quiet and respectable, and he's making it up to me. He's all I've got, since Weekes died, and he's taken Weekes's place in the house, and he's redeeming his past, and I love him more now than ever I did. But we were very poor, after Weekes died, because hardly anyone came to buy things here, and all Weekes's uncle's money had gone, bar a hundred pound or so, which is why I hoped Mr Lloyd-James might do something for us. I didn't want to beg, and I hadn't any real right to anything, but it would be only natural for him to help us, once he knew about little Jim. So I wrote and told him. And he came. And he heard what you've heard. And then he met Jim. I expect you'd like to, gentlemen? I can fetch him for you if you like."

Detterling nodded, as did Percival.

"Jim," called Meriel Weekes, and then went through the raffia curtain. "Jim," Detterling heard her say, "you're wanted."

The curtain parted. Somerset's face, as Detterling remembered it had been when Somerset was in his late twenties, was peering at them, grinning. His shoulders followed. Left arm gone, only a stump for the right. Then the torso, on an invalid chair pushed by Meriel Weekes. No legs. The face went on grinning as though it would never stop. And of course, Detterling now understood, it would never stop. A vegetable; living purely and quietly with mother at home, going straight.

"The car crash did this?"

"Yes."

"What . . . what did Somerset say?"

"He looked very hard at Jim for a long time. Then he said, 'My son,' and touched Jim on the cheek. Then he turned away and muttered. But I heard."

"What did he mutter?"

" 'God is not mocked'," said Meriel Weekes.

And then, Meriel told them, Somerset had left the shop for a good hour. When he came back, he said,

'You need never be really poor. Not with him to take care of. I've been to the Government welfare people down the road in Egham. They say you've never been near them. Why not?'

'I've got my pride,' Meriel had told him.

'Sink your pride,' said Somerset. 'They'll come and see you tomorrow. They'll either take him off your hands—'

'—Never—'

'—Or they'll make you a special allowance. For medical appliances, special care, and so on . . . quite apart from other benefits which are due to you. There should be considerable arrears to come. If they ask you why you never applied, say you didn't know you were entitled. If you have any difficulty, write to your M.P. He's a good man enough and he'll see you right. You can use my name; tell him you knew me and I advised you to approach him. That's all, I think,' Somerset had said; 'so I'll be going now.'

And he went.

" 'God is not mocked'," said Percival to Detterling, as they drove back to London. "What exactly did he mean? That he, the father, had been punished in the person of his son?"

"Partly. He also meant, I think, that no one ever escapes . . . and that even this would not be the end of it. If this horror was what came of a casual morning's fornication twenty-seven years ago, then anything might come from anything at any time. And yet again, there was the disappointment: his only son,

a petty, squalid and incompetent crook. And the comparison:
Somerset himself was also a crook, on an incomparably more
refined level, of course, but his moral failure had been of the
same kind. Like his son, Somerset had used people as if they
were things. He had got away with it so far, but here was God
reminding him that he had his eye on Somerset; reminding him,
too, of the hell that lay in store for all those like Somerset and
his son, which is to be loved and tended when helpless by the
very people whom they have deliberately injured or exploited:
the hell of being forgiven. To receive unrefusable charity bears
very hard on men like Somerset. It is the curse of the Detterlings," said Detterling, "but in the passive form. We Detterlings cannot serve selflessly: the Somersets cannot bear to be
selflessly served."

"But suicide, Detterling? Suicide because a son was paralysed in a motor smash?"

"Somerset had bred that thing on the wheelchair."

"But it's not as if the boy had been born like that."

"Somerset had bred him to be such that he had reached
that end. The shame was Somerset's."

"That's sheer Calvinism."

"Somerset was a Calvinist—or a Jansenist as they call it in
his Church. But like all Calvinists he believed that he himself
was exempt from the system, that God had made him special.
Now God was telling him different."

"Your friend Peter Morrison," said Percival after a pause,
"has a son who has been turned into an idiot by meningitis.
And yet no one has ever suggested that he would even for one
second consider suicide."

Detterling looked at the miniature Light Dragoon on horseback which he had purchased before leaving Meriel Weekes's
shop. He held it up to eye level to examine the detail of the
sabretache.

"Peter has another son," he said. "He has a wife. He still has
people to love him, people whom he can love. And he can
still love poor ruined Nickie, because he can remember him
as he was when he was whole. Perhaps Somerset, when he

heard about his child, began to hope for a son to love; but he could not love that thing on the chair for what it was, and he could not love it for its past, because he never knew it when it was lovable . . . if it ever was."

Detterling smiled at the toy Dragoon.

"That boy was a chip off the old block," he said; "and on its underside, where it had been hewn off, Somerset could see his own maggots."

There was another pause, during which Detterling peered very closely at the epaulettes of his Dragoon.

"As I understand your account of that Memorial Dinner," said Percival at last, "Canteloupe suggested that Somerset was in some sense immune from evil, that he was only experimenting with it, out of a purely objective interest."

"Somerset may have thought that too. But it wasn't true, Leonard. He could think himself immune from evil as long as he managed to guard himself against its effects. But when something he hadn't forseen got under his guard . . . then he got a mighty shock: at last he knew he was the same as everyone else, vulnerable, Leonard, because even he could not anticipate everything. Only God could do that."

"Back with your theory, Detterling?"

"Yes. When did he make his mistake . . . the fatal mistake which he never even noticed? When he got drunk? When he drank that glass of cheap sherry? When he was sick without getting himself to the loo? When he pleasured the skivvy? No, for my money, Leonard, the fatal mistake—the mistake which started all of this off and in the end destroyed Somerset—was a typical little act of meanness, so typical that of course he didn't notice it: trying to pass off half a crown on the Boys' Maid for a job that was always rated at five shillings. If he'd left the statutory five shillings, Meriel would not have looked for him that next morning and they would not have come together as they did. James Lloyd-James (for so he should truly be called) would neither have been gotten, nor born, nor later transformed into that grinning obscenity, the horror of which possessed and killed his father."

"All very neat and clever," said Percival; "but what am I going to tell them in Jermyn Street?"

"No need to labour the point," said Detterling. "Just tell them . . . that God is not mocked, and that God pulled the rug from under Somerset."

THE SURVIVORS

Contents

PART ONE

THE INHERITANCE

"SHIT," said Captain Detterling.

He spoke loud enough to be heard by the Bulgarian delegation at their table ten feet away, and in a tone that made his meaning very plain even to those of them who did not understand his vernacular. None of them, however, even so much as twitched. They simply sat on, attentive yet relaxed, their eyes fixed with bland and total respect on their Bulgarian comrade who was speaking up on the platform.

"It is the function and duty of all writers," came the anxious voice of the English translator through Detterling's earphones, "to participate in the political instruction of the people, in the ideological exemplification, that is, of the way in which the people must go. As for what way this is, doubt is no longer permissible or pardonable, unless it be caused by ignorance. It is therefore the duty of the writer to remove this ignorance, to assist in the struggle"—here the translator hesitated for some seconds—"to promote the amplification, the universal comprehensivisation, of Socialist Doctrine and Principle."

God, thought Detterling, what does this drivel sound like in other languages? He switched the arrow on the dial in front of him to Italian. A voluptuous voice fervently caressed the long abstract words as though about to bring them to orgasm. A degenerate tongue, the Italian, Detterling thought : its constant juxtaposition of the diminutive with the grandiose transposes everything, whether the most noble utterance or this jargon which we're hearing now, to the same level of trivial hysteria. No wonder the Italians are at once so conceited and so futile; their language compels them to live a libretto.

He turned the arrow to French. Absolute silence; how

appropriate—French, a precise and civilised language, had no equivalent for this rubbish, so the translator, one assumed, had simply given up. German : great throatfuls of congested inflections, ejaculated in a tone at once whining and aggressive. He removed his earphones to hear what the speech sounded like in Bulgarian itself, and hurriedly put them on again. Finally, for want of an alternative, he turned the arrow back to English.

"Now is the time," twittered the English translator (a female with an upper-class accent) "for all writers in the so-called 'free' countries of Western Europe and America to impeach the false and bourgeois, so-called 'liberal', concepts of freedom, in the name of which the capitalist masters of these countries contrive to hoodwink and prey upon the masses, and to proclaim the true freedom, which is conceived and actualised by the aspirations of the toiling proletariat."

"Shit," said Detterling once more.

The Bulgarians again ignored him, and all other ears in the chamber were blocked by earphones. Detterling sighed and turned to Fielding Gray, who was sitting next to him at the British delegates' table. Gray raised his one small eye in interrogation and eased back his headpiece to listen.

"Time for fresh air," said Detterling into the pink and crumpled ear.

"Ought we to go out in the middle of a speech? Discourteous to the speaker?"

"He's already been going on for twenty-five minutes. That's discourtesy *if* you like."

So Fielding Gray, amid glances of angry disapproval, followed Captain Detterling out of the Sala dello Scrutinio, in which the deliberations of the Annual Conference (1973) of the International PEN Club were being conducted, and into the courtyard of the Doges' Palace. Without a word they crossed the Piazzetta and settled themselves in the late afternoon sunlight that still loitered in front of Florian's.

"Seventy writers all in the same room," Detterling groaned at last, "and most of 'em foreigners."

"You didn't have to come."

"I thought I ought to see you all at it, just the once. As

you know, I'm only really interested in the social goings-on."

"They're even worse. You have to talk to people."

"That's what I intend. I might pick up something useful."

"Like what?"

"I might induce one of those ageing lady novelists to promise Stern & Detterling their memoirs."

"Most of 'em are too drunk to write any."

"They'll have kept diaries over the years. Or even better, I might get a manuscript from one of those Communists."

"Not if you can't be bothered to listen to their speeches."

"*That* was an official Communist. I'm interested in the kind that are planning to escape to the West and would be glad to find a little money and reputation waiting for them."

"That kind aren't allowed out to affairs like this."

"It's coming to affairs like this that turns them into that kind. They get a whiff of lovely bourgeois decadence, and then there's no holding them." Detterling broke off to order two John Collinses. "Stern & Detterling," he said, turning back to Fielding, "is prepared to sink quite a bit in a book by a renegade Communist. That's the main reason we're here in Venice."

"Gregory Stern said you were both here to attend that exhibition of European Book Production on San Giorgio."

"*And* to find a renegade Communist at the PEN Conference."

"You'll be lucky," said Fielding. "Every Communist writer here, however well regarded by the Party, has a kind of personal commissar in attendance. To see he doesn't hobnob with characters like you. You're a Tory M.P., remember. They've done their homework about all that, and no writer from behind the curtain, not even a potential renegade, will dare come within a mile of you. Any budding Pasternaks will have to be found by Gregory . . . who, incidentally, seems to be spending his entire time riding round the place in gondolas."

"That's Isobel's fault. She says that Venice is dying and they must look at it all for the last time."

"Isobel may have a point, I fancy. But I can't think the end will come *quite* as soon as she implies. At least I hope not," said Fielding, "as I've more or less decided to stay on for a year or two after the Conference is over."

"For a *year* or two?"

"I like decaying cities, and even dying ones, so long as they don't positively collapse on top of me. And *pace* Isobel, I don't think Venice will do that just yet. Another thing," said Fielding, caressing the cool shaft of his John Collins : "tax."

"Trouble with the Inland Revenue, old man?"

"Not yet, and I don't mean there should be. If you stay out of the way long enough, you don't have to file tax returns for the period of your absence. It's now September 1973. If I stay abroad until June or July 1975, say, I could save myself a lot of money."

"Funny. I never thought of you as being in the tax-evasion bracket."

"If it's legal, it's called *tax-avoidance*, Detterling. And I promise you I'm going to be strictly legal from now on. Too much worry the other way, believe me."

"So you have done some fiddles in your time?"

"Just one. Back in 1970, when I was working on Corfu with those film people, I got them to pay me in Zürich. Ten thousand pounds odd I've got there—and not a penny can I bring to England. One more reason for staying abroad a bit."

"But if *I* understand you, old man, it's income tax you really want to save. How's your income got so large all of a sudden? Time was when your novels barely kept you in booze."

"If you'd looked at your firm's accounts lately, Detterling, you'd know what's happened. My novels, as you observe, merely make gin-money. But the book on Conrad which you and Gregory commissioned for your Modern English Novelists series has turned into a gusher. The American rights alone," said Fielding bitterly, "are worth nearly twenty thousand quid. I shan't need to work again for years."

"You don't sound very happy about it all. Funny," said Detterling, "I always thought that Modern English Novelists series would be a loser. Good for prestige, but a financial loser."

"You must have heard what happened?"

"No. I've been away six months, remember, fact-finding for Canteloupe and that Ministry of his."

"But Gregory must have written—or told you since you got back?"

"There was some letter about tarting the series up. And Gregory did mumble something the other day about a gratifying response. But he was so eager to go off in his gondola with Isobel and Baedeker that he never got round to details."

"Well, he tarted the series up all right. He turned my book into a plushy great slab of a jet-set job with 128 pages of plates, most of them in colour. Isobel's idea. She'd been on about it a long time."

"Where did he find the money to go in for that sort of publishing?"

"I thought some of it might be yours."

"Oh no. I made my deposit in the firm years ago, and that was that."

"Perhaps he got some from Isobel—she had quite a bit when her father died. In any case, he found it. And *I* found," said Fielding Gray, "that my loving and dedicated literary study of the life and work of Joseph Conrad had been transformed into a kind of Bumper Annual Omnibus, full of tit and botty pics of South Sea Islanders."

"And now here you are, flying from the tax-man in consequence."

"I don't say I'm not glad of the money. Early middle age is an expensive time: one is old enough to have taste and still young enough to have appetite—a costly combination."

"Then why are you being so sour with Gregory for putting all this cash in your pocket?"

"Because he turned a serious book into something trivial."

"He didn't change your text, did he?"

"No. He just made sure that no reputable critic would give it serious attention. In the circles which I'd hoped to impress, my book on Conrad will just be written off as another piece of smarty-pants publishing."

"You can't have it both ways, Fielding. You can't get rich *and* be a Doctor of Letters."

"Oh, I know that. It's just that this way of getting rich seems so particularly shabby. Instead of being read by a few critical and appreciative people, and receiving in return a modest sum of money honestly earned, I am being paid a huge sum of money in return for being read by nobody. For nobody *reads* a book with that sort of get-up, Detterling; it just lies around to be glanced at. But even though I know this—and here's the really horrible thing about it all—I have nevertheless been developing a curious and most unwholesome conceit of myself; because a book with my name on it is selling by tens and hundreds of thousands, I have started to invest myself with great importance—although I know, in my heart, that it is spurious."

Fielding Gray drank at his John Collins; Detterling attempted no comment beyond a sceptical smile, as if to say, 'Stop posing'.

"No, no," said Fielding, who read the smile aright; "I mean what I'm saying. Listen, Detterling. As part of the sales campaign a certain amount of 'lionising' was organised for me—luncheons at the Connaught and so on. And do you know, I began to take the treatment quite seriously. Every now and then I had to shake myself all over, in order to remind myself that I wasn't the lion they were pretending I was, that I had simply, by pure chance, got caught up in a commercial process. And as the process intensified, so did I deteriorate. I forgot to remind myself of the truth; for hours, days at a time, I really thought I was the great writer they said I was. This sort of thing destroys a man, Detterling. I told you just now that I won't have to work for some time; but the truth is that I should find it almost impossible to work if I had to. My whole life lately has been a round of fêtes and speeches; I've been doing nothing whatever except sit in Buttock's Hotel and listen for the telephone to summon me to press interviews and television studios, and indeed I'd got to such a pitch that I felt bored and insulted if it didn't ring every ten minutes. That's why I came to Venice. September is not much of a time for literary lions in London, so I thought, 'I'll go to the PEN conference in Venice, they'll be all over me there'."

"And have they been?"

"No," said Fielding abruptly. "They're silly enough in

their own way, but they've too much sense for that. They don't go in for straw lions. So I'm beginning to be sane again —sane, but very sour, as you say, not because I'm denied the false praise that was ruining me, but because I'm denied the small degree of genuine recognition which I should have for my text on Conrad. The PEN people haven't been taken in by the ballyhoo, but because of the ballyhoo they haven't troubled to read my text either—and they're just the kind of people who should be appreciating it."

"I can't think," said Detterling, "why you want their appreciation. All those dreary, unctuous Reds, pissing out great pools of stale propaganda."

"There *are* more desirable elements in the PEN Club."

"Like those lady novelists you just accused of being tiddly all day long? But I take your point," said Detterling. "You're a poor little rich boy whom nobody loves—or not the right people and not for the right reasons. Boo-hoo, Fielding, boo-hoo-bloody-hoo. Pull yourself together and start another book."

"That's one reason why I'll probably stay on in Venice. There'll be fewer telephone calls to distract me, and I'm hoping this city will show me something to write about."

"It might," said Detterling. "If you stop whining and start looking, it just might. Good afternoon, Isobel . . . Gregory . . ."

Fielding and Detterling rose and rearranged chairs. Isobel Stern wrapped her long, gangling legs over one; her husband Gregory sat primly on the edge of another. Detterling beckoned a waiter and ordered more drinks.

"Phew," said Gregory; "we have walked all the way from the New Ghetto."

"What happened to your gondola?"

"Isobel dismissed it. She said we must see that part of Venice on foot. We must look close with our eyes, she said, to see how it is crumbling. I tell you, Fielding, Detterling, it is not crumbling, it is suppurating."

"Doomed," said Isobel.

"The Venice in Peril Fund—" Fielding began.

"—What fund?" said Isobel. "Only peanuts, unless the Italian Government does its bit. And can you imagine those

greedy wops spending money just to save something beautiful? They'd sooner put a motorway through the place."

"And ruin their tourist trade?"

"They hate tourists. They think of them as people who
have come to see a corpse."

"Who *pay* to see a corpse."

"Only they don't pay enough any more, and the corpse
is taking up the best bed. The Italians would sooner have a
nice, juicy, living slut in it," said Isobel, "something they can
fuck."

"Isobel, my wife, what *do* you mean?"

"I mean, Gregory my husband, that the eyeties are sick
of Venice and want something modern instead. Something
which appeals to *them* for a change: speedways and football
stadiums and enormous swimming pools. Or failing those,
a lot of factories in which they can make money. Anything,
in fact, but what they've got."

"Poor Fielding," said Detterling. "He's just decided to live
here for a bit, and I don't think speedways and factories are
quite what he's looking forward to."

"You are going to live in Venice?" said Gregory to
Fielding.

"For a year or two, perhaps."

"You've made him so rich by the way you've promoted
his book on Conrad," said Detterling, "that he can't afford
to live in England."

"No good ever came of living abroad," said Isobel. "A
man should stay where he has roots."

"Ah," said Detterling, "Fielding thinks his roots are being
poisoned. Gregory has corrupted him, he says, by turning
him from a poor novelist, who worked quietly in the country,
into a gilded metropolitan celebrity. He must stay abroad to
escape further contamination."

"Contamination?" said Gregory. "What nonsense,
Fielding, is this?"

Fielding, whose head was turned towards the glittering
façade of St Mark's, brought it slowly round and directed
his eye straight at Gregory.

"It's true," he said. "I can't sit still, I can't be quiet, I can't
work. And all because of this sham success with Conrad. I've

started to think and behave like a matinée idol . . . preening myself on doorsteps and waiting for the cameras to click."

"Balls," said Isobel. "All you need is a good kick in the arse."

"Please, Isobel. Is it the money," said Gregory, "that has done this?"

"No. I've earned big money before for a time—working on films. But there what I did was genuine, in its kind, and I was not corrupted. This is different; because what we've done—what *you've* done—with this book on Conrad is pure faking. You've faked me into fame, Gregory, and made me into something which I both adore and totally despise."

"The tragedy of the year," said Isobel: "poor little Fielding sobbing his heart out because he's suddenly famous and rich. See what you've done, Gregory? You and your vulgar wife. Listen, you," she said to Fielding: "it was my idea to jazz that book up because I smelt money in it and it's high time Gregory made some. If I'd left it to him he'd have gone on printing nice, liberal, literate and wholly unsellable books until he wound up in the gutter. And don't think Detterling would have bailed him out. Detterling's as mean as a crab-louse."

"Steady on, old girl," Detterling said.

"So Gregory needed to do something different," said Isobel, "and I showed him how, and now we're all making a packet. If you don't like the money, Fielding, don't go on squealing about it; just give it back."

"I've told you, it's not the money I mind—"

"—It's the damage to your poor sensitive soul," Isobel sneered. "For Christ's sake don't be so silly, Fielding. Just go home to England and get on with another book."

"There isn't another book," said Fielding stubbornly. "I can't see it anywhere, not yet. But I might find it here, and here, as I told you, I'm staying."

"In Venice." Isobel shuddered. "It's . . . it's like being in a graveyard full of broken tombs. Rather pretty to look at on a bright day, but to live in . . . Fielding," she said, suddenly changing her tone to one of persuasion and affection, "listen to what I'm saying. Can't you smell death in this place?"

Fielding shrugged at the suggestion but smiled in response to her obvious concern for him.

"I'm staying, Isobel," he said. "I think it may suit me."

"Well, don't say I didn't warn you. I tell you this town is rotting to death . . . in spirit as well as fabric. I feel it, Fielding."

"Isobel is sometimes psychic," said Gregory in an apologetic voice.

"I'm making Gregory take me home," she said : "I can't stand any more of it."

"When?" said Detterling sharply.

"Tomorrow."

"You never warned me," said Detterling to Gregory.

"I did not know until Isobel told me."

"A fat lot of help that is, Gregory. We're here to find new authors, remember? And now you're deserting me before we've even started."

"You must manage by yourself, my dear. After all, *you* have deserted me for all of the last six months."

"I was doing this enquiry for my cousin Canteloupe."

"None the less deserting me, my dear. But since we're on the subject, I confess I'd be intrigued to know exactly what you were up to."

"Yes," said Fielding. "What *were* you up to, Detterling? You've always kept clear of Government office : why did you take this on?"

"This was not a Government office."

"A job for a Ministry . . ."

"Strictly unofficial. I wasn't paid—though Canteloupe subbed up for my expenses. Out of his own pocket. I wasn't really working for the Ministry of Commerce but for Canteloupe personally."

"Cut the small print," said Isobel, "and tell us what you did."

A deep bell began to toll from the Campanile.

"Curfew," said Fielding.

"Only a show for the tourists," said Isobel, "but one day soon it'll be the real thing." And to Detterling : "Come on, Detterling. What was the dirty work you did for your noble cousin?"

"I never said it was dirty, and I only took it on to oblige Canteloupe. It was, in fact, an enquiry into something that had already happened."

"I see," said Isobel. "Cleaning up an old pile of dirt instead of starting a new one."

"On the contrary. Just making sure that there wasn't any dirt . . . or at least none visible."

"How dull."

"Far from it. In the summer of '72," said Detterling, "Canteloupe's Under-Secretary, Peter Morrison, pulled off a very neat coup at the Trade Convention in Strasbourg. No need to go into details, but the end of it was that Britain sold a huge amount of a new light metal alloy which we were keen to push—and one of the reasons we sold so much was that Peter had managed to discredit the products of our competitors. I can't tell you how he did it, but it was by means of a clever trick which Peter and Canteloupe think they might use again, with certain variations. Before they can do that, however, they have to be sure that no one has rumbled the trick . . . indeed that no one even suspects there *was* any trick. That was where I came in: they needed a substantial sort of chap with all the entrées—an M.P. like me—but one who doesn't count in that world and therefore wouldn't be noticed, to go all round the world listening in to what was being said about the '72 Convention and to find out if anyone was harbouring nasty thoughts about the sale of our light metal alloy. I was to be a fly on the wall—and I wasn't at all keen to take it on, because in my experience even the most discreet fly is apt to wind up under a swatter. But Canteloupe made a family obligation out of it, and I've always been interested in Peter Morrison's stratagems, so on condition that Canteloupe paid for me to do my travels *en prince* I agreed to have a try at it. And here I am, as you see, still unswatted, and happy to be able to report that no one appears to have spotted what Canteloupe and Morrison have been up to. So," he said to Isobel, "no dirt to be cleaned up; not so far, anyhow."

"Such hazards you went through," said Gregory. "I trust the Most Honourable the Marquis Canteloupe was happy with the news you brought home to him."

"In so far as he can be happy about anything.

Canteloupe, just now, is batting on a very dodgy wicket. He can't last much longer at the Ministry."

"Despite the success of our light metal alloy at Strasbourg?"

"That was over a year ago," said Detterling, "and Britain cannot live by light metal alloys alone. The cry is going up for a younger man who is—what's the jargon?—more in tune with the technological era in which we live."

"Not that anyone will do any better," said Gregory Stern. "Even the most brilliant technology, with the most abrasive young Minister behind it, will be little good unless the people are prepared to work and the Unions to cooperate. Just now I see no work, no cooperation anywhere."

"The people are bored," said Isobel. "They want some excitement. The only way of getting it is to precipitate disaster, and that's what everyone is busy doing. Demanding everything and giving nothing, and sitting back to see what will happen."

"Ai-yai," said Gregory: "death in Venice, doom in Britain."

"And trouble on its way to this table," said Isobel, as two Carabineri, wearing cocked hats and short swords, halted by them and saluted. "What have you boys been up to?"

"Signor Capitano Detterling?" one of the Carabineri said carefully. "Membair of the Ingleesh Parli-a-ment?"

"I am he," said Detterling.

Both men saluted again; one of them opened the pouch on his belt and produced an envelope.

"Thank you," said Detterling, and took it.

The Carabineri exchanged glances, then saluted once more and slithered away through the surrounding tables.

"Oh dear," said Detterling softly, "listen to this. 'CANTELOUPE DIED AT DESK FOUR OF CLOCK THIS AFTERNOON CARDIAC THROMBOSIS STOP PETER MORRISON.' He must have had it sent over some special network. Rather flattering that those police chappies knew who I was and where to find me."

"They always know that kind of thing in Venice," said Fielding; "rather frightening if you ask me. I think," he said, "that there's another sheet in that envelope."

"Yes. . . ."

Detterling unfolded a second message. He blinked, grinned rather wolfishly, then shook his head in puzzled acknowledgement.

"It's from the lawyers," he said. "They lost no time, I must say." He shook his head again, as if speculating on the logistic problems which the lawyers must have overcome in order to effect so swift a transmission. "Peter rang them at once, I suppose, and they must have asked him to relay this message to me the same way he sent his own."

"It must be very urgent."

"Not exactly. But certainly exigent."

"Well, what is it, Detterling?"

"Not Detterling," said Captain Detterling in a still, small voice : "not any more. You should call me . . . Canteloupe."

The Marquis Canteloupe was dead : long live the Marquis Canteloupe. In point of fact, as Fielding remarked to Detterling the next morning, both custom and courtesy forbade him to assume the title until his predecessor was buried. Detterling countered this by producing a telegram which had arrived from the lawyers a little while before and informed Detterling that under the terms of the deceased's will there was to be no burial service and that circumstances (mercifully unspecified) made it advisable to inter the body that very morning. Thus Detterling was spared the inconvenience of an immediate journey to England to attend the obsequies, and might call himself Canteloupe from that minute.

"But of course," he said, "I'll have to go home in a week or so in order to see into it all."

Meanwhile they began to piece together, from the copious letters and telegrams which arrived in the next few days, what had happened to bring about Detterling's unlooked-for inheritance. Canteloupe's son and only child, the Earl of Muscateer, had died many years since while an Officer Cadet in India; and until a very few days previously the heir presumptive had been Canteloupe's brother, Lord Alfred Sarum. But Lord Alfred, they had now learnt, had expired suddenly while attending his 113th drink cure, and since all Canteloupe's other siblings were also dead, this

had opened up the field a bit, as Detterling put it. Yet the
field, on inspection, proved to be exceedingly thin. Cousins
or uncles Canteloupe had none—except for that branch of
the family which descended from his great-great-great-
great-great aunt, Lady Julia Sarum, who had married a
certain Adolphus Detterling, of Richborough in the County
of Kent, Esquire, in 1810. Of this line the only survivor
was now Captain Detterling, and of course he could inherit only such titles as might descend through the Lady
Julia, his great-great-great-great grandmother.

The lawyers, nosing into the matter after Lord Alfred's
death, had at first opined that there was only one of the
family peerages to which Detterling might succeed—the
Barony of Sarum of Old Sarum. The two Viscountcies
(Sarum of Sherwood, and Rollesden-in-Silvis) could certainly not be transmitted through the female line; nor
could the Earldom of Muscateer. There remained only the
Marquisate, a rather late creation (1799), of which it was
assumed that it could descend only through issue male.
However, a junior partner of antiquarian tastes, idly reading through the original letters patent which conferred the
Marquisate, came across a clause which assigned a special
remainder, in default of heirs male, to the eldest daughter
of the 1st Marquis and to heirs male in direct line of suc-
cession from her. This eldest daughter was in fact the Lady
Julia Sarum (later Detterling) aforementioned, and an
examination of the family records made it clear why the
special remainder in her favour had been arranged: for
the 1st Marquis, at the time when he was so promoted for
his highly confidential services to the Crown, had no son
(his only male child having died while abroad, two years
previously) and a lunatic wife. In the event, however, the
special remainder was not invoked, as the mad marchioness
had killed herself by jumping from a window, and the
Marquis had married again and contrived, albeit very late
in life, to father a boy. Only now, some 170 years later,
was the remainder suddenly applicable, vested as it undoubtedly was in Captain Detterling, who accordingly became, by virtue of it, 6th Marquis Canteloupe of the
Estuary of the Severn.

"And also," as Detterling explained to Fielding Gray,

"19th Baron Sarum of Old Sarum, by reason of a different and more usual kind of remainder which Henry V assigned to all female descendants of the 1st Baron."

"But the Earldom and the Viscountcies," said Fielding, "are definitely extinct?"

"A pity, that," said Detterling : "but it doesn't do to be greedy. There are plenty of goodies without those."

The goodies not only included the Marquisate, the Barony, Canteloupe's house and park in Wiltshire, the theoretical right to every carp ever caught in the Severn, and a superb collection of rude books; they also comprehended Cant-Fun & Co. Ltd, one of the slickest and most successful 'Stately Home' carnivals in England, so organised as to screw the maximum of cash out of a credulous public and to inflict the minimum of inconvenience on the Marquis himself when in residence. In recent years Cant-Fun had paid for the entire upkeep of the Wiltshire house and estate, had shown an average profit of £300,000 annually, and had been so cunningly engrafted into the main body of the Canteloupe finances that death duties, as Detterling now learned from the accountants, would be extremely modest.

"It seems," said Detterling to Fielding, "that I've not really inherited Canteloupe's estate but the Chairmanship of the Company that runs it."

"Cant-Fun," Fielding said. "Only your cousin could have thought up a name as vile as that. The old philistine. Do you remember how he tore up that rose garden right in front of the house to put in an Amusement Arcade?"

"That was in his unregenerate days," said Detterling. "He got quite civilised towards the end. There was a man he met called Balbo Blakeney—a Fellow of Lancaster— who knew about houses and gardens. Balbo came to stay once or twice and showed him how to camouflage Cant-Fun. You'd hardly know it was there now, if it wasn't for the prole infants screeching. And I suppose that's a small price to pay for getting away with the death duties."

"I still don't quite see how that works."

"I don't actually inherit the *property*, or not so that I own it personally. Everything's tied up in the Company, which in some aspects is like a kind of Trust. There's a

Board responsible for it, and I become Chairman of the
Board, and as such I draw a vast sum in salary and expenses, enough to cover anything I could want within
reason and indeed well beyond it. But the point is that
every penny of the capital belongs, not to me, but to the
Company. Everything I get, including the right to live in
the house, I get because I'm the Chairman, not because
I'm the Marquis Canteloupe."

"No," said Fielding: "the Marquis of Cant-Fun."

"If you're going to make jokes like that, I shall think
you are jealous."

"Of course I'm jealous. I've always coveted a coronet
myself."

"Stick to your writing, and you may get a crown of
laurel."

"But not a Chairmanship to subsidise it. . . ."

There was a knock on the door of Fielding's sitting-
room, and a flunkey in liveries bowed himself in with a
letter. This turned out to be for Detterling.

"I must say, they do us well here at the Gritti," said
Detterling when the flunkey had gone. "The minute a
letter comes they bring it to you—wherever you are in the
hotel." His face clouded a little. "But how do you suppose,"
he said, "that they knew I was in your room?"

"I told you the other day, when the Carabineri delivered
those messages in the Piazza. In Venice they always know
where important people are. It's been their speciality for
centuries."

"You won't mind that . . . when you're living here?"

"I'm not the 6th Marquis Canteloupe. They won't
bother me."

"Such modesty. You were right. Venice *is* doing you
good. But don't overdo the self-abasement. It can be quite
as unwholesome as its opposite."

Detterling opened his letter. "From Carton Weir," he
announced.

"What's he on about?"

"Canteloupe's death—the manner of his dying."

For a minute or two Detterling read in silence. Then,
"Listen to this," he said. " '. . . The odd thing was that for
some weeks the old boy had been in the best possible form.

Back in July he'd been pretty depressed about the way things were running ("It's enough to put one off one's drink," he said once, and indeed it even seemed to be doing that), but about three weeks ago he perked up again and was full of ideas for the future. I think he was encouraged by the final report you sent in after your tour, telling him that no one seemed to have spotted the way he finessed the opposition at Strasbourg. "We're not done for yet," he said, and held a series of long conferences with Peter Morrison, at the end of which they'd both go away grinning like two cats who'd been at the baby's bottle. No doubt about it: he was in the pink. And then a few days ago his brother Alfred died—but he took that in his stride. "I've hardly seen him in twenty years," he told me; "silly, boring drunk—a good job he can never inherit." And after Alfred's funeral: "That's the last of my brothers and sisters gone," he said; "I've beaten the lot. A pretty poor lot they were, but I'm a long way the oldest, and it's something to have seen them all underground."

" 'And then he settled down again to do his plotting with Peter, and went on as merry as a martlet. The day he died he came into the Ministry at ten, looking fitter than ever. "What have I got on today?" he said. "Lunch with Sir Geoffery Bruce-Cohen, Minister," I told him: "at the Ritz." "Right," he said: "after I've had lunch with the old Shylock I'll just pop over the Park to see Maisie. So don't expect me back till tea-time." But as it happened he was back by half-past three . . . and looking rather dismal. "Lunch go off all right, Minister?" I said. "Lunch went off all right," he said; "the trouble is that *I* didn't go off all right when I went to see Maisie afterwards. Soft as a fish-cake." "Cheer up, Minister," I said: "we all have our off days." "I was looking forward to it like anything," he said, "all through lunch. But when I got there, I might as well have been made of plasticine." Then the phone went, and it was Peter Morrison wanting him. "Not just now, Carton," he said; "tell him to drop in at four. Now be a good fellow and leave me in peace." So then I left the poor old dear at his desk. Nothing else for it, I thought; he'll get over his depression by and by.

" 'But when I showed Peter in at four'," Detterling

read to Fielding, " 'he was sitting there dead. Peter took over then—called a doctor, rang the solicitor, sent those messages to you in Venice. Congratulations, by the way; I'd no idea you were in line for the title.

" 'You're not the only one to benefit: as you may or may not have heard, they've given the Ministry to Peter. Rather to my surprise he's taken me over along with the rest of it. I never thought he really liked me or trusted me, and I was all ready to pack up and go, but almost the first thing he did after they appointed him was to send for me and ask me to stay on. "I'm going to need you, Carton," he said; "you understand the way we work." Flattering. Or was it? Anyway, I'm still in my old billet, so all's well that ends well, you might say. Except that I miss Cante-loupe so dreadfully. He was often absolutely foul to me, and not a day passed without his telling me I was a fat old fairy, but we were together a very long time and he was such fun to be with. . . .' "

"So Peter's fallen on his feet," Fielding said.

"He was always bound to. But he hasn't had everything his own way lately . . . what with his elder boy gone potty and his land in Norfolk threatened. They're going to develop in that area, I'm told."

"I stayed with him there once, years ago. It was a very . . . seemly place. I wouldn't like it to be spoiled."

"It won't be, now he's Minister of Commerce. Some-where else will just happen to turn out more suitable. Time to go, Fielding."

"Go? Where?"

"This PEN Club party you said there was this evening. I'm still looking for Communists with manuscripts . . . or at least lady novelists with memoirs."

"You're going to go on with all that?"

"Certainly I am. I'm fond of Gregory and I'm fond of publishing," said Detterling, "and I shall have time on my hands. My seat in the Commons is gone and I don't sup-pose being Chairman of Cant-Fun is very hard work."

"You'll be sitting in the House of Lords . . ."

"Not much going on there. Off to the party," said Detterling. "Now Gregory's been dragged home by Isobel, I've got to do the work for us both."

The PEN Club party was being held in the Sala dell' Albergo of the Scuola San Rocco. No sooner had Detterling and Fielding got inside than they were boarded by two lady novelists, one middle-class and the other proletarian. Since they were too young to have written any memoirs worth mentioning, and since their books were already published by Stern & Detterling in any case, Detterling, who was anxious to break new ground, made some effort to circumvent them. But both of them were very excited, in their different ways, by his new title (intelligence of which had speedily run through the conference) and were also covertly fascinated by the celebrity, however meretricious, that had been recently attained by Fielding. So they made a strong frontal movement, trapped Detterling and Fielding firmly underneath Tintoretto's *Ecce Homo*, and settled down (as it seemed to Fielding) to make a night of it.

"Bloody lucky to be having this party here," said the proletarian, who was missing two important front teeth: "half the museums in Venice have been boarded up."

"No staff," said the bourgeois: "museum curators in Italy are wickedly underpaid."

"No cash to pay them, dearie. All drained off into the pockets of the politicians. . . . Tell me, Lord Canteloupe: what does it feel like to be a Marquis?"

"After walking all the way here," said Detterling, "it feels thirsty. If you'd let me get through to the bar—"

"—No need for that," said the bourgeois severely. "The waiters are coming round as quick as they can. In a crush like this it will help everyone if you stand still."

She then began a long lecture to Detterling on the iniquity of hereditary titles, while her colleague told Fielding all about her next novel, which was to contain several blow-by-blow descriptions of intercourse between an agricultural labourer and his nine-year-old daughter.

At long last, a waiter proffered a tray of tiny glasses of highly coloured liquids.

"John Collins?" suggested Detterling. The waiter shook his head malevolently. "Gin and tonic? Vodka and lime? Whisky-soda?"

"You'd better settle for Martini Rosso," said the prole,

taking a glass and passing it to Detterling; "the rest are poison."

She passed another to Fielding, who accepted it glumly.

"Attaboy," she said: "there's Sydney Offal. You know Syd?"

"No."

"Syd's a yank. Longest prick on the conference." She began to enlarge on the theme, breathily, while the bourgeois ordered Detterling to renounce his peerage, on the subject of which she was clearly manic. Detterling let his eyes wander, in search of discontented Communists or stylish Edwardian ladies, but saw only a scrawny Irish poetess with mauve hair who was straddling a chair and crying while a plump Italian critic gesticulated and pirouetted in front of her.

" . . . And a pair of ghoulies like basket balls," the prole was saying, as Fielding fiddled with his empty, sticky glass and prayed for rescue . . . which suddenly came darting from the region of *Christ before Pilate* in the form of a very young girl, who slid between Fielding and the prole like an eel and coiled herself round Detterling.

"*Lovely* Captain Detterling," she said; "I'm Baby Llewyllyn. I met you last year at Grantchester."

Baby Llewyllyn, Fielding observed, must now be about thirteen; she had gay little breasts, a page boy hair-cut, and long, loose stripling's thighs, about a furlong of which were visible beneath a tartan mini-mini-skirt and above matching tartan knee-socks. Like her mother, Patricia, she was strongly made as an entity yet curiously flabby in parts; the flesh of her thighs, though it looked spare and firm at one moment, could be seen to spread and wobble at the next, as she pressed her length against Detterling's; and the joints of her arms and legs had a quaint, gangling action which recalled her mother's sister, Isobel Stern.

"Poppa's here," she said. "He's just coming over." And then, with hostility, "Who are these people?"

"These ladies are Acarnania Mayling," said Detterling, indicating the bourgeois, "and Jessica Fubs."

"I know about them. Poppa says your books are soft, sticky crap"—to Mayling—"and yours are hot, runny crap"—to Fubs.

"And this gentleman," said Detterling, as Mayling and Fubs withdrew snarling, "is Major Fielding Gray."

"Poppa's spoken of you too," she said.

"So what kind of crap are my books?"

Baby laughed happily.

"He doesn't tell me that, because he says you're an old friend." She prised some of herself off Detterling and clamped it on to Fielding. "He says he *loves* you," she said.

Before Fielding could comment on this remark, which gave him great pleasure, Tom Llewyllyn came up.

"Evening, Canteloupe," he said quite seriously, "evening, Fielding. I hope Baby's behaving herself."

"Magnificently," said Fielding. "She's just routed Fubs and Mayling." Dear God, he thought, you do look old; you're forty-five, as I am, and you look over sixty . . . stooping like a hump-back, wrinkled and scraggy at the neck. "What brings you here, Tom?" he said. "We didn't know you were in Venice."

"We've only just come—and not for this PEN thing, though as I'm a member I thought I'd just drop in this evening. We're having a little holiday, Baby and I."

"I've got poppa all to myself," Baby said.

"Yes," said Tom, begging his two friends with his eyes not to ask where his wife, Patricia, was. "But not for long, poppet." Baby pouted fiercely, but Tom went on firmly, almost sternly, as if determined to make his point clear beyond possible doubt. "Baby must go back to England for school in a few days," he said. "I'm staying on here. I've got a Sabbatical Year from Lancaster, and I've decided to spend it researching into the decline and fall of the Serene Republic."

"Good, oh good," said Fielding, pursing his tiny warped mouth in his gladness. "I'm staying on too."

"Right," said Tom after a pause, as if he had summed and discounted possible objections and was now giving his (slightly reluctant) permission. And then, as if realising that this was niggardly, "Good, Fielding," he said.

He's worried, thought Fielding, lest I might disrupt his life here in some way; he may 'love' me, as Baby says, but he's never really trusted me since I let him down over that Greek affair in 1962. . . . Further speculation along these lines was interrupted by the reappearance of the waiter with the tray.

"Perfectly revolting drinks," said Tom. "Do you think we might go somewhere else and have dinner?"

"There's a buffet," said Baby, who liked to show she was well up with what was going on.

"A cold buffet," said Fielding, "they shuttle the same stuff round from function to function until at last it gets eaten."

"That's settled then," said Detterling, who had decided that the auspices of the evening were against his finding any literary prospect worth waiting for. "I know rather a nice place near the Rialto Bridge. You must all three be the guests of Cant-Fun."

"Cant-Fun?" said Baby.

As they walked to the Rialto Bridge, Detterling explained Cant-Fun to Tom and Baby. Baby took a very intelligent interest.

"So what it comes to," she said, "is that you pretend to the Government that you only live there because you run the Company."

"That's about it."

"But you won't really run it, will you? I mean, I know you're called the Chairman, but there'll be lots of other people doing the real work?"

"There's a Board. Trustees—or that's what they amount to. Solicitors and so on."

"But if they ever turned nasty," said Baby, "they could stop you from being Chairman?"

"Shrewd point," said Fielding.

"We shall be very careful," said Detterling, "that no one nasty gets on to the Board."

"I should hope so. Because when you have a son," said Baby, "you'll want to arrange for him to be Chairman after you die."

"I suppose so. I can't say I've thought of that much."

"But of course you'll want to have a son," said Baby, and squeezed Detterling's hand, "so of course you'll have to have a wife. I think that I should *love* to be Lady Canteloupe."

"I'll bear you in mind."

"I think you're so sexy."

"That'll do, Tullia," said Tom, "you've made your point."

"Tullia?" said Detterling.

"Baby's real name. I use it if she's being silly or childish."

"I wasn't being silly or childish," Baby giggled, "I was being grown up."

Whereupon they arrived at the restaurant. By the time they had surveyed the place and engaged a table (*al fresco*, by the side of the Grand Canal), Baby had dropped the topic of her matrimonial ambitions and redirected her talents and energies to the task of planning her menu.

"Parma ham and melon, tomato soup, ravioli, grilled scampi, and roast veal," said Baby when invited to order.

"Are you sure that will be enough?"

"With pudding and cheese, of course."

While Baby went through her first three courses, the others, who were waiting to begin at the scampi, drank long iced drinks such as had not been provided by the PEN Club and talked of the historical research which Tom was to do in Venice.

"The decline and fall of the Serenissima," said Fielding, "rather a long order?"

"I don't propose myself as the Gibbon of Venice," said Tom. "I merely intend to pick out and analyse certain moral and political mistakes which have from time to time damaged the Republic. For example : Ruskin maintains that in one sense the Republic started to decline very early—as soon, in fact, as it lost the first fine fervour of its primitive Christian faith. Most scholars see this as an absurd exaggeration, and point out that this was just the stage at which Venice started to flourish as a mercantile and imperial power. But I think that Ruskin deserves a certain, admittedly much qualified, support. One result of the falling off in faith which Ruskin so much deplored was that Doge Dandolo was condoned and applauded by his people when he perverted the Fourth Crusade into an expedition for the conquest of Constantinople. Splendid, said all the Venetians : lots of lovely Byzantine loot, large territories won from the Roman Empire of the East—to say nothing of fat fees for shipping the Crusaders where they hadn't intended to go. But in the end what Doge Dandolo really achieved was the laying open of Byzantine territory, not so much to the Venetians, who hadn't enough citizens to administer it, but to the Turks, who were thus enabled to expand in wealth and power until they became the Republic's most ferocious enemy. And so an early failure in morals and religion led, over the centuries, to commercial and strategic disaster."

"It's like poor Mummy always used to say," said Baby, looking up from her soup: "we are 'tied and bound with the chain of our sins'."

Not the least astonishing thing about this observation, Fielding thought, was the way in which Baby referred to her mother as being totally finished and done with, if not indeed actually dead. But once again he saw that Tom's eyes were pleading that nobody should enquire about Patricia, so he coaxed the conversation away from this dangerous area and back to Tom's academic affairs.

"What do they say about this at Lancaster?" he asked. "Are they happy you should spend your time on this subject?"

"I've got a Sabbatical Year," said Tom, "and I'm free to use it as I wish."

"That wouldn't stop Provost Constable giving his opinion."

"He takes the view that since my book on power has been well received, I can safely be left to choose my own subjects for the future."

"A gross *non sequitur*," said Detterling, "but then I never took Constable very seriously. The man has a massive complacency which he deludes himself into thinking of as moral integrity."

"You could be right," said Tom, "but a lot of important people share his delusion. He's to have a Life Peerage very soon."

"From a Conservative Government?"

"Why not? It makes the Tories feel good to create a socialist peer from time to time, and Constable's socialism is safely back in the Attlee vintage. The great point is," said Tom, "that Constable will oppose all modish and egalitarian schemes of education, and will do so the more impressively for speaking from the Labour benches."

"Do you value his approval," said Fielding to Tom, "of your reseach here, I mean?"

"Not particularly . . . though of course it's convenient. The truth is," said Tom, "that I'm not very concerned about my research . . . not just now at any rate. What I'm really after is an excuse to spend a year in Venice."

"Why?"

"Mond," said Tom, "Daniel Mond. You remember him, Fielding?"

"Vividly. What has he got to do with it?"

"He'll be joining me before long, I think."

"I still don't see—"

. . . But further enquiry into this matter was now prevented by a cry of ecstasy from Baby.

"Ooooh, look," she piped, "on the Canal."

A magnificent gondola was coming from the direction of the Rialto Bridge; it was now nearly opposite where they sat and about twenty yards out in the Canal. The immediate comparison which occurred to Fielding was with Cleopatra's barge. From the poop to the cabin the hull of the vessel was ornamented, not indeed with beaten gold, but with an intricate lattice of silver that flashed and sparkled in the evening light and, aided by its broken reflection in the choppy Canal, made the rear half of the gondola seem in some sort to burn, on and into the water. The cabin or *felzo* itself was not of the usual near-rectangular structure, but resembled a tiny tented pavilion, such as a pigmy knight might retire into during a tournament, with a mock battlement from which flew a banner displaying a yellow heraldic beast on a red background. There was one gondolier at bow and one at stern; both of them were dressed in red pantaloons and short, tight tunics quartered in red and yellow. Forward of the pavilion two men were sitting on chairs with high, straight backs; and on a couch in front of them sprawled a pretty, dimpled boy, a Cupid of some seventeen summers, drinking from a goblet. As this tableau was ferried past, one of the seated men raised a hand briefly in the direction of the dinner party, but without turning his head.

"Jesus," said Baby, "that *boy*."

She started to skip along the quay on which they were

sitting, keeping pace with the gondola and waving across at it. "You saw who they were?" said Detterling to Fielding.

"One of them. Max de Freville. The one who waved—if you can call it that. The other was in the shadow of the tent."

"Lykiadopoulos. . . ."

"His partner. . . ."

"And the third, one presumes, is Lykiadopoulos's current boy. Rather a high standard—I agree with Baby. I wonder," said Detterling, "what Max and Lyki are up to in Venice."

"Will Baby be all right?" said Tom, following her with his eyes. "What happens along this quay?"

"Nothing. In about forty yards there's a side canal blocking the way. She'll have to come back here."

"While she's gone," said Tom rather nervously to Detterling, "I want to ask you something. You'll have to go home in a few days, you said just now, to see into Cant-Fun and the rest of it?"

"That's right."

"Can you take Baby back for me and dump her with Isobel in London? She likes you, and I don't want her to travel alone—for obvious reasons, I think. I can't go with her myself, because Daniel Mond may be here at any time, and it's important I should be here to meet him when he arrives."

Why, thought Fielding, who had already been intrigued by Tom's earlier reference to Daniel; why can't Daniel take care of himself for a few hours? But Tom clearly did not intend to say any more of Daniel Mond just now; it was Baby he wished to talk of.

"So if you'd see her to Isobel's," Tom said, "I'd be most grateful. You see, it's not just that she's so precocious, but she's innocent with it. She doesn't realise the sort of . . . unpleasantness . . . which she might get into if she carries on as she does."

"Don't worry," said Detterling, "I'll take her back for you."

"Thank you," said Tom.

He looked along the quayside. Under a lamp at the end of it, Baby was to be seen hitched up over a parapet, showing a pert little bum and exiguous knickers, and craning down what must be the side canal of which Detterling had spoken.

"I don't know," said Tom, "*why* she's like she is. Isobel was a bit the same when she was young, all flirty and knowing, but not . . . not so *radical* about it as Baby seems to be. Mind you, Canteloupe, she's much better than she was a year ago when you last met her, but she's still . . . rather a worry."

"So I imagine. What happens when she gets back to England?"

"Isobel will pack her off to school. It's a special sort of school which I found out about after Patricia—that is, after we decided Baby ought to go away. We were lucky to find a suitable place for her, for Baby, I mean." Tom, thought Fielding, has rather lost his grip over all this. "They have ways," Tom said uncertainly, "of calming them down."

What ways, Fielding longed to ask; and whom, exactly, were they calming down? But Baby was now cantering back along the quay, eager to be at her scampi.

"They went along a little canal up there," she said, helping herself to half a pint of sauce tartare, "and stopped a short way down it, and got out of the gondola on to some steps. That boy has got something the matter with his leg. It makes him limp horribly."

"Sounds like the Palazzo Albani," Detterling said. "I thought it was empty."

"Perhaps they've hired it."

"If so they'll be here for some time. I thought they had their hands full on Corfu. All those hotels they're building there . . . to say nothing of their interest in the Casino."

"The season's almost over on Corfu," Fielding said.

"But if you're building anything in Greece, you stay close and watch as sharp as Argus. Otherwise not one brick goes on to another. Lyki knows that even if Max doesn't."

"I think," said Baby brightly, "that that boy belongs to one of the gentlemen."

"That's my guess too," said Detterling. "Mr Lykiadopoulos has a tooth for boys like that."

"Which of them is Mr Lykiadopoulos? The straight one or the small round one?"

"The small round one."

"Yes," said Baby. "He was helping the boy out of the boat. He wouldn't let the gondoliers get near him."

"What happened then?"

"A sort of Major-Domo man came out of a big door. With a lantern. Which wasn't necessary because there was a light over the steps."

"Fantasy," said Tom. "The gondola, the renaissance liveries, the Major-Domo, the lantern . . . sheer fantasy."

"They've both got a streak of it. You should see the tomb Max put up for Angela in the British Cemetery on Corfu. But that's a different kind of fantasy from the pantomime we saw just now; this lot smells of Lyki more than of Max de Freville. Lyki always liked Venice . . . or what he thought was Venice. I wonder," said Detterling, "I wonder what those two are up to."

Detterling's question was to be answered soon enough. The very next morning, at ten o'clock, the telephone rang in his drawing-room and the concierge asked his permission to send up the Signor Max de Freville.

"Morning, Canteloupe," said de Freville as he was shown in, pronouncing the name in the same tone of polite acceptance as Tom had adopted the previous evening. "I knew you'd be staying in the Gritti."

"Good of you to call. When did you and Lyki arrive in Venice?"

"A day or two ago. We only realised you were here when we spotted you and your party last night."

"I gather you've hired the Albani," Detterling said. "Does that flash gondola of yours go with it?"

"That gondola is Lyki's. He had it built to his own specification years ago . . . in 1959, I think, when he was running the Baccarat Bank at the Casino here."

"Tell him it defies the sumptuary laws of the Venetian Republic. The cabin is not of regulation design, and that metal-work all over the hull is an exhibition disallowed even to noblemen."

"Do the sumptuary laws still apply? I thought they went with the last Doge."

"Perhaps they did and perhaps they didn't. But the Venetians are in a very odd mood, Max, and this is no time for conspicuous display by foreigners."

"I'll tell Lyki you said so. But I don't think he'll take any notice. You know what Greeks are, Canteloupe : no tact and no taste."

"Since we're talking of taste and tact, how are you and Lyki getting on with your plans to wreck Corfu?"

A hurt expression appeared on Max de Freville's face. The deep furrow, which dipped from his nostrils to the corners of his mouth, opened like wounds.

"You know I'm trying to play that down," he said morosely. "Angela's always hated what we're doing to the island, and I'm trying to placate her by limiting our operations."

"From what I hear, you're building as many hotels as ever. You've even put one on the beach at Ermones. Nausicaa's beach," said Detterling. "You wouldn't even leave that alone."

"Lyki insisted and I couldn't stop him. But I'll tell you what," said Max de Freville, becoming visibly more cheerful, "that hotel at Ermones may well be the last. Things are falling apart on Corfu. Greek inflation is making nonsense of available capital, and there aren't enough tourists even to fill the hotels that are up already."

"Why so pleased about it, Max? You surely don't want to go broke?"

"I shan't go broke. We've got other investments—including a large share of that film of the Odyssey which was made on Corfu three years back. I'm told it's doing rather well."

"It'll need to—if it's to make up for all your hotels going smash."

"I don't mind being poorer, much poorer," said Max, "if only I can do what Angela wishes—stop Lyki from turning the whole island into a lump of concrete."

"Then stop him," said Detterling, uneasily reflecting that Angela had now been dead for nearly three years.

"It's difficult. In name, he's head of the whole concern—I had to concede that to make the thing workable under Greek law. So if he wants to go on building—which he still does—he can only be stopped, in the end, by lack of cash. Which is just what I'm hoping will happen."

"I see. . . . And so what brings you to Venice?"

"Lyki brings me to Venice. He didn't want to leave me behind on my own, because he's long since rumbled my change of heart and thinks I might deliberately screw things up on Corfu even worse than they are already."

"Then why did he leave the place at all? What brings *Lyki* to Venice?"

"Ah," said Max de Freville, wrinkling his nose part in amusement and part in annoyance, "you may well ask."

"And shall I be answered, Max?"

"I don't see why not, though it isn't for everyone's ears. Keep it under your coronet, Canteloupe, if you please. The long and the short of it all is that we have, or soon will have, a very trying liquidity problem. New projects, as I say, are likely to be postponed or cancelled—and even then, with the present recession what it is, we shall barely have enough to keep afloat. So Lykiadopoulos has been doing some arithmetic, and taking into account the probable rate of inflation from now on, he has concluded that in order to be safe we shall need another million quid in the kitty by next April."

"What's all this to do with Venice?"

"He hopes to find the money here," said Max de Freville. "I mentioned a few minutes back that he ran a Baccarat Bank in Venice in 1959. He made a lot of money then, and he hopes to make even more now. Tomorrow he's going to see the Directors of the Municipal Casino, hoping to persuade them to let him run a full-scale Baccarat Bank from October through to March, with our assets on Corfu as his security."

"Dwindling assets."

"And very rapidly dwindling at that. But although Lyki's worried sick about tomorrow's interview with the Directors, I think he'll have his way with them. Any dish Lyki cooks up has the right smell, and he's a specialist in presentation."

"But surely," said Detterling, "you two own a substantial interest in the Casino on Corfu. Wouldn't it be much easier to set this bank up there?"

"The Casino on Corfu is peanuts. In Venice they still gamble with big money."

"Big enough to bring him in a million?"

"That's what he's hoping."

"And what are your hopes, Max?"

"I shall just watch and wait. If Lyki wins his million, then we shall have enough to safeguard our existing installations. So far, so good: there's no getting rid of the bloody things now they're built, so better they're kept going than rot to pieces. What worries me is the chance that he might win much more than we need to tick over and have cash to spare for his beastly new projects."

"So what you'd like is for him to win enough to keep everything cosy—"

"—Anything up to eleven or twelve hundred thousand—"

"—But no more."

"That's about it."

"Unlikely that he'll win more," said Detterling. "Eleven or twelve hundred thousand is a very long order."

"He'll have six months. The minimum stake for the punters will be very stiff. Big Baccarat Banks are few and far between these days, so this one will attract attention; and there's still a lot of people about with money to lose."

"I get the impression they're no longer interested in losing it. This kind of thing's going out, Max."

"Going, perhaps, but not gone."

"All right. Along come the few remaining big spenders and start betting in maximums. How high is that?"

"Five million lire, if the Directors will allow it. Ten million on special days."

"Three and a half thousand quid, that makes, and seven thousand for festivals. Suppose they get lucky and clean Lykiadopoulos out?"

"They won't do that."

"How can you be sure?"

"I've known Lyki a very long time. However lucky other people get, he always gets luckier."

"That's sheer bravado, Max. Lyki can be broken like anyone else. What happens if he is?"

"We'll see when the time comes."

"You seem very fatalistic about it all."

"Why not? I don't see much future left, Canteloupe, for our kind of people. It's all coming to an end for us. Closing time in the Playgrounds of the West, as somebody once said. But there is just a little while left, and now I'm going to spend the next six months of it in a beautiful palace in the most beautiful city in the world. I'll settle for that—and leave the problems till they come. The chances are there'll be nothing I can do about them anyway."

He smiled at Detterling, who shook his head in deprecation. But Max went on smiling, and gradually a dreamy look—almost, Detterling would have said, a soppy look— spread all over his face.

"But there is one problem," Max went on, "which I shall attend to immediately. The state of this city. I'm going to see what I can do to help the Venice in Peril fund. Angela will like that; the place has always been one of her favourites. I'm going to look around and see what, in my opinion, are the things which most urgently need doing, and then decide which of them, from a practical point of view, *can actually be done*. There's a lot of such things which can't possibly be done because it's too late and the cost's too high; but there's also a lot of quite important jobs which could still be managed, even on the relatively small sums which I can contribute. I shall raise what I can and send it in to the fund, with a special report, recommending where and to what my money would be best applied."

"Why bother?" Detterling drawled. "If the Playgrounds of the West are closing, as you say, and if, in any case, people like you and me are going to be turned out of them, why spend money and effort on their preservation?"

"I want Angela to see that I have tried," said Max in a shrill voice. "I know I shall be beaten in the end, but to please *her*, Canteloupe, I must try. Anyway, I shall need some occupation," he went on, in a somewhat saner tone. "I have no real part to play in Lykiadopoulos's arrangements for this bank."

The telephone rang. Detterling picked up the receiver and listened.

"Very well," he said, and rang off. "Fielding Gray," he said to Max de Freville. "Are you prepared to be civil to him?"

"More or less. Whatever he did to Angela, he's had his punishment. I know she's forgiven him."

"Good," said Detterling evenly. "He's staying in Venice for some time, and now I come to think of it, you might get him to help you conduct this survey of yours. He'd be useful, and it would do him good."

"Has he the right kind of approach? Literary tastes rather than visual, I should have thought."

"At any rate, try him."

"All right, I'll try him. When he gets here, I'll take you both off for a look at the Albani. If he is appreciative . . . in the right way . . . then he could be my man. After all, he's very sensitive—or so Angela's always said."

At the same time that morning as Detterling and Max de Freville were talking in the Gritti, Daniel Mond finished his packing in Lancaster College, Cambridge, and telephoned to engage a taxi to meet him presently at the Porters' Lodge. Everything was in order : he had been granted leave of absence by the Provost; he had informed his bedmaker and said all his goodbyes; he had arranged that someone else should take his tutorials in mathematics when Full Term began; and he had sent a telegram to Tom Llewyllyn in Venice, warning him that he would arrive by the late afternoon train on the next day. Now all that remained was to make sure that he left behind nothing which he would be needing. He carried his suitcase from his bedroom into his sitting-room, and looked carefully round.

It was astonishing, Daniel thought, how little he had acquired, apart from books, since he first came to live in this set in 1953. Twenty years, and all he had achieved by way of decoration was a mediocre print of the college chapel, an eight-day clock (a present from a pupil) which no longer worked, a framed photograph of Tom Llewyllyn and himself standing on the college bridge, and the regimental badge, mounted on a small wooden shield, of the 49th Earl Hamilton's Light Dragoons.

One by one he looked at these. No; nothing he would need. Time to go.

But as he walked towards the door, he halted, put down his case, and returned to look once more at the mounted badge. 'The old skull and coronet,' he muttered to himself, and thought of Corporal-Major Chead and Trooper Lamb and Mugger in the stores; of Giles Glastonbury and Geddes the Squadron barber, of Mick Motley and Captain Fielding Gray. What was it Corpy Chead had said when he gave him that badge years ago? 'You can polish all you want, friend . . . but that skull will keep on grinning.' Yes, that was it. I wonder, he thought, what Corpy Chead is doing now.

Time to go. He put out his hand almost guiltily, took up the wooden shield, and slipped it into the pocket of his jacket. He carried his suitcase outside on to the stairs, closed the inner door, hesitated briefly, and then sported the oak. But did one *sport* it, he thought, when one was going away? Or did one sport it, properly speaking, only when oneself was inside and behind it? In which case, he supposed, when one was going away one merely closed it. In any case at all, his oak was now shut.

He stepped out over the dewy autumn grass by the river, walked slowly up the path which went by the Provost's Lodge and the College Hall, then on to the lawn of the Great Court, and paused by the central statue of the Founder. 'Beate Henrice,' he whispered, 'ora pro nobis', although he did not believe in God. As he walked on, Jacquiz Helmutt came in through the Porters' Lodge. Since Daniel had said goodbye to Jacquiz the previous night, it was rather embarrassing to meet him like this, so he smiled vaguely and made to walk straight on; but Jacquiz confronted him full-face and barred his way.

"Goodbye again, Danny," Jacquiz said. "I hope you'll soon be feeling better."

"Thank you, Jacquiz," said Daniel, the tiny voice grating from his ruined throat.

"Give Tom my best wishes and have a nice rest in Venice. We'll miss you when Full Term starts. Any idea when you'll be back?"

"At God's good pleasure," rasped Daniel thinly, although he did not believe in God.

"Er—well—au revoir," said Jacquiz, and moved away quickly, as if he had suddenly thought of something important which he must do at once.

Time to go.

The Porter on duty was Wilfred, who smiled and waved

at Daniel in his usual friendly way but did not, being a man of rare courtesy, bother Daniel with questions either about his going or his coming back.

"Taxi's ready waiting, sir," said Wilfred. "Want a hand with your case?"

"No, thank you. It's very light."

"Well, sir : cheerio."

"Cheerio, Wilfred," Daniel said.

The taxi was waiting on the college stones outside the Lodge. Had he remembered to pack his thick fawn jersey with the roll collar, the one that Mrs Constable, the Provost's wife, had given him? 'For protection against the fen air,' Elvira Constable had said : 'it's very treacherous.' And so, Daniel thought, was the air in Venice. But there was nothing he could do about the jersey. It would look odd if he opened his case on the stones to find out whether it was inside, and in any event he could not go back for it now.

The Palazzo Albani, as Max de Freville explained to Fielding and Detterling on the way there, was up for hire because Benito Albani and his wife, sole surviving members of the Venetian branch of the Albani dei Conti Monteverdi, had left Venice some years back and gone to live in Siena, where the family had its origins. Not only was the Palazzo for hire, it was also for sale if anyone would buy it; but this was not in the least likely, since the building, while undeniably both curious and attractive, was also sprawling, intricate, unsound, incommodious and exceedingly expensive to maintain. It was, said Max, only through the perverse whim of Lykiadopoulos that they had taken the place; however pleased with it he (Max) might be for antiquarian and aesthetic reasons, it was, from a domestic point of view, at once an extravagance and a nightmare.

Max's judgements, both adverse and favourable, began, to receive illustration from the moment they disembarked from their motor-boat on to the steps of the entrance in the Rio Dolfin. As Baby Llewyllyn had observed the previous evening, there was a lantern over the entrance; but what Baby had not been able to see from a distance was that this was at the centre of a circle formed by seven small projecting stones, which were carved into grotesque but very humorous miniatures of the seven deadly sins.

"How Ruskin would have hated them," said Fielding. "He always deplored the way the Venetians saw vice—as funny instead of wicked."

Max gave Fielding a thoughtful look. The Major-Domo on whom Baby had reported, splendid in wig, yellow coat piped in red, and silk breeches and stockings, opened the door from within and walked backwards, with arms spread daintily, bowing. They were now in a large, crude hall which, Max explained, took up the whole of the ground floor, having been used for many centuries, in accordance with the Venetian custom, as a warehouse. It was now absolutely empty except for one wooden bench.

"Quite uninhabitable," said Max: "cold, damp and hardly any windows. God knows what kind of state the Albani's merchandise got into when it was stored here . . . but of course the water kept much lower then."

"The Albani weren't above trade?" asked Fielding.

"No Venetian has ever been above trade. . . . There's another door at the far end for pedestrians, leading into the Calle Alba, but it's not at all the thing to arrive or leave on foot."

They went up a flight of plain stone stairs, which lacked rail or balusters, along a stone corridor, through a padded door, and into a circular ante-room. The few chairs looked as though they would collapse if an infant sat on them, and the hangings (Fielding noticed) were frankly tatty. There were no windows, only doors, since the ante-room, Max told them, was dead in the centre of the piano nobile and was surrounded on all sides by other rooms, a ceremonial dining-room to the left, kitchens to the rear, and for the rest Max's own sitting-room (which looked out over the Rio Dolfin), his bedroom, bathroom and dressing-room, and a small den in which his man-servant performed the offices of valeting. The guided tour was clearly to be of 'public' rooms only, for Max did not offer to show them his own set but led them straight into the dining-room on the left.

This was spectacular. It ran the whole length (from the

Rio Dolfin to the Calle Alba) of the Palazzo, making a long
rectangle which was broken only by a convex curve, formed
by a segment of the ante-room, in the central portion of the
inner wall. All along this wall were bracketed candelabra,
those on the circumference of the curve being of nine
branches (in tiers of five, three and one) and of sumptuous
design. The doorway (in the centre of the convexity) was
surmounted by a pediment which displayed a frieze of the
deserted Ariadne; Ariadne herself, weeping and rending
her piquant breasts, stood upright from base to apex, while
Theseus' ship was slipping away into the left-hand angle
and Bacchus and his crew were distantly emerging from
the angle on the right. The tale was continued in the pediment which topped the high mantel over the fire-place at
the far end of the room : in this frieze Ariadne and Bacchus
and his entire gang, including the obese Silenus, were involved in a complicated orgy, a great feature of which was
the rapt expression on the face of a leopard who was being
orally pleasured by a pre-pubescent but priapic faun.

"*That*," said Max, "the Albani had to keep covered. By
Dogal decree."

All of this was beguiling enough; but the chief excellence
of the room lay not in the room itself, not in the candelabra
nor in the friezes, nor even in the magnificent black table
that ran on legs carved as gods and heroes for thirty yards
down the middle; it lay in the view which was to be had
from any of the seven windows which were set along the
outer side wall. Framed between thin stone shafts which
supported ogival canopies, they were absolutely plain both
in surface and in substance; and what one saw through
them was this :

On the right a wall, which rose sheer beside the waters
of the Rio Dolfin to a height of twenty feet and was an
immediate continuation of the façade of the Palazzo. To
the left of this wall, an enclosed garden. In the centre of
the garden a gravel path, forming a perfect square and
flanked by rose bushes and statuary; within the square an
unkempt lawn; and at its centre a fountain—a nymph
pouring from an urn, looking sadly at the ground as well
she might, for her urn was dry and no waters ran. Outside and all round the square, a pretty wilderness of shrubs

and tall grasses and trees, ilex and lady-birch, apple and cherry; and through the wilderness little tracks (much overgrown) running to little clearings (now hard to define) in which were garden seats of elegant design and tainted metal. To the left of the garden a wall (on the other side of which, thought Detterling, must run the Calle Alba) matching, in height and texture, the wall which separated the garden from the Rio Dolfin. At the far end of the garden the tall side, masked by trees up to forty feet but above that absolutely blank, of the next building along the Rio.

And there was one thing more of note. On the far side of the formal square path, set well back in the wilderness and surrounded by a cluster of tiny plane trees, stood a round tower. This was perhaps forty feet high, pierced by small but frequent windows, and crowned, like the turret of a French castle, by a cone which bore a weather vane, this being in the shape of a mounted and fully armoured knight, the point of whose lance indicated whence the wind blew to Venice.

"What's that?" Detterling asked of Max de Freville. "A summerhouse?"

"A pleasure pavilion. Supper-room on the ground floor, well-appointed bedroom above it. Built by the same Albani as commissioned the Ariadne friezes. Young Piero—Lyki's boy—wanted to have it for himself when we got here, but Lyki likes his boys under his eye and under the same roof, so he told Piero that the tower wasn't hygienic—no plumbing. Piero said he could use a commode, as they did in the days when it was built, and Lyki said that Piero wasn't living in the slums of Syracuse any more and must forget the filthy habits he learned there, and there was nearly a nasty row. Luckily Piero's a sensible little boy, so in the end he shut up and moved in where Lyki told him—on the third floor of the Palazzo. Lyki's on the second. We'll go on up there now."

"So the tower in the garden is empty," said Fielding, as they walked up the plain stone stairway to a stone corridor on the second floor. "Just as well perhaps. Let the ghosts take their pleasures undisturbed."

Once again, Max gave him a thoughtful look; then he

led the way through a padded door into an ante-room very much the same as the one on the floor beneath.

"Same arrangement all the way up," said Max. "On the right are Lyki's private rooms, and on the left a drawing-room."

Lykiadopoulos, rotund and glossy, came out of a door on their right and bounced up to them as if made of rubber. Although his acquaintance with Detterling and Fielding was very slight, he greeted them with enthusiasm.

"My dear Lord Canteloupe, my dear Major Gray. Welcome to our beautiful house. But there is nothing worth looking at on this floor, we shall go up to see the portraits . . . and you shall meet our Piero."

They mounted a third flight of plain stone steps, went along yet another stone corridor, through yet another padded door, and into a third circular ante-room.

"Piero," called Lykiadopoulos in a high voice, "you may come out, my birdie. Come out and meet our guests."

After a few moments a door in front of them opened and the boy Piero, wearing wide blue trousers and a short yellow jacket of velvet, limped across the ante-room to-wards them.

"You are welcome," he said to Fielding and Detterling in a low, modest voice.

His thin childish face and long dark hair, which swept back over his ears and tapered to a little tail down the back of his neck, reminded Fielding of an acolyte he had once seen in a Beardsley drawing of Venus at her toilette. But unlike the acolyte Piero did not simper or leer or giggle; when introduced to Detterling and Fielding he shook hands very correctly and looked them both gravely and full in the face.

"Your friends will want to see the portraits," he said to Lykiadopoulos, and led the way out of the ante-room and into a chamber identical in shape and dimensions with the dining-room on the first floor. It was absolutely empty, except for a long row of portraits down the inner wall.

"The Albani portraits," said Max de Freville.

"All by mediocre hands," said Lykiadopoulos, "and not valuable, but a complete record of the family, from the man who built the Palazzo down to the man who is hiring it to us today."

"*Simpatici*," Piero said. "They have pleasant looks, have they not?"

Slowly they moved from the fifteenth-century Albani who had founded the Palazzo, past a number of calm and knowing faces, until they came to a picture much larger than the rest, a family group which must have been painted (Fielding reckoned) towards the end of the eighteenth century. Father and mother seated; two small children on the floor in front of them; a boy of about Piero's age, and of somewhat the same grave yet childish cast of countenance, standing behind the mother; a girl perhaps a year older, very fresh in the cheeks, standing behind the father; and, standing behind and between the boy and girl, an alien figure—a young man in his middle twenties, comely enough to look at but conveying with his green eyes and strongly set mouth a definite impression of pride and even arrogance that was wholly lacking in the other persons in the picture or in any of the Albani portraits which Fielding and Detterling had yet seen. For while the Albani faces down the centuries suggested that their owners were given to the quiet and steady pursuit of tasteful and available pleasures, the features of the young man at the rear of the family group indicated an inclination to whim and a readiness to dictate.

"Who's that?" Fielding said. "A stranger in the nest."

"We do not know," said Piero. "The husband and wife are Fernando and Maria Albani. The two little ones are twins, Francesco and Francesca. The girl, the eldest child, was called Euphemia, and the boy, like me, Piero. But the man between them, *bello ma non simpatico*, him we do not know."

"Funny," said Detterling: "he has a look of Canteloupe's dead boy, Muscateer. Mind you, Muscateer had a much kinder face and he was only nineteen when he died; but still, if he'd grown, he might have been rather like that."

"Your memory goes back a long way," said Max. "Canteloupe's boy Muscateer died in 1946."

"I watched him dying," Detterling said.

"Who was this . . . Muscateer?" Piero asked.

Fielding started to explain. Captain Detterling, now Lord Canteloupe, had been a distant cousin of the late Lord Canteloupe, who had had a son called Lord Muscateer, who had died of jaundice while serving his King in India.

"Jaundice," said Piero, as they lagged behind the rest of the party, "what is that? A plague, a fever, such as kills men in hot countries?"

"No. Hepatitis. An illness of the liver . . . hepatico," Fielding hazarded.

This Piero understood.

"One does not die of that," he said.

"Muscateer did."

"In India. . . . Poor Muscateer, so far from his home. Why was he named Muscateer," said Piero, evidently anxious to know, "when his father was named Canteloupe?"

"In England," said Fielding, "the eldest son of an important lord is called by the second of his father's titles."

"I see. And this Captain Detterling, now Lord Canteloupe—has he a son?"

"No. He is not married."

"But when he marries and has a son, that son will be called Muscateer? Because Captain Detterling is Lord Canteloupe, is also Lord Muscateer."

Piero was so pleased at having mastered the principle that Fielding had not the heart to explain why it did not, in the case of Detterling, apply.

"I wish *I* was called Lord Muscateer," Piero went on. He touched Fielding's arm and led the way across the room to the windows which looked down on the garden. "Look," he said: "that tower. That would be my castle. To be called Lord Muscateer and live in a little castle. . . ."

"You live in a very fine Palazzo."

"Yes, but for how long?"

Piero glanced down the room towards Lykiadopoulos, then turned his face to look levelly at Fielding. Fielding, who took the point, gently shrugged his shoulders.

"Mr Lykiadopoulos," said Piero, "is kind but very strict. He would not let me live in the tower. He will not like you and me talking too long now. Come."

Piero and Fielding walked down the room to join

Lykiadopoulos, Detterling and Max in front of the final portrait, that of Benito Albani, absentee owner of the Palazzo. Fielding looked at the typical Albani face: agreeable, sceptical, placid, indicative of a self-indulgent disposition kindly and carefully schooled by its possessor.

"Why did he leave for Siena?" Fielding asked.

"They say," said Max, "that he found Venice no longer to be real. The Albani have always dealt in terms of realities, and Benito was put out when none was left. I'm told he said that living in Venice was like living in a dream, which did not suit him, as dreams cannot be controlled by intelligence."

"A pretty cool lot, these Albani."

"*Ma simpatici*," insisted Piero.

"One can be both."

They all walked down the stone corridor towards the stairs. There was yet another flight going up, and Detterling, who was in the lead, made to ascend this.

"No," said Lykiadopoulos with (Fielding thought) unnecessary earnestness. "There is only the servants' rooms up there. The attics."

Piero looked at Fielding and gave him, for whatever reason, a wide grin. This was the first time Piero had smiled, and on the whole, Fielding felt, he did better not to; he smiled like a whore, venal, insinuating, obscene. But it seemed that Piero knew this himself; for after only a split second the grin disappeared totally and Piero became his grave and modest self again. I wonder, thought Fielding, what he found so funny as to make him forget himself; what can there be up that stairway?

Clearly he was not to find out. For,

"Now you have seen all," said Lykiadopoulos, leading the way quickly down the stone steps. "I have work. Max will telephone for a motor-boat for you." He stopped suddenly and turned, then called up to Piero, who stood uncertainly on the top stair of the flight.

"Do not come down, little one," Lykiadopoulos called. "You will only tire your poor leg. Our guests will forgive you, that you do not see them off. Go to your room."

"When will you take me to the Piazza?"

"This afternoon, this evening. Now go to your room."

Piero lifted a hand, to salute Detterling and Fielding, and limped away down the corridor.

"Nicely mannered boy, that," said Detterling as they all continued their descent.

"Yes. Good morning, Lord Canteloupe, Major Gray." Lykiadopoulos turned down the corridor which led to his own apartments. "You will forgive me that I too do not see you off. There is a lot of work."

"Funny," said Detterling, as Max led him and Fielding on downwards : "he seemed delighted to see us, but now he can't get rid of us too quickly."

"He didn't like it," said Fielding, "when you tried to go up to the attics."

Max twitched slightly at this observation, as if he both resented it and appreciated the acumen behind it.

"It's only," Max said in a cajoling voice, "that he's nervous. He's got a lot on his mind—this interview with the Directors tomorrow, and all the preparations he'll have to make to get his bank set up. When that's all settled, we'll both want to see a lot of you here. We'll give a dinner soon. I'm hoping," he said to Fielding, "to go about Venice these next weeks seeing what a bit of money might do to stop the rot. Canteloupe here thinks you might be interested in helping me."

"Why not? If you can let bygones be bygones, so can I."

"Then you'll hear from me later. But one thing, Fielding. When you come here, do not interest yourself in Piero."

"I suppose I can be civil ?"

"Civil but distant, if you please. Anything else would anger Lyki; he knows your sort. As I say, Lyki's got a lot on his mind just now," said Max de Freville, "and it would be . . . unfortunate . . . if he were to get upset."

When Daniel Mond arrived in Venice the next evening, Tom and Baby met him at the station. Baby kissed Daniel shyly and chastely (for he always had a quietening effect on her) and Tom picked up his suitcase.

"Not much luggage," Baby said.

"Not much need," said Daniel.

But lightly burdened though they were, Tom hired a motor-boat (largely because Baby's conduct on public transport was not always discreet) and from this they disembarked at a quay near the Campo di San Giovanni e San Paolo.

"We're in the Pensione San Paolo," said Tom, "just behind the church."

"I always liked this part of Venice," said Daniel, "even that brute Colleoni."

"I think Colleoni's lovely," said Baby. " 'A brow like Mars to threaten and command'."

"The trouble is," said Tom to Daniel, ignoring Baby's cultural show-off, "that the San Paolo is closing for the winter in a few days. We'll have to look out for something else."

"Anything quiet will do."

They booked Daniel in at the Pensione San Paolo, then returned to the Campo and sat down at a table, in the shadow of Colleoni, for a drink. A few minutes later they were joined by Fielding and Detterling, in accordance with an arrangement made with Fielding by Tom that morning.

'He'll be tired,' Tom had said on the telephone, 'but he'll be glad to see you. Please be very easy with him. And please bring Canteloupe with you.'

'He hardly knows Canteloupe.'

'That's just the point. It'll make it all look more natural and casual than if you come alone.'

'I don't see it.'

'If you come alone,' Tom had said, 'it'll look as if you've come especially as an old friend for a privileged inspection.'

'Tom . . . you're not making much sense.'

'Never mind, Fielding. Just do as I ask.'

And so Fielding had done. But as he arrived with Detterling now, and looked at Daniel, who gave a serene smile of greeting, he wondered, rather crossly and not for the first time, what all this fuss and fiddle-faddle were about. If Daniel wished to join Tom in Venice, why could he not have fixed a definite date and just come, like anybody else? Why had Tom been kept waiting on Daniel's pleasure, uncertain when Daniel would arrive and yet insistent that he must be there to meet him? And why so much solicitude about how and with whom Fielding should present himself to Daniel that evening?

"Canteloupe will take Baby home when he goes," Tom was now explaining to Daniel, "so I can stay put in Venice from now on. We can start looking for digs in a day or two and move into them when Baby leaves."

Daniel nodded. He seemed to take it for granted (Fielding thought) that some such arrangement should have been made about Baby and that from now on Tom should be entirely at his disposal.

"What a pity," said Baby to Detterling, "that we can't go home on a boat. That might take *weeks*."

"Alas," said Detterling courteously, "the world is too much with us." Then to Tom, "What's all this about looking for digs? I thought you were settled."

Tom told him about the closure of the San Paolo.

"This habit of closing places out of season is getting to be an absolute curse," Detterling said. "It means re-engaging the servants every spring—or worse, engaging new servants —so that they don't begin to understand what they're doing until the season's nearly over again."

"I think," said Tom, "that the San Paolo is closing for modernisation."

"Which means there'll be four rooms the size of boot cupboards for every one room they had before."

"Very optimistic," said Fielding, "to spend money modernising a hotel in Venice just now."

"But the fact is," said Baby, who had an eye to essentials, "that it *is* being closed and Poppa must find somewhere else. And just as well, if you ask me. The San Paolo's a real dump. There was a spider dropped out of my shower."

"Speak no ill of the San Paolo," said Tom. "Once, when I was an undergraduate, the owner lent me enough money to feed myself on the way home to England. Currency was very tight in those days, and he knew he couldn't possibly see me or his money again for at least a year."

"If he's an old friend," said Daniel, "he might suggest somewhere for us to go."

"He sold out and vanished years ago," said Tom, "though I still stay there for old times' sake."

"You know," said Detterling, "I think I might have the answer for you."

"Somewhere quiet and moderately priced," said Daniel. "Which will take us for an indefinite period."

"And I must have a table big enough to spread my work on," said Tom.

"And so, one assumes, must Mr Mond."

"Mr Mond," said Daniel, "can do such work as he has on his lap."

"Well, I think I know something," said Detterling. "Something which meets all your conditions and is rather out of the ordinary too. I can't promise, but I can let you know about it for certain in twenty-four hours."

"Very kind, Lord Canteloupe," Daniel murmured.

"The least I can do. The last time you needed my help I rather let you down. In Baden Baden, if you remember?"*

"Very clearly. But I don't know that it was your fault. Anyway, it was a long time ago . . . over twenty years."

"I shall try to do better by you this time," said Detterling. "Please leave it to me."

"It is," said Tom, not looking at Detterling but gazing warily past him at the pedestal of Colleoni's statue, "perhaps more a matter for Daniel and me."

"You can always go somewhere else," said Detterling coolly, "if you don't like the place I hope to arrange."

"What do you hope to arrange?"

"I'd sooner not say until I'm sure I can arrange it."

"Rather odd of you," said Tom in a brittle voice.

A football, kicked by one of a crowd of little boys who were playing in the Campo, bounced into Tom's lap. He stood up and threw it angrily from him, over the rails which guarded Colleoni's plinth. The boys looked at him reproachfully, and one of the eldest began carefully climbing over the rails to retrieve their toy.

"Poor little boy," said Baby annoyingly.

"You shut up."

"Tom," said Daniel, and rested his hand for a second on Tom's shoulder. "I'm rather tired and I'd like to go in and rest."

"Sorry," muttered Tom.

Daniel finished his drink and rose.

"I understand, Lord Canteloupe," he said to Detterling,

*See *The Sabre Squadron* p. 216 and *passim*.

"why you don't want to tell us what you have in mind for us. It's rather special, isn't it, and you don't want us to be disappointed if you can't, after all, arrange for us to go there?"

"That's about it," said Detterling, looking pleased.

"Then kindly go ahead and do your best," said Daniel. "It's very civil of you to offer. If you say it's special—"

"—Out of the ordinary, I said—"

"—Out of the ordinary, then I'm sure we shall like it if we can have it." And to Tom, "It will save us both a lot of trouble."

"Of course," said Tom. "I was being silly. Come on, Tullia. We'll go in now with Daniel."

"I want to stay with Lord Canteloupe," Baby said.

"Go with your father when he asks you," said Detterling levelly.

Baby went. Detterling and Fielding remained sitting tête-à-tête in the Campo. An empty barge passed down the nearby canal in the dusk. The little footballers were suddenly gone. A man and a woman in black crossed the Campo very slowly and went into the entrance of the Scuola San Marco, between the two vast sheets of sacking that hung on scaffolds in front of the façade.

"I'm told that façade has been hidden for nearly a year," said Fielding. "God knows when they'll finish whatever they're doing."

"Pity."

"Yes. Though of course the sacking is not inappropriate, since the Scuola is now a hospital. One always tends to forget that."

"I don't suppose the Venetians forget it."

"No. . . . What did you make of Daniel Mond?"

"A mild man. A peace-maker," Detterling said.

"We certainly needed one just now. I wonder what's got into Tom. His behaviour was most peculiar—like an affronted nanny."

"No doubt it will all be made plain in time. Anyway," said Detterling, "it's none of my business. But I do like Mond, from the little I've seen of him, and that's why I volunteered to make arrangements about their diggings. I've had rather a nice idea."

"What is it, Canteloupe?"

"You'll know as soon as they do . . . if it comes off." Detterling picked up his empty glass and clinked it against another. "Time to get back to the Gritti," he said.

"Why can't you tell me what you're trying to arrange for them?" said Fielding huffily.

"You're getting as prickly as Tom." Detterling paid the waiter who had answered their summons. "I prefer not to discuss my vision—for vision it is—until I have been able to realise it. A very sound rule, Fielding; you, as an artist of sorts, should be able to appreciate that. An unrealised vision is very vulnerable : it is easily spoiled or dirtied, easily reasoned or mocked away. One should keep it secret until one has given it a form solid enough to stand against the malice of time and chance . . . and the human race."

However anxious Detterling might be to guard his vision, he had no choice but to discuss it with those on whose good will he must depend to give it substance. The next morning he went to see Max de Freville and Lykiadopoulos in the Palazzo Albani.

"The word 'Casino'," he began deviously, "has three meanings in this country : an establishment with gaming-rooms; a common brothel; or, in a prior connotation, a 'little house' (diminutive of 'casa') built for the purposes of more or less disreputable private pleasures."

"I dare say," said Max. "What of it?"

"But the pleasures need not necessarily be disreputable," Detterling continued. " 'A little house' could be used to enjoy the pleasures of reflection, scholarship or conversation. Or, indeed, of quiet habitation."

"No doubt. What is the point of this exegesis?"

"The point," said Detterling, "is that you and Lyki possess just such a little house or casino—that tower in your garden; and that I know two people who would thoroughly appreciate it. Should they be allowed to live there, the arrangement would be . . . aesthetically apt."

There was a long silence. Max looked at Detterling with suspicion, as though fearing that he was perpetrating some obscure joke. Lykiadopoulos was poker-faced.

"Who are they?" he said.

"Tom Llewyllyn is here in Venice—you saw him dining

with me the other night. He has been joined by his friend
Daniel Mond, a mathematics don of his college. They are
looking for somewhere to live quietly together during the
winter."

"I know neither of them," said Lykiadopoulos.

"But Max knows Llewyllyn, and I know both. I can
vouch for them. You would be doing more than a kindness;
by installing them in your tower you would, let me repeat,
be creating an aesthetically pleasing scene."

"Not very pleasing for them," said Max. "There is no
running water for a start."

"You have servants who could carry them water. They
would rather like that. It will remind them of their undergraduate days just after the war, when the young gentlemen still had bowls and ewers in their bedrooms."

"And chamber-pots," said Max. "They'd be needing
them too. Where would they empty them? These days one
cannot ask Italian servants to carry full jerries about."

"Ah," said Detterling. "As to *that*, I thought some
chemical device might be installed. I'd gladly pay for it, and
there is plenty of time to have it done. They wouldn't want
to move in till their hotel closes next week."

"Very obliging of them," said Max. "Meals?"

"This part of Venice is full of cafés and restaurants."

"I do not quite understand," said Lykiadopoulos. "What
are they doing here, these two friends of yours?"

"They both have cause to spend the winter in Venice.
Tom Llewyllyn has research to do. As for Mond's reasons,
they have not been told to me and it would be discourteous,
I fancy, to enquire very closely into them; but I think they
are of a kind that might entitle him to consideration."

"Are they poor, that you wish us to lodge them in such
quarters? That tower is for summer pleasure," said
Lykiadopoulos, "not for winter dwelling."

"They are not rich but neither are they poor, and they
could certainly afford a decent hotel for as long as they will
be here. But the thing is," said Detterling, "that they both
have—how shall I put it?—a flavour of the medieval
scholar, or even of the monk, about them. So they will not
mind, in fact they will rather enjoy, a little discomfort, and
in any case they will soon make themselves snug. And then

the cloistered setting . . . a little tower in a walled garden . . . will suit their temperaments. Of all people in the world, they will understand what such a place has to offer."

Lykiadopoulos nodded.

"Very well," he said, "and why not? It will take perhaps a week to arrange that beds and furniture may be placed there, and that this sanitary 'chemical device', for which you say you will pay, may be satisfactorily installed. Tell your friends they may move into our garden casino after one week. And during that week they shall come here to dinner so that I may make their acquaintance first."

"You're sure you want them here?" said Max.

"Not particularly. But I want to stop Piero's hankering. Day after day he is at me, 'why can he not live in that tower?' If it is full of other people, he will know he cannot live there and will be quiet. So that is settled, Max. And now," said Lykiadopoulos, beaming on Detterling, "since we are talking of casinos, I have interesting news. Those responsible for the Municipal Casino here have finally acceded to my request that I run a Baccarat Bank this winter."

"When do you start?"

"When they change over from the Summer Casino, out on the Lido, to their winter premises on the Grand Canal. In just over three weeks."

"On the Grand Canal? It's still the Palazzo Vendramin they use?"

"Oh yes indeed."

"As far as I remember," said Detterling, "the gaming-rooms there are very pretty but rather pokey. Where are they going to fit you in?"

"That is a problem. Hitherto there have been Baccarat Banks only out on the Lido. To accommodate a table for eighteen persons and myself and the croupiers—to say nothing of the spectators—is not easy in the present rooms in the Palazzo Vendramin. So they are to open a new chamber one floor up, and I am to bear one half of the expense."

"I don't see why you should," said Max. "They'll be taking five per cent every time your bank wins a coup, which will amount to a huge sum before the winter's done. The least they can do is fit up a suitable room for you."

"Ah, but I am being very fussy, Max my friend. I am

insisting on the most luxurious fittings, and on special arrangements for the service of food and drink so that my clientele do not have to descend to the bar and buffet below."

"I still think the management should pay. They'll collect the profits from the catering."

"Maybe not all of them," said Lykiadopoulos. "It is one of the many details that have still to be settled. But the important thing is that in principle we are agreed that my bank should commence on October the sixth. Already advertisements are being prepared, and letters will be sent to prominent gamblers on the books of the Casino."

"What one must ask oneself," said Detterling, "is will enough of them come?"

"Why should they not?"

"Venice can be very putting-off in the winter, very damp and bleak—and all the worse now it's positively falling apart. And then there is always the danger of another 1966. But I think your worst enemy," said Detterling, "will be indifference. People just don't seem to go in for persistently high play any more—or at any rate not as persistent and as high as you'll be hoping for. The big games have all dried up in London. The high tables in the French Casinos are very poorly attended, by comparison with ten years ago. Somehow the whole thing seems to be losing its appeal. It is no longer considered amusing to drop really big money at the tables, or not by those that have the big money to drop. The rich, as a breed, are changing: they have become . . . less visible, tighter and more discreet. They've had to, in order to survive."

"And you, Lord Canteloupe," said Lykiadopoulos, "have you become tight and discreet?"

"I always was," said Detterling. "You ask Max. He'll tell you how tightly I used to play in his chemmy games in London back in the fifties. I never risked more than a few hundred the whole evening, and very seldom that. Eh, Max?"

"But you did come and play. Shall you have a go at Lyki's bank when it starts?"

"It would be a pleasure to see you there," said Lykiadopoulos. "The presence of an English marquis on the opening night would do much for the tone and would attract extra customers."

"I might drop in as time goes on," said Detterling. "But not until much later in the winter, and certainly not on the opening night. I've got to go home and look into my new estate. Tight and discreet, you see. I'm flying back to London next week."

"Please tell me exactly when," said Lykiadopoulos. "I want to arrange a day for this dinner your two friends are to come to."

"I'm flying next Wednesday."

"Shall we say Monday for dinner then? The seventeenth. We will make of it a farewell for you, a welcome for your friends, and also a celebration that I am given permission for my Baccarat Bank."

"Can we ask Fielding Gray?" said Max. "I want to talk to him about our inspection of Venice."

"Certainly we can ask him, Max my friend. But I hope you are not preparing to be *too* liberal in your gifts to the fund for preservation."

"Liberal or not," Max answered sharply, "I shall be giving only my own money."

Lykiadopoulos shrugged gently, as if to imply (Detterling thought) that Max's money, as an entity separate from their joint interests, no longer existed. Max coloured.

"My money," he insisted, "or money that I myself have raised for Venice. There must be ways of doing that."

"Most of them are being thoroughly explored by others," said Lykiadopoulos smoothly. He turned to Detterling. "Then that is settled, Lord Canteloupe. Dinner on Monday the seventeenth. You yourself and Major Gray, and your two friends who are to come into our tower. You will kindly engage them for me. Eight o'clock for eight-thirty."

"Just one thing," said Detterling. "Can Tom Llewyllyn bring his daughter?"

"His daughter?"

"The little girl you saw from your gondola the other night. She's called Tullia—usually known as Baby."

"Baby," said Lykiadopoulos in quiet deprecation.

"She ran after us that evening," said Max, "and absolutely goggled into the gondola."

"It was a very intriguing sight," said Detterling, "for a child of her age."

"It was very rude behaviour for a child of any age. Also"—Max glanced at Lykiadopoulos—"I fancy she's rather ... forward ... for hers."

He's trying to ingratiate himself with Lykiadopoulos, Detterling thought : he's trying to make up for that spat about the money by warning Lykiadopoulos that Baby might raise naughty ideas in Piero. Max, thought Detterling, must be very much under Lykiadopoulos's thumb—or even his heel. Aloud he said :

"I'm taking her back to London with me on the Wednesday. We can't just leave her alone on the second last night of her holiday."

"Do you promise that she will be . . . *sage* . . . if she comes?" asked Lykiadopoulos.

"She'll be good," said Detterling. "I'll tell her she's invited as a special treat before she goes home, but that the invitation is conditional on her behaving quietly. She understands that kind of bargain."

"Does she?" said Lykiadopoulos. "I'm told that very few of the young understand bargains these days and even fewer trouble to keep them."

"She'll behave nicely if I ask her to," said Detterling, "for my sake."

In fact he knew very well that Baby, though anxious to please him *ceteris paribus*, could not be relied on to behave nicely for his or anybody's sake. By issuing his guarantee he had put his personal credit with Max and Lykiadopoulos very much at risk. This he had done, not out of affection for Baby, but out of his sense of what was fair and proper : it was neither fair nor proper that any thirteen-year-old girl should be abandoned for a whole evening just at the end of her holidays; therefore Baby must come to this dinner; therefore he, Detterling, was prepared to enter into an undertaking, though he knew it to be imprudent, on her behalf. Whatever happens, he thought grimly, she'll enjoy the party : she's the kind that always does.

Lykiadopoulos, who had been watching Detterling's face, now nodded at him slowly, as if to say that he was privy to Detterling's process of thought, which he respected as a man of feeling but somewhat resented as Baby's future host.

"Very well," he said with courteous reluctance. "Ask Mr Llewyllyn to bring Tullia on the seventeenth. In view of her extreme youth we will dine earlier than I said before. All should come at seven o'clock for seven-thirty. Informal dress. . . ."

". . . So I suppose this will do," said Baby Llewyllyn to Detterling, pulling at her tartan skirt.

"You wouldn't by any chance have something a bit longer?"

"No. My only other one is even shorter. Don't you like seeing my legs?"

"I'm thinking of Mr Lykiadopoulos. He might think that that outfit could, let us say, *confuse* Piero."

"Piero?"

"The boy you saw in the gondola."

"What a pretty name. Why does he limp, that boy?"

"I haven't asked. Come on, we're there."

Detterling and Baby jostled their way off the vaporetto and stood looking up at the façade of San Giorgio Maggiore. Detterling had called on Tom and Daniel earlier that morning, to tell them about the dinner at the Palazzo Albani, and had found Baby kicking her heels in the foyer of the Pensione. Apparently Daniel wasn't feeling well and Tom was busy looking after him; and so Detterling, acting on the same principle as had made him insist that Baby should be asked to Lykiadopoulos's dinner, had volunteered to take her on for the day.

"How lovely," Baby said now. "Thank you for bringing me. I've seen San Giorgio from over the water, of course, but never close to."

"Funny. I should have thought your father would have brought you."

"Oh, Poppa doesn't care for Palladio. He thinks his buildings are smug."

"But you like them?"

"I find them . . . satisfying," Baby said. She took his hand. "Come on," she said, "let's go inside."

She continued to hold his hand as they walked into the

church, but he did not find this embarrassing. She was not up to her tricks, he realised; she was simply being friendly. Perhaps he was beginning to have a good effect on Baby; he certainly hoped so, as he did not want any trouble on the way back to London.

"We must see the Tintorettos," Baby was saying, "in the chancel. At least, most of the work is by Tintoretto, but he was very old when he painted them, so some of his pupils probably had to help."

"You seem to know a lot about it."

"I read it up in the guide book. One should always read the guide book," Baby instructed him, "before going to a place, to prepare oneself, and then again when one gets back, to remind oneself what one has seen and fix it in one's head."

"A very good rule. Did you make it up for yourself?"

"No. Uncle Gregory Stern told me. He often takes me to see things. I think he fancies me."

"Don't talk like that, Tullia," said Detterling, in a tone so sharp that it surprised both of them.

"Why not?" she said, letting go of his hand. "If it's true."

"Because it isn't true, and because in any case it spoils things. You . . . you spoil yourself when you talk like that."

Baby gave Detterling a long and careful look.

"You mean," she said, "that you don't like me when I talk like that. But I've done it before, and you haven't complained. Why start now?"

"Because I didn't care before. That is, I hardly knew you before. I've been thinking," he hurriedly changed the subject, "about that dinner. You'll want to look grown-up."

"Do *you* want me to look grown-up?"

"I think the best thing," said Detterling, evading the question, "will be a trouser suit. That will be very sensible from every point of view."

"I haven't got a trouser suit."

"I'll get you one."

"Thank you," she said coolly. "Now look at these Tintorettos. The guide book says they're best seen from the altar rails."

There was something here that puzzled him, something small and innocuous, yet which offended his sense of logic.

"Tullia," he said, "you haven't got that guide book with you?"

"No, my lord." She laughed and spread her hands, then took one of his again. "Uncle Gregory says one should always leave the guide book at home, because otherwise one will probably lose it somewhere and guide books are very expensive. Uncle Gregory," she said, "is a generous man but mean in small matters. Still, he's quite right about this, because if you bring the book you keep looking at it and not at what you came for."

"But if you haven't got the book with you now, how do you know about these pictures?"

"I told you just now, silly. I read about them before we came, like Uncle Gregory said to do. Now please be quiet and look at them."

"But Baby," he persisted, "you didn't know I was going to bring you to San Giorgio until we left your hotel. So how could you have re—"

"—I knew I would be coming here last night," she said patiently, "though I didn't know it would be with you. So I read all about it before I went to sleep."

"*How* did you know?"

Baby shrugged.

"One does sometimes," she said. "Auntie Isobel says it's the same with her. Now please be quiet, my lord, and let's look at these lovely pictures."

"These pictures, my birdie, you are for ever looking at these pictures," said Lykiadopoulos to Piero, who was gazing at the family group round Fernando and Maria Albani. "They are not well done. This one is one of the worst. By the end of the eighteenth century there were few good artists in Venice, and the man who painted this was not among them."

"I am puzzled, Lykiaki," said Piero. "That young man at the back does not belong. Who is he?"

"You have asked me before, and I have told you : I do not know, and it cannot matter."

"Lord Canteloupe said he was like his cousin Muscateer, who died in India."

"A fancy."

"Lykiaki," said Piero, turning from the family group, "why can I not have that tower—just during the day? I could go there when you are busy."

"What would you do there?"

"I could make it a pleasant place to be in. Arrange it and decorate it . . . if I may have a little money."

"A little money you may have perhaps, my birdie, but you may not have the tower. Others are coming to live there. Two friends of Lord Canteloupe."

Piero glowed with disappointment.

"What friends?"

"Two *professori*. An old acquaintance of Max, called Tom Llewyllyn, an historian, as I think. And a mathematician called Mond."

"Why would two *professori* want to live in that tower?"

"Lord Canteloupe says they will appreciate it."

"So would I . . . appreciate it."

"The matter is settled, Piero. The two *professori* are coming to dinner on Monday, and with them Lord Canteloupe and the writer you have met here with him—Major Gray."

"The man with the wounded face."

"Also a little girl, Mr Llewyllyn's daughter. She was the one who waved at our gondola the other evening."

"Is she coming to live in the tower?"

"She is going back to England, to school. Why do you ask?"

"Because she is a very pretty little girl," said Piero.

"What is that to you?"

"I shall enjoy looking at her."

"Look all you wish, my birdie, and let it stop there . . . unless you would sooner be back in Syracuse than here in Venice."

"What harm can looking do if she is going back to England?"

"None. I tell you, you may look all you wish. But do not touch, Piero *mio*. Little girls are not for touching."

"Why should I want to touch?"

"Because you are hot, you boys from Sicily. But hot boys from Sicily who touch little English misses"—Lykiadopoulos lingered on the words with some relish—"end up in prison."

"I know what you would really like, Lyki *mou*. You would like for me to touch her, and for her to touch me, while you were watching. You would like to see my fingers go into her tight little knickers, and her hand reach to stroke my—"

Lykiadopoulos slapped Piero very hard on one cheek.

"You have sung enough of that song, my birdie. Of course," said Lykiadopoulos calmly, "you are quite right. But we may not think of such things."

"We may think of them, if we may not do them. But I would gladly do that, or anything you wanted, to give you pleasure. I am here to give you pleasure, Lykiaki, and yet you ask nothing of me. All the time I have been with you, many months now, you have asked me to do nothing. What do you wish of me?"

"To be my little lame birdie, that is all. Time was, Piero *mio*, when I would have demanded pleasure from you every day, every night. But now it is enough to know that you are there . . . and to know, also, that you are hot, oh, so hot, but cannot touch anyone else because I will not allow you."

"And yet you say it would give you pleasure to watch me touch someone else. So why do you not do this? You are rich, it is easily arranged, a girl, or another boy if you wish, or a man—"

Once again Lykiadopoulos struck Piero on the cheek.

"I said, enough of that song. These things are not permitted, for they are sin, and though I have sinned myself in the past, I shall sin no more and I shall save you from sinning. Your poor ruined leg shall be a token that you are not for coupling, and that you are bound, by the will of God and by your fear of me, to be forever clean."

After a long silence, Piero said:

"I would sooner love you than fear you."

"Your fear is the expression of your love."

"A sad way of loving."

"The most desperately and deeply felt, the most profound way of all. Only through abiding fear can there be abiding love . . . the love I wish from you."

"Can I not love you just because you have been kind to me?"

"You can love me for that, but not only for that. You

must also fear and obey. And one of the things in which you will obey me is this : you must not sulk because you cannot have the tower, and when these *professori* come to dinner, *caro*, you must show them that they will be most welcome there."

"I shall do my best," said Piero, "since you have asked me."

"My birdie, I have commanded you," Lykiadopoulos replied.

"And so," said Piero to Daniel Mond, "now that you have seen the tower, you will be glad to live in it ?"

"It looked enchanting in the dusk. And Mr Lykiadopoulos has made very handsome arrangements inside it."

"You will be all right with paraffin lamps ?"

"I like them. They remind me of when I was a soldier."

"You, a soldier ?" said Piero dubiously.

"Well, not exactly. But once I spent some days with soldiers on a big manoeuvre. We had paraffin lamps in our tents. They made a small circle of very clear light, I remember, light you could easily read by, but they left the rest of the tent dark and mysterious. And yet one felt completely safe inside the circle . . . as though there were an invisible wall, put there by a magician, to keep out the creatures of the night. It was a very cosy experience."

"I think I know what you mean," Piero said, and started to smile at Daniel. Almost as soon as his smile began, however, he closed his lips sharply to shut it away, as if he had suddenly remembered, Daniel thought, that he had carious teeth or rotten gums which he must on no account reveal. But since he showed his teeth and gums quite unashamedly when he was talking, it could not be these that troubled him. So why, Daniel wondered, is he afraid to smile ?

"Why do you smile ?" Daniel asked.

"I did not smile."

"You were just going to."

"I was thinking . . . in my home in Syracuse we had paraffin lamps because there were no other kind. So I knew what you meant when you said their light made one feel so safe—though of course we longed to be rich and have the electricity."

"You speak English remarkably well, for a boy from Sicily."

Again Piero started to smile and again he clamped his lips shut.

"There you go again. You were just going to smile at me, but you stopped. Did you think I was making fun of you? I meant it. Your English is excellent."

"I have had opportunity since . . . since I knew Mr Lykiadopoulos."

"Good. Then smile."

"No. Why should I?"

"If you don't, I shall think I have offended you. Please smile."

"Very well," said Piero, and smiled. Daniel, despite himself, shrank slightly, and as the others at the table observed the smiling boy, they stopped talking, one by one. A long silence followed, which was at last broken by Baby Llewyllyn.

"Christ," she said, "what's up with you? You look like Lazarus saying 'Hullo there' from his grave."

Up to this stage of the evening, everything had gone smoothly. Tom and Daniel had been shown the tower and were as pleased with it as Detterling had hoped. For Lykiadopoulos had taken trouble and shown taste : each of the two main rooms had been furnished and arranged as a bed-sitting-room for one person; they were well warmed by oil heaters, comfortably carpeted, prettily hung about with pictures and curtains, and immaculately clean. ('This is what I should have wanted to do,' Piero had said aside to Lykiadopoulos, 'but with my own hands.') The chemical sanitation (which came with Detterling's compliments, as promised) had been installed in what had once served as kitchen and pantry to the former dining-room (now to be Daniel's apartment) on the ground floor; Tom would have to walk downstairs from his own room and then through Daniel's in order to come at it, but a certain amount of inconvenience was to be expected of such an establishment, and Tom and Daniel had known each other too long and too well to worry about niceties of privacy. For the rest, hot water would be brought over from the Palazzo every day at 8.30 a.m. and 7 p.m.; baths were to be had on request in Max's bathroom ('Or in mine,' Piero whispered to Daniel); and for meals Tom and Daniel would quite simply go out, proceeding through a door in the garden wall which opened into the Calle Alba. He would give them the key of this door, Lykiadopoulos said, as soon as they moved in—which, it was agreed, they were to do on the Wednesday afternoon, after Detterling had been seen off with Baby. This settled, and certain minor problems, such as the collection of laundry, having been raised and resolved, the party had crossed the garden to the Palazzo ('I wish I could live in that tower, it's so *snug*,' Baby said) and mounted to the dining-room on the first floor for dinner.

A round table had been set for the party's accommodation between the head of the long table and the fire-place, in which there was an extravagant log fire. They dined by the light of candles which had been carefully deployed (Detterling noticed) so as to leave the obscene carving on the pediment above the fireplace in complete darkness, out of respect, no doubt, for the tender years if not the innocence of Miss Tullia Llewyllyn. Baby, seated on the right of Lykiadopoulos, got along very well with him. Modest and composed, looking three years older in her new trouser suit than she did in her tartan outfit, she behaved beautifully and conducted a knowledgeable conversation with her host about the Titians in the Accademia, comparing them with those in the National Gallery in London. In other respects also the dinner had gone on swimmingly. As delicious courses and exquisite wines came and went, Fielding Gray and Max de Freville discussed their forthcoming excursions in Venice; Tom and Detterling discussed Tom's reasearch and the future publishing ventures of Stern and Detterling (Detterling had still not found either a Communist who wished to default or a Senior Lady Novelist with available memoirs); and Daniel had been very contented to talk with Piero of the tower and to try to make out something of the boy's provenance. Later on, conversation had become general, had for a while waxed genial, and had then reverted, without any sense of strain or failure, to the former duologues. Everything, in fact, had been as friendly, as

civilised, as enjoyable as the most dutiful host could hope or
the most exigeant guest require . . . until, that is, Piero began
to smile at Daniel's behest and Baby broke the ensuing
silence by comparing the boy from Syracuse with the risen
Lazarus.

"Or Lazarus rolled into Mary Magdalene," Baby now
emended herself, "if you see what I mean."

They all did; for Piero, as Fielding Gray had noticed on
his previous visit to the Palazzo, smiled like a whore,
a whore, moreover, who was desperate for custom. But
offensive, not to say cruel, as Baby's remark undeniably was,
and embarrassing, even excruciating, as the situation had
suddenly become for Piero, it should not have been beyond
the powers of the six very experienced men who were also
at the table to set matters right. One child carried away by
wine and by her personal success in conversation with her
host, had shown off, gone too far, and in so doing had insulted another child : nothing here surely (thought
Detterling) which a little adult tact and firmness could not
correct. The trouble was that too many adults now applied
themselves, too obviously and too earnestly, to mutually con-
trarious processes of correction.

Daniel, full of guilt at his own clumsy persistence in demanding a smile of Piero and thus initiating the incident,
was the first to try.

"Very odd," he said, "the effects produced by candle-
light. Chiaroscuro can make a nightmare of the most
familiar domestic scene."

This, though somewhat donnish, was not all a bad im-
provisation. All might have been well, had not Tom, much
ashamed as a father, leaned right across the table to Baby
and told her very sharply to apologise; and had not
Lykiadopoulos, much affronted as a lover, said that evil lay
in the eye of the beholder. Max de Freville then added his
quotum to the prevailing distress and anger by observing
that it was nice to see Piero smile 'for a change', as he often
wondered why he never did so. While everyone began to
digest the several injurious implications of this kindly intended remark, Detterling decided on a policy of total
silence and Fielding Gray determined on one of total
candour.

"Don't let's be silly about this," he said. "There's something badly wrong, physical or mental, with every single one of us at this table. I myself have a hideously deformed face, a self-pitying disposition, and a near-absolute addiction to drink. Max is pathologically obsessed with a dead woman, whom he couldn't fuck when she was living; Lykiadopoulos hopes to make money by preying, in the meanest and nastiest way, on the most contemptible failing of his fellow creatures; Daniel talks, or rather croaks, like a sick frog; Canteloupe is callous, cowardly, corrupt and viciously smug; Tom could only ever copulate with his wife when she put on an act like a kitchen maid in heat for the butcher's boy (quick, quick, we can do it under the stairs); and Baby is a greedy and conceited little bitch. So why, in this company," he said to Piero, "it should worry you or anybody else that you happen to smile like a seventy-year-old street walker I cannot begin to imagine."

Having delivered himself of this lot, Fielding rose from the table.

"If you'll all excuse me," he said, "I'll go upstairs and look at those portraits."

"I think I'll come too," said Baby. Her cheeks were shining and she looked very excited.

"Tullia—" Tom began anxiously.

"—She'll come to no harm with me," said Fielding as he made for the door. "These days," he turned to add, "I can't get hard after seven in the evening. Liquor."

"I didn't mean—" Tom began again.

"Yes, you did. That's what the trouble is with the wretched child. You keep thinking she's going to get up to something, and she senses it and starts thinking so herself. It's your thoughts, Tom, which are infecting her. Treat her normal and she'll behave normal." And to Baby, "Come on, then, if you're coming."

"I meant," said Tom, "that in your present mood you may say some more unpleasant things to her. More things like all you've said already."

"In my present mood I shall say only the truth—which is all I've said already. If you don't want her to hear the truth, tell her to sit down."

"Go with him," said Tom to Baby.

"I was going anyway."

She walked down the room to Fielding, who opened the door for her.

"See you all later," she said.

"Well," said Lykiadopoulos after the door had closed, "he's quite a speaker, that Major Gray. He's quite right about my Baccarat Bank, of course : it really is a most despicable proceeding."

Slowly they began to collect themselves while Lykiadopoulos, the perfect host, kept the conversation going by discoursing of the preparations for his despicable Bank.

"Nice looking lot," said Baby to Fielding as they walked down the line of Albani portraits : "fond of a little fun, I'd say."

"You'd be right," said Fielding. They paused before the picture of a sixteenth-century grandee who held a rose in one hand and the lead of his pet monkey in the other. "Expensive fun at that," Fielding added.

"And knew a thing or two about how to get it. But these paintings aren't up to much," Baby said. "That monkey could be made of straw for all the life it's showing."

"The Albani, though they were wealthy and loved pleasure, had a mean streak in them. They liked getting things at a cut rate. In the sixteenth century they could have found a very good portrait painter, but they used this one —Rocco da Malamocco—because he was a distant connection and was prepared to knock off ten per cent."

"Rocco da Malamocco," Baby rhymed. "What a very silly name. How do you know all this?"

"I've been investigating the Albani. There's a very good public library here—the Biblioteca Marciana—full of annals of the city and its families. '*Insignis et iucundus*,' says one chronicler of this fellow in the picture, '*pecuniae tamen cautor* : distinguished and agreeable but sparing of his money'. Another writer calls him '*avarus*', but he was an enemy."

"*Avarus*," said Baby : "grasping?"

"Worse; downright greedy."

"Ah," said Baby, "like me."

She grinned at him and hooked her hand into his arm, propelling him on to the next portrait.

"That was quite a mouthful," said Baby. " 'Greedy and conceited', you called me. Do you really think that?"

"You're certainly greedy for food—"

"—That's because I don't get enough love," she said slyly.

"And you're conceited about your appearance."

"Do you like my trouser suit?"

"I prefer the little-girl get-up."

"You like little girls?"

"Yes."

"Even when they're greedy and conceited?"

"I like looking at them, Baby."

"Good," she said. "I enjoy being looked at. All girls do. There's nothing unnatural about it—though Poppa seems to think so."

"He's afraid that if you overdo your enjoyment, you may run into a nasty spot of trouble."

"I should just run out again, from anything nasty. You know, one thing you said was quite right. If only Poppa wouldn't worry about me, there'd be nothing to worry about. He makes me nervous, though I love him very much. But he doesn't love me all that much, I think, although he fusses; he only brought me to Venice out of a sense of duty, because of Mummy and everything that's happened just lately. I expect you know all about that."

Fielding didn't, having not seen or heard of Patricia Llewyllyn since 1971, and he longed to ask Baby to bring him up to date. But he felt this would be unwise and unkind. Although he had spoken so frankly before her, in the dining-room, about her parents' past relations, that had been in the heat of the moment and he was now inclined to regret it. Baby, for all her apparent sophistication, was very young, and he was beginning to understand what Tom had meant when he claimed that beneath all the tartish antics the child was still innocent. For while Baby knew that people often behaved in an abandoned way and did very peculiar things, she also believed (or so Fielding sensed) that it was all jolly and kindly and pretty, all in delicate shades of pink and cream like a tasteful pornographic painting, that it was soft and giggly, jokey and tickly, in a word, idyllic. Lust (as opposed to mere randiness), dirt, disease and stink—these had no place in Baby's tender little Eden, nor did violence or betrayal, pain or *tristitia.* 'I should just run out again, from anything nasty,' Baby had said. But would she see it coming? Would she start running in time? All in all, Fielding felt, he must be very careful with Baby : not indeed fussy, like Tom, but sympathetic. There was no unsaying what he had said in the dining-room but he was most reluctant, now, to draw Baby into what was evidently, to judge from Tom's reticence about Patricia since he had appeared in Venice, a very perilous area. Perhaps Baby was equally reluctant to enter it, for she was already sailing off on a new bearing.

". . . You know," she was saying breathlessly, "I sometimes think Poppa likes Daniel more than he likes anybody. Not that I mind, but I do feel a bit jealous of them being together in that tower. They'll buy a kettle and give little tea parties, and you'll come and so will Piero, though not Mr Lykiadopoulos or Mr de Freville. And you'll all sit there, waiting hours for the kettle to boil on one of those oil-heaters, talking men's talk as the evening comes down on the garden; and later on you'll wonder where to go out to dinner, and Poppa will wrap up Daniel against the cold when it's time to go, and Piero will be sad because he'll have to have dinner in the Palazzo with Mr Lykiadopoulos instead of coming with all of you, but he'll cheer up when Daniel asks him for tea again the next afternoon. . . . And all the time I shall be hundreds of miles away in England, trying to do my prep or whatever they call it at my new school, but thinking of Venice, thinking of you and Poppa and Daniel and—"

"—Stop enjoying yourself, sweetheart," Fielding said, "and look at this picture." He pointed to the family group round Fernando and Maria. "What do you make of it?"

"Sentimental," said Baby after some thought. "Those two little kids might be made of marshmallow. And really bad anatomy. The girl at the back has got a triangular tit."

"An effect of the draperies, perhaps?"

"Ugly. Bad workmanship. But there is one thing about this picture," Baby said : "that young man at the very back, between the boy and the girl. *He* comes alive all right—the only one that does. And very bad news he was, if you ask me."

"I'd hoped you'd notice him." Fielding stepped in front of Baby to study the group more closely. "The trouble is, I can't find out anything about him. A contemporary gossip-writer describes the picture, but simply refers to the fellow at the back as 'a friend of the family', without naming him. Yet he must have been a very special friend to be included in a family group. Had the Albani adopted him? Or was he some kind of very superior tutor? Or was he the *cicisbeo*?"

"What's a *cicisbeo*?"

"The recognised lover—often in the fullest sense—of a married woman. Sometimes he lived with the family and went everywhere with it. The husband would be complaisant, because he would prefer to go out for his goodies; and so the wife would be very grateful for the *cicisbeo*'s attentions. He had a definite and respected place in society. In the days of arranged marriages, when husband and wife were often totally indifferent to each other, it was a very sensible system."

"Well, this one looks like a bully to me," Baby said. "A bully and possibly a blackmailer as well."

"Someone who'd made his way into the household and couldn't be got rid of?"

"And had them all afraid of him."

"Yes. . . . A *cicisbeo* who had gone rogue on them, perhaps? I'm inclined to think not, though. The convention required that the *cicisbeo* should be more or less of an age with the lady, and this chap is much younger than the Signora Albani."

"That wouldn't have stopped him being her lover."

"It would have stopped him being her acceptable, her *legitimate* lover. In which case he would have been a family scandal. In which case he would hardly have appeared in this picture." Fielding sighed. "I must do more research into it all," he said. "What do you make of the boy? He was called Piero, by the way."

"Dripping wet," said Baby.

"But rather beautiful."

"A little like Mr Lykiadopoulos's Piero—but brought up soft. I'll tell you what :—I want to go to the loo," Baby said. "Where is it?"

"They all have private ones in their own apartments."

"There must be one for guests."

Baby crossed her trousered legs and lifted one foot from the ground, miming urgent need.

"If you went downstairs to the dining-room and asked Max or Mr Lykiadopoulos. . . ."

Baby pouted miserably. "Infra dig," she said, "like a bub at a nursery party."

"I know," said Fielding : "on the next floor up—the top floor—there are the servants' quarters. There's bound to be a loo there, and the servants will still be busy downstairs, so they won't bother you."

"Phew, thanks," gasped Baby and hurried off.

Fielding went on looking at the family group. What was it Lykiadopoulos had said about the top floor? 'Just attics and servants' quarters'—only that. But Piero had found something funny in this remark. So what was up there to amuse him? Perhaps sharp-eyed Baby Llewyllyn would find out . . . a little girl looking for the lavatory, not knowing which door it was. Fielding grinned at the alien in the portrait. "And as for you, you bastard," he said, "I'm going to find you out as well." He stood there, gazing into the narrow green eyes of the unknown young man who was his quarry, and pleasurably wondering, as the minutes ticked away, what was keeping Baby Llewyllyn for so long upstairs.

In the dining-room Lykiadopoulos talked on about his Baccarat Bank.

"There will be two sessions *per diem*," he said, as he poured himself brandy and passed on the bottle. "From half-past four to seven, and from half-past ten to one a.m., giving time for us to go through three shoes in each session, each shoe to be of seven packs. But on the opening day—Saturday, October the sixth—there will be only the later session, a longer one from ten-thirty to two, preceded by a gala dinner for specially invited guests. You're sure," he said to Detterling, "that you wouldn't like to attend?"

"I can't, I'm afraid. I shall be tied up in England."

"I think I can promise that your air fare would be paid—first-class, of course—if you cared to come out just for that weekend."

"Very civil of you," said Detterling, "but I prefer to pay for my own tickets, especially when they're first-class. It makes life simpler, you see. In any case, I shan't be leaving England at all for at least a month."

"Then the opening night will be the poorer without you," Lykiadopoulos deferred gracefully.

"And I shall be the richer without it, I dare say. But I'll try to pop in during the winter, if only for the pleasure of watching you in action."

"In action," said Daniel: "forgive my ignorance, but what does the action in Baccarat consist of?"

Max now gave an account of this, necessarily rather lengthy and provoking little grunts of annoyance from Piero, who interrupted from time to time to protest that the game was merely childish. Daniel, however, being interested in the mathematics that governed games of chance, listened with attention.

"Unless my calculations are at fault," he said when Max had finished, "the odds are slightly but definitely in Mr Lykiadopoulos's favour as the banker."

"Yes," said Max. "The only trouble is that every time Lyki wins a coup, five per cent is deducted from the sum won, there and then, to cover taxes, expenses and the Casino's commission."

"Thus the only party that is sure to win," said Piero, "is the Casino itself. The whole affair is not only despicable, as you said, Lykiaki, it is the merest folly."

"I must be the judge of that."

"But do you not *know* that it is so?" Piero persisted.

"I know that once before, here in Venice, I won several hundred thousand pounds from such a bank. The stakes were much smaller then—"

"—So now you think you will win more. Suppose you have ill luck," said Piero, red in the face with drink and irritation, "suppose God looks down and says, 'Why should that fat Lyki win money, who has so much already, I will make it all go to the other players'."

"That would be very unfair of God, my birdie. The other

players will be no more deserving than I am, and some of them will be much richer."

"But still, it might happen. God enjoys being unfair : he enjoys taking things away from people, even if he only gives them to somebody richer instead. It is the sort of thing that someone who made this horrible world would think to be funny. To those who need he seldom gives, but he takes from all alike—whatever they love most, he takes it. You love most your money, so he will take that. And if he does, it will serve you right."

"You must make up your mind with whom you are so angry : with me, or with God ?"

"With both of you. With God for making a bad world, and with you for making it worse. You have all you need; why not be content with that ?"

"Times are difficult, my dear."

"Not for you," said Piero. "If you would only cease from making Corfu hideous with those hotels, you would still have enough money to be happy. It is those hotels—"

"—I do not wish to discuss them in front of our friends—"

"—It is for those hotels, to keep them going, to build up more, that you have come here like a jackal to scavenge."

"We will not talk of this."

"Shall we not say the truth ? It is those hot—"

"—You are drunk," said Lykiadopoulos, at last losing patience, "you are silly with drink."

"Do not say that." Piero was now suddenly threatened (Tom thought) with such loss of face as would be unbearable by a Sicilian. "I am never drunk."

"You are a little boy, full of ignorance and drink."

"*Do not say that,*" Piero shouted.

"Shall we not say the truth ? The drink is talking from your belly like a devil possessing you."

Piero's face gobbled with fear.

"That is wicked," he yelped, making a sign against the evil eye. "To talk of devils is to raise them."

"See how he babbles," jeered Lykiadopoulos, inviting the rest of the table to join him against Piero, "this brave boy from Sicily who believes in devils."

"So do you," said Piero, recovering his spirit. "I have seen him on his knees," he said to all at the table, "trembling and sweating with terror and begging God to deliver him from the evil one. Upstairs, on the top floor, he has a special—"

"—You be quiet," said Max de Freville. "Be quiet, do you hear?"

"Trembling and sweating," said Piero, pointing to Lykiadopoulos. He thrust his face over the table. "Lykioula *mou*," he spat.

Daniel, who knew that 'oula' was the Greek form of femine diminutive, patted Piero on the hand and croaked,

"That's enough for one evening. Tell your friend you are sorry, then take me upstairs to see the Albani portraits."

There was a long silence.

"I am sorry," said Piero sullenly to Lykiadopoulos.

"No, not like that," said Daniel, "say it as you mean it."

"I am sorry. Lyki, I am sorry."

Lykiadopoulos showed no sign of hearing.

"As your guest," said Daniel, "your guest for the first time, I ask you to accept Piero's apology."

"If he will say he was at fault, he shall be forgiven."

"Go on," said Daniel to Piero.

Silence.

Daniel rose.

"I wish to see those portraits," he said to Piero. "We cannot go until you are forgiven."

"I was at fault," blurted Piero. He bit his lip and started to cry.

"Tears," said Daniel to Lykiadopoulos; "will that do?"

"Tears of sorrow or tears of temper?" said Lykiadopoulos.

"Shame," said Piero.

Lykiadopoulos hesitated.

"Then you may go with Mr Mond," he said.

Daniel bundled Piero across the room and through the door. For the second time that evening Lykiadopoulos started to soothe his guests with suitable discourse, this time (in Detterling's honour) about the state of cricket in Corfu and the success of To Krikit Phestibal in which several notable English clubs had fielded elevens against the islanders earlier that very month.

As soon as Daniel and Piero were on the stone stairs, Piero recovered.

"I have never slept with him," he declared to Daniel.

"I don't care either way about that."

"But I never have. See," he said, as they came to the second floor, "he has his rooms along this corridor here. Mine are above."

When they had mounted to the third floor, Piero led Daniel into the circular ante-room, then through a door at the far end of it and into a bedroom.

"I sleep here, always here," Piero insisted. "I have my own sitting-room on one side of this and my own bathroom on the other." He opened doors into both. "You must come and have baths when you wish—but better that he should not know."

"Then better that I should not come."

"We will see. He is jealous. He wishes to keep me in a prison. That is why he calls me his birdie: he has me in a cage. Not a small one, a big one, with trees and flowers—how do you say?—"

"—An aviary—"

"—An aviary. This palace. A very beautiful aviary; but always, beyond the leaves and the branches, there are iron bars, network—"

"—Netting—"

"—To hold me in. I cannot leave this floor to go down-stairs but he will know it. He will not stop me, but he will know it and perhaps he will follow me. I may go into the garden, but otherwise I may not leave the palace without him."

"He has said so?"

"No. But it is so. When I did once go out by myself, he punished me. I wished to go to the Accademia, for the pictures. Often I asked him to take me, but he was always too busy, so one morning I decided to walk there, though it is not easy for me to walk. When I got there, he was wait-ing with the gondola. 'You are tired, birdie,' he said: 'I have come to take you home.' 'I wish to see the pictures.' 'You are too tired. You shall see them another day with me.' And he made me come back with him. Since then we have not yet been to the Accademia. So instead I look at the portraits here. He is always telling me how bad they are, but never does he take me to see others."

"He has a lot on his mind."

"That Baccarat Bank. Paah. But I should not have spoken as I did. It will do no good, and I shall be punished again."

"He forgave you."

"Perhaps, but he will also punish me. I should not have called him 'Lykioula'. Especially not that."

"If things became really bad, you could always leave him."

"Leave him? Where for?"

"Your home in Sicily."

"He sends money to my family there. They would sooner have the money than have me. It is time we went to see the portraits."

Piero led the way back through the ante-room and into the long salon where the portraits hung. As Piero and Daniel entered, Fielding Gray turned towards them.

"Is Miss Llewyllyn not with you?" asked Piero.

"She went to the loo."

"Loo?"

"Lavatory."

"Which lavatory? There is only mine on this floor, in my bathroom, and she was not there just now."

"I told her to go upstairs. To the servants' quarters."

Piero's eyes opened very wide.

"She should not go up there. I mean, there is no lavatory there."

"No loo in the servants' quarters?"

"No. That is," Piero stammered, "their quarters have been changed. Anyway, there is no . . . no loo up there now."

"Perhaps that explains," said Fielding, looking carefully at Piero, "why she has been gone so long. I expect she's still looking."

Piero's eyes opened yet wider.

"She has been gone a long time?"

"Nearly half an hour."

"*Gesu-Maria*," said Piero. "You are sure she went up-stairs?"

"That's where I told her to go."

"Then I must find her at once. You will excuse me, Mr Mond, Major Gray."

He hobbled off with urgency, leaving the door of the salon open in his haste. His footsteps receded over the parquetry of the ante-room floor, signalling his impediment (clack, pause, clack-clack, pause, clack-clack); the padded door, which led to the passage and the stairway, swung to behind him with a muted thump.

"What do you suppose all that is about?" asked Daniel.

"The top floor here is a sensitive area. They let that out without meaning to when Canteloupe and I were being shown round the other day."

"And so . . . you sent that child up to find out what's there?"

"Yes. She doesn't know it, of course. She's simply look-ing for a loo. Or she *was*," said Fielding with satisfaction.

"You've not forgotten how to use people, I see."

"I'm curious, Danny. I'm curious about a lot of other things as well. About you, for a start. Before you appeared in Venice, Tom was going on as if you were bringing the crown jewels with you. 'I must be here to meet Daniel. No, I don't know when he's coming, but I must be here when he arrives.' You'd have thought he was expecting some kind of Messiah. What's the mystery, Daniel?"

"No mystery, Fielding. I've always wanted to spend some time in Venice, and with things as they are I thought I'd better come now."

"Before the whole bag of tricks sinks into the lagoon?"

"You could put it like that. I've never taken a Sabbatical in twenty years, so the College Council was prepared to release me."

"You've got a Sabbatical Year, then, like Tom?"

"Not exactly. Fellows proceeding on a Sabbatical under-take to do some special research, for which they would not normally have the opportunity, while they are away. I am under no such obligation."

"They've given you a holiday? In return for long service and good conduct?"

"They released me for a while," said Daniel, with an edge of irritation to what was left of his voice, "because they knew—or at least Provost Constable knew—that I wished to go to Venice while Tom was living there."

"Tom puts it the other way round. He said, just the other day, that he was living in Venice because he knew you wished to come here. He chose the Serenissima for his research, he said, as an excuse to sit in Venice and wait for you . . . and then to stay with after you came. Which comes first, Danny : Tom's hen or your egg?"

"Why are you so anxious to know?"

"Because I'm looking for a subject for my next novel. I've been rather . . . rather sterile . . . these last months, and Detterling is anxious to put me to work again. For my own good, he says, and he's probably right. So I'm latching on to anything which I find at all odd, in the hope that it'll give me a start. Your situation and Tom's might give me a very promising start."

"Oh no, Fielding," said Daniel with real pain, "don't put me in another of your books."

"Not you, Daniel. Your *situation*, I said. That's what I'm interested in."

"So was it the last time—with *Operation Apocalypse*— or so you've always pretended. But you were so cruel and false, Fielding : cruel and false to *me*."

"As I've told you before, it wasn't you. It was a character in a fiction : a mere combination of words."

"Sophistry, Fielding. Oh Fielding," said Daniel in a thin, despairing voice, "please don't use me again. Please."

Daniel's fingers twitched along the high silk scarf which protected his throat. He had sounded (Fielding thought) like the last satyr in the forest, piping his scrawny dirge while the Christians felled his shrine to build a church.

"Never mind, Daniel," he said. "I'll not hurt you . . . . But I'd like your opinion on another little mystery, which could be the sort of thing I need."

He took Daniel up to the picture of the Albani family group, and began to explain about the stranger in its midst.

"Miss Llewyllyn," called Piero. "Miss Tullia Llewyllyn?"

The top floor of the Palazzo Albani consisted of a single-

storey penthouse divided by a corridor. On either side of
the corridor were three doors, two of those on Piero's left
being, as he well knew, locked. He opened the only unlocked door on the left and switched on the light: an un-
shaded bulb dangled from the ceiling, showing a room
empty save for an old rocking-chair. Then he tried, one
after the other, the three rooms on his right. Two of them
were stacked with empty crates, trunks and suitcases which
had come to the Palazzo in Lykiadopoulos's elaborate
baggage train. The third was full of toys, abandoned
Albani toys, Piero presumed: two magnificent rocking-
horses, a model railway with scenic background on a wide
shelf all round the walls, a four-foot long replica of an
ocean-going liner (this done with detailed expertise, the
kind of thing he had sometimes seen in the windows of the
more expensive shipping offices in Syracuse), and a collection of military uniforms, built for a child of seven or eight,
which were carefully draped over wickerwork frames in
two ranks of four.

But in all of this there was no sign of Baby Llewyllyn.

"Miss Llewyllyn," he called along the corridor.

If he assumed that Baby was still on the top floor, there
was now only one place where she could be. He limped to
the end of the corridor, opened a door which faced him,
and stepped out on to the palace leads. There was a flat
margin, about twenty yards wide, between the four walls of
the penthouse and a battlement (fifteen feet high and
perforated with narrow Gothic apertures) which rose from
all four sides of the palace roof. Somewhere in that leaded
margin, he thought, he must find Baby.

"Miss Llewyllyn . . . Tullia . . . *Baby*."

"Here," said Baby's voice.

She was peering through one of the apertures which
looked down on to the Rio Dolfin. The opening was taller
than she was and slightly broader. She's had a lot to drink
for a little girl, he thought: she could have fallen
through.

"Come away from there," he said. "What are you doing
on this roof?"

Baby's dim figure turned from the battlement and
skipped across the leads to join him in the strip of light

which was coming through the open door of the penthouse.

"I came out here to widdle," Baby said. "There was nowhere else I could do it."

Piero winced. Although he had not led a sheltered life, he was not used to being addressed by young females in such very direct terms on this particular topic.

"But Major Gray says you've been up here half an hour," he said. "It couldn't have taken you all that time just . . . just to do it."

"Ah," said Baby, "I've been looking at something."

"Looking down at the canal?" asked Piero hopefully.

"Of course not, silly. Or not for long. *You* must know, since you live here. Perhaps you can explain."

She took him by the hand and led him round the corner of the penthouse, down that side of it on which were the two locked rooms. With her free hand she pointed through a window.

"This," she said, "I can understand."

Against the right-hand wall of the room, as seen through the window, was an altar surrounded and surmounted by eikons, which glittered dimly, gold and red and blue, in the light of a sanctuary lamp.

"A shrine," said Baby; "a chapel."

"You should not have seen this. Mr Lykiadopoulos wishes nobody to know of it. Those eikons are very valuable."

"Well, I shan't steal them. I'd like to look at them more closely, though. You haven't got a key to that room?"

"No."

"Well then : come on and tell me about the next thing."

She pulled him along the wall to the next window.

"Now this," she said, "really does need a bit of explaining."

'This' was a sculpture, perhaps a third of life-size, of a fat and lightly clad lady in early middle age. She was reclining under a cupola, propping her leering face up with one arm and reaching with the other to take a wine cup from a tray which was being held out to her by a group of four skinny boys who had hair-styles rather like Piero's. The boys were quite naked : each of them had one hand under the tray and was using the fingers of the other, with a kind of lewd delicacy, to amuse his already rampant genitalia. This interesting tableau was set on a square dais of wood and lit by four pairs of altar candles, each pair being at one corner of the dais.

"You should certainly not have seen this," said Piero. "It is not right."

"Don't be silly. I know what boys do with those things of theirs—Mummy told me years ago. I often wish I had one myself," said Baby; "it looks great fun."

"Mr de Freville would be furious. It is his."

"What is it?"

"This too is a shrine. That sculpture is a copy of the tomb of a dead lady friend of Mr de Freville. The tomb—it is much bigger than this—is in the British Cemetery in Corfu."

"You mean . . . those boys are going on like that in a cemetery?"

"That bit is different. In the cemetery the boys do not have . . . those things of theirs . . . at all."

"How horrid. That," said Baby, "must look really nasty. But this is rather pretty, in a way."

"When he is in Corfu, Mr de Freville goes every day to the tomb. Here in Venice he comes up to this room instead. The candles are always lit. He . . . he talks to the lady," said Piero. "I heard him once, one night when I was up here looking down at the canal. Very late it was, three in the morning. He was talking on and on. I could not hear what he was saying, because the window was closed as it is now, but I could hear his voice because it was all shrill. I came to the window and looked through it. He was kneeling by her side, weeping and babbling in this high funny voice."

"Poor Mr de Freville."

"You must not tell anyone you have been here. You promise?"

"I promise," said Baby, crossing two fingers of her free hand behind her back.

"And now we must go before anybody comes. Mr Lykiadopoulos would not like us to be alone together."

"You're afraid of him?"

"Yes."

"Come on then. Poor Piero," said Baby, as they moved away from the window. "Everyone in this house seems to have problems. I wouldn't wonder if Mr Lykiadopoulos's are worse than anybody's."

They walked down the corridor of the penthouse, Baby being careful to suit her pace to his.

"What a pity," she said. "This wonderful palace, and nothing but misery and worry inside it."

"It will be better, for me at least, now that your father and Mr Mond are coming to the tower."

They started descending the stairs to Piero's floor and the picture gallery. Piero released his hand from Baby's.

"I'm sorry," he said, "but we are nearly back with the others."

In the dining-room the conversation had turned on to Daniel Mond.

"A mathematician, you say," said Max de Freville to Tom. "Distinguished?"

"Not very. Something went wrong with his original line of research and he could never find anything else. I have an impression that he never really tried . . . that he didn't want to find anything because he was afraid lest it might be too dangerous."

"Dangerous?" said Lykiadopoulos.

"It was all before I first knew him," said Tom, "and it's not easy to get him to talk of it. As far as I can make out, he was tipped, back in the early fifties, to be *the* mathematician of his generation. He was a pupil of Dirange's, his research was brilliant, so they say—"

"But you've just told us it went wrong," said Max.

"Not in the sense that he failed. He succeeded all too well. It turned out that what he had discovered was not just a new operation in pure mathematics, as he had thought; it was something which, potentially at least, had a disastrous application to practical physics."

"A bigger and better nuclear bang?"

*"Something of the kind, but far worse. Daniel, it seems, deciphered a mathematical notation which had been in-

*See *The Sabre Squadron*, pp. 8 to 12 and *passim*.

vented by a German called Dortmund. Dortmund had died without explaining it to anyone, and for years nobody could crack the code, so eventually Daniel, the young white hope, was put on by Professor Dirange to get to the bottom of it. Now Daniel, as I say, had assumed that it was all to do with some new theorem of pure mathematics. But it wasn't. What Dortmund had discovered, and Daniel now uncovered, was a method of examining the behaviour of particles at any given moment in their existence . . . of examining this behaviour so minutely that he was on the way to revealing what power ultimately held all particles, and therefore all matter, together."

"And so also on the way to revealing what could pull it apart?"

"Yes. Enormous forces, far greater than those released in any nuclear explosion, were involved. For Daniel had come close to finding what it is that binds the entire universe. At this stage, certain people guessed, more or less, what he was on to, and put him under pressure to show them the new method. It was his patriotic duty, they said. On the contrary, he said, it was his duty to humanity to keep silent. And keep silent he did, though he half-killed himself— quite literally—in order to do so. I don't know the details —none of his friends does. But I know something horrible happened to his throat, which is why he speaks as he does. . . . So that is what went wrong with Daniel's research, and why he never had the heart to take up anything else. He came back to Lancaster, after it was all over, and settled down simply to teach conventional mathematics in conventional areas. And that is all he has done in the last twenty years."

"With nothing to show for it," said Max, "when he might have made history."

"Or perhaps unmade it altogether," said Detterling. "His predicament was hardly enviable. But all that was a long time ago," he went on, his tone glibly recommending that old, unhappy things should be forgot by all right-minded people. "Whatever may or may not have happened then, he looks a contented man to me now. Any man who succeeds in being contented," he said to Max, "is quite successful enough. No need to make history."

"He has been a fine teacher," said Tom, "and he has published some useful textbooks for undergraduates. For the rest, he has lived with his friends, and at peace."

"At peace?" said Lykiadopoulos. He turned to Detterling. "Contented, you say? Not entirely, I think. Every now and then his eyes hold great pain. I have only known him since an hour or two, but I have seen this."

"His throat often hurts him," said Tom.

"There is also a different kind of pain. Or perhaps not pain : yearning. For what does he yearn?"

"He wishes," said Tom, "to be able to believe in God."

"Why can he not?" asked Lykiadopoulos.

"Because of his early work. It wasn't only that this work might have been used to tear the world apart. There was another, a different horror lurking at the back of it . . . a kind of metaphysical obscenity. You see, his method—or rather Dortmund's—would have enabled him to take a particle of matter, and then, by minutely investigating its behaviour and the causes of this behaviour, to follow it back through all its career to the beginning of time . . . to analyse what happened at its birth, *i.e.* what happened at the birth of the universe itself. He never tried to do this, or not consciously, because he was afraid. But he thinks part of his mind followed the trail back through time, followed it despite his fear, because one night he had a dream in which he was taken back, step by step, and shown the beginning, the explosion into being, of the universe. *And then he was also shown what had been before the universe.* Just for an instant, before he awoke, he saw what had been before space and time began."

"And what was that?" said Max de Freville. "Some kind of primaeval atom from which the explosion had come?"

"No. Nullity. Nothingness. Not even emptiness, for there was not yet space to be empty. It was like sleep or unconsciousness; total non-existence."

"Which, nevertheless, he could in some sense observe?"

"He . . . conceived it. But how, he asked himself, had existence sprung from nullity? Because if there were total nullity, nothing whatever could have been born in it or emerged from it."

" 'In the beginning was the Word'," quoted Lykiado-poulos.

"There was no Word. He was sure of that. No God, no presence, just nothingness. And yet there had been birth; he himself had just witnessed it. He had seen the explosion, and now he was seeing the nullity which alone had preceded it and out of which, therefore, it must have come."

"God's work," insisted Lykiadopoulos. "What else?"

"No. Not God's work," said Tom. "God's death. For there could only be one explanation, Daniel decided. The nullity which preceded the universe only commenced when there *was* a universe to precede. The explosion which was the birth of the universe had created nullity in retrospect. Before the universe began there *must* have been something, which we may call God. But God, in creating the universe, had destroyed himself—he had become the universe, and so left a blank, a nullity, where he himself had once been."

"But surely," said Max, "if Daniel was privileged to go back before the universe began, he must have found the God, or the Something, that was there before it."

"No. Because although he was allowed back into the past, he was of the universe and therefore went back into the past as it had become since the creation of the universe. Once God had become the universe he could no longer project himself back into the past, for Daniel's benefit, or appear as he had in fact been in that past. God was now the universe; what had been God was now nullity to those allowed back to see it. Or that was how it seemed to Daniel. It was the only way of explaining how total nullity had produced a universe."

"A stupid nightmare," said Lykiadopoulos. "But even if the nightmare was a vision of the truth, Mr Mond can still believe in God, because he says that God became the universe. Therefore the universe is God."

"No. In becoming the universe God abdicated. He destroyed himself *as God*. He turned what he had been, his true self, into nullity and thereby forfeited the Godlike qualities which pertained to him. The universe which he has become is also his grave. He has no control in it or over it. God, as God, is dead."

"Yet we are all bits of him."

"Bits of his corpse. Not of the true God."

"Why did God do it then?" said Detterling. "Why did he commit suicide?"

"Daniel says the only person who could answer that question would be the true God who no longer exists to answer it. It is conceivable," said Tom, "that he got bored with his own perfection."

When Piero and Baby returned together to the portrait gallery, Daniel and Fielding were still standing in front of the Albani family group.

"Ah," said Fielding to Piero, "you found her."

"Yes," said Piero flatly.

"Then should we not," said Daniel, "be getting back to the rest of the party?"

"Hang on a mo," Baby said. "I haven't yet seen all the pictures."

After briefly recharging her memory of the family group, Baby began on the nineteenth-century offerings. Fielding hovered after her. Piero joined Daniel.

"I shall let you know," whispered Piero, "if it is all right for you to come to my rooms. Mr Lykiadopoulos told me to make you welcome, but I am not sure how much I shall be allowed to see you."

"I'm very tired," grated Daniel; "please let us go downstairs." Then, seeing that Piero was hurt by his neglect of the whispered confidence, "If I cannot come here," Daniel managed, "you can always come to the tower."

"If I am allowed . . ."

Daniel took hold, rather heavily, of Piero's arm. As they began to move towards the door, Piero staggered slightly on his bad leg.

"I am sorry," he said; "please do not let go." He looked nervously back at Fielding and Baby. "You will be coming now?" he called.

"In a minute," Baby carolled. "He's scared," she said to Fielding, "that I might go upstairs again. Or show you what's there."

"What is there?"

"I shan't tell you. I promised Piero not. And besides,"

she teased, "it was mean of you to tell me there was a loo up there."

"Wasn't there?"

"No. I had to go out on the roof."

"So one can get on to the roof, can one? What else did you find out?"

"That Piero is a very polite, kind boy, and he's afraid of Mr Lykiadopoulos, who is very religious. That Mr de Freville is very sad about a lady who died a while ago, and comes and talks to her statue. There," said Baby: "I haven't actually broken my promise, have I? Anyway, I had my fingers crossed."

"I knew that lady," Fielding said.

"She's the one you mentioned downstairs? The one he couldn't fuck when she was alive, you said. Why couldn't he? Your turn to tell me something."

"I think he liked her too much," Fielding speculated. "He knew that if he fucked her it would be different, and he wanted it to stay the same. He—"

—Clack, pause, clack-clack, pause, clack-clack. Piero coming back along the corridor to move them on.

"Go on," said Baby.

"He didn't want to try to have too much," said Fielding. "He was right. I loved somebody once, and my mistake . . . my lethal mistake . . . was to try to have too much."

"Quick, Major Gray," came Piero's voice down the gallery. "Quick, to the stairs. There is something wrong with Mr Mond."

Daniel was in the pine forest near the Warlocks' Grotto, where he knew he must meet Captain Fielding Gray and his driver, Trooper Lamb. They were to picnic in the Grotto, near Dortmund's grave. Fielding and Lamb were driving up the track (with the picnic hamper) in Fielding's land-rover, but Daniel had chosen to walk up the hill through the trees.

But now he could not find the way. The trees were in circle upon circle around him, all evenly spaced, and in the gap between any two of them another stood sentinel just behind, so that after a few yards their ranks were impenetrable by the eye and for all Daniel knew they might spread away to the end of the world. His only hope was to pick the right direction in which to make for the Warlocks' Grotto, where he would find food and wine and Michael Lamb and Fielding Gray.

'Fielding,' he called.

But the trees would not let his voice through any more than they would let his eye.

'Oh, Fielding....'

And now he could hear the howling of the dogs, still distant but nearer every second. Which way should he run? If he could hear the dogs, surely Fielding could hear him.

'*Fielding.*'

But he knew he was not heard, or not by Fielding.

Daniel ran. At first he thought he was running away from the howling of the dogs, but soon he realised that the howling was all round him, filling his ears, his head, his throat with noise and pain.

'Fielding, oh Fielding,' he sobbed, 'why did you let me come alone?'

He sank down towards the soft floor of pine needles. He would lie here till the dogs came. But even this brief comfort was denied him, because the floor of the forest was as hard and cold as stone.

'Oh, Fielding,' he moaned.

"I'm here, Danny," said Fielding. "Help me get him down the stairs"—this to Piero. And to Baby Llewyllyn, "Tell someone to ring for a doctor."

"You shouldn't move him," Baby said.

"I'm all right," said Daniel. "Just one of my spells. No doctor, please. I'll just stay here a moment, and then we can go on down." His face was running with sweat and his colour was grey-green. "No fuss," he croaked; "but ask them to have a boat ready so that I can go home."

Baby went on down to deliver the message. Piero squatted on the stairs behind Daniel and began to massage his neck, one hand resting lightly on each shoulder, the thumbs working from the shoulder-blades to the top of the spine and then round to the ears.

"Daniel," Piero said; "Daniele."

Slowly the colour came back into Daniel's cheeks.

"Daniele. Oh, Daniel. Daniele."

Ten minutes later the dinner guests were embarked from the Palazzo Albani and were waved on their way by Lykiadopoulos and Max de Freville, though not by Piero, who retreated to his rooms as soon as the boat was announced. They got Daniel back to the Pensione San Paolo without any further trouble and saw him to bed. Then they went to Tom's room for a night-cap. Baby served the drinks from Tom's dressing-table : whisky for the grown-ups, cola for herself.

"Daniel likes that tower," said Tom. "Good."

"Piero will be good for Daniel," said Fielding.

"And Daniel will be good for Piero," said Baby. "Piero is afraid of Mr Lykiadopoulos. Daniel will protect him."

"Tell them what you told me," said Fielding to Baby, "about when you went to the loo."

Baby told them. She did not tell them exactly what she had seen, because, as she explained, she did not want to break faith with Piero. But she had had her fingers crossed, and so she might tell them as much as she had already told Fielding.

"Yes," said Detterling when Baby had finished, "Lykia-dopoulos has always been pious on the side, and Max's thing about poor Angela is obviously getting worse and worse. When I saw him in Corfu last year he was only visit-ing her grave. But now it seems he tries to cart her about with him. A statue, you say ?" he said to Baby.

"A small one," said Baby. "I don't think Piero would like me to say more. Nor would Mr de Freville."

"Thank you, Tullia," said Tom, "that was all very in-teresting. Now say goodnight."

"Must I ?" Baby wheedled.

"Yes," said Detterling.

Baby kissed her father on the lips and Detterling on his cheek. As she came towards Fielding Gray, he held out his hand for her to shake, thinking that she would not want to kiss a face like his. But she ignored his hand and kissed, not indeed his face, but his hair.

"Nice hair," Baby murmured, and quietly left the room.

"Baby did well at dinner," said Detterling. "Kept her end up with Lyki. A pity about that gaffe with the boy, but he seems to have forgiven her, telling her all that about Lyki and Max. You tore us all off a pretty fierce strip," he said to Fielding.

"I was sick of all that pussy-footing. No one saying what he meant. I had a whole lot more of it from Daniel later on."

"Don't you bully Daniel," said Tom.

"I wasn't. I was just asking him a few questions—about why he's come to Venice and so on. He was as sly and shifty as a sewer rat."

"Your enquiries were impertinent."

"Why?"

"Fielding," said Tom, "can't you see that Daniel is vulnerable? That attack he had tonight before we came home—"

"—He's always had attacks of one kind and another ever since I've known him—even before that business with his throat. He was always being sick or turning green or starting to cry or—"

"—Fielding. Are you so totally dedicated to yourself that you notice nothing at all about other people?"

"I notice what they tell me. Daniel said it was 'just one of his spells', not to fuss. No point in calling a doctor, he said."

"No, none. You see, Fielding, every now and then his throat hurts him so much that he faints, as he did tonight. Nothing a doctor can do. He has a drug to deaden the pain, but he takes it as seldom as possible because it makes him— well—peculiar, inconsequent, and he prefers to be of the company, to understand what's going on. So he delays taking his drug for as long as he can, and then the pain comes at him."

"Well, I'm very sorry to hear it."

"You must hear more. What have you noticed of Daniel's . . . demeanour . . . since we have been here?"

"Whatever this pain in his throat, he looks pretty contented most of the time. Sometimes he seems quite fatuous with content, positively gorged with it."

"Yes. That is the effect of the drug. If he gets the dose just right, he is in a comfortable, drowsy state but fully able to follow conversations and so on. Contented. But if he has taken too much, or if he has only just taken it, he is what you call gorged or fatuous and I should call vague or withdrawn. That is what he is anxious to avoid."

"Will his throat ever get better?" Detterling asked. "I should have thought Venice was the last place to bring it. All this damp. This bad, marshy air. Polluted too, these days."

"He wanted to come to Venice for the peace."

"That I understood. That's what made me think of that tower for him. But in the circumstances, is Venice wise?"

"It's what he wants," said Tom. "That is why I arranged to spend the winter here. So that when he came, there should be somebody here to take care of him."

"If you want to do that," said Fielding, "get him out of Venice. Canteloupe's obviously right."

"Where should I take him? Venice or Cambridge are the only places he wishes to be, and he cannot stay in Cambridge for fear of embarrassing them. While he is taking this drug, he cannot be relied on to teach effectively."

"Anyway," said Fielding, "Cambridge and the fens are just as bad for throats. For heaven's sake, Tom, take him somewhere suitable. Up in the mountains, perhaps . . . or somewhere warm. The doctors must know what would be best."

"They say Venice is best, because it is what he wants. When a man must be dead in a few months," said Tom, "you no longer bother about giving him healthy air. If you love him, you give him what he wants."

PART TWO

WINTER QUARTERS

A sad tale's best for winter.
I have one of sprites and goblins.

Shakespeare, *The Winter's Tale*
Act II, Scene i

"GOODBYE, Poppa . . . Daniel . . . Fielding." Baby
Llewyllyn waved at the receding group on the steps of the
Gritti. The three men in the group waved back and turned
away. "Goodbye," called Baby, and choked ominously.

"Come and sit down," said Detterling, and led her into
the cabin of the motor-boat which he had engaged to
carry them across the lagoon to the airport. "There," he
said : "don't cry, or you'll have me starting."

"I can't imagine you crying," snuffled Baby, and
managed a smile.

"I do from time to time, I assure you. Heigh-ho," he
sighed after a pause, "goodbye to Venice, and nothing
achieved."

"What did you hope to achieve?"

"I was meant to be looking for authors. Renegade reds at
the PEN conference, or old ladies who were tickled in their
cots by Henry James. But I've been too frivolous to find
any."

"You haven't been frivolous at all. It's just that too much
else was going on. Your being made a lord so suddenly, and
then that gang at the Palazzo, and getting that tower for
Poppa and Daniel."

As they passed the cemetery island of San Michele, they

watched some men in black unload a coffin from a funeral
barge on to the landing stage.

"Tricky work," said Detterling; "they wouldn't want to
drop it in the water."

"That reminds me," Baby said. "That lady Mr de Freville used to be so fond of. Angela . . . ?"

". . . Angela Tuck."

"You said, and Piero said, that he goes to her grave on
Corfu to tell her things. What sort of things, do you think?"

"He's unhappy because Lykiadopoulos makes him do
things she wouldn't have liked. Putting up ugly buildings
near beaches, cutting down trees for roads and car
parks. . . ."

"Why doesn't he stop Mr Lykiadopoulos?"

"He can't. Mr Lykiadopoulos is stronger."

They passed an islet on which was a tumble-down farmhouse and a few acres of reed and wild grasses. A boat-
house sprawled down a mud embankment and into the
lagoon, the waters of which filled it to within a few feet of
the roof.

"I should like to live there," said Baby; "on that little
island, in the farmhouse. In a way, it would be rather like
living in that tower in the Palazzo garden."

"I know what you mean."

"It was kind of Mr Lykiadopoulos to let Poppa live there
with Daniel. But I do not like Mr Lykiadopoulos. He won't
do any harm to Poppa or Daniel, I think, but he is bad for
Piero and Mr de Freville. And it may be," said Baby, "that
he is bad for you."

"What harm can he do me? I shall be in London?"

"But you'll be coming back to Venice," said Baby. "You'll
be coming back to make sure Daniel is all right in that
tower."

"Perhaps, yes."

"Then please be careful, my lord, of Mr Lykiadopoulos."

"You don't have to call me 'my lord'. In fact you
shouldn't."

"I like to. Sometimes it's a joke; sometimes it's because I
like to. You *will* be careful of Mr Lykiadopoulos?"

"You mean . . . I ought to steer clear of his Baccarat
Bank?"

"No," said Baby, "I don't think it's exactly that. It's another danger."

"Danger?"

"It isn't clear. It's still some way off, you see." A gondola nosed out of the tall reeds to their left; a man in a grey cap sat fishing from it. Baby came close to Detterling. "It isn't clear," she repeated, "but it's there."

"Thank you for letting me know."

"Don't make fun."

"I wasn't making fun."

For a while they sat in silence as the motor-boat swished along a channel through the reed beds. Then Baby said:

"Poppa will be with Daniel. Uncle Gregory and Auntie Isobel will be kind to me, of course. But . . . ?"

". . . Yes. I shall come."

"Often?"

"If you wish it."

"If you please, my lord," Baby said.

"I do hope Baby's going to be all right at this school," said Detterling to Gregory and Isobel Stern in their house in Chelsea.

They had all had a delicious dinner cooked by Isobel, after which Baby, worn out with flying and with eating, had voluntarily retired to bed.

"She's got to go somewhere," said Isobel gloomily, "what with Tom off in Venice and Patricia . . . well . . . permanently out of the way."

"What exactly happened about Patricia?" asked Detterling. "I was in the East when she was taken off, on my mission for poor old Canteloupe. I never heard the full story."

"Boys, my dear," said Gregory: "young ones. Lots and lots of young boys."

"But surely, you don't have a woman put away . . . 'permanently' . . . just because she likes boys?"

Since neither Isobel not Gregory seemed eager to answer, Detterling now began to approach the question from another angle.

"Fielding Gray said something rather curious in Venice the other day," he told them. "He said Tom liked Patricia

to behave like 'a kitchen-maid in heat'—that it was only any
good for Tom if she did behave like that."

"She got to like it too," said Isobel flatly. "Then Tom
stopped liking it—or anything else in that line, so I gather—
about six or seven years ago. He left her high and dry. Or
rather, high and wet."

"Oh Isobel my wife, such a vulgar thing to say of your
own sister."

"Go on, Isobel," said Detterling.

But once again reluctance prevailed, and once again
Detterling was compelled to abandon the direct approach
and come crawling in from the flank.

"Well, how was it," he said, "that Fielding Gray knew
all about the 'kitchen-maid' bit? He's a very old friend of
Tom's, but I can hardly think Tom told him."

"Patty told him," said Isobel. "They had an affair together."

"I never knew that."

"Even you, Canteloupe, do not know everything,"
Gregory said.

"It was in the summer of 'seventy-one," said Isobel;
"they had a nice little bunk-up down at Broughton Staithe."

Clearly, thought Detterling, Isobel had little objection to
talking about her sister's peculiarities or infidelities *as such*;
it was only about this business of the 'boys' that she was
reticent. Well, let her get on at her own pace, he thought;
she'll have to come to it in time.

"Tom was at some conference of history dons," Isobel
was saying, "and Patty took Baby to Broughton for the sea
air. Fielding was alone in his house there (it was long after
Harriet had pushed off) writing his book on Conrad. And
then one day he met Patricia and Baby as they were trail-
ing across the golf links to the beach. Up till then they'd
hardly known each other, and Patricia hadn't even register-
ed that Fielding lived at Broughton—or so she told me later,
and I believe it. But now . . . well, they took one look at each
other over Baby's head, and what they both read in the
other's face was, 'God, I need some sex and you'll just
about do for it.' They didn't need to say anything explicit,
they couldn't in front of Baby; they simply exchanged a few
vapidities, in the course of which he mentioned where his

house was. So that evening, after Baby was in bed in their lodgings, Patricia tramped along the lane to Fielding's house, and two whiskies and fifteen minutes later he was riding her past the post for the first time. She couldn't stay long because her landlady locked up at eleven—typical of Patty, to be too mean to stay in a proper hotel—but that suited Fielding down to the ground. He didn't want a lump like her in his bed half the night—she knew that well enough for herself, she told me; which was another thing typical of Patty—she was dead honest when you came down to it. So it was hot, quick, sloshy short-timers every evening for the ten days she was in Broughton, and when, after a week or so, he didn't come up to scratch too easily, she used to excite him by telling him about what she did with Tom—or *had* done with Tom before he gave out on her some years before. And on the last night, when that no longer worked, she told him about some horny undergraduate she'd had it off with a time or two. . . ."

Isobel paused, but now that she was well into her narrative she was bound, as Detterling had foreseen, to continue, Just as a driver, who has many excellent reasons for stopping the car, nevertheless finds himself compelled to drive on, despite his hunger for lunch, despite the squeals of the children who are clutching their parts in the back, until he comes to the ideal place to halt; so Isobel must now keep going, whatever her misgivings, until she reached the only destination that was fully appropriate—the end of Patricia's story.

"So when Patricia went back to Grantchester," Isobel went on, "they said goodbye and thank you, and that, one might have thought, was that. No harm done, quite the reverse. Both of them much the better for it . . . but neither of them likely to go trekking all across Norfolk and Cambridgeshire for another helping. It had been very convenient, and now it was over. The trouble was, it wasn't over with Patricia. Not that she wanted Fielding again, for he was nowhere near being up to her demands; and yet he had not entirely failed her; he had responded, for a time, with just enough skill and enthusiasm and what she called *inspiration* to hint to her how fascinating sex could be, and indeed *would* be, given a man of Fielding's strange and creative sexual

aura who was twenty-five years younger. In short, Fielding
had roused her imagination more than he had pleased her
body. He had made her hunger for someone who must certainly be younger and stronger and far more beautiful than
he but must *also* have his—Fielding's—uncanny talent for
investing sexual activity with a new and enchanted atmos-
phere. This she found hard to describe, but it seems to have
been a feeling she had with him that she was taking part in
something insidious and forbidden, not just ordinary
mutual pleasuring or copulation, but something deliciously
and magically perverse, like a mythical piece of metamorphosis or incest, which was at the same time both unnatural
and paradisial. With Fielding, however, this feeling never
anything like reached the heights (or depths) she thought
it could have reached, because his physical performance was
so lax. Where was she to find someone who was both
physically proficient *and* endowed with Fielding's brand of
sorcery?

"Now, I've already told you that in order to excite Fielding, to get him going when he was bored with her, she'd
reminisced about her goings-on with an undergraduate.
He'd been gone from Cambridge for some time, this young
man, but now she began to wonder if she shouldn't look for
another one like him, because a clever and sympathetic
undergraduate might be able to provide just this extra
sexual dimension for which she was hankering. The trouble
was, it was rather unfair on Tom to go drumming up young
men on his college doorstep; and anyway she wasn't all that
to look at any more, so she might have a lot of difficulty pulling them in. But she had a really murderous itch on, poor
Patty did, like Pasiphaë for her bull or Phaedra for Hip-
polytus, and somebody young and beautiful she must have
. . . somebody young and beautiful and as enchantingly perverse as Fielding Gray.

"Then she remembered something she'd once heard
about adolescent boys. They're so randy, she'd heard, so full
of fresh juices, that they don't much care what they do or
whom they do it with provided they get a nice feeling at the
end of their pricks. Unlike twenty-year-olds, who are beginning to discriminate, they just want to come as often as
they can and never mind where. That's not saying, of

course, that they'll do it with any old slag who comes up to them—they're too wary for that—but once they know who a person is, and so long as that person behaves pleasantly and is presentable in the broadest sense, they don't at all mind being invited to hang their trousers up to dry when they come in out of the rain and being given a nice long rub down. And then they're pretty to look at, and they can go on and on, and, above all, they're accustomed to take orders at that age and indeed prefer to take them; so that although she could hardly expect them to manifest of themselves that weird and arcane *esprit* of which she'd had such tantalising whiffs from Fielding, she knew they would happily comply with whatever she suggested in her pursuit of it. She would have to conjure up the demon herself, but at least a fresh eager boy (provided she didn't frighten him) would give unstinting cooperation."

"And so," said Detterling, "she started spotting out adolescent boys up in London. Since she was a well-mannered upper-class woman, when she chose to be, and quite definitely 'presentable in the broadest sense', they soon came round to her all right. And then, of course, they came round to her London flat."

"Who told you?"

"Jonathan Gamp. Over a year ago. But," said Detterling, "the story was, then, that her little friends were all over sixteen, which made it legal, and though she sometimes asked two or three of them to come along at the same time, she handled them all too discreetly to give rise to scandal."

"She handled them strictly one at a time, if that's what you mean. Apparently group sex wasn't her answer. There was no question of illicit orgies."

"Then why all the bother later on?"

Isobel took a deep breath.

"Have you ever seen that picture by Bronzino in the National Gallery?" she said. "It's called Venus, Cupid and —What's the rest, Gregory? You'd know."

"Venus, Cupid, Folly and Time," Gregory said.

"Apt," said Isobel crisply. "Well, there's a little smirking cherub throwing rose petals about and a horrible old man lowering in the background. Venus is kneeling down among the rose petals, and Cupid is bending over to kiss her. But it isn't going to be just a nice kiss for Mummy, it's going to be something very different, because they're both smiling in that certain way, and Venus is already popping her tongue out, and Cupid is fondling one of her tits. He's about fourteen, Cupid is, and a real dish, with his plump curvy rump sticking out behind him, and his whole body all silky and sexy and taut. You can't see his cock because it's hidden between his thighs, but there's a tiny wisp of dark hair running out which is more suggestive than any penis ever painted. So that's what the cherub is smirking about and the old man is lowering about : Venus and her newly pubescent son are just about to have it away among the rose petals. There's a light, bright, thrilling madness about it all—just the sort of thing, Patricia told me, that she got hints of when she was with Fielding. And as time went on, what she began to want was what was happening in that picture : to frolic among the rose petals, not just with any adolescent boy she managed to pick up, but with her own pubescent son . . . which, as you well know, she has not got.

"Then in 1972 something new started up, something about which she did *not* tell me herself. Baby reported to Gregory on one of their outings that Mummy had taken to having very funny conversations with her, 'telling her things', as Baby put it. After a little probing, it emerged that Patricia, under pretence of telling Baby the facts of life, was describing her own fantasies. She told Baby that if she'd been a little boy, Mummy would have shown him what to do now he was growing up, and she gave a pretty detailed account of the imagined course of instruction. You see what she was at ? She was trying to get the incestuous kick she wanted by corrupting her own child—only verbally, but quite effectively for all that. Naturally enough—*un*naturally enough —Baby got a lot of ideas into her head and started to behave a bit oddly. She noticed how excited Patricia became during their sessions, and she also noticed that Patricia was going off to London increasingly often, so she put two and two together and started her own line in fantasies about what her Mummy was up to in the big city. This made her behave odder, and the end of it was she was sent home from school in the middle of one bright morning, carrying a polite but firm letter for Tom which said that she'd better not come back the next day—or ever. At this stage Tom, who already knew that something was wrong but had deliberately tried not to realise what, was compelled to have a show-down with Patricia. How much he got out of her I do not know, because by this time I was out of Patty's confidence—I'd told her rather sharply to pull herself together and she'd bitterly resented my 'unkindness', as she called it. Anyway, whatever Patty told Tom, the upshot was that he engaged a governess for Baby and encouraged Patricia to stay out of the way in London . . . which she began to do for longer and longer periods, until by the beginning of this year she was hardly in Grantchester at all. Baby was jealous about this at first, but she got fond of the governess, and started to simmer down, and there's been a marked improvement in her ever since."

"There certainly has," said Detterling. "I went to see Tom and Baby in Grantchester back in May last year—just after Baby was sacked from school, it must have been. Baby was a really atrocious child, and poor Tom looked about ninety."

"Both of them started to recover as soon as Patty removed herself to London. Gregory and I helped a bit—we've always been fond of the child, even at her worst, not having one of our own. We used to take her on holidays and expeditions and so on when the governess had time off. I think it did her good to be away from Tom as well as from her mother. Tom means well by Tullia, but he broods over her."

"Agreed. . . . But meanwhile," said Detterling, "what of Patricia? She was living alone in London, I suppose . . . and you and she weren't talking?"

"No. I made one last effort, but she just wouldn't see sense. All she kept saying was, 'I'll find him. I know I'll find him.' 'You be careful where you look,' I said, and was told to get out and mind my own business. There was nothing I could do. There was no question, yet, of having her confined unless she went of her own will. You see, she'd done nothing—nothing palpable—which could be put up against her. It's not against any law to talk to your daughter about sex or to entertain sixteen-year-old boys in your flat, if they're willing to come there. And willing they certainly were. A couple of 'em were moving up the stairs as I went down after my last missionary visit, and they were positively pink with pleasure. So after that I just settled down to wait for whatever was going to happen." Isobel paused and drank some whisky from her glass. Then, "Lobes," she said suddenly, as if announcing an important clue: "ear-lobes."

"What?"

"When Patty and I get really excited, we nibble and we nip. We particularly like nipping ear-lobes. Right, Gregory?"

"And very nice it is, Isobel."

"Gregory may enjoy it," said Isobel to Detterling, "but there are those that don't, as you'll see in a minute. Well, time went on, and then one afternoon about three months ago, midsummer's day it was, the telephone rang and there was Patty clacking away on the other end of it. We hadn't spoken for weeks, but now here she was, positively honking with excitement. She'd found what she was looking for, she said, and she wanted me to come round to her place and see him. Why? I asked her. So that I could see for myself, she said, that she hadn't been wasting her time. So that I should understand that those that seek will, in the end, find. That dream she'd had, of being Venus in the Bronzino picture—that dream had come true. I could come and see for myself.

"So I went. Rather fast, because I didn't like the sound of it. Light, bright madness, I said to you just now about that picture; well, there was all of that in Patty's voice. When I got there twenty minutes later, the door of her flat was ajar and she was looking out of it, wearing slacks and a shirt (which didn't suit her) and with her finger over her lips.

" 'He's asleep,' she whispered; 'come and see.'

"On the bed, lying on his side, was a perfect little beauty, limbs like Cupid in the picture, the same round and rather fat bottom, the same silky flanks, and a little dark bush, hardly more than a fleck of it. And the face in profile on the pillow . . . well, it was a pretty close boyish approximation to Baby's. This boy could have been Baby's brother; and so Patricia had her dream, she had a son, a son whom she could . . . 'show what to do now he was growing up'. By the look of it, she'd been showing him pretty energetically, because he was absolutely flaked out.

" 'How old ?' I said.

" 'Seventeen.'

" 'You're sure ?'

" 'Yes. I know he looks much younger, but I've seen his provisional driving licence. I always make them prove they're old enough.'

"This made me burst out laughing. Poor old Patty, I thought, a gone woman if ever there was one, but still retaining this one vestige of caution and respectability, clinging to this one last rule as a bankrupt clings to a tea-pot that the sheriff's men have somehow overlooked.

" 'Shush,' she said; 'you'll wake him.'

" 'Where did you find him ?'

" 'At the Baths. He's got a half-holiday from school.'

"Yes, I thought, you'd know all about half-holidays by now, when to go to the Baths.

" 'Well,' I said, not knowing what else to say, 'don't do him to death. He looks absolutely whacked.'

" 'That's the swimming,' she said. 'I haven't done anything yet. I'm waiting for him to wake up.'

" 'He knows what he's here for ?'

" 'Oh yes. He let me undress him. He liked that, but he asked if he could go to sleep before—you know.'

"By this time I thought our absurd conversation had gone on long enough. The plain facts, whatever Patty's fantasy might be, were these : she was about to take her pleasure with a healthy and willing seventeen-year-old boy, who was having a nice rest on the bed first. That was all. Nothing to be done. No sense in making a fuss. I'd just better go away and leave her to it. To tell the truth I was getting rather excited myself—"

"—Oh Isobel, Isobel," Gregory said.

"Sorry, my old darling, but that boy was such a peach, such a soft fleshy peach with down on, and looking at him lying there just waiting to be eaten was more than I could stand. So I said goodbye and good luck to Patricia, and I went . . . leaving her to her big moment.

"And a really big moment it must have been," said Isobel. "I suppose all the ingredients were just right. Youth and strength, both refreshed by sleep. Beauty. The eerie feeling which she remembered having with Fielding and had always wanted again—the feeling of taking part in a forbidden yet divine mystery : in this case, Venus making love to her own son. And then think of the sheer perverse lustfulness of it all. Patty peeling off her slacks . . . standing over the bed . . . coaxing the cries of pleasure from the little boy whom she imagined as flesh of her flesh. . . . Oh yes," said Isobel, "she must have had a very big moment indeed. You see, Canteloupe, for all our love of nipping and biting, I've never drawn blood—have I, Gregory?—and Patty once told me that though she did sometimes bite through the skin, it was only a little way and only if she was very excited indeed. But this time," Isobel said, "this time with the boy from the Baths who looked like Baby," Isobel said, "*this time,*" Isobel said, "she bit his whole right ear off and bloody near killed him with it. When she came to and realised what she'd done, she bandaged him somehow with a towel, and she called an ambulance, and the ambulance men called the police, and the police called me and Gregory, and nobody thought of calling Tom, and in the middle of the hubbub she gave a little moan, just a tiny moan, and told them to take her away."

"And so now," said Detterling after a long silence, "she'll be in an asylum for good and all ?"

"For as long as anyone can foresee. Apparently she thinks, now, that that boy really was her son. She thinks she seduced and nearly killed her own son, and she's torn between terrible remorse and desire to make it up to him— by seducing him all over again, but this time without savaging him. I suppose the shock finally did for her— when the blood began to spurt. . . ."

"How much does Baby know ?"

"She's been told there was a horrible accident," said Gregory; "that Patricia among others was very badly injured and is unlikely ever to come back from hospital. She seems to accept that. She's had the great good sense not to ask any questions."

"One thing is clear," said Detterling : "she's much better off without her mother. And I don't think she'll suffer from being away from Tom for a bit."

"Tom's jittery after everything that's happened," said Isobel, "and who shall blame him ? God knows what ideas

Patricia put into that child's head before she left home."

"Better forget about all that and let her forget it. She looks a tough child to me," Detterling said. "If she's treated just like anyone else, and doesn't feel that anxious eyes are following her the whole time, she'll be all right."

"Well, we shall see what we shall see," said Gregory, who seemed a trifle irritated at the confidence with which Detterling was prescribing.

"What is very important," said Detterling, "is this school she's going to. What's it like?"

"That's the trouble," said Isobel: "it's one of those expensive places where the rich park their problems. God knows how Tom can afford it."

"Some of his early books are in the fashion again," Gregory said; 'he's making very nice money out of them this year."

"More's the pity," said Isobel, "if it means he can go on sending Baby to this school. It's the sort of place," she explained to Detterling, "which is battened on by psychiatrists who pay the head a fat commission for recommending that the children should have treatment. All fads and no learning."

"That's the last thing Baby needs. A psychiatrist would just stir her up again—and then announce she needed ten years' deep analysis."

"Tom's told them 'no psychiatry'. We made him. But we couldn't get him to send her to a normal school," said Isobel, "though these days, with a bit of push, she could probably be got into one. He thinks she may still be . . . peculiar . . . and he wants a school which offers special care for peculiar children."

"Of course she'll be peculiar," said Detterling, "if she realises she's being specially cared for."

"So we told Tom. He wouldn't agree. He's got dreadful guilt about what happened—he thinks he betrayed Baby and Patricia by his own neglect—and he wants to feel he's doing something out of the way, i.e. something very expensive, to make amends. Self-sacrifice, you see."

"Only it's not himself he's sacrificing, it's Baby."

"Well, one will see," said Gregory, still sounding as if he resented Detterling's interference.

"Yes, one will see," said Detterling, "and very soon at that. She's asked me to go and see her."

"We shall all go to see her," said Gregory stiffly.

"Well then," said Detterling, deciding that a little soft-soaping was now called for, "Tom trusts you and Isobel more than anyone on earth. If you tell him that this school is definitely not doing her good—"

"—That we cannot tell him until we know it to be so. I do not understand why you are so . . . taken up . . . with my niece Tullia. You hardly know her."

"I saw a bit of her in Venice," said Detterling carefully, "and I rather liked what I saw."

"Oh. And what of your other business in Venice? Finding authors for us. You had, perhaps, a little time left over for that?"

"That was your business too. Only you ratted on it."

"Boys, boys, boys," said Isobel. "Such speech we cannot have," she said, imitating Gregory: "there must be civil words."

"Of course there must," said Gregory: "more whisky, Canteloupe?"

"If you please. Quite a lot. As it happened," said Detterling, "I became rather preoccupied with one thing and another, and anyway all that PEN crowd went away not so very long after you did. But I've briefed Fielding to keep his eye open for us—"

"—That is no good. Writers do not procure the services of other writers any more than bishops procure the services of saints. There is too much professional jealousy."

"Well at least," said Detterling, "Fielding seems to be working again. Or on the verge of it. He thinks he's on to a new story."

"What kind of story?"

"Mystery man in a family portrait—late eighteenth-century. No one seems to know who he was or why he's in the picture. Obviously it must have been known once, but none of the surviving records have anything to say about the chap. Why not?"

"Is this fact or fiction?" asked Gregory.

"Fact, so far. If Fielding can't find out anything more, he'll have to make up the rest. But if he can discover who the fellow was there might be an amusing biography in it."

"*If* he was someone who is worth a biography," said Gregory.

"If he wasn't, there can still be a good novel."

"I think," said Isobel in a thoughtful voice, "that for all our sakes Fielding Gray should not start writing a costume piece. If he makes it up, it will probably be ridiculous, and if he finds out what really happened, he may disturb troublesome ghosts."

"Good heavens, Isobel my wife, is no one ever to do research for fear of raising ghosts?"

"Sad," she said. "Such sad ghosts."

"What are you saying, Isobel?"

Isobel did not answer.

"Isobel . . . *Isobel* . . . what is this you are saying?"

Isobel shook her head.

"It is not clear to me," she muttered. "I am very tired and I must go upstairs."

"Bloody blue murder," said Max de Freville to Fielding Gray : "to do anything for this heap would cost millions."

'This heap' was the Palazzo Castagna-Samuele, a high and narrow seventeenth-century edifice languishing over a scurfy little Rio and long since ready to subside into an easeful death by drowning. Max and Fielding were surveying it at an angle from the Ponte del Ghetto Vecchio, their view being somewhat impeded by assorted articles of underwear which hung drying on a line slung athwart the waters of the Rio.

"It might be possible to restore the façade," said Fielding, "without bothering about what's behind it. The façade is all that matters here."

"That way, the whole damn city will turn into a façade."

"I know. Half the buildings have been rotten inside for decades. This one certainly has," said Fielding, "so there'd be no cause to feel guilty about abandoning the interior."

A loose shutter, caught by the evening breeze, flapped feebly back against the wall, showing a window behind which was utter blackness. The sun caught the window, which responded, or rather failed to respond, like the pupil of a sightless eye to an optician's flashlight. Then, after a

few moments, the sun sank behind the ragged roof-line of
the buildings behind them. Although it at once became very
chilly on the bridge, neither man moved : for the sickness
of the Palazzo Castagna-Samuele compelled respect as well
as melancholy; and just as Max and Fielding would have
felt it impolite to walk noisily or eagerly from the bedside
of a declining man, so they would now allow themselves
only the most gradual and decorous, almost imperceptible,
withdrawal from the house which they were examining.

"What sort of state do you suppose the foundations are
in ?" asked Max.

"They could be better than the fabric. They were built
to withstand water, whereas the fabric was not designed
to resist all this filthy air pollution from Mestre. At any
rate it might be worth having a survey done. If you could
raise a respectable sum for the Fund and also send in a
surveyor's report which said the foundations were in quite
good nick, they might put up the balance needed to restore
the façade."

"How important is this building ?"

"As architecture it's no more than merely handsome. But
it has a curious history. A Jewish doctor, Josephus Samuele,
built it for a courtesan called La Castagna. Since Jews
were not allowed to build palaces—only tenements—and
since they were forbidden to have carnal intercourse with
Christian women, including whores, there are some interesting questions to be asked."

"Like, why was Samuele allowed to get away with it ?"

"Yes. One answer is that he was the confidential physician
who was treating the Doge's daughter for the clap. According to another story, La Castagna had a reputation as a
witch, so no one wanted to offend her or her lover."

"Wouldn't they have burnt her ?"

"One would have thought so. But according to this
version, she put it about that she was the reincarnation—or
even the zombie—of Medea herself, the Queen of Witches,
and as such indestructible."

"A likely tale."

"The chronicler Andrea di Cannaregio says it was widely
believed. In any event, the Inquisition was told to lay off
La Castagna, though there may have been several different

reasons for that. Apparently she was pretty generous with her favours even after she moved in with Samuele, who was a complaisant protector if ever there was one. One theory says he encouraged her to have as many affairs as possible, and then hung about behind the curtains taking notes and making sketches, as he was a pioneer sexologist who wanted to record variations in coital behaviour. Unfortunately La Castagna burnt all his papers after he died. Like most harlots, she was subject to fits of prudery."

"I don't know that any of this justifies expensive restorations to the Palazzo."

"Oh, his descendants were a pretty odd lot too. They included a distinguished architect who is reputed to have bought the children of poor parents in order to bury them alive under the cornerstones of his buildings—an ancient form of sacrifice which was intended to propitiate primitive gods of earth and weather. He built several villas in the Veneto, all of which have survived in good order, so the superstition may have had something in it."

"Where do you pick up all these stories?"

"The Biblioteca Marciana. It's full of gossiping histories and the like. The nuisance is, I can't find out anything at all about the one person I'm really concerned with just now. I mean that stranger in the picture in your gallery— the late eighteenth-century family group of Albani. I know a good deal about the picture, who painted it and so on, and quite a lot about Fernando and Maria Albani, and the ages of all the four children—but not a word can I find, anywhere, about that stranger at the back of the picture. All the records and references are written as if he simply didn't exist, as if there were only the six Albani figures in the painting and no one had ever seen a seventh."

"It's getting late," observed Max, dropping his voice to a whisper as if afraid lest the Palazzo Castagna-Samuele might hear him; "we'd better be going."

They moved slowly on across the bridge and down a broad Calle. Golden Hebrew letters arched over a door on the corner in front of them; a very small boy scampered past with a little round cap on his head and ringlets hanging over both ears."

"Orthodox," said Fielding. "There can't be many of

them left. Who *can* that man be," he said, turning earnestly
to Max, "that man in the picture?"

"Why are you so keen to find out?"

"Because everything is against my finding out. Because
there's a conspiracy of silence on the subject."

"Benito Albani—the one who let the Palazzo to Lyki—
he may know."

"Do you know his address?"

"Only that he lives in Siena. But Lyki will have the exact
address—or the lawyer's. I'll get it from him and send it to
the Gritti for you."

"Not there. I'm moving out. Into the Gabrielli for the
winter."

"Yes," said Max, part as in malice, part as approving a
sensible course of action; "the Gabrielli will only cost you
half."

"It's not that. It's just that the Gabrielli is more appropriate. Middle-class people like myself," said Fielding, "even
when they're highly paid writers, have no business in
places like the Gritti for very long. To stay there for the
winter would be to promote myself above my proper
station—an easy and tempting thing to do when one is
abroad, but dishonest and destructive."

"All those years with Hamilton's Horse," said Max,
"and you still think of yourself as middle-class?"

"In origin. You should have seen my parents. . . . Anyway, please send Benito Albani's address to the Gabrielli.
I'll have moved in by tea-time tomorrow."

"I can't guarantee to send it tomorrow. Lyki's in a
tremendous whirl, getting ready for this Baccarat Bank.
Sometimes I don't see him for twenty-four hours on
end."

"As soon as you can then."

"I'll do my best. But there's another thing about Lyki
which won't help. He's in a very uncertain temper—and
not just because of the Baccarat Bank. I think . . . that
Daniel Mond bothers him. Tom and Daniel have been in
that tower for over a week now, and everything's going well
on the surface, but I think that Lyki is—well—discomposed
by Daniel. It's as if he suspected that Daniel saw too far into
his concerns."

"Daniel will have no interest whatever in Lyki's concerns."

"I know that. So does Lyki. But what he feels—he hasn't put it into words, but I've known him for years and I can usually tell—what he feels is that *if* Daniel ever should take a look at his affairs he's capable of seeing much farther into them than Lyki would care for."

"What is there to see? Baccarat, Piero, hotels in Corfu—all rather out of the ordinary run, I grant you, but nothing, by contemporary standards, to cause serious trouble or discredit."

"In the end there's always something to cause serious trouble or discredit. You know that."

"Yes. . . . On second thoughts, save yourself the trouble of sending that address to the Gabrielli, and leave it with Tom and Daniel in the tower. I'll be popping in on them in a couple of days."

"Warn Daniel to be careful . . . not to annoy Lyki in any way."

"Daniel always annoys a certain kind of person, which kind includes Lykiadopoulos for one and myself for another. He is good, Daniel is, and he makes the likes of Lykiadopoulos and me feel guilty and inferior. That's all this whole thing of Lyki's is about. Tell him to do as I do—to try to treat the uneasiness which Daniel arouses in him as therapeutic. I'll be coming along to the tower for a dose of this purgative therapy on the afternoon of the day after tomorrow," Fielding said, "and I'll very much hope that by then you will have found me Benito Albani's address."

In order to reach the tower in the garden of the Palazzo Albani, it was necessary, unless one had a key to the door which led into the garden from the Calle Alba, to go through the Palazzo itself. Fielding decided it would look better to arrive there by water. When he informed the Major-Domo, who met him on the landing stage, that he wanted 'i signori Mond e Llewyllyn', the man gave him a look as of one who was being put upon and showed him through to the garden with neither the respect nor the elegance which he had manifested on previous occasions. Fielding decided to say nothing of this to Tom and

Daniel. What he did say was that it would be tiresome having to go through the Palazzo every time he came to see them.

"I know," said Tom; "but Lykiadopoulos insists on our keeping the door into the Calle Alba locked up."

"There's no bell there?"

"No. When you're coming in future, you must let us know roughly what time. Then I can wait by the garden door and let you in when you knock."

This settled, Fielding enquired after Tom and Daniel's domestic arrangements. These, it appeared, were satisfactory : the tower was warm, the sanitary device was up to its office, and the beds were comfortable. Hot water came in from the Palazzo at the stipulated hours, borne by a cheerful female from the kitchen who had taken a maternal fancy to them. For the rest, they had decided to use Daniel's room, the one downstairs, for 'entertaining', and they had purchased a kettle. This Tom now filled from a white ewer and placed on one of the oil heaters to boil.

And how did they pass the day? Well, they went to a café in the Calle Alba for coffee at nine-ish, read during the morning in their separate rooms, had a light lunch at another café which did snacks, slept a little in the early afternoon, then went on a local sightseeing expedition (to the Frari, perhaps, in which there was enough to be seen to last them a life-time), and came home at about four-thirty for tea. More reading after tea unless, as today, there was a guest; a bath at seven-thirty for one of them (they took it in turns) in Max's bathroom; then dinner in one of the restaurants near the Rialto, and back home to whisky and bed.

"Very quiet, you see," said Daniel.

"I suppose you see quite a lot of Max and Lykiadopoulos?"

"No. Max occasionally, when we go to his bathroom. Lykiadopoulos only once, when he came on a rather formal visit to enquire whether we'd settled in all right."

Odd, thought Fielding (remembering what Max had told him), that Lykiadopoulos should be 'discomposed' by Daniel after meeting him only twice—at the dinner, and on this 'formal' visit to the tower. But never mind Lykiadopoulos for the present. The topic which Fielding really wished to get on to was the far more inviting one of the boy Piero. However, he was wary of naming him immediately lest injurious deductions be drawn by his hosts from his eagerness; and he therefore raised another subject which, he thought, might serve as a way of bringing discussion round to the young Sicilian without indecorous precipitation. "I hear hooligans have been smashing your college chapel about," he said.

There had been an item in the English papers about this six days before. The offertory chest in Lancaster College chapel had been busted open and rifled, and a tomb in a chantry off the choir had been, for no ascertainable reason, savaged with a pick.

"We had a letter about that today," said Daniel; "from Balbo Blakeney. They think it was done by some of our own undergraduates."

"But surely," said Fielding, "term doesn't start till October."

"That wouldn't prevent some of 'em from sneaking back to do their dirty work during the vacation," said Tom. "There are quite a few students of Lancaster just now who resent the chapel because, they say, it stands for a repressive faith and, even worse, causes the college to maintain a private school for the choristers."

"I thought Lancaster had flushed out all that left-wing nonsense."

"There's been less of it, but these days you're never quite rid of it."

"But is there any hard evidence to connect your own students with this affair?"

"Yes. An anonymous note to the Provost said that the money had been sent to Oxfam, and that similar action against the chapel would be repeated unless the choir school was closed by Christmas and he himself gave an undertaking not to accept a Life Peerage. It's pretty widely known that he'll probably be offered one this autumn."

"I see," said Fielding. "The argument is that only a member of the college would care whether he took his Barony or not?"

"What is more, the note bore the motto, 'A Red Rose

for Lancaster'. There is always a possibility," said Tom,
"that one of the young and more dissident Fellows had a
hand in it. A Fellow might be in a good position to steal a
key to the chapel."

"I don't see Provost Constable scaring very easily," said
Fielding.

"No," grated Daniel. "Balbo says that the Provost has
hired a private security agency to guard the chapel and
track down the offenders; and that he has intimated to the
agency that if they find anyone up to any new mischief he
doesn't much mind how hard they hit him."

"He'd better be careful," said Fielding : "these days that
sort of talk could prevent even a Conservative Prime
Minister from giving him a peerage."

"Constable's too grand a man to care about any Prime
Minister."

"You're on his side in this?" said Fielding. "I should
have thought you would have deprecated violence—and in
a sacred place at that."

"Sacred places, of all places, must be protected. The only
way you can be sure of controlling a violent man," said
Daniel, "is to knock him unconscious. Nothing else is
certain. And if you hit him too hard and kill him by mistake, he has only himself to blame."

"Daniel, my Daniel," mocked Fielding, "what would the
National Council for Civil Liberties say? You're not dealing with criminals, my dear, or hadn't you heard? These
fine young men are politically dedicated idealists."

"Then the harder you need to hit them. Violence is no
less to be prevented because it is political in motive, and
idealists are far more dangerous than criminals. Criminals
stop when they've got what they wanted. Idealists never
stop because they can never attain their ideal."

Daniel put his hand up to stroke the silk scarf over his
throat, which had clearly not benefited from the vehemence
of his last speech. Tom started fussing around with the
kettle, which showed no signs of boiling. Fielding wondered
how he could slant the present subject of delinquent youth
in general in such a way as to bring Daniel smoothly and
naturally on to the subject of Piero in particular. This had
been his aim in raising the Lancaster desecrations, but the

turn which the discussion had now taken was unhelpful. Whatever Piero might be, he was clearly neither violent nor idealistic. However, Fielding's problem now solved itself, in a sense : there was a light tap on the door, and into the room limped Piero.

"Mr Lykiadopoulos has gone out," he announced to all present, "and so I could come."

"Good," said Daniel : "the kettle's boiling for tea."

"He has told me not to pester you," said Piero : "he says I must not come to this tower or even go into the garden without asking his permission first. He would not have let me come this afternoon . . . but now he has gone out to that Casino to make more arrangements, and he will not know. He thinks the servants will tell him if I disobey him, but like me they are Italian and they will not betray me to a Greek."

He did not, however, sound absolutely sure of this.

"As far as we're concerned," said Tom stolidly, "you're always welcome."

"He says I am a nuisance to you, and that is why I may not use the garden without asking him first. But really he is punishing me for what I said at that dinner."

Piero sat down on the arm of Daniel's chair and placed the finger of one hand lightly over Daniel's wrist.

"Yet he says," Piero went on, "that I may go out with you, should you wish. Although he does not like me to see you here in the garden or in the house, he says he does not mind how often we go together to churches or galleries or restaurants . . . should you wish to go."

"Interesting," observed Fielding. "It seems he does not mind how well you know Tom and Daniel provided you do not know them on his territory. In other words, he wants them to keep their distance from him. By more or less forbidding you to see them here but encouraging you to go out with them, he is sending them a message. He is telling them to look away from the Palazzo; he is telling them that they will enjoy his confidence, of which you, Piero, are the symbol, so long—and only so long—as they turn their attentions away from himself and his immediate precinct."

"Then why," said Tom, "did he allow us to come and live in it?"

"To keep me from having this tower," said Piero, "and also, perhaps, out of kindness. But he did not realise, when he made the arrangement, what sort of person was coming. He did not know about Daniel."

"Did not know what about Daniel?"

"That . . . that Daniel sees certain people a long way through their skin," said Piero awkwardly.

"You flatter me," said Daniel.

"But now he knows this," said Piero, "it is rather, I think, as Major Gray has described. He cannot change the arrangement about the tower, he would not wish to, because he made it with Mr de Freville's friend, Lord Canteloupe; but he does not like . . . being looked at . . . by Daniel. He does not like to be discussed by Daniel. Now, if I see Daniel and Tom here, on Mr Lykiadopoulos's ground, it is Mr Lykiadopoulis whom we shall discuss, as we are now doing. But if I go with them to churches and museums, there will be other things to talk of."

"I'd sooner talk of other things now," said Daniel.

"Very well. Let us talk of the places we shall go to in Venice, now it is permitted. You do," said Piero, "you do want to come with me?"

"Of course," said Daniel.

"The kettle has nearly boiled," Tom now told them all, "but there is nothing to eat. I will go and buy some biscuits. Bear me company, Fielding."

As Fielding and Tom crossed the little wilderness towards the garden wall, Tom said:

"For a little while Daniel will be able to go to places. Later on he will not."

He took a key from his pocket and unlocked a green door in the wall.

"So then," said Fielding, "the less Daniel can leave the tower, the more Piero will want to come to it. Which Lykiadopoulos will not like."

"He may not mind when he knows what is happening to Daniel."

"Will he want to have Daniel . . . dying in his garden?"

"Daniel says that Lykiadopoulos will not object to that. Nor, he thinks, will Max. Although they are both superstitious men, they are not frightened of death as such, only lest it should deprive them of something. Daniel's death, he says, will deprive them of nothing."

Tom opened the green door; they stepped through into the Calle Alba; Tom locked the door behind them. Bewildered by the bustle in the Calle after the peace of the garden, Fielding followed Tom in silence until they came to a wide Campo. Just beyond the entrance to this was a little grocery store, the outside of which was much hung about with flasked wine of dubious provenance and thick-skinned salami sausages. While Tom bought the biscuits, Fielding went to examine the well-head at the centre of the Campo.

"What will Piero do," said Fielding after Tom had rejoined him, "when *he* knows that Daniel is dying?"

Tom put down his packet of biscuits on the metal cover of the well-head.

"I cannot concern myself too much about Piero," he said. "I only hope he won't be a nuisance."

"You dislike Piero," said Fielding.

"Yes. But I shall do my best to be pleasant to him because Daniel seems fond of him."

"How deep does that go?"

"You are in a very prying mood today, Fielding. Come on. They'll be expecting us back."

When Tom and Fielding had regained the garden, Fielding said:

"I should rather like to have Piero. But I shan't even try. You know why not?"

"Because you haven't a chance."

"On the contrary. My face makes people pity me. You'd be surprised how many people come to bed with me out of pity, or rather, out of a combination of pity and disgust, which they—and I—often find hugely exciting. I might well get Piero that way."

"All right. Then why won't you try?"

"Because Piero's pity would be of a kind dangerous and degrading to both of us. It would be the pity of the priest for the victim. That's why I asked what Piero will do when he knows Daniel is dying. If he starts to pity him, and if I am right about his particular brand of pity, it could be an ugly spectacle."

"That's enough for one afternoon, Fielding. I shall be bearing the brunt of all this. I've chosen to do it, so I've asked for everything I get; but you will not make the task easier for me by prematurely airing your clever, beastly theories about what may or may not happen. You will only confuse and depress me. Please leave me to cope with the problems as and when they crop up."

When Fielding and Tom entered the tower, Daniel said, "Piero and I have thought of such a good expedition. There's a church called the Madonna dell' Orto—

"—A long way up beyond the Fondamente Nuove," said Piero. "It has a cloister, they say. Daniel would like that."

"There are Tintorettos," responded Daniel. "The kettle is boiling, Tom. It was the church of Tintoretto's own parish."

"There is a Last Judgement by him," said Piero, "all sorts of bodies coming alive again." He lay down on the carpet and performed a mock-gruesome pantomime of this phenomenon.

"And it is not far from the Ghetto," Daniel said. "Perhaps I should see that."

"I was up there with Max the other day," said Fielding; "beautiful but sad. And dirty with it."

"We could go to the church by boat," said Daniel, "and then walk down through the Ghetto to the Grand Canal—it's not too far for us, I think—and catch the vaporetto home. . . . The kettle is boiling, Tom."

Although Daniel was sitting just by the boiling kettle, he made no attempt, Fielding observed, to do anything about it. Tom, who had been ponderously measuring tea into a teapot, now crossed the room, lent over Daniel with some difficulty to reach the kettle, and carried it back to the teapot.

"It should be a very good expedition," Tom said. "Shit. I've forgotten those bloody biscuits. We must have left them on that well," he said to Fielding.

"We do not much need them," said Piero, who was now capering about on the carpet and clearly cared for nothing save the projected trip to the Madonna dell' Orto. "Tell me, Major Gray, when you went with Mr de Freville, did you go to the church or only to the Ghetto?"

"Only to the Ghetto. There's a peculiar palace there which might be restored if the Save Venice Fund ever got the money. I'm not sure whether or not Max thought it would be worth the trouble; he was in a non-committal mood. Which reminds me : did Max leave a note for me?"

"Yes," said Daniel, taking an envelope from his breast pocket. "He gave it me when I went for a bath last night. Just as well you mentioned it, or I'd have forgotten. It seems easy to forget things here," he murmured uneasily; "messages, biscuits, time itself—"

"—Good," said Fielding, purposely breaking in on Daniel before he could enlarge his catalogue, "it's Benito Albani's address in Siena."

"What do you want with that?" said Tom.

"I thought he might know something about that stranger in the painting."

Tom began to hand round cups of tea. Piero followed up with the sugar bowl.

"I've not seen the picture yet," said Tom. "I didn't get up there that night when we dined, and I haven't cared to ask since."

"I will show it to you some time," said Piero.

"Perhaps," said Tom, offering lemon to Daniel. "Baby told me about it before she left," he said carefully. "She said she thought there might be a good reason why you could not discover anything . . . anything about this stranger, I mean. She implied that it was just as well."

"Come, come," said Fielding, "and you a scholar."

"Someone seems to have taken care," said Tom, "that all record of this man should have disappeared. This was almost certainly the work of the Albani family. If so, why should Benito Albani be willing to tell you anything?"

"Because it all goes back over 170 years. At one time the family may have been anxious to suppress information about Mister X, but by now, surely, there can't be anything they'd wish to hide."

"That depends what it is."

"Why do you say 'Mister X' and not 'Signor'?" said Piero.

"Just a manner of speaking. Though come to that he certainly looks more English than Italian."

"Look," said Tom; "it's an intriguing little mystery, from what I've heard, but probably the solution is quite banal. So why not make one up for yourself—if you're going to write a novel about it. You'd do it very well."

"And that way you would not impinge," said Daniel, "on what doesn't concern you."

"I should like to find out the truth," Fielding said.

"You've shown very little respect for *that* in the years I've known you," croaked Daniel.

"I tried to tell the truth about Conrad in my biography. After years of writing novels, you see, I've become rather bored with lies. And so now, Daniel, I should like to follow up an historical truth. You just remarked," said Fielding, turning to Tom, "that the truth in this case was probably very banal. But a little earlier, you told us that Baby reckoned there might be quite a lot to it—and not very pleasant at that, or so she seems to have hinted."

"She was showing off to me, I expect. She often does. Anyway she had nothing to go on."

"I'm inclined to trust Baby's instinct. She has a good eye," Fielding said. "She may not have had much to go on, but enough, I dare say, to warrant a polite letter of enquiry to Benito Albani . . . now that I have his address."

He flourished Max's note and put it in his pocket.

"But suppose that he is—how do you say?—evading?" said Piero.

"Not quite : evasive," corrected Daniel with an encouraging nod of his head.

"Then I shall at least know," said Fielding, "that he has cause in this matter for evasion . . . and therefore that I have cause for pursuit."

"Things are going to be a bit different from now, Corporal," said Detterling to his man-servant in London.

"So I had surmised, my lord."

"We shall still keep this place in Albany going for when we're up here. But quite a lot of the time we shall be at the house in Wiltshire. Do you fancy being butler there, by the way?"

"Thank you, my lord, but no. Personal servant has always been my place, and I've no wish to step out of it now."

"Wise man. Very few people realise that promotion is often a prime cause of misery, particularly for men in middle age. It takes them into a sphere which is beyond their competence and reduces them to nervous wrecks."

"Exactly so, my lord."

"So personal servant you'll remain, but I'm going to increase your money. Valeting a peer of the realm warrants more than valeting a mere M.P."

"Your lordship is very generous."

"No, just much richer. Now then : immediate plans. I'll need another ten days in London to sort things out with the lawyers and the College of Arms. If there are no snags, we'll leave for the country on Wednesday, October three."

"Are there likely to be snags, my lord?"

"No. If one considers what a devious line of inheritance it is, it's surprising how smoothly things are going. Most of the stuff is routine—except for one thing : the patent for the first marquis was drawn spelling 'marquis' with an 'i'. I want to be marquess with an 'e' and a second 's'."

"The two ranks are indentical?"

"Yes. But 'marquess' looks nicer on paper."

"There will surely be no difficulty then?"

"You'd think not. But the Heralds incline to the view that I should stick to the spelling in the original letters patent."

"I see. But I cannot imagine, my lord, that we shall overstay our time in London merely to supervise the substitution of an 'e' for an 'i' and the addition of a second 's'."

"I suppose not. You know, Corporal, your style has changed. You may not want to be a butler but you're beginning to talk like one."

"As your lordship observed a few minutes ago, there is a difference between being valet to a peer of the realm and being valet to a mere M.P."

"Well, so long as you're happy...."

"Never happier, my lord. We are to leave London on Wednesday, October three, you say. At what o'clock?"

"Estimated time of departure, Corporal, is o-nine-forty-five hours."

"Covers for the furniture, my lord?"

"No. We shall be back and forth pretty often. Which reminds me : I shall probably be going to Venice again in November or December. Some particular friends of mine are there this winter. Do you wish to accompany me or would you prefer to remain in England ?"

"I should prefer to be instructed, my lord, rather than consulted. It makes me feel more secure."

"Very well. I'd better take you. It's the sort of thing they may expect of me now. But that's not for weeks yet. Smoked trout and cheese soufflé for lunch tomorrow, please; I shall be dining out in the evening. I think that's all for now."

"Then have I your lordship's permission to retire ?"

"Yes, Corporal. Fall out, please."

"The personal servant of a marquis, my lord, does not fall out; he retires."

"Very well; you have my permission to retire."

"Thank you, my lord. Goodnight, my lord."

"Goodnight, Corporal."

For many years now, ever since he had left the Army and come to his present employment, Detterling's man-servant, when bidden goodnight, had turned smartly to the right and marched straight from the room, as was the custom in his (and Detterling's) old regiment. Now and for the first time, however, he put his right hand over his heart, bowed, then backed slowly off (reminding Detterling of Lykiadopoulos's Major-Domo) and did not turn his face from his master until he was out of the door. Oh well, thought Detterling; if that's how he wants to go on, why should I object ?

"And so, Max my friend, everything is all set," said Lykiadopoulos in Venice. "The guests whom I wished to be invited have all accepted for the dinner on the opening night; all the places at the *Table de Banque* are already taken for the first session; and it is thought that there will be a number of very substantial punters playing from the floor."

"I'm glad you're pleased," Max de Freville said.

"It is very urgent I should do well, Max. I have had to-day the figures for our concerns in Corfu. Inflation, over the last two months, has run even higher than we thought.

If our concerns are to remain healthy, I must win the equivalent of three million dollars by April."

"And if you don't?"

"You and I will not starve, my friend; but many of our employees will. I do not want that for my people. We must keep our hotels open on Corfu, and in order to be safe in doing so we must have three million dollars by the spring."

"Rather more than you were originally aiming at."

"Because inflation in Greece, as I say, is running even higher than we feared."

"Three million dollars," said Max. "Nearly two thousand million lire. It's a long order, Lyki."

"There is one new factor in my favour. The management of the Casino have agreed that the maximum stake against the bank for any one individual punter at any one coup should be increased to ten million lire on ordinary days and fifteen million at weekends and holidays."

"Fifteen million, eh? Ten thousand quid. Very nice if you're winning, Lyki. But if the cards go sour on you. . . ."

"I shall have bad patches, of course. But with the security that is behind me, I can weather those. In the long run, as you very well know, the odds are with me."

"But if you had a particularly fierce reverse in the short run? They're very grasping, the management of this Casino, Lyki: that's why they're letting the stakes march so tall—bigger and better five per cents for them. But on the same reckoning, if they saw you take a real walloping one evening I wouldn't put it past them to ask for a payment in cash. Now, what securities have you given them?"

"The deeds of several of our hotels in Corfu, and of other properties. It would take a very big walloping to come anywhere near reaching what they are worth."

"Granted. The fact remains that if things go badly for you the management *might* ask for cash at some stage, and once it was known that any of our properties was up for a quick sale, their value would slump like a snowman in Hades."

"I think, Max, that I can keep the Casino management happy as long as they hold those deeds. There is only one thing which worries me."

Lykiadopoulos went to the window and looked down on

the Rio Dolphin. He gave a very long sigh and broke it off
with a quick hiss, like a tyre being tested for pressure.

"Arabs," he said, turning back towards Max de Freville.

"Arabs?"

"Arabs and their oil money. It is rumoured some may
come to play against my bank."

"Well, that's what you want. Really rich punters."

"These are too rich. They will *all* of them play in
maximums *all* the time. A bad run while I was playing
against them could be very painful indeed. And there is another thing. These Arabs—the ones that may come here—
were on the French Riviera during the summer playing
Roulette and Trente-et-Quarante. When they lost, they
would request that the maximum stake should be raised still
higher, and that the game should continue beyond the advertised hours. . . ."

". . . Thinking that since their money was more or less
limitless, they only needed time to start winning?"

"Precisely. One cannot operate a bank if such privileges
be allowed to the punters. The Casino managements in
France, I am glad to say, were very firm. They did not raise
the maximum stakes and they did not stay open beyond the
normal time. But what I am afraid of, Max my friend, is
this. If those Arabs come here, and ask *here* that the stakes
be raised and the hours of play extended, the Casino
management might be inclined to give way. Italians are
different from the French in these matters; they have far
less regard for regulation and procedure. And then the
management here in Venice would be keen to please such
wealthy clients and tempt them and their kind more and
more away from France."

"If such a thing were to happen, you, as banker, could
always insist that the conditions originally agreed should be
kept to."

"Yes, I could—and make enemies of these Arabs. I think
they would accept a refusal from the management to
change the procedure, but they might not like it if the
refusal came from me. Such men make vexatious enemies."

"In short," said Max, "win or lose, those Arabs will be a
big pain in your arse."

"In my neck, if you please, Max. Yes, a very big pain. Because, as you yourself observed, their money is limitless. Every day more of it gushes out of the ground : it is *infinite*. This destroys all the usual assumptions as to the long-term odds and so forth. Once one is dealing with infinity, as every schoolboy knows, the usual laws of mathematics cease to be applicable."

"What shall you do, Lyki ?"

"Wait and see whether they come. They may well not. But if they do come," said Lykiadopoulos, "then I must acquaint myself with that branch of mathematics—there is such a branch, I believe—which attempts to regulate the region of the infinite."

"It's a branch of metaphysics, Lyki, rather than mathematics."

"Then I shall now go upstairs to my dear chapel and pray for metaphysical guidance," said Lykiadopoulos. He grinned and waddled towards the door. "From God at least," he announced as he departed, "even infinitude can have no secrets."

Egregious Sir,
began the letter which Fielding Gray received from the Albani lawyers in Siena :

My esteemed client, Signor Benito Albani dei Conti Monteverdi, has passed to me your recent enquiry and requested of me to answer you.

This we can only do within the competence of our records here in Siena. These demonstrate as follows :

1) In October of 1796 our client, the Conte Monteverdi, then head of the Monteverdi family and a resident of Siena, received a visit from his Venetian cousin, Signor Fernando Albani dei Conti Monteverdi. Signor Fernando carried with him a small facsimile of the family painting to which you refer. This, he said, he had come particularly to show to His Excellence the Conte; for he wished him to look on the figure of the young man at the back of the picture. This he declared to be an Englishman of the name of Humbert fitzAvon, who was affianced to the Signor Fernando's daughter, the Signorina Euphemia. It was the Signor Fernando's wish that the Conte Monteverdi, as head of the family, should adopt Humbert fitzAvon as his son.

2) When asked why he had brought with him only a picture of the young man instead of conducting him to Siena in person, Signor Fernando Albani averred that it was unwise for an Englishman to travel openly in Italy at that period. It was, he said, the very uncertainty of Mr fitzAvon's situation in Italy which made him anxious that the young man should be legally adopted by the Conte before marriage into the Albani family.

3) When asked for further information about Mr fitzAvon, Signor Fernando stated that he had known Mr fitzAvon in Venice for some two years and was satisfied that he had a respectable fortune at his disposal. He had nothing to say, however, on Mr fitzAvon's standing or relatives in England, and when pressed in this matter could only assert that Mr fitzAvon was a gentleman, an orphan from an early age, and that he had attended Oxford University.

4) Such a meagre indication of Mr fitzAvon's provenance was considered by the Conte Monteverdi to be unsatisfactory. Having first taken the advice of the partners at the head of our house at that time, he declared his refusal to consider any further the adoption of Mr fitzAvon.

In conclusion, my present client, the Signor Benito Albani, has asked me to assert to you that nothing more is known of the matter. It is, however, generally believed in the family that Mr fitzAvon left Venice shortly after Signor Fernando's return from Siena, and that the Signorina Euphemia was subsequently placed in a convent.

> We Beg to Remain,
> Egregious Sir,
> Your most Respectful—

"—Et cetera, et cetera," said Fielding as he folded up the letter.

There was a thoughtful silence in the Casino dei Due Professori (the name by which Tom and Daniel's tower was now beginning to be called by the inhabitants of the Palazzo Albani and its neighbourhood). Tom lifted the kettle off an oil-heater, warily tested it with his palm, and put it back.

"Nowhere near boiling," he said.

Piero, who was sitting by Daniel and making sandwiches for tea in the English manner, put down his knife
and said, "In Sicily we say that there are three kinds of
truth : the truth one tells to the taxes man, the truth one
tells to one's acquaintance, and the truth one tells to God.
The first is for deceit and no one would think of believing it,
not the taxes man or anyone else. The second is for *bella
figura*—what one's acquaintance should think if they are to
respect one. Only the third is really true, and not always
that, because a certain sort of Sicilian will lie even to God.
That letter from the Albani lawyer in Siena is telling you
the second kind of truth. They assume you are too intelligent to be satisfied with the first kind, while the third—the
real—kind is of course none of your business : so they are
telling you the second kind, which is what people tell to their
acquaintance and their acquaintance, for the sake of politeness, at least pretend to accept."

"A plausibly edited version ?" said Tom.

"Yes," said Piero. "True in what it says but leaving much
unsaid. Admitting the existence of shadowy places—to
make it seem the more honest—but casting little light among
the shadows." Piero turned to Fielding. "Yes, Major Gray,
they are telling you, there was indeed such a young man as
you ask about, rather mysterious, as you say, and for a time
he was quite closely connected with our family; but in the
end the family's better judgement prevailed to reject him,
and after that he disappeared."

Piero went on making the sandwiches in the way he had
been taught by Daniel.

"We have been told nothing positive about him," said
Tom, "except that he was an English orphan of education
and gentle birth with an adequate estate, this latter apparently in money. You see how cleverly the thing has been
angled. The young man in the picture, from being a
mysterious stranger whose presence might have sinister implications, becomes simply a prosaic and quite well-heeled
Englishman of whom the Conte Monteverdi pronounced that
he didn't realy measure up to Monteverdi standards and must
therefore be sent packing. For that's how the matter is now
presented : Italian grandees examine and then dismiss an
English gentleman who aspired to marry with them. The

story not only refutes scandal but actually confers credit on the family for being formidable and fastidious."

"Exactly," said Piero. "It promotes *bella figura*. 'Promotes' is right?" He looked at Daniel for approval of his idiom.

"Don't take risks in our language," Daniel said with a cautionary smile. "That one came off. Next time you may fall flat on your face—not good for *bella figura*. . . . They make no difficulties, you notice," he went on to the company at large. "There is no suggestion that Fielding is sticking his nose where it isn't wanted. A strictly factual letter, purporting to tell him everything on record."

"But making it very plain," said Fielding, "that that's my lot. Where do I go for honey?"

"You could always accept the version you've been given. It *might* be true."

"No. You've only got to look at that portrait. That young man . . . fitzAvon, as they call him . . . is not the sort to be seen off just like that by a mere—by a mere—"

"—By a mere bunch of wops?" Piero suggested.

"And another thing," said Fielding: "I want to know what happened at the beginning."

"You mean," said Piero, "how Mr fitzAvon ever got mixed up with this particular bunch of wops in the first place."

"Yes. I don't believe he just picked up somebody's handkerchief while on a Sunday afternoon walk. That picture—he'd thrust his way into it, and all of them, even the two little children, knew it."

"Perhaps you are reading too much into that picture," said Daniel. "Anyway, you seem to be at a dead end now."

"Try the British consulate," said Tom. "As that letter implies, 1796 was not the most propitious time for an Englishman to be in Italy. Napoleon menaced the whole country, and the fall of the Serenissima itself was only months away. Perhaps fitzAvon was on some special mission, or carried special papers . . . in which case he would have had to report himself to the British representative in Venice, to say nothing of Venetian officials. There may still be some record in diplomatic or state archives."

"Yes," said Fielding. "According to what Fernando told

the Count Monteverdi, in 1796 he had already known fitzAvon for two years. Which means fitzAvon must have arrived here not later than 1794 . . . when things were already very tricky in Italy, so that he might well have had to be specially accredited, but before things finally broke down in Venice, so that records were still being properly kept here. Bureaucrats may help me out where the local historians have failed me."

"I shouldn't bank on it," said Daniel. "Can you really imagine that a file of the kind Tom is thinking of would survive for 180 years? Or that anyone could find it if it had?"

Nevertheless, while Daniel and Piero discussed their forthcoming trip to the Church of Madonna dell' Orto, Fielding listened very carefully to Tom, who now instructed him in the special skills and vanities of bureaucratic archivists and how to exploit these in his search.

Captain Detterling, on arrival at his house in Wiltshire, surveyed it and saw that it was good; he surveyed his furniture, his books, his pictures, his gardens, his home park and his outlying territories, and saw that they were good; he surveyed the Cant-Fun installations and saw that even these, in their fashion, were good : for they had been so cleverly arranged and tricked about on the advice of his late cousin's friend, Balbo Blakeney, that while they might still entice the vulgar, who arrived by the trippers' entrance, they were invisible from the drive used by His Lordship or the apartments in which he lodged.

'Lodged', indeed, was the *mot juste*, and here was his only cause for dissatisfaction. As Fielding Gray had suggested in Venice, he was not so much Lord Canteloupe as Lord Cant-Fun. Although the grosser appurtenances of Cant-Fun had been tastefully camouflaged, its influence and organisation were everywhere. There could be no doubt of it : the Marquess Canteloupe (he had had his way with the Heralds about the 'e' and the second 's') was lodger and not lord in his mansion . . . which, in any case, was not his mansion; legally it belonged to Cant-Fun & Co. Ltd, and only because he was Chairman of the Board of that company was he graciously (or rather grudgingly, he sometimes thought) allowed a suite, much as in an hotel, for his accommodation. His very servants, except for the Corporal, were on the company pay-roll; and if he could not assert the rights of a proprietor, no more could he assert those of his office as Chairman—because, as he very soon discovered, there were none, except to draw a massive income and operate a vast expense account. He had no reckonable authority; only by courtesy of the company was a certain deference conceded to him. He was asked to render no services, and was indeed competent to render none. He was not even required to sign the company's cheques.

But if Cant-Fun could do without him, it could not get rid of him. The employees might think that they served only the company, but the company, in the last resort, served only the Lord Canteloupe. It existed, in practice if not in theory, only to provide the Lord Canteloupe with money and goods. So cannily had the terms of the trust been drawn that the one right which was his—to be supplied—was inalienable; the lawyers had seen to that. In principle, it was true, the members of the Board might vote him out of his seat at their head; but if they did so, they were deemed also to have voted for a dissolution of the Board itself and with it the dissolution of their handsome salaries. The matter was abundantly clear: Detterling might be without power or function in his domain, but of his revenues he was truly King. These he now surveyed, and saw that they were good.

Thinking his state over, then, Detterling decided, all in all, that it would do. Though resentful, for a while, that no one valued his opinion or sought his decision, he was bound to admit to himself that administration (as opposed to intrigue) was neither to his taste nor to his talent; let those that understood such things get on with them for his benefit. And again, although it saddened him slightly that he was tolerated rather than obeyed in his ancestral (however deviously ancestral) home, he saw the very real advantages of his position; for if he could not command, neither need he care. The company would attend to such tedious chores as maintaining the fabric, restoring the plumbing and seeing to the welfare of the numerous personnel.

And so Captain Detterling surveyed his Marquessate and saw, on the whole, that it was good. He was magnificent yet he was free of responsibility. Free, indeed—but free for what? How was he to fill his days?

Of this he thought as he walked in his rose garden (though it belonged, of course, to the company, trippers were not allowed to obtrude into it, and it might pass, if anything might, for his own) on one blue and elegiac autumn afternoon. He had done with the House of Commons; he was not inclined to attend, more than occasionally, the charade that was now the House of Lords. Although he would continue as an active partner with Gregory Stern in the publishing house that bore their names, this had always been a hobby with him rather than a profession, and he did not think Gregory would thank him if he made more of it now. Again, while he was a reader of books and a passable amateur scholar of the Greek and Latin classics, his interest in literature was too casual to constitute a *raison d'être*. Charitable works he despised as hypocritical interference; entertaining he disliked, except for small dinner parties; county society bored him, and London society irritated him past bearing. There had been a time when he enjoyed, as he would have put it, 'observing the upper-class scene', but these days most of those in it seemed to him either querulous or trendy, without dignity and without humour, witty indeed on occasion but for the most part lacking the gift of irony, which of all human qualities he valued highest. The only people he still enjoyed observing were certain old acquaintances who had retained a kind of disillusioned elegance over the years; and of these the most rewarding, Somerset Lloyd-James, was dead. With what, with whom should he amuse himself, he wondered, as he watched the sun go down behind the company's trees. Should he travel? But there was little pleasure in the greatest journey unless there was someone to wave one off and wave one home again: someone to miss a little; someone to need a little. He needed, in his middle age, to need someone. Still more, perhaps, he needed someone to need him.

And then, with a sudden stirring of his muscles from knee to navel, he remembered that there was someone who needed him, if only for the time being. He went straight indoors to telephone the Head Master of Baby Llewyllyn's school in Devon, was allowed to speak to Baby herself, and heard her voice rise with happiness as she said, yes, oh yes, of course she could come out with him the next Saturday afternoon.

Daniel and Piero's expedition to the Church of the Madonna dell' Orto started with a disappointment. They had planned to stop at the Accademia on their way and look at the cycle of splendid paintings in which Carpaccio displays the ridiculous history of St Ursula. But although the Accademia was open, the entrance to the room they wanted was blocked.

"*Chiuso*," they were told bluntly and could get no explanation.

"It is the shortage of staff," Piero told Daniel, "though they do not like to say this."

"That is no excuse," said Daniel petulantly. "They should close some less important room."

"That is just it," said Piero; "less important rooms do not need to be guarded so carefully. The Carpaccios must be watched all the time."

"Then they should find someone to watch them. Good heavens," grated Daniel as they returned to their boat, "people come for thousands of miles to see those pictures— only to be told 'chiuso'."

"But we have not come thousands of miles," said Piero soothingly, "and we may try another day. And this morning, if you like, we may see other Carpaccios at the Scuola San Giorgio near the Riva. It is on our way."

"I don't want to see other Carpaccios," grizzled Daniel; "I want to see the St Ursula ones, and I want to see them now."

"Stop being a baby," said Piero, "and I will show you something special instead." And some time later, as their boat cruised along the Fondamente Nuove, "You see that pink house," he said, "on the corner of the basin and the Lagoon?"

"Yes," grumped Daniel.

"It is called the Casino degli Spiriti. It too is among trees

and in a garden, like your Casino . . . though yours is much
smaller. This one is so called because a group of friends
would meet here, in the summer afternoons, and walk in the
garden talking of philosophy, of the Good and the Beautiful."

The pink Casino came nearer. It did not look philosophic
and intellectual, Daniel decided, but rather jolly in a
commonplace way.

"Nevertheless," said Piero, answering the unspoken
thought, "it was of the deep things that they would talk."

"I doubt it," said Daniel, "if they were Venetians."

"But it is so, *Daniele caro*. That is why they were called
the Spiriti—because it was of such matters that they spoke."

The boat turned left, out of the Lagoon and into the
basin.

"But later," said Piero, "there was a story that it is called
the Spiriti because ghosts come here, across the Lagoon
from San Michele. Fools," he said; "there may indeed be
ghosts here, but they come from a cemetery much closer
than San Michele."

"There is no other cemetery."

"I will show you."

Piero spoke to the boatman, who was about to turn
across the basin towards a small canal which opened over
to their right. The man straightened the boat and drove on
into the neck of the basin and down to a second canal on
the right, in the mouth of which he held the boat steady.
A small bridge arched almost over their heads, and a
cowled Franciscan who was crossing it paused to look down
at them.

"That huge building to the left of this little canal," said
Piero, "that is the old school of the Misericordia. A little
way along . . . there . . . is an angle in the wall which makes
an alcove. There is grass as you see, and much thick
bramble, and at the edge of the bramble is set a white stone.
Do you see it?"

"I see it."

"Inside the bramble there must be more such stones, although we cannot see them. This little alcove was a cemetery, or so I say, and it is from here the ghosts rise who walk
in the garden of the Spirits."

"How did you first find this place?"

"I have never been here before. Before you and Tom came, I was not allowed out, you remember."

"Then how did you know it was here?"

Piero blushed slightly.

"From Miss Llewyllyn," he said, "Miss Tullia Llewyllyn. She had been here when she was in Venezia, and she has written from England to tell me of it, as she also told me of the Casino degli Spiriti. She said . . . that they are sad ghosts who come from here, and they go to the garden of the Spiriti because there they may feel memories of happiness, not their own happiness because they had none, but that of the friends who walked in the garden long ago. Come, we must go on, or they will close the church before we have had time to see it."

Again Piero spoke to the boatman. They passed under the bridge, from which the friar had now departed, and after a little while they turned right under another bridge and then left, and stopped by a small quay.

"La Chiesa della Madonna dell' Orto," Piero said, and raised both arms to greet an opulent façade much encumbered with statuary. "Miss Mary McCarthy writes in her book of Venice that it is a great favourite with the English."

"You've been reading Mary McCarthy?"

"Baby Llewyllyn sent me the book with her letter. She says Miss McCarthy knows much of this quarter and I should read her."

"Have you got the book with you?"

"No. Baby said I must read it before coming and then again when I get home. While I am here, she said, I must use my eyes. First we will go inside the church, and then we must visit the cloister."

To Daniel's relief, the interior of the church was less elaborate than its façade. Even so, he found it difficult to understand why the English were supposed to be so fond of the place. Ugly girders traversed the nave above his head; the Tintorettos by the altar were ill-lit and somewhat hectoring in aspect; there was brickwork of an unendearing pink. He told himself that he was in an uncooperative mood, probably because of his earlier annoyance at being cheated of the Carpaccios, and that he must try harder to be appreciative. Piero would be disappointed if he did not enjoy himself. But try as he might, he could not dissipate his hostility to the building and its contents. The marble columns, which much impressed Piero, seemed to him to be dull and (since they needed girders to hold them in place) bogus. The celebrated Cima over one of the side altars he thought artificial and absurd : what were all these saints doing, so superior and self-satisfied, standing under a crumbling colonnade in the middle of nowhere? Why didn't they get moving and do something to prove their sanctity or at least to earn their daily bread? They weren't even talking to one another, merely being pensive—about their own excellence, no doubt.

"I like that little hill town at the back," said Piero, "and the landscape is so pretty."

"But what's the point of that group in the foreground?" snapped Daniel, being pettish and knowing it, unable to stop himself. "An ecclesiastical corner-gang of useless idlers. What are they *doing* there?"

Piero looked at him in pretended consternation and then laughed.

"What would you expect them to be doing?" he said. "Masturbating one another?"

The idea of their all beginning to do just that, with the same grave and smug expressions still on their faces, cheered Daniel up. He gave a thin smile.

"That's better," said Piero; "now let us go to the cloister."

The entrance to this was just to the left of the church as they came out of it. The door in the wall was locked.

"Somehow," said Daniel, "nothing seems to be turning out quite right this morning."

"Don't say that," said Piero, distressed. He pushed miserably at the door, which did not give an inch.

"I never saw a door look more locked. Let's go back to the boat."

"The boat has gone," Piero gulped. "I told the man to go before we went into the church."

"You let the boat go?"

"I thought we were to walk down through the Ghetto and take a vaporetto home."

"I'm too tired to walk anywhere."

"Why did you not say so before?"

"How could I know you were going to be so stupid about the boat?"

"But we had *agreed*, Daniel, that we were to walk down—"

"—Only if we felt up to it. Of all the stupid, selfish, thoughtless—"

"—*Prego, Signori*," said a voice behind them.

The speaker was the cowled friar who had earlier watched them from the bridge near the basin. He was holding up a key and trying to get past them to the door. Daniel and Piero stood aside.

The Franciscan unlocked the door and held it open for them. Daniel and Piero hesitated.

"We may as well go in," said Piero.

"I suppose so," griped Daniel.

Nodding their thanks to the friar, they stepped into the cloister. The friar closed the door, showed them how to unlatch it from the inside, and then walked quickly away towards an opening that led off the cloister at the far end. Daniel and Piero stood and looked around them.

"There, *Daniele mio*," Piero said.

And now Daniel began to understand why the Madonna dell' Orto had always been loved by the English. The cloister was not remarkable; the stonework was ordinary and the plot of grass in the middle was badly kept, consisting mostly of bald patches and sagging weeds: but the place was for some reason deeply satisfying. It was all that such a place should be; its arcades invited one to saunter; its proportions dispensed ease to the mind.

Daniel and Piero walked slowly to the end of the gallery which ran along the south wall of the church, then turned right, and came to the opening through which the friar had disappeared. He was standing in a tiny, sawdusty court on the far side of the opening, in conversation with a workman who was hammering tacks into a complicated framework of wood. The workman looked up and saw Daniel and Piero; he said something sharp to the friar but was apparently soothed by the answer.

"He asked why we were let in," said Piero. "The friar said we would do no harm."

"Surely," said Daniel, "this cloister belongs to the church. Why should we not come in?"

The friar turned towards Daniel.

"He rents this corner as a workshop from the priest," the friar said. "He does not like to be disturbed. If the cloister is open the local boys come in and play football and break things."

"We shall not play football," said Daniel.

"So I inferred," said the friar.

"You speak very good English, Father."

"Brother. I am English. Brother Hugh."

"What is he making?"

"He is making an aviary for our island."

"Your island?"

"San Francesco del Deserto—near Torcello. We have a convent there, which is also a kind of rest-house for our brothers from elsewhere who are tired, and a school of preparation for novices. These days there are few novices. But there are a lot of birds. You may remember that the Founder of our Order was partial to birds. We keep many species, some of which need protection. Hence this aviary."

"Brother Hugh. Hugh Balliston."

"I was wondering whether you would recognise me, Daniel. My vows precluded me from reminding you of our previous and worldly acquaintance. But since you have penetrated under my hood, I see no reason to deny it."

"Who is this?" said Piero.

"This is Mr Hugh Balliston—

"—Just Brother Hugh, if you please—"

"—And he was once, not very long ago, a student at my college in Cambridge. A very good student," Daniel said, turning from Piero to the friar. "There has been speculation about what happened to you after you went down."

"Now you know."

"Why, Hugh? You had a splendid degree, you had every prospect—"

"—Don't ask me to explain, Daniel. It's much too difficult. But I can tell you this much. You remember what happened to Hetta Frith?"*

"Yes."

"Well, the full . . . the full meaning of it caught up with me a few years later. The impact was delayed; when it came it was horrible."

"But it wasn't really your fault. The guilt lay with Mayerston."

"Don't instruct me about guilt, Danny. I'm the expert." Brother Hugh ran his hand down his habit and looked very carefully at Daniel. "Or am I? Either way, we'll now leave the matter, if you please. And indeed I must now leave here, since it seems this contraption is ready. I'm due back on the island early this afternoon."

"Tom Llewyllyn is in Venice," Daniel said.

"Then perhaps I shall see him some time. And perhaps not."

"Do you come over often?"

"Every few days I drive a small barge over, to do necessary errands for the convent."

"Then we could arrange—"

"—No, Daniel. I'm afraid we could not. I can't make arrangements of that kind."

"We could all come to the island to see you," blurted Piero, who looked as if he might cry.

"You could come, and you'd be made most welcome, but there's no knowing whether you'd see me. You'd see whomever they sent to the door to show you round."

"But surely . . . your Order is not as strict as that."

"*I* am as strict as that," said the friar. "Did I hear you saying just now that you were too tired to walk any further?"

"You did."

"Then it is my duty to render an office of corporal charity and give you a lift home in my barge."

"You will honour us by taking a meal?" said Piero.

"No, thank you. I'm expected on the island. So," said the friar, "we'll just get this aviary aboard and then we'll be off. See how cleverly he's made it. Exactly the right use of space and shape, as near as possible an asylum without

*See *Places Where They Sing*, passim.

being a prison. Come on, the barge is a few yards down
from the church. Where am I to take you?"

In the end, since Brother Hugh's barge was too cumbrous to ride easily down the Rio Dolphin to the Palazzo,
he dropped them at a quay by the Rialto Bridge. He had
been too preoccupied with steering to speak to them by the
way, and so now,

"When do I see you again?" asked Daniel as the friar
helped him up over the gunnels.

"Don't be awkward, Danny. You heard what I told you."

Meanwhile, Piero had remembered something which
Daniel had forgotten.

"For the good brothers of St Francis," he said, leaning
down from the quay and scrabbling a 10,000 lire note into
the friar's hand.

"Thank you, my pretty one. We need everything we can
get." The friar raised his arm in farewell. "We shall pray
for you both on our island, my brothers and I."

"All set for Saturday night?" said Max de Freville to
Lykiadopoulos on the Thursday before the latter's Baccarat
Bank was due to open.

"I think so. The new decor is sumptuous, the Casino
personnel are making a considerable effort about the dinner,
and the arrangements for the game itself are highly satisfactory. There is, however, one cause . . . I will not say for
concern, but for serious thought."

"Those Arabs you were talking of the other day?"

"Yes," said Lykiadopoulos. "They are not coming just
yet, but it appears that they have reserved very heavily at
the Bauer-Grünwald for early November."

"How many of them are coming?"

"That is not clear. So far they have made no communication to the Casino. All we know is what we have from the
manager of the Bauer-Grünwald, who has told us in confidence that two Arab princes of substance have engaged
accommodation for themselves and their entourages from
Friday, November the second for periods undefined but
which in neither case are to be less then ten days. No precise numbers have been given: each prince has simply
booked an entire floor. Now, my dear Max, one may

readily assume that Their two Highnesses will come to play against my bank; but how many members of their entourages will they permit or encourage to come with them?"

"Ask me another," Max said. "But presumably places are now being booked at your table a long way in advance?"

"Certainly."

"Then if these Arabs want to play they'll have to declare themselves to the Casino before very long."

"Not necessarily. If all the proper places were booked when they came, they could always ask for chairs behind those of the other players, and play from those. It is a great nuisance when many people do that, but it cannot be stopped. And those of them humble enough to stand could play from the floor."

"In short, however many of them want to play, they'll find a means of playing."

"Right, Max my friend. Now, if there were only the two princes, it would not be really dangerous. But if there were, say, ten more of their people, all playing on or near the maximum stake, as these Arabs are inclined to do, of ten thousand pounds a coup, then the affair would be very nervous for me. I must make certain preparations, I think."

"You mean . . . add more securities to those which you're putting up already?"

"I would not wish to, though it may be asked. No. As we were saying the last time we spoke of this, I must consider more deeply the mathematics . . . or the metaphysics . . . of a situation in which the resources of my opponents are approaching the infinite. I must have my equations ready. Tomorrow I go to Padua, to see a Professor of my old acquaintance at the University there."

"You have a mathematician in the house—or at least in the tower. He is a metaphysician too, if I am not mistaken."

"I would not wish to involve Mr Mond. He is here to be quiet, I think, and must not be disturbed. Besides, I doubt his competence in that very specialised branch of learning to which I must address myself."

"The theory of chance, I suppose? I should have thought Mond was well up to that."

"Something rather more arcane than the theory of chance, Max. My professor and I must discuss an old dis-

cipline of the savants, which was once much prized both
by mathematicians *and* by metaphysicians, but is now
commonly ignored by both, and among them, no doubt, by
Mr Mond."

"I wonder how they all are in Venice," said Baby Llewyllyn
to Detterling, as they sat over tea in Ye Merlin's Pantrie on
Saturday afternoon.

"I haven't heard anything."

"I have, just a little. I wrote to Piero to tell him about
some places in Venice, and he wrote back to say that
Daniel and he would be going to them quite soon. But I
haven't heard how they got on yet."

"Why did you write to Piero of all people?" Detterling
asked.

"He was kind to me. And then I want to keep in touch
with Venice. I've written to Poppa, of course, and to
Major Gray. Whatever happened to his face?"

"A bomb in Cyprus. There was a local truce, but even
so a Greek Cypriot threw a bomb, and of course Fielding
wasn't ready."

"How unfair," Baby said.

"But not surprising. Greek Cypriots are the nastiest
people in Europe. Even the Greeks think so, though they
don't often admit it."

"One teacher at our school—"

"—Be accurate, Baby. A master or a mistress?"

"They don't like being called masters or mistresses. They
like being called teachers."

"That sort, are they? Well, a man or a woman?"

"A woman. She says that Greek Cypriots are a fine, free-
dom-loving folk who have been exploited for centuries by
Venetians and Turks and us British."

"When did she say this?"

"In a history lesson. She was telling us how marvellous
it was that since 1945 people all over the world have been
throwing off the shackles of imperialism—particularly
British imperialism. That's how she came on to Cyprus."

"She deserves to be raped by a Cypriot."

Baby giggled.

"I knew that would annoy you," she said. "Most things

at my school would annoy you. A lot of them annoy me too."

"What sort of things?"

"The teaching's so wet, for a start. It's difficult to explain this, but they just don't tell me what I want to know. Art Appreciation for instance—we do a lot of that, and the other day we were doing Claude Lorrain. We were shown a beautiful, dreamy painting of ships in a harbour and buildings with tall columns on the edge of the water. The teacher—a man this time—started talking about Claude's love of harbour scenes, and his nostalgia for a vanished world, and the romantic light. So then I asked what the picture was called, and he said it was called *Ulysses' Mission to Chryses*, because Claude often chose legendary subjects, it was part of the nostalgia thing. What *was* Ulysses' mission to Chryses, I asked, because although I knew a bit about his journeys I hadn't heard of this one. So he said it was a complicated story and didn't really matter—the point was the harbour and the nostalgia and the light, all that all over again. But *what* was Ulysses doing there, I asked, and *why* had he come to see Chryses, and *who* was Chryses anyhow? And then he got quite cross, this teacher did, and told me just to look at the picture and respond creatively to it. But you see, my lord, that was just what I wanted to do, and of course I know that means looking at it, but it *also* means knowing what it's supposed to be about, all the guide-booky things like that, so that one can understand roughly what was in the artist's mind when he was painting."

"Agreed," said Detterling. "In this case your man probably didn't know the answer."

"It's all in the *Oxford Companion to Classical Literature*," said Baby. "He could have read it there, as I did afterwards. It's the same with other subjects," she went on, "more scones, please, waitress, they don't teach you the hard and exact and necessary things you need to know or practise. It's all soft and flabby. In English Literature, for example, it's always 'How do you react?' and 'What do you feel?', never 'What does he mean?' or 'How is the poem constructed?'."

"In one word," said Detterling, "you want discipline."

"I want to be made to work," Baby said. "I'm sick of just

being told to express my own feelings about this, that or the other. How can you express anything unless you know something to express and learn the rules of expressing it? I want to play games," she said, tucking into the new plate of scones, "as they do at other schools, because if you don't get proper exercise you won't have a good appetite. I want to have tests and marks and competitions," she said, flourishing the jam spoon, "so that I can know that I'm the best."

"And if you turn out not to be?"

"Then I shall make myself keep on until I am."

"That's my girl," said Detterling, rather wanting to cheer; "I'll see what can be done."

At much the same time that Saturday, Piero and Fielding Gray arrived for tea with Tom and Daniel in the Casino dei due Professori. This had become a habit agreeable to all four of them, though Piero could only attend when Lykiadopoulos was not at home (for Lykiadopoulos, while allowing and encouraging Piero to go on expeditions with Tom and Daniel, still forbade him to 'pester' them in the tower or the garden). This afternoon, of course, Lykiado-poulos was well out of the way at the Casino, supervising the final preparations for the dinner and the opening session of his bank. None of these at the tea-party in the tower had been invited to the dinner (nor had expected to be), but Tom and Fielding proposed to go to the gaming-rooms that evening and watch Lykiadopoulos in action at the Baccarat Table.

"It could be amusing," said Fielding, "and God knows I need some amusement. I've been slaving away at those archives all week long and not a sniff of Mr Humbert fitz-Avon. The consular staff are sick of the sight of me. This afternoon they gave me a letter of introduction to the Italian chappy who's in charge of the City records—a pretty broad hint to take myself off there."

He put his hand in his pocket to make sure he had the letter safe, and brought it out, along with another one which he dropped on the floor. Tom picked it up for him.

"That's Baby's writing," said Tom in a carefully neutral voice which nonetheless suggested that an explanation was required.

"Is it? I collected it from the Gritti on my way here. A lot of people don't know I've moved." He looked at the postmark. "It must have been at the Gritti some time," he said, facing down Tom's curiosity. "I ought to go there more often. Come to that, they ought to send my stuff on to the Gabrielli—they know perfectly well that I'm there. It's typical of these places: once you've paid and left you can drop dead for what they care."

"Come on, Fielding," said Tom. "Let's hear what Baby's got to say for herself."

Fielding put the letter of introduction back in his pocket and opened Baby's. He read out loud her first phrases of greeting, then paused and read on in silence, irritated, puzzled, sceptical by turns, but always attentive.

"She writes a lively letter, your Tullia," he said to Tom when he had finished it, "in a fair round hand. But I'm not quite sure what you'll make of it. 'Now, listen, Fielding'," he read out to them all, " 'and don't laugh at me. Last night I had a dream. I was in the Palazzo Albani with you, looking at those paintings, and I wanted to go to the loo, and you told me, just as you did after that dinner, that I'd find one on the top floor. So up I went, but the stairs and the top floor were all different: I found myself going up a ladder and climbing out through a hatch; and instead of a penthouse, there was just one little tiny hut in the middle of the roof. Well, this hut certainly looked like an outdoor lav, so I dashed over and opened the door. But it wasn't a lav at all, it was a miniature version of a room that really is up there— I went into it when I was exploring that night—a room which is full of toys. Beautiful toys, some of them, and two lovely old rocking horses, which were just the same in my dream as they had been when I really saw them, only of course much smaller.

" 'And in this room somebody was crying. Not a child, as you might expect in a room full of toys, but a man, quite an old man, I thought, was crying his heart away. And after a bit, though I couldn't see him, I knew who he was: he was the father of the children in that picture which interested you so much—Fernando Albani. He had come to look at his children's rocking horses—only he wasn't *up there with me*, he was wherever the rocking horses had been when he was really alive, in a nursery somewhere on a lower floor, and he was deciding that it would be best to store the horses away. At first I thought that was because his children were grown up and gone, and this was what was making him sad. But then I knew it wasn't this, it was something quite different, something really horrible, which he didn't want anyone to know about and was somehow connected with those rocking horses. It was almost as if the horses had seen something dreadful and he was afraid that unless he hid them away they might open their mouths and tell people. I knew, too, that he was ashamed as well as sad, most bitterly ashamed, but still, try as I might, I could not find out the cause of this. Then suddenly he stopped crying and was gone . . . and there I was, looking at the little rocking horses and wanting to pee like mad. I woke up at once, but I only just made it, because at this school, though it's meant to be so modern, the night loos are down a corridor a million miles long.

" 'Fielding, don't think that I'm silly, but since you're interested in Fernando's family and that man at the back of the painting, why not have a good look at those rocking horses? Piero knows just where they are. I mean, if Fernando in my dream was afraid they might tell somebody something, why shouldn't they tell you?' "

After a silence Tom said :

"She never mentioned a room with toys while she was still here."

"She didn't tell us anything much about what she'd seen," said Fielding, "because she'd promised Piero not to."

"I should not have minded her telling you about the toyroom," said Piero; "and now . . . that we all know each other as we do, I should not mind your knowing about the other things that are up there, though I shall not tell you just at this minute. The only thing is that you must never go up there. Mr Lykiadopoulos and Mr de Freville would be angry."

"Then how am I to examine those horses?" said Fielding.

"You really think it's worth following up?" said Tom.

"I do."

"You think those horses might open their mouths and tell you something?"

"Not literally. But they could be a clue of some kind."

"I'm afraid you cannot go up to see them," said Piero. "No one can go up there."

"You," said Fielding. "You can go up there."

"Yes. But what would I do if I did?"

"You would look very carefully at those rocking horses, and see if they suggest anything to you that is out of the ordinary."

"Very well," said Piero; "if you promise not to be cross if you are disappointed in my report. Since that kettle is so slow, I shall go now."

"Very civil of him," said Tom when Piero had gone, "going off on a fool's errand so readily."

"Your daughter is very percipient," Fielding countered; "so is Piero, though in a different kind of way. In this instance the combination may turn out to be helpful."

"Perception is one thing," said Tom; "but you seem to be crediting Tullia with some sort of second sight."

"Let's say . . . that I think her imagination, aided by her intelligence, assists her to make particularly sensitive speculations. If her mind had been working on the mystery of the stranger in that picture, there is no reason why it should not have reached certain conclusions and presented them to her in a dream. Have you ever heard of a man called Rivers?"

"Psychologist," said Daniel; "flourished in the early decades of this century. A kind of common-sense English edition of Freud."

"Right. He was in charge of mental cases at the Military Hospital where they put Siegfried Sassoon during the 1914 war. But that's by the way. In Rivers' published work he makes it very clear that he believes that our minds often sort out problems while we're asleep and then we dream the answer—or what the mind thinks is the answer. He adduces several alleged cases as proof. Now, if this faculty were especially intense, it might well produce the sort of dream experience described by Baby. What her mind was telling her, in a highly metaphorical way, was that the presence of a stranger in that picture, plus the fact that nobody can or will tell us anything about him, adds up to the possibility of some kind of disaster which involved the stranger and one or more of the Albani children, thus very much grieving their father. And so, her mind is telling her, if you want a clue to it all, take a good look at the children or, since they are long dead, at the places and things once associated with them."

"These, I suppose, being collectively symbolised by the rocking horses," said Tom. "But I cannot see how they themselves could possibly help you."

"Nor can I. But they make somewhere to start."

"Pretty tenuous thinking."

"Perhaps," said Fielding. "But there could just be something in it. You see," he said hesitantly, "although I've tried to give a rational explanation, I also believe it to be at least possible that Baby has something . . . something extra . . . going for her in this field. Extra-sensory perception would be a respectable name for it."

"Not to me, it wouldn't," said Tom. "I resent having my daughter exploited as a witch."

"No one's exploited her," said Fielding. "I never asked her to write to me, about her dreams or anything else."

"Well," said Daniel the peace-maker, "granted that Baby may be able to help you by tuning in on some unusual wave-length, what has Piero to offer? You had hopes, you said, of the combination."

"Piero's main asset at the moment is that he alone of us is allowed up to that top floor. But I should also say that he has the gift of very speedy and very accurate practical awareness. If there is anything odd to be seen up there, Piero will see it—just as he'd see a coin lying in the gutter. It's part of his survival kit, like his ability to parrot English."

"Unfair," said Daniel. "His excellent use of English comes from his ability to understand the mental processes which lie behind our idioms."

"If you like. Whichever way you put it, there's no doubt that he's very quick to hook on to new usages. That's his speciality: *hooking on* to things. He doesn't have to be told twice. If he plays his cards right, I see a great future for Piero."

"I don't," said Daniel; "he's vulnerable."

"We all are. The thing about Piero is that he's smart

enough to know where he's vulnerable and to take constant
and necessary measures for his protection."

"I wonder how he got that limp," said Tom.

"Street accident," said Daniel, "or so he told me. A cart
ran over his leg when he was small and it was never properly set. Vulnerable, you see. Any other street boy would
have avoided that cart by instinct."

"But not any other street boy would have cleverly turned
an ugly limp into an important part of his charm."

The door opened and Piero appeared, looking uneasy.

"I found nothing, nothing indicative," he said, glancing
at Daniel to receive his approval of the word, "about those
rocking horses. But then it occurred to me that though
dreams often tell us things, they do not tell us exactly."

He gave a look that expressed genuine deprecation of this
insight and sharp distaste for what he had achieved by it.

"In that room are uniforms hanging on frames, a child's
uniforms. Some of them are of the Cavalry. Cavalry, I
thought; horses. One of these uniforms had a kind of
wallet."

"A sabretrache," said Fielding.

"A sabretrache," repeated Piero carefully, storing this
rare word away. "Inside it was this. It may or may not be
of interest to you."

He put his hand under the waistband of his trousers and
drew out a sheaf of rustling papers, quarto size.

"No need to look so miserable about it," said Fielding;
"let's have a look."

Then he saw what had upset Piero. On the top sheet, as
Piero passed the sheaf to him, was a line of writing, probably a title or description, in bold capital characters of a
kind known to him but not at all familiar : underneath was
a detailed and delicate water-colour painting, life-scale, of a
cluster of some five or six crocuses, in the middle of which
burgeoned a flower that was not a crocus but an erect phallus, beautifully and variously tinted over the bulb by a
band of primary chancres.

PART THREE

A BEAST IN VIEW

LYKIADOPOULOS fingered a card face down from the Baccarat shoe and slid it to his right. He fingered another card to his left, and a third he kept in front of himself. He then repeated the process, after which he watched the senior croupier as the latter scooped up the two cards on the right with a long spade of plywood and set them down before a little old lady in a mauve dress who had staked fifteen million lire and was playing the cards for the punters on her half of the table. The little old lady picked up her cards with reverent tenderness, as if lifting a newly discovered papyrus which might crumble to pieces at any moment, and examined them with enormous concentration, as though fearful lest she might overlook some apocalyptic message contained in them.

"*Non*," she said, "no card."

Lovingly she lowered the two cards face down on to the table.

The croupier now scooped up the cards on Lykiadopoulos's left and presented them to a near-pithecoid German who had staked only two million lire but was the most highly committed player among his comrades on the other half of the table. He seized the cards, flexed them brutally, squeezed one out from under the other and flung them down.

"*Carta*," he grunted.

But before he could have the card for which he had asked, Lykiadopoulis must show his own. He slid them apart with his two index fingers and flicked them both on to their backs, revealing a Queen and an eight.

"Another natural," said Fielding to Tom. "He's having a pretty decent run."

The senior croupier checked the old lady's cards (a five and a two) and then the pithecoid's (two tens). The junior croupier swept all the stakes on the table into a heap in the centre and with a few flicks of his wrist had all the plaques piled according to their respective denominations, which ranged from 100,000 lire, represented by a modest blue rectangle no larger than a wafer of butterscotch, up to the permitted maximum of fifteen million, which was celebrated by triumphant figures of gold set in a slab of ivory a foot long.

The senior croupier checked the piles of plaques.

"*Cinquanta milioni,*" he proclaimed.

"Thirty-three thousand quid," said Fielding to Tom.

The croupier scribbled on a coupon, tore it from a book, thrust it through a slot in the table, and sent three plaques of medium size after it.

"Less five per cent," said Tom.

Tom and Fielding were leaning over a bronze rail which encircled the Table de Banque at a distance of about five yards. Inside the rail were the seated players (eighteen of them at the table and another three or four snuggling up as near as possible on extra chairs) and a mob of infantry (as Fielding had nicknamed them) who prowled about restlessly and from time to time tossed plaques over the heads of those seated and on to the enticing green baize. By leaning over the rail from outside Fielding and Tom declared themselves as spectators only; but this class was by no means contemptible, as there was a special admission fee of twenty-five thousand lire to be paid before one could even poke one's nose into the 'private' rooms in which the bank was being conducted. Fielding might have grudged the money, had it not been for the sumptuous decorations which Lykiadopoulos had commissioned and supervised during the last few weeks. The theme of these was Metamorphosis : the walls were decked round with Ovidian scenes, at once delicate and voluptuous, of nymphs sprouting leaves or feathers to the frustration of the inflamed gods who pursued them; while carpets, chair-backs, looking-glass frames and even ashtrays carried supplementary legends of lesser importance but greater indecency.

Only the Table de Banque itself was strictly functional

and innocent of venereal addition; and at this the play had now been going on steadily for half an hour. According to Fielding's rough estimate, Lykiadopoulos, who had started badly but then produced a series of naturals, had won on average three coups in every five so far played and was about a hundred and fifty million lire ahead. The betting on Lykiadopoulos's left had been mostly in millions and half-millions; on his right it had been rather higher, though only the little old lady in mauve was consistently betting in maximums.

"You know," Fielding now said to Tom, "if a few more of them started betting as high as they're allowed to, this game would get very fierce indeed."

"It's quite fierce enough already. I'm not a prig, I trust, but I still retain vestiges of my youthful socialism, and it makes me uneasy to see billions of lire shunted back and forth over this table just to make a Venetian holiday."

"But do admit : the spectacle is rather splendid. Lykiadopoulos has won again, if I'm not mistaken."

"*Settanta milioni*," called the croupier, and then, as an afterthought, "*e tre cento mila*."

Lykiadopoulos looked modestly, indeed primly, in front of him, clasping his hands together almost as if in prayer.

"*Prego, Signore*," called the senior croupier, initiating the next coup.

Lykiadopoulos's right hand slid out of his left, snaked across the green baize, reared up in front of the Baccarat shoe and darted out one quick finger to flick a card down from the frame.

"The way he does that," said Tom, "is curiously offensive."

"The movement of the hand and the finger?"

"Yes. It reminds me of a particularly nasty gesture they make in Corsica to cast the evil eye."

"The evil eye," said Fielding in sudden excitement. "That's it. It must be."

"What must be what?"

"That picture on the front of the manuscript Piero found this afternoon. It's an example of the standard magical use of an obscene object to ward off unwanted intruders. Not quite the same thing as casting the evil eye, because in this case the idea is to protect oneself or one's property rather than to broadcast malice; but it's pretty sinister all the same. What that diseased limb among the flowers means is, 'Watch out, or you'll be picking something nasty'."

"A kind of curse? But why should anyone write a manuscript and then put a notice saying '*Don't* read on' at the very beginning?"

"We don't yet know what the MS is. It might be some kind of heirloom—a family document which they wanted to preserve but didn't want just anyone to look at. Or it could be a will, or some piece of pure pottiness about buried treasure, or directions how to find the unmarked grave of a criminal or a suicide—it could be anything. Or nothing."

"But of course you're going to have a go at it?"

"Of course. If Piero and Daniel hadn't been so upset by that phallus on the front I'd have started there and then. As it is, it's now safe in the Gabrielli, and I shall start on it tomorrow."

"But if you're right," said Tom, "about that thing on the front page . . . if it is a warning . . . then surely Piero and Daniel were very wise to behave as they did. They refused to have that MS examined or discussed in their presence because, they said, it repelled them. On your theory they had good reason to be repelled. It's what they were meant to be—and you too, Fielding. Doesn't that make you nervous?"

"Because I have explained a superstition, it doesn't mean that I share it. And I'm sure you don't, Tom."

"I don't share the superstition. But the use of that appalling sign . . . according to you . . . does indicate that somebody at some time was anxious that that MS should not be widely read. Perhaps there was good cause for his anxiety. Perhaps one should not pry."

"Oh, come, Tom, come. If no one ever pried our libraries and museums would be empty. You're a scholar— you *live* by prying."

"But you are not a scholar, Fielding. You're just inquisitive."

"I don't think curiosity will kill this cat. In any case, I imagine that that sign is only a modified warning. The use of such symbols, remember, was to protect property from the malignant, not to bar men of integrity. In this case, the probable intention is just to stop that MS from falling into the wrong hands."

"What makes you think that yours are the right hands?"

"Look," said Fielding, "it is at least possible that that MS may have something to do with Fernando and his family and that stranger in whom I am interested. If so, it might save me the trouble of going through hundreds more archives, and after the experience of the past few days that is something I am keen to avoid. And so tomorrow morning I start reading. All right?"

"That's up to you . . . and I don't say I shan't be interested to hear what you find, if you're ready to take the risk."

"You cannot believe that there's a risk."

"Let me just repeat that Piero and Daniel don't like the smell of it . . . and then leave it at that. But there's another thing, Fielding: the letters on that cover looked like a Greek script of some kind. Why should anything to do with Fernando and his family be written in Greek? Or is the text in something different?"

"No. I had a brief look through in the Gabrielli before meeting you for dinner. It's all in Greek, and a very awkward style of lettering at that. Some sort of decorative late Byzantine type. But the words and the syntax seemed very simple from what little I saw. Schoolroom Greek, *nursery* Greek, Tom. You see?"

"I suppose so. If that MS consists of Greek exercises, say, done by the Albani children . . . and then discarded in the nursery where they were written, tucked away in any old place for want of a waste paper basket . . . yes, that might explain how it came where Piero found it. But what could you learn from children's Greek proses? And *why* that horrible thing on the top page?"

"Why indeed? Perhaps we shall know before very long. . . . By the look of it, my dear, Lyki has nearly come to the end of the first shoe. Let's get into the bar before the rush."

The bar had been decorated in much the same style as the Salle de Baccara, but here was not so much Metamorphosis as Metempsychosis. The murals carried a somewhat camp version of the Platonic myth of the after-life, displaying the descent of a group of human souls, their trial before the nether judges, and their subsequent rebirth as beasts or reptiles.

"A curious motif for a bar," commented Fielding. "I wonder what on earth he's put in the restaurant."

"The elevation of pure souls through the hierarchy of Ideas to the level of the True and the Beautiful," said Lykiadopoulos, who had just come up behind them. "Good evening, Mr Llewyllyn, Major Gray."

"Good evening, Mr Lykiadopoulos. And in what style is the ascent of the pure souls portrayed?"

"The same as this. A frivolous style, I admit, but appropriate, in my view, to the fumbling notions of a mere heathen philosopher. My intention, you see, was to present a kind of pagan Human Comedy: the inferno in the Baccarat room, the Purgatory in here, and Paradise in the restaurant. I am afraid the allegory will be wasted on most of the customers, but not on you two gentlemen, I think. How did you enjoy watching the game?"

"It was very instructive," said Tom. "I hope you are happy with the outcome."

Lykiadopoulos shrugged.

"I do not think you approve," he said in a courteous and indifferent tone; "but then neither do I. Mr Mond is not here, I see?"

"He is tired this evening."

"It is just as well that he has not come," said Lykiadopoulos. "The company would not suit his sensitivities. Do you think," he went on with the tiniest hint of anxiety in his voice, "that Mr Mond will come some other time?"

"I very much doubt it," said Tom.

"And yet," said Lykiadopoulos, with the gingerly persistence of one probing an incipient pimple, "he did express an interest in the game . . . that night when you all came to dinner."

"Like all mathematicians," said Fielding, "he is always interested to hear about unfamiliar games, because the rules of these constitute new sets of dimensions, so to speak, and make for new quirks of chance inside them."

Max de Freville came up to them.

"Just arrived," he said. "How goes it, Lyki?"

"Fair, Max, fair," muttered Lykiadopoulos. Then, turning back to Fielding, "So Mr Mond's interest in my bank is purely theoretical?" he asked.

"His interest—what there is of it—is not in your bank at all, nor even in the game as such, but in the mathematical ideas it suggests to him."

"I always wanted to be a mathematician," said Max de Freville, "but I just wasn't up to it."

"But," said Lykiadopoulos, ignoring Max's autobiographical fragment, "if Mr Mond is interested in such ideas, he could come here to the Casino and observe some actual passages of real play. The calculation of the odds against any given series of results, for example—would that not amuse him?"

"Not much," said Tom. "He has—forgive me—more absorbing problems to consider."

"But of course," said Lykiadopoulos with genial self-deprecation. "How stupid of me to think Mr Mond should be much concerned. He expressed a polite interest in the game and perhaps entertained himself for half an hour the next morning with a few mathematical excursions which it might suggest; but that is all, eh?"

He still seemed in need of reassurance.

"I should say so," said Tom.

"Lucky chap," said Max de Freville. "With that sort of mind he need never be bored."

Lykiadopoulos, who had visibly relaxed after Tom had spoken, now tightened up again and shook his head sharply from left to right. A liveried footman approached and bowed. Lykiadopoulos acknowledged the bow with a quick wave of his hand and followed the man out of the bar without any further word to those about him.

"He's off back to the table," said Max. "You must forgive him if he's a bit edgy this evening. It's a prickly business, running a bank, and he's anxious to get off to a good start."

"He's done well enough so far."

"And he'll need to go on like that. In a few weeks some high-flying Arabs are coming, and the more he can stack up now, the better. What about some supper? Lyki tells me the food in the special restaurant they've put in is quite something."

"So, apparently, are the murals," said Fielding: "the ascent of the pure souls, he told us, to the True and the Beautiful."

"Poor Lyki," said Max; "he's always hankered after that. But he's incurably earth-bound if ever anybody was. It's all Plato's fault," he went on as they entered the restaurant, "for presenting the love of the ideal as a kind of spiritual pederasty. Plato only intended a metaphor, but old queens like Lyki get themselves into delicious and deliberate muddles about it, and end up by thinking that the True and the Beautiful just means a more than usually pretty little boy."

They all looked up at the murals. Sure enough, enthroned at the top of the end wall, above the layers of the geometrical Ideas through which the pure souls (pneumatic water babies) floated dreamily upwards, sat a naked, very white, and pre-pubescent Piero.

"You see what I mean," said Max. "The True and the Beautiful—a high class fancy boy with his hairs shaved off. No more appropriate, logically and philosophically, than a grilled lobster—which would make a much better God in a restaurant."

In the Casino dei due Professori, Piero said to Daniel:

"Why did you not go with the others to the gambling?"

"I've seen gambling once, and that was enough."

"Where was that?"

"Years ago, in a place in Germany. It wasn't a proper Casino, just a low nightclub where they played some wretched game with a ball and a wooden board with numbered holes in it. In Hanover it was, a club called the Oo-Woo Stube."

"What a peculiar name."

"It was a very peculiar place. There was an obscene cabaret, I remember—uncommon, back in the 'fifties. I was taken there by Fielding Gray and some of his friends. He was still in the Army then. We had a horrible row with a German, who called me a disgusting Jew. Perhaps that's why I've never been able to stand gambling establishments —I associate them with that German."

"What was Major Gray like in those days?"

"Good-looking. Overbearing. A discontented officer in a smart cavalry regiment."

"Ah. That was how he knew that word this afternoon . . . sabretrache. What do you think is in those papers, Daniel?"

Daniel shifted restlessly in his chair.

"I dare say we shall know soon enough," he said. "Fielding is a determined man."

"He should be careful."

"Because of that . . . that sign on the top page, you mean? That won't stop him," said Daniel, and jerked his head sharply, warning Piero that he had had enough of the subject.

"I do not understand," said Piero, breaking the silence which followed, "why you were in Germany with Major Gray. You were not in the Army?"

"No. It's a long story."

Daniel's head jerked again, several times. His body twisted in the chair. His hand went to his throat, then flew away from it and pointed across the room.

"That drawer," he gasped. "There's a packet of powders. Put one in water."

"There is no water in the jug."

"Cold tea. . . ."

Piero poured the remnants of the afternoon's tea into a dirty cup and emptied a sachet of powder into it. Daniel seized the cup and gulped. He breathed heavily, writhed a little, and was still. Piero came up behind him and started to massage his scalp.

"What is the matter, Daniel?"

"Nothing . . . now."

"The pain will come again, I think."

"Yes. But not for a while. And there are always the powders."

"The pain will come more and more. The powders will help less and less, and then not at all."

"Before then I shall be dead. It is time I told you."

"Ah," said Piero coolly; and then again, "Ah." He lowered both hands and stroked Daniel's ears. "I shall not tell Mr Lykiadopoulos or Mr de Freville. Nor will we talk of it any more. Daniel . . . do you wish that I should be kind to you?"

"You are being kind to me."

"I could be much more kind than this."

"To please a dying man?"

"I said, we will not talk of that. I have wished to be kind to you for many days now. But until this evening there was no chance for me to say it."

"Soon I shall sleep a little. When I wake I shall need all my strength. Please do not rouse me, Piero. Comfort me, as you have been doing. Do not seek to rouse me."

"Very well," said Piero, and raised his hands from Daniel's ears back to his scalp.

When Tom, Fielding and Max had finished eating their supper underneath the True and the Beautiful, they returned to the Salle de Baccara. Lykiadopoulos, who was now going through the third shoe of cards, still appeared to be winning, though not in such large amounts as when Tom and Fielding had watched him previously. The little old lady in mauve had departed, and her place had been taken by a dark, cross young woman who was betting in plaques of only half a million, these being reluctantly supplied by a stout middle-aged party who was standing behind her. Fielding wondered idly whether the old lady in mauve had been cleaned out or merely bored.

"God knows," said Tom, when Fielding asked his opinion in this, "but the play seems very tame now she's gone."

"The punters are holding back," said Max, "because Lyki's been having a good streak. They'll sniff the air until they think they can smell his luck turning sour, and then weigh in hard. That could be interesting . . . particularly if they get it wrong. You see that Lyki's now putting on a pinched look and sitting rather hunched?"

"Yes."

"He's doing it on purpose, to make them think that *he* thinks that he's going to start losing. This could encourage them to bet heavier while his luck still lasts."

"But will it last?"

"You can never tell, of course. But obviously Lyki thinks

it will. When he reckons he's in for a bad patch he starts grinning like a vampire to put them off."

"They must see through him after a time."

"Then he does it the other way round. Double bluff. And when that's stale, he goes into an entirely new range of expressions. Impassive one minute, jittery the next—they always bet high if they think the banker's jittery—humble, arrogant and even crazy. It's a non-stop performance."

"Well, I'm afraid I can't stay for any more of it tonight," said Fielding. "I've got a long day tomorrow on that manuscript," he added to Tom.

"What manuscript?" said Max.

Silently Fielding cursed his clumsiness. Lyki and Max must not know that he was in possession of something taken from the forbidden part of their house; taken by Piero, it was true, but at his, Fielding's, bidding.

"Something I found in the Biblioteca the other day," he lied; "didn't I tell you?"

"No. Something to do with that man in the picture?"

"Perhaps. I don't know yet."

"How are you getting on with all that?"

"I'm getting nowhere," said Fielding. "It's time we had another trot round Venice . . . if you're still interested in making restorations."

"I'll give you a ring next week. I've got several ideas for raising money."

"Perhaps Lykiadopoulos will help?"

As Fielding spoke the senior croupier announced a handsome win for the bank.

"Not a penny," said Max. "Anyhow, I want to do it myself."

"Come on," said Tom to Fielding; "I must get back to Daniel."

Tom and Fielding, having descended to the ground floor of the Casino, decided to walk together to the Rialto, where their ways would part.

"I shall be glad when this winter is over," said Tom as they crossed the bridge into the Campo Santa Fosca. "I'm scared, Fielding."

"Scared of Daniel's death?"

"Scared of his dying. Of what may happen first. It's because I'm scared that I choked you off when you started to talk of it the other day . . . of how that boy may behave and so on. I'm sorry, Fielding. I should have listened. You were saying that if Piero starts to pity Daniel it could be an ugly spectacle. What then?"

"There will be loss of dignity. It is important that Daniel should do this with dignity, Tom. You see that statue over there—Paolo Sarpi?"

"Sarpi the Servite. Sarpi the rebel and reformer. I can't imagine he's much to your taste, Fielding."

"No, but he was an impressive man. You remember what he said? 'I never tell lies but I do not tell everyone the truth.' That has always been Daniel's way, Tom. He has never told lies but he has always seen fit to keep much of what he knew to himself. And so it is now. He is keeping his feelings, his troubles, his fears, his pain as far as possible to himself, and this, Tom, is the true dignity. But if once Piero shows him pity, it may weaken his resolve; he may be tempted to let it all out—to voice his fears, complain of his troubles, to whine about his fate."

"Perhaps Piero will not pity him when he knows he is dying. Perhaps he will shun him."

"That would be better, even if it hurt Daniel."

"Then what am I to do, Fielding?"

"We must find Daniel something to do. If he is occupied, he might be proof against Piero's pity, or his disgust—whichever it turns out to be."

"What possible occupation can we find him? Soon he will be too ill to leave the tower."

"I was thinking this evening of what Piero said some time back—that Lykiadopoulos is somehow afraid of Daniel, afraid lest Daniel might see through his skin and find him out. Max, too, has said something of the kind. What reminded me of this was the anxiety Lykiadopoulos showed, when he spoke to us in the bar, about the possibility that Daniel might come to watch the play. He kept on reverting to it. So you don't think Mr Mond will come here, he said; and then, a few minutes later, are you *sure* that he won't come? Three or four times he asked that, though each time in a slightly different way. It was as though he had some secret which he thought Daniel might penetrate. If so, why not occupy Daniel by getting him to do so?"

"I've told you. Before long Daniel will not even be able to go out. Anyway, what should he care about Lykiadopoulos's secrets?"

"It was just a thought. Lykiadopoulos's sort of secrets might be particularly diverting."

They crossed a bridge and turned sharply into a narrow passage.

"As long as Lykiadopoulos is afraid of Daniel," Fielding went on after a while, "it will be a sign that Daniel still has his powers, powers which depend on his still being himself and so in good part depend on his dignity. Perhaps Lykiadopoulos has told his boy to destroy Daniel's dignity, by whatever means, so that he need have nothing more to fear. Or perhaps he has told Piero to spy on Daniel."

"He has forbidden Piero the tower."

"So Piero says. And comes there almost every day."

"You are devising conspiracies like a Jacobean dramatist."

"Yes. We'd better let it rest for a bit and see what happens. I'll have plenty to do with that manuscript to translate."

"That manuscript. Do you really think it can help you?"

"Why not?" They came to the steps of the Rialto Bridge. "Remember Tullia's dream."

Tom started up the steps, shaking his head.

"I shall be glad when this winter is done," he called down softly; "plots, dreams, diseases . . . gamblers and their catamites. . . ."

"The stuff of Venice," Fielding called back, and went on his own way.

In London, Detterling said to Isobel and Gregory Stern:

"I've found just the sort of school she says she wants, and they're willing to take her straight away. So what about it?"

"After Christmas perhaps," said Gregory.

"She wants to move now. She wants to *start*."

"Tom would forfeit this term's fees at the present school and have to pay them in full at the new one."

"I'll see he's not the loser."

"Perhaps," said Gregory, "he might not care for such a benefaction. He might even consider it to savour of interference."

"I think Canteloupe is right," said Isobel, who had so far been silent. "If we simply tell Tom that the present school has turned out unsuitable, that we've found a good new place, and that we've made it all right about the fees, he'll be satisfied."

"But, Isobel my wife, we must get his permission before we move her."

"No," said Isobel; "let's not worry him just now. Let's serve it up as a *fait accompli*. He will trust us to have done what is best."

"The school she is at will not release her," said Gregory, "until they have it from her father in writing."

"They'll release her," said Isobel, "if the Most Honourable the Marquess Canteloupe of the Estuary of the Severn asks them to. He might have to pay them a big fat sweetener, from the sound of the place, but since he's so keen about Baby's future I don't think that will bother him."

"No," said Detterling, "it won't."

"Very well," said Gregory; "since you both seem so sure of your ground, I suppose I must agree to what you propose."

"To what Baby herself has proposed," Detterling said.

"So what is this new school you have found for her?"

"Radigund's School, near Dorchester."

"Radigund," said Isobel, "Queen of the Amazons."

"Motto," said Detterling, "from Lucretius. *Nil fit de nilo* —nothing comes from nothing. Headmistress: Miss Clodia Wentworth Rex, M.A. (Hons. Cantab.)—as tough and as beautiful as any Amazon of them all. Extensive woods and playing fields, hockey, lacrosse, cricket, Eton fives, squash racquets, tennis, badminton and swimming—in an open-air pool, unheated, no cosseting. Equitation as an extra on request; occasional attendance arranged at meets of the Devon and Dorset Stag Hounds under personal supervision of Miss Wentworth Rex. Seven open awards to the Universities (by which Miss Wentworth Rex means only Oxford and Cambridge) during the last academic year."

"Fees?" said Gregory.

"You old *Jew*," said Isobel.

"Stiff," said Detterling, "but no stiffer than the school she's at now."

"Uniform?" said Isobel.

"Daughter of *Eve*," said Gregory.

"Grey shorts and knee stockings," said Detterling, "with white shirts and blue jerseys. The school tie is worn with this ensemble on Sundays and November the eleventh; dresses only on formal occasions. School song: *Drake's Drum*. No termly exeat; girls may be visited but not taken out on the fifth and eighth Sundays of term—only. Miss Wentworth Rex does not believe in disruption."

"I find it rather suspicious," said Gregory, "that she is so readily able to find a place for Tullia after the current term has started."

"That was a stroke of sheer good luck," Detterling said. "One of the junior girls has just broken her neck while out with the Devon and Dorset Stag Hounds."

'*Ἐγω Φερνανδος Ἀλμπανι,*' read Fielding in his room in the Gabrielli, '*νυν πεντηκοντα ἐτη βιωσας, ἐγραψα ταδε, ἀτε τους παιδας ἐμους την των ἀρχαιων Ἑλληνων γλωτταν διδαξων* . . . I, Fernando Albani, being now fifty years of age, wrote what follows, in order to teach my children the language of the ancient Greeks.'

Just underneath this was written 'MAIUS MDCCC' (May 1800), the Latin intervention being explicable, Fielding thought, by Fernando's ignorance, common in amateur scholars, of the Greek way of expressing such tedious technicalities as dates. Under this again was a sentence which had been written in ink of a different colour from that used on the rest of the page and in rather cramped letters, as though the writer had penned them, with some difficulty, in a gap between passages previously completed.

'*Παῦτα ταυτα γεγραφα, ὡς δουλος ὠν της ἀληθειας, ἰνα ἐκεινοι οὐς ἀν θελη ὁ Θεος ἰδωσι και ἐπιστωνται* . . . . All these things I have written, as the slave of truth, that those whomsoever God wills may see and comprehend.'

Tucked beneath this observation, in ink of the same colour was the date 'AUGUSTUS MDCCC'. This, as well as the sentiment expressed and the cramped writing, proclaimed that the sentence was an afterthought: clearly Fernando, having started with the intention of writing a Greek Primer for his children (the two younger children in the picture, thought Fielding, as the elder ones would have been fully adult by 1800 and indeed well before), had later decided that his work might appeal to a wider audience ('those whomsoever God wills') and had added his extra preface accordingly. This might reflect the vanity of an author, who was touting his MS round for publication, or it might amount to a prayer from Fernando that he would be properly understood—that his readers, whoever they might be, would 'see and comprehend'. In either event, thought Fielding, it could be taken to imply that Fernando was conscious of having in some way transcended his original purpose.

After the date of the second preface, the MS reverted to ink of the standard colour and now displayed a title in Greek capitals—the same title, and in the same elaborate style of lettering, as was written on the cover sheet above the abominable group of flowers.

ʹΗ ΤΟΥ ΝΕΟΥ ΛΥΚΟΥ ʹΙΣΤΟΡΙΑ

THE STORY OF THE YOUNG WOLF

No difficulty here, thought Fielding. Plainly, Fernando intended to demonstrate the correct use of ancient Greek idioms through the medium either of a fable or a nature tract, the better to engage his children's interest. He had written an old-fashioned Reader; very well, now to read it. . . .

The story began, simply enough, with the introduction of The Mighty Wolf (ʹΟ Κρατων Λυκος) who was King of a Mountain in the Far North. To The Mighty Wolf were born two children, a male and a female, the former of whom, the Wolf-Prince or Lording of the Forest, was at once announced as the hero of the coming tale. Clearly a fable, then, rather than natural history; so far, so good. At this stage, however, the story became tiresome and prolix, for it entered into the details of the Wolf-Prince's upbringing. Fernando was obviously seeking to improve his children (and perhaps to impress the wider audience seemingly anticipated by his second preface) by laying down, in the manner of Xenophon or Cicero, the correct style of a gentleman's training. And the Wolf-Prince's training was interminable. Quite apart from the usual academic and moral disciplines of the period, he was put through a long and elaborate course, to prepare him for his duties as Lording of the Forest, in the Customs and Science of the Hunt, and another course in Tactical Deployment and Encampment of the Pack. He was later sent to a University for well-born wolf-cubs (thus giving Fernando the opportunity to express his copious notions on the proper conduct of such places of learning) after which he returned home for a final going-over in preparation for his despatch on the lupine equivalent of the Grand Tour.

At this point Fielding began to flag. Although the Greek was simple, clear and undemanding in its vocabulary, the florid and finicky type of lettering wearied him, and the very simplicity of the language, with its constant repetition of the same elementary constructions, made it exceedingly monotonous. To top it all, the tedium of the subject matter (for Fernando's views on paedeutics were in no way novel) began to irritate Fielding almost beyond bearing. He now started to feel at his crutch the thick sweat and lurking tumescence which were always, with him, a sign that mental desperation was about to lead to physical orgasm, which in turn would be followed by several degrading hours of intellectual apathy and sloth.

However, before the crisis finally overwhelmed him he was saved by pure chance. A few days before the Wolf-Prince was to depart on his Grand Tour, one of his tutors took him into the Forest to make certain he was still well up on his hunting lore. In the ensuing passage, Fernando, for the first time, used a word which Fielding did not remember. The Wolf-Prince was described as 'διαφοιτῶν' among the trees. Trying to ignore his erection, which was now swollen dangerously close to climax and defeat, and turning with some effort to the Greek Lexicon which he had borrowed from the Biblioteca Marciana before settling to his task, Fielding found that the word was a technical hunting term which meant 'running up and down to catch the scent'. Immediately after it, for some reason, Fernando had written a similar word, 'ζαφοιτυων', in brackets. Further consultation of the Lexicon revealed that this was the old Aeolic form of διαφοιτων. Why bother to put that in, Fielding thought; Fernando was simply showing off. Clearly, a man who had such a limited vocabulary that he did not know the Greek equivalents for May and August would have been only too glad to make a big bang when using one of the few rare words he did know, and might well have added a dialect form in brackets to ram his point right home; it was all of a piece with his intolerable display of his ideas on education—in short, sheer conceit. Still, it was an attractive word, ζαφοιτνων, thought Fielding, with an interesting meaning; and as he looked at it once more chance, or inspiration, caused him to picture it in English letters, a translation he sometimes effected with Greek words that appealed to him. As he built up the word on the tablet of his mind, the letters shifted and flickered, stirring some memory, hinting at something familiar here. He wrote the word down, both in Greek letters and in English:

ζ α φ ο ι τ υ ω ν

z a ph o i t u o n

He surveyed the letters. Something was there for him, waiting for him to pluck it out. But what? What? His penis was beginning to throb. Any moment now he would squalidly come. Quickly. 'z', 'a', 'ph' . . . *or 'f'*, 'i' and 't'. Surely; leave out the 'a' and transpose the 'z': phitz . . . *or fitz*. What letters were left? 'a' . . . 'o' . . . 'u' . . . 'o' . . . 'n'. But the first 'o' and the 'u' made the Greek diphthong 'ου', for which it was permissible to substitute an English 'v'—a reasonable if rough phonetic equivalent in the present combination, after the 'a' and before the second 'o'. Thus the Greek 'αουων' became the English 'avon' . . . and the whole turned to 'fitzavon', or, of course, fitzAvon . . . which was, surely was, the name given in the recent letter from the Albani lawyers as being that of the stranger in the picture of whom he had written to enquire. Fielding's penis, undischarged, ceased to throb and curled away to nothing as he checked his discovery, all danger of degradation now gone. Success had restored intellect to primacy. Now there was hope. For of one thing he could be certain: there was some kind of trail. However Fernando's story meandered about, there was, there must be, some sense in which the Wolf-Prince, the Lording of the Forest, stood for the man whom the Albani lawyers in Siena had named as Humbert fitzAvon. Fernando had planted the clue, and had indeed pointed directly at it, that those 'whomsoever God willed might see and comprehend'. Be patient, Fielding told himself; only be patient and play out the game in Fernando's way, for there is no other.

"Those Carpaccios we could not see the other day," said Piero to Daniel, "when the room at the Accademia was closed. I have enquired, and I know the room will be open on Friday."

"What about it?" said Daniel.

"We could go to see them then. We could also go to see the other Carpaccios at the Scuola San Giorgio. It would make an interesting morning."

"A very long morning. Anyway, not on Friday, I think."

"Why not, Daniel?"

"Friday is the thirteenth. Unlucky."

"Saturday is the thirteenth. Friday is the twelfth."

"Not Friday, *caro*. Next week perhaps."

"Next week the Carpaccios at the Accademia may be closed again. Why not Friday, Daniel?"

"Because I shall not be well. There is beginning to be a rhythm in all this, *caro*. For several days I am all right and may need only a few of those powders. Then there will be a bad day, but with more of the powders I can see it through. Then there will be a very bad day, of which I will not speak. Friday will be one of those days."

"And after that you will start to be better?"

"Yes. Only each time the bad days come they are worse than before, and it takes me longer to recover."

"Oh," said Piero flatly. "Then I shall find out whether the Carpaccios will be open on Tuesday or Wednesday of next week."

"All right," said Tom to Fielding: "I accept that Fernando seems deliberately to have drawn attention to that odd Greek word, and I accept that it is an anagram of fitzAvon. I also accept that since the Greek word is a participle describing an action of the Wolf-Prince, we can equate the Wolf-Prince, provisionally at least, with Humbert fitzAvon; and of course we know from that lawyer's letter that he is the stranger in the painting. But now for a few awkward questions."

"Very well."

"First, if Fernando wanted to write about fitzAvon, why did he write in Greek? And why cast the thing as a fable?"

"On the showing of the first brief preface," Fielding said, "he simply set out to write a story in elementary Greek to practise his two younger children in translation. On the showing of the second preface—the one in the different ink—he later realised that his fable had somehow . . . taken him over . . . and had changed into a disguised history of fitzAvon—with whom, for any number of reasons, he was obsessed. To judge from what I have read of the story—"

"—More of that in a moment. First let us be clear about what Fernando was trying to do. This clue, the word 'ζαφοιτνων', that identifies the Wolf-Prince as fitzAvon—it appears relatively early in the narrative. So Fernando Albani must have realised, even so early as that, that he was, in truth, writing about fitzAvon; otherwise he would not have left so deliberate a clue to that effect. But whom was this clue for? For the two children? If I remember rightly what you've told me, they were twins, Francesco and Francesca, who were about seven years old at the time when the family group was painted. Now, according to that lawyer's letter, Fernando first met fitzAvon late in 1794, and took a copy of the painting to the Count Monteverdi in Siena in the autumn of 1796. The painting, therefore, was almost certainly done in 1795 or '96. This means that the twins, seven years old then, were about twelve years old in 1800, when Fernando was writing his Greek fable. In which case he could hardly have expected them to spot his clue, unless they were very bright indeed; and in any event, if he had wanted them to know that the Wolf-Prince was fitzAvon, he could simply have told them so without playing word games. So whom is that clue for? And come to that, why the disguise in the first place?"

"Because what was to be told was scandalous and disgraceful. I haven't finished the fable yet," Fielding said, "but even as far as I've got the story is pretty shocking— once you transpose it into human terms, that is. Simply as an animal adventure it is no more than merely meaty—"

"—Fit for twelve-year-olds?"

"Yes, *so long* as it is read as an animal adventure. Now, suppose Fernando had promised his children a Greek Reader in the form of a fable, he would have wished, being a good parent, to carry the thing through in a suitable and consistent manner. As an animal story it had started and as such it must continue. But on my theory, as it stands so far, when he realised that he was also telling the story of fitzAvon, he inserted a clue to that effect, hoping that his children might come back to the fable when they were older and more perceptive, and learn the unpleasant truth they could not be told while still young. Fernando also hoped, if I am right about the second preface, that others too might learn this truth—'those whomsoever God wills'— at some future date. In short, Tom : while he did not want his children, or anyone else, to find out straight away about a recent and appalling family scandal, he did wish the matter to be placed on record, so that posterity might have at least some chance to learn of it. It was his duty to his family to suppress the facts for the time being; it was also his duty, as a man of truth, to make sure that those facts remained, however remotely, available."

"Why? What's so important about them?"

"Nothing yet. Spectacular they may be, but not in any sense important. Perhaps their importance may be revealed later. Remember, Tom : I've scarcely read half of the text yet."

"Very well," said Tom. "Take me through it as far as you've gone."

"With pleasure. As I was telling you when you inter-

rupted with all your questions, the Wolf-Prince was sent to
a wolves' University and then came home to be prepared
for his Grand Tour. There follows the hunting scene, with
the verbal clue to the Wolf-Prince's identity as fitzAvon,
and after it a long lecture from the Mighty Wolf about the
dangers of foreign parts, in the course of which he dis-
penses a great deal of Polonian advice. And then, at last,
the Wolf-Prince, Lording of the Forest, sets out on his
travels...."

Detterling drove Baby Llewyllyn from the school she was
leaving in Devon to the new one near Dorchester.

"I'm glad to get out of *that* place. Was it difficult to
arrange?" Baby said.

"Not really."

In fact, however, the progressive Headmaster and his
wife (a female lout in long skirt and sandals) had insisted
that Detterling pay three terms' fees in lieu of notice. They
had become very fond of Baby, they snarled, and had been
looking forward to having her under their care for the next
four or five years. Since custom and the law only required
one term's fees in lieu of notice, and since a letter from
Tom, as parent, authorising Baby's removal, would have
compelled the school to release Baby on that consideration,
Detterling had briefly reviewed the idea of telling Tom what
was afoot and asking him to write. But all that would have
taken time and time, he thought, was not on Baby's side :
she only had to fix some silly crush on a boy or a male
teacher, a thing which any girl of her age might do at any
second, and she would want to stay where she was after all.
So he had signed a cheque on the instant, helped Baby to
pack her kit, and here they were now on their way to
Dorchester.

"They'll fit you out with the uniform when you get to
Radigund's," Detterling told her; "they're all ready for
you."

"Miss Clodia Wentworth Rex sounds jolly grand," Baby
said, looking at the brochure which Detterling had given
her. "Do you think I should do equitation? It's good for
the thigh muscles."

"I shouldn't do it just for that."

"I'll see what kind of other girls do it, and then decide. It might annoy Poppa if I went stag-hunting."

"Why should it?"

"He's still a socialist in his old-fashioned way and he sometimes comes all over socialist about the most ridiculous things."

"Then be on the safe side and drop equitation. No point in upsetting your Poppa."

"Does he know about all this—my changing schools, I mean?"

"Not yet, no. Your Aunt Isobel and I thought it better not to worry him until it was all actually done. He's got his hands full as it is."

"Yes," said Baby, "full of Daniel Mond. Poppa will need help later. Fielding Gray won't be much use; he'll just glide away somehow. And as for Piero, he's very young."

"You know about Daniel then?"

"Of course, my lord. I wasn't born yesterday or even last week. You'll be there to help Poppa when it happens?"

"If he wants me. I shall be going to Venice fairly soon to see how things are getting on."

As they drove up to the Tudor manor house in which Miss Wentworth Rex presided over the eighty odd members of the Headmistress' House (where Baby was to be) they passed two little girls who were trotting along in grey shorts.

"It's the sort of place where they make you run everywhere before six in the evening," Detterling said.

"I wonder what I'll look like in shorts."

"You will make a brave boy."

The car stopped.

"Like Rosalind or Viola, you mean?"

"Say Viola. Then I can be your Orsino. 'If ever thou shalt love,' Detterling quoted, 'In the sweet pangs of it remember me. . . . How dost thou like this tune?'"

"Oh, good my lord," whispered Baby, and kissed him on the temple.

Together they unloaded Baby's luggage, saying nothing.

"Drive away now," said Baby: "I must go in there by myself."

". . . And so," said Fielding to Tom, glancing at the MS, "the Wolf-Prince comes to the border of his father's territory and decides to spend the night there before crossing into foreign lands and beginning the Grand Tour proper. If we think of the Wolf-Prince as fitzAvon, it all fits quite well, I think."

"Yes. For Mountain in the Far North we can read England, which fitzAvon is now about to leave, having received the education of an eighteenth-century English gentleman. So here he is, just before finally leaving. What happens now?"

"The Wolf-Prince falls in with bad companions over night. They all gorge themselves on the flesh of wild goats. Then one of them complains that it's too tough and asks the others if they've ever tasted lamb. The real delicacy, he tells them, is lamb which has been taken from the mother's womb before birth. So they all break into a sheepfold, find some pregnant ewes and gobble the unborn lambs. At first the Wolf-Prince hangs back, but the flesh the others are eating looks so delicious that finally he can resist it no longer. Then the sheep-dog comes along to see what's up, and the young wolves tear him to pieces and drink his blood."

"Meaty stuff for twelve-year-olds, as you said."

"It turns out that the sheep-dog and his sheep are under the protection of The Mighty Wolf, King of the Mountain, who has an agreement with the sheep-dog that his flocks shall not be molested provided that he sends in so many sheep a year as tribute to the royal household. So The Mighty Wolf is furious with his son, who has not only assisted in crimes of theft and murder, but has further dishonoured his royal birth by preying on defenceless beasts instead of hunting wild ones."

"I thought wolves always preyed on defenceless beasts if they could."

"Not royal wolves. Or not Fernando's."

"But presumably The Mighty Wolf ate the sheep that came in as tribute."

"That was different. Accepting tribute was one thing; breaking into a sheepfold and eating unborn lambs was quite another."

"And how do we read all this in terms of fitzAvon's adventures?"

"As something pretty fierce, I'd say. A drunken orgy followed by child-rape, perhaps . . . that or something not far off. They got bored with the goaty old whores and sought out the tender little lambs. Despite the freedom allowed to the gentry in those days, they obviously went much too far, and wound up killing the night-watchman who'd come to investigate. How serious it was we can see by going back to the Wolf-Prince. He is told that he's put himself so far beyond the pale that he will be condemned to death by the Wolf Council and that not even The Mighty Wolf, his father, can protect him. But the Wolf-Prince has a huge fit of repentance, and The Mighty Wolf manages to arrange that his son shall be allowed to leave the country in secret, on condition he undertakes a dangerous mission of *sub rosa* lupine diplomacy, which will keep him out of the way until the row dies down. And so now, instead of setting out on a Grand Tour, the Wolf-Prince is sent packing straight off through perilous country which is threatened by The Mighty Wolf's enemy, the Wolf Imperial, to the distant city of the Marsh Wolves . . . which could, of course, mean Venice. And that's as far as I've got."

"We deduce, provisionally, that what fitzAvon had done was so awful that he was threatened with hanging, but that someone important intervened and arranged for him to go away and get lost in a country under the threat of war—*i.e.* in an Italy which was about to be invaded by Buonaparte— and to fill in the time with a cloak and dagger mission to the Venetians?"

"That seems a reasonable equivalent."

"But *who* intervened, Fielding? Unlike the Wolf-Prince, fitzAvon was an orphan. Or so Fernando told His Excellency the Count Monteverdi . . . according to your letter from the lawyers in Siena."

"There could have been a guardian, or influential friends of the family to help him. Come to that, he may very well not have been an orphan at all. That lawyer's letter implied that what Fernando told the Count was very far from being the truth, and of course we now see why. He could hardly tell the Count, if there was to be any hope

of an adoption, the real reason why fitzAvon had come to
Venice. Nor could he tell him anything accurate about
fitzAvon's family in England, in case the Count made
enquiries and found out about the scandal. In fact it is very
likely, I should say now, that fitzAvon was a false name
assumed for concealment."

"Then how did *Fernando* find out about the scandal?
And why did he not reject fitzAvon once he knew
about it?"

"Questions to be answered in our next instalment, Tom.
Somehow, fitzAvon must have established a pretty strong
hold on the Albani family in Venice—you can see that from
the painting—and somehow the truth about him must have
come to Fernando in such a manner and at such a time as
to be acceptable . . . if only acceptable perforce."

"Well, I hope the rest of the story is going to be worth all
your trouble."

"I should say—wouldn't you?—that fitzAvon's travels
have got off to a very promising start."

"With child-rape and murder? After that there doesn't
seem much left to go on to."

"Oh, plenty, I assure you. If I know my fitzAvon—and
I think that I am beginning to—he'll do much better for
us than that."

When Baby entered the Tudor manor house she found herself in a wide hall. On her left was a door which bore a
highly polished brass tablet: HEADMISTRESS. Baby
knocked and went in.

When she had closed the door behind her, she turned
into the room and saw a tall, handsome lady, a kind of
female version of Prince Philip (Baby thought), who was
putting a large book back on a shelf.

"And who might you be?" said the lady, though she knew
perfectly well, since she was expecting Baby and had observed her arrival through the window.

"I'm Tullia Llewyllyn, ma'am."

"Are you indeed?"

The lady advanced, holding out a hand and smiling.
Baby, without knowing why, did something which her
mother had taught her to do long ago but which she had not

done for years now : as she took the lady's hand she dropped
a little curtsy. Considering her lack of practice (she thought)
she made quite a good job of it. Anyway, the lady looked
pleased enough.

"I am Clodia Wentworth Rex," the lady said, "and you
address me, not as 'ma'am', but as 'Headmistress'." She
looked Baby up and down and round and about, and then
up and down again. "You've got a bit of flab on you," she
said, "but you'll do. You'll do very well, Tullia Llewyllyn."

"Thank you, Headmistress."

"Did no one bring you here?" asked the Headmistress,
knowing the answer.

"Lord Canteloupe drove me down. He's gone now."

"Has he indeed? Why didn't he come in?"

"Because I told him not to."

"Why did you do that?"

"Because it would not have been the same if he'd been
here when I first met you."

The Headmistress considered this for some time.

"Your luggage is outside?" she said at last.

"Yes, Headmistress."

"Come on then, Tullia Llewyllyn. I'll give you a hand
with it."

Detterling had decided, on his way home from Dorchester
into Wiltshire, to send Tom a long telegram about what had
been done with Baby. A telephone call, which would neces-
sitate Tom's being summoned from the tower into the
Palazzo, would be awkward; a letter would take too long.
Now the thing was done, Tom must know at once.

As Detterling was walking after dinner in his rose garden,
deciding on the style and composition of the telegram, his
manservant came through the darkness and requested an
interview.

"It's like this, my lord," he said, as he fell into step with
his master; "I find that I should be grateful if your lordship would desist from addressing me as 'Corporal'."

"I've called you 'Corporal' since you came to me."

"Things are different now, my lord. The military title
lays me open to mockery from the other servants. As you
know, my lord, these are merely contractor's personnel, em-

ployed by the company, and they do not understand proper discipline."

"Very well. What am I to call you?"

"The plain surname would be too peremptory these days, my lord. On the other hand, the addition of 'Mister' before the surname would be merely vulgar."

"Your Christian name then?"

"Unsuitable, my lord. My Christian name is 'Tommy'."

"Suppose I called you 'Thomas'?"

"That is not my name, my lord. I was christened as 'Tommy'."

"Then what on earth would you like me to call you? Indeed what *can* I call you?"

"I have thought of this with great care, my lord, and I have decided on the title of 'Chamberlain'."

"*Chamberlain?*"

"On the dictionary definition, my lord, a chamberlain is the chamber attendant of a king or a lord. I think you must agree that I qualify."

"Yes, but don't you think something a little less archaic would be better? What about 'Steward'?"

"Inexact, my lord. I do not cater for your lordship's household."

"In London you do."

"But your lordship's *seat* is here in Wiltshire. Anyway, the title of Steward is now cheapened by its application to delinquent boys who serve fried fish on channel steamers."

"You don't think the other servants will laugh? I mean, if they laughed at 'Corporal' they might find 'Chamberlain' mildly comic as well."

"The dogs bark, my lord, but the caravan moves on. I find the title of Chamberlain so satisfactory that I am prepared to be mocked for it. I am no longer prepared to be mocked as a mere Corporal."

"So be it then."

"I am greatly beholden to your lordship. Good night, my lord."

"Good night . . . Chamberlain."

The Chamberlain bowed and backed off out of the rose garden. Had Detterling not known that his old friend and servant was a teetotaller, he would have assumed that he was drunk. He very much wished he could assume this, as the alternative appeared to be that the Corporal was going potty. If so, he must of course be humoured unless and until he became violent; for a man with his length of service could not be lightly put down or turned off. All the same, Detterling did not look forward to asking one of the other servants to fetch or find his Chamberlain. Shall I say '*the* Chamberlain' or '*my* Chamberlain', he wondered. He could of course just say 'Fetch Tommy', or whatever the other servants called him, but this would be to let him down behind his back. Detterling shivered, partly from the chill of the October night and partly from a sudden spasm of despair at human folly, and went indoors to telephone his cable to Tom Llewyllyn.

The cable arrived the next day at the Casino dei due Professori just as Tom and Daniel returned from a light lunch at a local café. Meals were getting to be rather a problem, as Daniel was less and less inclined to make the effort to go out for them, and Tom was more and more determined to keep him up to the mark for as long as possible.

'Just bring me back a sandwich,' Daniel would say.

'You must eat properly.'

'I've no appetite, Tom.'

'You must eat, Danny....'

On this particular day they had had a wretched luncheon of over-cooked omelettes, and Daniel went straight off to be sick as soon as they were back in the tower. What with this, and what with the sullen demeanour of the Major-Domo, who had brought the telegram over from the Palazzo, Tom felt low. After he had gone upstairs to his room and read the telegram, he felt even lower.

It was not that he objected to what had been done with Baby; far from it. Although he had formerly regarded Baby as a 'special' case and so had insisted on a 'special' school for her, he had come to doubt the wisdom of that decision while Baby had been with him in Venice; and if she had now been moved, at her own request, to a place at which she would (so Detterling assured him) learn much more and be much happier, it was quite all right with Tom. Nor was he in any way resentful that he had not been consulted; for he well knew that if such things were to be done, they were best very quickly done. Nor, finally, was he jealous of those who had acted for him, or fearful lest Baby's gratitude to them should divert her affection from himself; he was too big a man for that.

What bothered Tom was his own futility : his futility in choosing the wrong school for Baby in the first place; his futility in not changing his decision when he had begun to realise how well Baby was shaping now that Patricia was out of the way; and his futility, after Baby had left Venice for England, in simply putting the matter from him. He had, of course, the excuse of his preoccupation with Daniel. But in this area too he felt futile. He was letting Piero do the work for him, because himself he was too feeble to cope. Nor could he claim that much effort was going into his research—the research which, in any case, had been only a pretext for coming to Venice. All in all, he was just flabbily footling about, achieving nothing for those people he loved most (Daniel, Baby and himself) and having apparently abrogated both authority and control in the affairs of all three of them.

As if all this wasn't enough to depress him, he now found himself thinking of poor, sad Patricia in the lunatic asylum. Normally he thought of her little, and then with thankfulness. For years before the disaster Patricia and he had been diverging : after a last violent flare-up in the early sixties all sexual relations had long since ceased between them; and many other causes had alienated and later entirely divided them. Patricia had become at first noticeably and then pathologically mean about money; she had begun to depreciate and then to mock savagely at his colleagues, at his concern with the affairs of Lancaster, at his intellectual and academic success; she had exercised a creepy and damaging influence over Baby during several crucial years of her childhood. So that when the Furies came to destroy Patricia, Tom had rejoiced both that his girl had been rid of a demon and that he himself would henceforth be spared a great burden of anxiety, inconvenience and hate. Nor had he ceased to rejoice in the months that had passed since. But this afternoon, as happened just occasionally, he remembered Patricia as she had been on the day when he married with her, loyal, loving and proud; he remembered the early years of what had been a true affection, intelligently served on both sides, and a true pleasure, hot and strong and loud with words of lust; and, remembering these things, he thought also of the poor fluttering and babbling thing in the asylum, and bowed his head.

But not for long. First, he made himself fetch paper and pen and write letters of assent and thanks to Detterling and Isobel. Next he wrote, more easily now, to his daughter to wish her luck. Then, mindful of past failures and future perils, he descended to Daniel's room, to try what he could do for him. Because he had failed in skill and virtue, he need not, he must not, fail his friend in love.

After the Wolf-Prince had been smuggled off on his mission, his adventures, Fielding found, were for some time very dull. Although he was supposedly travelling through perilous and almost embattled lands, the narrative eschewed danger or excitement and provided instead a crudely informative documentary about the terrain between Nice and the Veneto, both of which, along with all the places *en route*, were now openly named by Fernando. The Wolf-Prince apparently reached Nice by ship and proceeded across Italy by the main roads, staying as he went in important towns and cities. To explain this sudden emergence into the actual world, Fielding conjectured that Fernando had decided to use the journey as an opportunity of teaching his children some geography (after all, he still purported to be writing a work of education) and at the same time as a means of making absolutely clear, to such mature readers as had understood the clue to the story, precisely where fitzAvon was going. To avoid any possible confusion, VENEZIA was spelt out in Roman letters instead of Greek and repeatedly named by the Wolf-Prince as his destination; and only when the point had been laboured *ad nauseam* did the story at last return to the terms and territory of fable. Thus the Wolf-Prince, having engaged rooms for the night in a posting-house in Vicenza and having ordered a carriage to take him on to Venice the next day, had nevertheless reverted, by the following afternoon, to procedures more proper to his species, being discovered slinking through the reed beds towards the nearby City of the Marsh-Wolves, 'which lay by the Ocean of the Winds'.

Once the Wolf-Prince had arrived in the city, the inhabitants of which appeared to live more in the manner of water-rats than of wolves, the tale livened up considerably. The Wolf-Prince's mission, it appeared, was to carry secret oral instructions to his father's representative at the court of the Grand Wolf of the Marshes. These had to do with action to be taken and policy to be followed in the various contingencies which might arise if the Wolf Imperial pursued a projected campaign eastwards and attacked the City of the Marsh-Wolves. Having delivered these instructions, the Wolf-Prince was simply to stay on in the city, ready to assist The Mighty Wolf's representative to carry out his master's bidding in the light of whatever events might ensue. In other words, thought Fielding, fitzAvon came to Venice with secret orders for His Britannic Majesty's Minister in residence about what he was to do if Buonaparte crossed Italy and threatened Venice. For the rest, fitzAvon's brief was to hang about in Venice on the ostensible pretext that there might be further duties for him, thus ensuring that he kept some 300 leagues out of sight and out of mind of anyone, back in England, who might have it in for him on account of the atrocity he had committed there. So far, so good; very good, in fact.

But even more interesting than the story of the Wolf-Prince's mission (the conduct of which did not, of its nature, engage much of his energy) was Fernando's description of the young blade's diversions off duty. Predictably, the Wolf-Prince soon came by dubious and debauched companions, with whom he indulged in appalling revelries in dens along the bank of the river. But although the scope and kind of fitzAvon's iniquities could hardly be mistaken, Fernando continued, doubtless out of regard for the tender years of his children, to clothe his deeds in the disguise of animal metaphor. His actions were reported, as they had been in the earlier scene of depravity, in terms of ferocity rather than of sexuality. Now, however, the vocabulary, still simple but more ample, told its own tale : instead of his former monotonous use of the all-purpose word 'κακος' or 'evil', Fernando was resorting to such words as 'lustful' or 'corrupt' and to such phrases as 'with enticing movement of the limbs'. It was quite clear, if one paid close attention to the text, that fitzAvon was sampling the whole Venetian repertoire of sexual talent, at every level from elegant dalliance with the most famous courtesans down to zestful ruttings in the most infamous stews. And then, as Fielding read on, the Wolf-Prince and his friends made plans to organise a vast banquet of 'luxurious flesh, forbidden fowl and dainty sweetmeats' in their favourite waterside den—all unaware that a treacherous jackal had reported them to the stern Conclave of Black Wolves, whose office it was to preserve in the city the ancient lupine virtues. Which being interpreted, thought Fielding, can only mean that fitzAvon and his chums were getting up a sumptuous all-rounders' orgy in a friendly bordel, not knowing that one of their servants had peached to the Officers (formerly, if no longer, *Black* Dominican Friars) of the Holy Inquisition. . . .

" . . . And so," Fielding told Tom over lunch the next day, "there they all were capering about in the bawdy house, when the doors suddenly flew open and in poured the men from the Holy Office to arrest them. Consternation and bare botties everywhere. Brawls and denunciations. But fitzAvon, who knew a thing or two about Venice by then, was off and away by a back passage before anyone spotted him, pausing only to assist a young man—a *very* young man—whom he rather liked the look of. As it is given in animal terms, 'The Wolf-Prince descried a cub, who was almost grown but was too young and weak to save himself in such affairs as this; and the Wolf-Prince, having pity for the cub, led him out by the hidden way and brought him to safety'.

"Later on, when they were well clear of the fracas, the cub introduced himself as the eldest son of a wolf who was very important in the city, though in fact the family had originated elsewhere. They were called the White Wolves of the Green Mountains—a near enough correspondence to the Albani dei Monteverdi."

"And so that was how fitzAvon came to meet Ferdando,

said Tom. "He rescued his son and heir from arrest in a
brothel. And here is where the story which you're after
really begins."

"Unfortunately," sighed Fielding, "it is also where
Fernando's manuscript ends. Or almost. After the rescue
there is only one paragraph left. This just states, in so many
words, that the cub brought the Wolf-Prince to his father,
who was grateful and entertained him much among his
family. The family looked on the Wolf-Prince with favour;
the cub and the Wolf-Prince became blood brothers; the
Wolf-Prince took a liking to the cub's sister, who returned
it; and the pair of them declared their mutual love. And
that's that . . . except for an indication that at this stage
the Wolf-Prince was pretty much of a mystery to all of
them. 'He could not yet tell his true name and parentage
because of the troubled times,' writes Fernando. This may
explain why there's no mention of any plans for a wedding.
The last sentence, apart from a P.S. addressed by Fernando
to the twins, is simply : 'And so it came about that the Wolf-
Prince told his love to the White Wolf-Maiden, and she
told her love to him, little knowing to whom she told
it'."

"This P.S.," said Tom after a pause : "what does
Fernando say there?"

" 'These things I have written for you in my chamber in
the tower in the garden. Take what I have written when
you go hence, and read. I shall write more of these matters
while you are gone. When you return new pages will await
you, against such time as you may read them, among the
books in the tower.' It is dated," said Fielding, "SEPTEM-
BER MDCCC. September 1800."

"Plague," said Tom the historian. "In the autumn of
1800 there was plague in Venice. He must have sent the
twins away, and finished off the first bit of his story in a
hurry so that they could take it with them."

"Why would he stay behind himself?"

"Business," said Tom. "In time of plague there are many
complications. Banks and merchants collapse, and later on
perhaps there are looters. He had to take care of his property and look after his money."

"So he packed his children off with this MS, and pro-

mised to write more which they would find, should anything happen to him, among the books in your tower . . .
all of which, of course, have long since vanished. He was
planning a second instalment," Fielding said, "which they
could read when they were older and wiser. And which,
perhaps, others could read too . . . anyone who got hold
of this"—he plonked his hand down on the MS—"and
learnt from the postcript where to find the continuation."

"What form," said Tom, "would the next instalment
have taken? Would he have gone on with his fable?"

"If we are right," said Fielding, "we have now reached
just the point where the story really hots up. fitzAvon has
performed a service for the Albani family and now moves in
on them. He has the elder son right under his thumb, and
the elder daughter has fallen in love with him. Clearly,
there are the makings of real trouble here—given fitzAvon
was the brute he appears to be—and scandal and disaster
are looming. Now we have posited that Fernando began
to write a Greek Reader for his younger children, found
himself writing the biography of fitzAvon in the form of an
animal fable, and decided to continue so that the children
and possibly others should have a fair chance of later access
to the truth which, for the time being, must stay disguised.
In short, Tom, Fernando had got himself into a dreadful
mess. He wanted the children to know—but not yet. He
wanted the truth to be left to posterity, but he was committed to telling it in a code that would become increasingly
difficult to decipher as the years went on and as all points
of reference gradually became obscured. What was more,
this code was already proving immensely cumbersome for
himself to operate. So what does he do now? I think he
says: 'To hell with writing this Greek rubbish; the twins
are off to the mainland, so they can take it with them, as
far as it's got, and make what they can of it, and that gives
me the chance to change my horses and tell the rest of the
story in plain words. That Greek bit is unlikely to have
made them much wiser, they probably won't get the point
for years yet—but whenever they do they can come to the
tower where the sequel will be waiting for them, and by
that time they'll be old enough to know the worst. Meanwhile, there's plague threatening Venice, so I'd better get

on with writing the rest of it while I still can.' I think that's
what he says—and does."

"You could be right," said Tom. "A pity that we shall
never see the second instalment, whatever form it took. *Did
Fernando Albani die of the plague?*"

"No. He lived, according to the records, until 1812."

"Then he could certainly have finished his work. But we
have no way of finding it. Either it stayed in the tower
among the books there, and was removed and destroyed
with them years ago; or the children got hold of it . . . and
did what with it?"

"Hid it away perhaps . . . just as they, or somebody, hid
away the first part. We found that, but we can't expect
such luck a second time."

"No," said Tom. "Or can we? *That phallus,*" he said.

"What about it?"

"It's got to be explained some time."

"I thought we were more or less agreed. It's some sort
of warning to tread carefully. It's certainly worked on
Daniel and Piero. They haven't even asked me how I'm
getting on. Have they asked you?"

"No. But I think it's the MS itself they're shy of—the
paper on which that thing is painted. I dare say they'll
listen to the story—if ever we get to the end of it."

"I wouldn't be so sure. I think they're in favour of
letting sleeping dogs lie."

"But since you're so determined to wake them," said
Tom, "let me put to you the following proposition. Whatever that phallus may or may not mean, it would certainly
not have been on the cover sheet of the MS when Fernando
gave it to his two twelve-year-old children. Somebody must
have painted it on later."

"All right. Who and when?"

"We can only guess. But first let us hypothesise a little.
Let us assume that the two younger children were given
that MS, with the declared purpose of furthering their
Greek, and that they took it with them in the autumn of
1800 to the family villa in the Veneto or wherever they
were sent to avoid the plague. Let us assume that they read
it, did not take the clue about fitzAvon (though they probably remembered him quite clearly), and then wrote the

whole thing off as a piece of silly old Papa's boring educational rubbish. However, they wouldn't want to hurt his feelings, so when he sends for them to return from the Veneto they bring the MS with them and put it in a cupboard in the schoolroom, ready to be trotted out if he asks about it. Meanwhile Papa, they know, has been working on a second instalment, which, according to the P.S. at the end of the first, is stored away in the tower in the garden. But they certainly don't want to read another load of what they assume will be the same old ballocks, so they deliberately 'forget' about it; and Papa says to himself, well, if they're not interested, so be it, they haven't yet seen what I'm really at and just as well, I never wanted them to know as early as this and I'll leave it all till later.

"So the years go on, and then in 1812 Fernando dies—"

"—Rather suddenly," said Fielding. "According to the gossip books, of a 'flux'."

"But nevertheless," said Tom, "he has time on his death bed to say to Francesco, 'Take another look at that Greek story I wrote for you and your sister when you were children, and this time pay attention.'' So Francesco, who by now is rising twenty-five, goes to the schoolroom, blows the dust off the MS, and has another gander."

Yes, thought Fielding, that could be right. He thought of Francesco: Francesco sneaking away from the others who were kneeling round his father's corpse, tiptoeing through one of the circular ante-rooms with a candlestick in his hand. The chanting of the priest died away behind him, he went into a stone corridor, up or down some stairs and into the old schoolroom, set down the candlestick, looked round and remembered the rocking horses (which if Baby's dream was anything to go by, Fielding thought, had been sent up to the attic by Fernando many years before); he smiled at the miniature uniforms, then went to the cupboard where the MS had been dumped when he and his twin sister came back from the villa in the Veneto, early in 1801, that would have been, after a sharp winter had rid Venice of the incipient plague. Francesco took up the MS, gave a sob as he thought how little attention he and Francesca had paid it despite all the trouble the kind old man had taken, and began to read. . . .

". . . And this time," said Tom, "the penny dropped. Or at any rate Francesco got inquisitive enough to follow the instructions in the postscript and to dig out Part Two from among the books in his father's study in the tower. And what did he find? In your view and, on balance, in mine, he found an undisguised narrative of what happened after fitzAvon had ingratiated himself with the family. Euphemia, the older girl, is in love with fitzAvon; Piero, the older boy, is fitzAvon's close friend, his 'blood brother', bound to him by their memory of a sensational orgy and their escape from the Inquisitors' men; the two parents, whether or not they like the look of fitzAvon, must show their gratitude, and the more so as they understand that fitzAvon has an undoubted hold on them through his knowledge of Piero's delinquent habits. This is where the second part of the story begins. And Francesco, though fascinated, doesn't much like it. At the time when all this was happening, back in 1794, he'd been a tiny little boy who adored his big brother and sister, and now he's about to learn what they were really up to in the intervals of coming to the nursery and dandling him on their knees. . . ."

"But where are they *now*," said Fielding, "his big brother and sister? What has happened to Piero and Euphemia? Are they kneeling with the others round Papa's corpse? Or have they gone away? Or what?"

"According to that lawyer's letter," said Tom, "fitzAvon left Venice for ever shortly after the Count Monteverdi refused Fernando's request to adopt him, and Euphemia went into a convent. But *could* one go into a convent in 1796 or '7 when Buonaparte was banging on the door of Venice? And anyway, what about Piero? If you ask me, what that letter said was just an official gloss. The real answers lie in the second MS, the one which Francesco has now found in the tower after his father's death. If that story has the kind of ending which you and I think it has, the answers will not be pleasant. I think we can assume that Piero and Euphemia had long since disappeared, and that the younger children had been given some suitable and anodyne explanation. But now, Fielding, in 1812, Francesco is about to find out what really happened."

"And is not, as you say, going to care for it."

"No. So let us continue to hypothesise. Francesco now reads about whatever disaster fitzAvon brought on the family, and takes his twin sister into his confidence—after all, the story was written for both of them—and they decide, being dutiful children, to honour their father's intention. This is that, while the story should not be shouted from the roof-tops, it should be available to posterity if posterity should have the wit to find it out. A civilised attitude, I think : the truth can be hidden from the vulgar but it must not be allowed altogether to lapse; an account must be rendered in order that history may be complete. Only God knows all things, but man should at least have the opportunity to discover as many as possible. This, to judge from the second preface to the MS which we *do* have, is obviously what Fernando thought and now his children think so too. So what are they to do? Here, Fielding, one becomes very speculative. But *I* think that Francesco and Francesca decided to leave the first MS in the nursery-schoolroom, in a casual but not necessarily obvious place—"

"—In that sabretrache?"

"Why not? And then they had to think very carefully what to do with the second, which contained the real meat of the matter. Now, anyone who did find and read the first MS would be directed by its postscript to look in the tower for the second. But this, think Francesco and Francesca, is too easy; anyway, there may by now be excellent reasons for not leaving the second MS in the tower any longer. Possibly the tower is damp and the MS will be damaged if left there; or possibly Francesco, now the paramount male in the household if his elder brother has vanished, has a mind to use the tower . . . for certain purposes, as a handy place for entertaining while his mother is still alive and encumbering the Palazzo itself . . . and does not wish the MS to be kicking about in the tower while he is giving his parties there. Possibly this, that or a hundred other reasons. So the second MS, they decide, is not to go back to the tower; *but*, to keep faith with their father, they must insert a clue as to its whereabouts in the first MS, so that anyone who gets that far—"

"—As we have done—"

"—So that anyone who gets that far, *as we have done*,

may have a fair chance to know it all. Now then : have you seen anything, in any part of the narrative of the first MS, which might have been written in by another hand later ?"

"No. All corrections are made in the same ink and in the same hand as the text—made, that is, while the text was being written. The only thing in ink of a different colour is Fernando's brief second preface, dated August 1800. And that can't be any help."

"No. But is it the *only* thing in ink of a different colour ?"

"Yes . . . unless you count that phallus, which is in water colours."

"But I *do* count that phallus, Fielding. It is the only thing there is to count—the only addition to the original MS, and therefore the only possible thing that Francesco could have put there to be the clue we are after."

"*If* he did. *If* such a clue exists."

"We must believe it does, or we have no hope at all. So we are back, where my hypothesising began, with that phallus. Why should a well-conditioned young man, as we imagine Francesco to have been, think of painting on that cover sheet a flower piece with a prick in the middle of it ?"

"Well, why ?"

"Because whatever else you may say of it, it would certainly be noticed. Almost anything else might be overlooked as mere decoration or doodling, but a phallus in that state is bound to receive attention."

"Not after the first shock of the thing."

"But for long enough—long enough for whoever sees it to notice that it is covered with primary lesions. Such a horrible thing is not forgotten, Fielding; it was not intended to be forgotten; it was intended, first, to arouse strong if horrified curiosity—'read this but read it with caution'—"

"—That I might accept—"

"—And secondly, Fielding, to give anyone who did find and read it a clue where to look for a sequel."

"Not the most helpful clue I've ever been given."

"But at least, as I say, unforgettable. One is compelled to think of it; its very violence ensures that. And if one goes

on thinking of it long enough, it will sooner or later give
up its secret."

"I wish I had your faith."

"Try, Fielding. Try, as I am trying."

But there was no will left in Fielding's face.

"It's no good," he said : "one may as well recognise a
dead end when one sees it."

He rose from the lunch table and stretched.

"I'm due to meet Max de Freville in twenty minutes,"
he said, "at Florian's in the Piazza. We're going to have
another look at a Palace which interests him. In the
Ghetto. Want to come?"

"Why not?" said Tom. "I could do with some fresh air."
He glanced down at the manuscript on the table.
" *'Mentula magna minax'*," he muttered.

"Catullus."

"Yes. 'A huge, menacing prick'. It's got to stand for
something, Fielding . . . if you'll excuse the pun."

"Where is Tom this afternoon?" said Piero, arriving in the
tower for tea.

"He went to have lunch with Fielding Gray in the
Gabrielli. Fielding called in here this morning, bursting
with news about that MS you found. I said I didn't want
to hear it; but Tom did, so they went off together for
lunch."

"They will be coming back in time for tea?"

"I don't know."

"Because if they do not come back, I shall make and pour
it for you. But I cannot start until we are sure, because
Tom would think I was presuming to take his place."

"Then let's leave it for a bit," said Daniel. "I wish you'd
never found that manuscript."

"So do I. But at the time I was just trying to help Major
Gray, and I did not think properly about that . . . that sign.
I only thought, 'I do not like this'. If I had thought longer,
I should have put the papers back where I found them and
pretended that I had found nothing. And yet, Daniel, I
do not know that those papers can do any harm. The
writing on the front had been done a long time ago; so
whatever is in them—it must all be over now."

"Nothing is necessarily over," said Daniel, "however long ago it was."

Daniel had been wrong when he told Piero that Fielding and Tom were lunching at the Gabrielli. Although that had been their declared intention, Fielding had later remarked that he ate a lot of his meals there in the normal course and would welcome a change. So they had left the Gabrielli after having a drink in the bar and walked a few yards up the Riva degli Schiavoni to the Campiello del Vin, at the far end of which was (and is) the Trattoria Malamocco, well known for its plain but excellent table.

And so, now that it was time for Fielding to meet Max, they left the Malamocco, went back to the Gabrielli to park the MS in Fielding's room, and then again passed by the Campiello del Vin on their way to the Piazza.

"A very decent spot of lunch," said Fielding, looking down the Campiello at the Trattoria which they had left a few minutes before.

"It was Mary McCarthy's favourite place," said Tom, "when she was here writing *Venice Observed*."

"Malamocco," reflected Fielding. "I've heard the name recently. In another connexion, I mean."

"No doubt. It's a port on the Lido. Once very important," said Tom in a lecturing tone, "but destroyed by an earthquake in the twelfth century, after which it—"

"—No," said Fielding, suddenly impatient, "nothing to do with that."

"Sorry I spoke," said Tom, and sniffed loudly.

They trailed up the Riva degli Schiavoni, both of them cross after too much noon-day wine.

"It made Baby laugh," Fielding said, after some time, "because it sounded so silly."

"*What* sounded so silly?" snapped Tom.

"A name. Somebody da Malamocco."

"Precisely," said Tom, at once pained and smug. "Somebody from the port of Malamocco."

"*Rocco* da Malamocco," said Fielding, ignoring Tom's exhibition of self-righteousness. "He painted one of those portraits in the Palazzo Albani. Baby and I looked at it that night we all had dinner there."

They turned into the Piazzetta.

"I've never seen the portraits," said Tom in a deprived manner.

"They're not up to much. This one by Rocco is of a sixteenth-century chap who's holding a rose in one hand and a monkey on a lead with the other."

"Very interesting, I'm sure."

They trudged down the arcade towards Florian's.

"A monkey for lechery," gobbled Fielding, "and a red rose for the pox. Common symbolism all over Europe."

"What are you blithering about?"

"Shit," shouted Fielding as they entered Florian's. "It's right under our bloody noses."

Some elderly Americans looked startled. Max rose from a table, with a deprecating air, to greet them.

"Rocco da Malamocco," boomed Fielding: "the letters in the middle make CODA MALA. *Coda* is a variant of *cauda*, *cauda* means a 'tail' or in obscene sense a 'prick'. *Coda mala*—a bad, rotten or diseased prick. I must be off."

And he was. The Americans gaped at the discomfited Tom. Max patted him rather hopelessly on the shoulder.

"Fielding's gone," Tom said stupidly.

"But he was going to come with me to the Ghetto," said Max.

"I know. He asked me to come too."

"What's got into him?"

"I think . . . that he thinks . . . that he might have made a discovery which he had almost despaired of making."

Something to do with that portrait, thought Tom, pulling himself together. He's gone to the Palazzo Albani to investigate. Perhaps it will be best if I keep Max occupied; because then, with Lykiadopoulos off at the Casino, Fielding will have the place to himself. Better for him like that, thought Tom; for after all, the first MS, which started all this off, was taken from a forbidden part of the Palazzo without anybody's permission, and Fielding might be embarrassed if he had to make explanations. Aloud he said,

"Well, let's have a coffee and go to the Ghetto without him."

"Very kind of you," said Max courteously, "to keep me company."

"I think," said Daniel to Piero in the tower, "that you can start making the tea now. Since Tom's as late as this he won't mind."

Piero took the kettle off the oil-heater and poured a little water to warm the pot.

"That's right," said Daniel.

"The Carpaccios in the Accademia—the St Ursula ones —will be open on Wednesday," Piero said. "Will you come with me that morning? And then to see the others at the Scuola San Giorgio?"

"I'll come to the Accademia, and then see how I feel."

Piero began to measure out the tea.

"It would be a pity to miss the Scuola."

"There will be other days."

"Let us hope so."

Piero poured boiling water on to the tea in the pot and began to stir.

"Don't stir it."

"Why not?"

"It's said to be middle-class."

"It makes it stronger."

"To make it stronger you must let it stand."

"That takes longer, and we are already late having it."

"Precisely; but that is a middle-class consideration."

Fielding Gray came into the tower.

"I've read that MS," he said without preamble: "as I hoped, it's about the stranger in that picture."

Daniel and Piero regarded him with displeasure.

"But it's incomplete," Fielding said. "There's another MS I must have—or something of the sort. I think I know how to find it."

Piero fetched a third cup and poured tea for the three of them. Fielding explained that the phallus on the cover sheet of the first MS must be pointing to the sixteenth-century portrait of the man with the rose and the monkey. A monkey for lechery, he said as he had said to Tom; a red rose for the pox.

"Rocco da Malamocco," he repeated in conclusion:

"*coda mala* in the middle. That phallus must mean that we are to look at Rocco's painting."

"*Who* is to look at Rocco's painting?" said Piero.

"Is there anyone in the house?"

"Only the servants."

"Then will you take me there?"

"No. I should not have gone where you told me the first time. I shall not help you now. Whatever else that horrible sign may have meant, to me it is a sign to stand away. And to Daniel."

"You agree with that, Daniel?" Fielding said.

"Yes."

"I could go by myself."

"You would not be allowed up to the portraits," Piero said, "unless Mr Lykiadopoulos or Mr de Freville or I myself were with you."

"Then please come with me, Piero. I can't give up now. I must get to the bottom of it. Surely, Daniel, you understand?"

"Oh yes. I too once wanted, very much, to get to the bottom of something. I did . . . and then I wished I hadn't. Leave this alone, Fielding."

"But *this* is different. Your thing was scientific—it could have been abused. But this is just a very minor historical mystery."

"It may reveal more than you know. It may open up something else which should not be opened up. My thing, as you call it—that too was just a minor mystery when it started. A minor mystery of mathematical notation which, if solved, might possibly suggest new methods for use in the most abstract realms of pure mathematics. Instead of which, Fielding, it opened up a new way to hell."

"But all I want to know is what happened to some people who have been dead for well over a century."

"Dead in their own private hells. If you open up the way to those hells, who knows what you may let out?"

"Daniel. . . . This record has been deliberately left behind. There is a preface to the first MS which says it is written for whomsoever God wills to read it."

"A pretty formidable curse it sounds."

"Daniel, you are seeing this too darkly."

"I wish I wasn't seeing it at all. I'm too tired to argue. Do what you want, Fielding. Piero, take him to that painting."

"No," said Piero, "I won't. You are right, Daniel. Hidden things should stay hidden."

"If Fielding is determined," said Daniel, "he will in any case uncover them. We shan't stop him for long. Better go with him now and do as he asks."

"No."

"*Please*, Piero," Daniel croaked. "I can't bear this conversation any more."

"Very well." Piero turned to Fielding. "Come along, Major Gray," he said. "But understand this. If you stir up ghosts, I shall do everything I can to help them to rest again, because my master, Mr Lykiadopoulos, will not want them in his house. So much will be my duty."

"What do you mean?" said Fielding.

"I do not want to help you. I am helping you only because I know you will bully Daniel until I do as you ask. So I will come with you now to the gallery—but on this understanding: should the ghosts whom you are summoning demand some payment for their journey before they will return, I shall help them to get it because it is just that they should have it."

"You are saying," said Fielding, "that they may want their own back on me for poking my nose in?"

"They may want something of somebody, and if so they must be given it. That is the condition of raising them."

"There will be no ghosts," said Fielding, "and if there are I know how to deal with them on my own terms."

"I shall help them to get theirs. It will be the safer way for me. Now come with me, Major Gray, to the portrait gallery."

"It has a lot of charm," said Tom to Max de Freville as they looked at the Palazzo Castagna-Samuele in the fading light.

"My mind's almost made up. You see, Tom, I don't want to do anything obvious. But to save a back-street curiosity like this—I know Angela approves of the idea."

"How will you go about it?"

"Angela agrees with me that I should raise the money for a survey of the fabric and the foundations. If the report is hopeful, then I shall pass it on to the organisers of the Venice in Peril fund, with some more money if I can get it. I think they'll take the hint."

"So the next step is to find money. Not easy these days. The rich are in a mess, Max."

"Angela thinks that Fielding Gray ought to help."

"How? He's doing well just now, but he hasn't got *this* kind of money."

"She wasn't very precise. She thinks he might produce some idea . . . some new method of raising cash. After all, he owes a debt to both of us."

Tom let this pass. He had heard various rumours as to the part that Fielding had played in bringing about Angela's death,* and he would have liked an accurate account; but Max's vague reference to the affair did not give him enough excuse for detailed enquiry. This being so, he preferred that the subject of Angela should be dropped altogether.

"How's Lyki's bank going?" Tom said.

"I can't expect any money from him."

"I was just wondering how he was getting on."

"Very fair, I'd say." Max looked at his watch. "If we walk down to the Casino now, we can watch the end of his afternoon session."

Tom, who had seen and smelt enough of the filthy Rio which flowed round the Ghetto, was glad to assent. As they walked, Max said :

"All that excitement of Fielding's in Florian's just now. . . . Was it something to do with this mystery of his—about the stranger in the family picture?"

"Yes."

"I don't suppose any harm can come of it. But it *is* an Albani affair, and the Albani *do* rent the palace to us. So if something nasty comes out from under a stone, they might be cross with Lyki and me for letting Fielding meddle."

"He's been doing most of his meddling in the public library. They can't complain of that."

*See *Come Like Shadows, passim.*

"But he did get his first notion about this business from looking at that picture in the Palazzo."

And that's not all he's had from the Palazzo, thought Tom; not by a long chalk. Sooner or later, if anything more turned up, Lyki and Max might have some right to know what was going on.

"We gave him the address of Benito Albani in Siena," Max went on; "thinking back, I'm not sure that was wise."

"Very little came out of that; only a lawyer's letter more or less dismissing the whole thing."

"But Fielding's still on the trail?"

"Yes."

"Well . . . just so long as he doesn't bother Benito or the lawyers again. It might make trouble. But I think," said Max, "that Lyki and I ought to know if anything startling comes of it. After all, we do live in the place."

"I can tell you this, Max. Either nothing will come of it, or else Fielding will have his answer very soon. That's why he was so excited."

"Well," said Max, "in a sense you live in the Palazzo too. So you'll see that Lyki and I know anything that we should."

"Yes. I'll see that you know anything that you should."

"Well," said Piero to Fielding in the portrait gallery, "there is your sixteenth-century portrait. There"—he tapped the canvas—"is the red rose, and there is the monkey. What now?"

Fielding looked at the portrait. The man's face, indifferently painted though it was, suggested intelligence, self-control and worldly humour: it did not (for how should it?) suggest the whereabouts of what Fielding sought. What help, he asked himself, had he expected? The phallus had told him, so he thought, to come to the painting by Rocco da Malamocco: but as Piero said, what now?

"Will the picture come away from the wall?"

"Not easily, no. The frame is set into the woodwork round it."

"Test it."

Piero tried the frame. It remained quite steady. He ran

his hand along the base, pulling, pushing, probing this way and that.

"It is very firm," he said contentedly.

"Look down there. Just below."

A few inches below the picture a small gilded and wreathed medallion was fixed on to the panelling:

TOMMASO ALBANI 1507–1560

it read; and underneath, in smaller letters;

Rocco da Malamocco pinxit

Clearly, the medallion was of far later date than the painting, and had been placed there by some member of the family who had taken an interest in the portraits, had perhaps had them cleaned and catalogued. Then why, Fielding asked himself, looking along the row of faces on the wall, had not this pious person placed commemorative plaques under all the paintings, as he had under Rocco's—and, Fielding now saw, under Rocco's alone. He felt the medallion. He pressed it. No response.

"You try," he said to Piero.

Piero felt delicately round the gilt surface with his fingers, then tried the chiselled wreath which surrounded it.

"Nothing," he said. But Fielding heard him catch his breath.

"Try again."

Piero hesitated, then scrabbled with his finger-nails at the wreath. Fielding shrugged and walked down the line of portraits. Why is he suddenly so clumsy, Fielding thought: one moment his touch was as tender as a girl's, the next he was clawing like an impatient dog at a door; he was trying not to show that he had found something. Fielding stopped and looked at fitzAvon, where he stood at the back of the family group: he wanted to appear relaxed, Fielding thought, but underneath he was as fierce and tense as a cat about to leap—even this painter had caught that. After a brief look at the rest of the family, all smug and wooden (as though frozen into an appearance of content by fear of him that watched them from behind), Fielding turned from the Piero in the canvas to the Piero in the flesh . . . who was now standing away from the wall and shaking his head. I must do what he did the first time he tried that wreath, Fielding thought. He went to the medallion, placed his fingers round the wreath, managed to ease the tips underneath it; then he pulled wreath and medallion together gently out from the wall. They were backed by a cylinder, which slid out behind them like a drawer. The cylinder was about a foot long; from the far end of it Fielding drew out a scroll of paper. Piero widened his mouth, bared his teeth, and then spat, pointing the first and fourth fingers of his left hand towards the floor. Fielding pursed his thin, pink little mouth into a grin of triumph, then tucked the scroll into the waistband of his trousers, as Piero, he remembered, had done with the first MS. Once more Piero spat and pointed his two fingers at the floor.

"I'll just put this device back," Fielding said. He inserted the end of the cylinder into the opening in the wall and eased it inwards until the medallion, once again, sat right up against the panelling as though fastened to it. "There," he said; "I don't think anyone will notice that it's been interfered with. Do you, Piero?"

"You have no right to those papers, Major Gray."

"I have every right. They were left there that 'whomsoever God willed' should find them. It seems that God has chosen me."

As Max and Tom entered the Casino from the Calle Vendramin, they were aware that the doorman saluted with unusual briskness. The lift-man, who took them up to the special floor on which Lykiadopoulos operated his bank, was positively leering with pleasure. Even the woman in the cloakroom, who normally radiated malignance, seemed to be happy about something and gave them tabs for their overcoats with a most uncommon good grace.

"There's a new air about the place," said Max.

In the passage to the bar people hustled to and fro, laughing and chattering and waving. In the bar itself eager waiters darted about with trays, serving a clientele of at least three times the usual number, while the head barman, deploying bottles and cocktail-shakers with the skill and speed of an expert conjurer, pattered away with animation to nearby drinkers.

"An air of carnival," said Max. "What's got into everybody?"

When they entered the Salle de Baccara itself, they found out. As they wriggled their way through a dense crowd, excitement throbbed all about them and noises of oohing and aahing and Madonna-mia-ing rose shrill ahead of them; and as they broke through at last to the rail, they were almost dazzled by the profusion of brilliant plaques that lay strewn across the table and by the clusters of white robes which billowed on either side of Lykiadopoulos and threatened at any moment (Tom thought) to swirl right over him.

"Jesus Christ," said Max, "it's the bloody Arabs. They weren't expected till November."

An Arab next to Lykiadopoulos turned his cards face upwards. There was a sound, somewhere between a high-pitched humming and a howl, from the spectators. Lykiadopoulos sat very still in his seat, while a delicate dewy red patina spread over both his cheeks.

"Part of his act?" said Tom to Max, remembering the latter's disquisition about this on the bank's opening night. "Or genuine, would you say?"

Max shook his head and affected not to hear. While the humming of the spectators slowly quietened, Max and Tom watched the croupiers, who were doggedly paying out to the punters on both halves of the table.

PART FOUR

THE KILL

AS SOON AS he had made his discovery in the portrait gallery in the Palazzo Albani, Fielding Gray returned to the Gabrielli Hotel. He did not even pause to look in again on Daniel in the tower, for Piero, he knew, would have accompanied him there, and he had had enough of Piero's disagreeable behaviour for one day. He simply walked out of the Palazzo into the Calle Alba and hence to the Accademia Bridge, where he caught a vaporetto which would take him the rest of his way home. Neither while he was waiting for the vaporetto nor while he was on it did he attempt to examine the scroll of paper which he had found, for the excellent reason that some of it might have blown away. The scroll stayed firmly tucked into the waist of his trousers, and only when he was in his room in the Gabrielli, with the door locked behind him, did he at last allow himself to extract and unroll it.

The sheets were covered with small and precise writing, not in Italian, as he had surmised, but in French. The moment he thought about it, the reason for this was plain: French would be understood by Fernando Albani's children, and by educated people of the kind to which the memoir was addressed, but it would not be understood by servants who might have happened on the sheets in the tower where they had at first been deposited. Although the French was more sophisticated than Fernando's Greek had been, it was not difficult to read and tended to avoid hypothesis or qualification. The opening paragraph (there was no title) was quite admirably blunt.

'I, Fernando Albani, offer the following account of the shameful events within my household between the years 1794 and 1797. The public evidence has been concealed in order to prevent or at least defer open disgrace. But I wish my younger children to know all, as a warning to be wary of their Albani blood. This blood has always been reported to be cool and wholesome; my story will suggest other possibilities. For the rest, it is written to preserve the truth for such as may come on it at some future time; the account is therefore rendered as truthfully as I would render it to God Himself.'

This was much the same declaration of motive as had prefaced the first MS, Fielding thought : the truth must be recorded in order that 'such as may come on it at some future time' (*cf.* 'those whomsoever God wills') may be fully and accurately informed. Very well; what was there to know?

'This history,' Fernando continued, 'concerns a young Englishman who first came under my eyes in the last months of 1794, introducing himself in the name of Humbert fitz-Avon and as being of reckonable family. In an earlier tract and in another tongue I have written, under guise of a fable, of all that befell this young man in his life before he came here to Venice and before we knew him. I based that account on what he told me of his life and career as our acquaintance progressed; and it is of this acquaintance, how it quickened and then ripened into fruits of poison, that I must now write here.'

As the text continued, Fielding began to build a picture of fitzAvon in his intercourse with the Albani family in the early days after the first meeting. Where Fernando did not state, he most amply insinuated; where he omitted a concrete detail, he established it by the very manner of his omission; where he had not seen, he implied beyond doubt what he had conceived. A little imagination swelled the words into flesh and blood; a little insight transformed Fernando's hints and suggestions, his reported and compressed exchanges, into voices, conversations and whole scenes. . . .

'. . . My son tells me you have done him a great service, Mr fitzAvon. We are grateful, my wife and I.'

'I was glad to be of use, Signore. A pleasant boy like your son should not be made to pay too high for one act of folly committed while he is still so young.'

'As to that . . . act of folly . . . I rely on your discretion.'

'You may do so. Discretion is a small thing to give, Signore, in exchange for the friendship of yourself and your family.'

'You are most welcome here, Mr fitzAvon. Consider this house to be yours and everything that is in it. . . .'

. . . An invitation which was to be taken all too literally. For only a few days later :

'Why *were* you at that bordel, Piero ?'

'I was curious, Umberto. A friend told me what was arranged there.'

'Did he indeed? Shall we walk in the garden and out to the tower?'

'If you like, Umberto.'

And they strolled in the garden, passing Fernando, who was coming back from the tower towards the house.

'We are going to the tower, father.'

'By all means, but please do not disturb anything in my study. I am happy to see you here today, Mr fitzAvon.'

'It is so pleasant in your garden, Signore. There are few gardens in Venice.'

'I'm glad you enjoy it. You must excuse me. Good afternoon, Mr fitzAvon, and Piero.'

'Your father will not be coming back to the tower, Piero ?'

'No. He has business this afternoon.'

'Good. Let us walk a little and then go there. So, Piero. You were interested about what would happen at the bordel. Was your curiosity satisfied ?'

'There was not enough time, Umberto. Those men came to spoil it.'

'What did you see before they came ?'

'Men with women.'

'Was anyone with you ?'

'No. I kept in the background. I was only there to watch.'

'I see. Come into the tower. . . . And now tell me. Where you excited by what you saw before those men came ?'

'Of course.'

'And you are excited now, remembering it ?'

'Yes, Umberto.'

'Let me try you. Yes, you *are* excited, Piero.'

'I think you too are excited, Umberto.'

'Try me then . . . *gently*, Piero. You Italian boys can be

very rough. That's better. Do you trust me, Piero? Will you
do what I say?'

'Yes. Only show me.'

'All you need do is stay still. For I think, *this* time, that it
will be best for you . . . like this. Quite still, Piero. My pleasure, *this* time, is to give you pleasure. So I kiss you there,
and there, and there . . . such a soft skin you have . . . yes,
you may stroke my hair, Piero . . . while I am kissing you
. . . here.'

And a few days after that :

'I thought perhaps I should find you alone, Signora. I
passed Signor Albani on my way in.'

'I am very often alone, Mr fitzAvon. I expected you before now.'

'Why?'

'Because of the way you have looked at me. You made
sure the others would not see, and then looked at me.'

'I wonder what I meant.'

'Do not mock me, Mr fitzAvon. From the time you first
looked at me, I have waited for this. I am impatient. My
husband is no longer young, and *I am impatient.* Come
with me. Behind that screen is a little door, and behind the
door there is—'

'—One moment, Signora. Please don't move yet. Let me
sit here beside you and let us talk for a little. Like this. What
beautiful arms you have. Beautiful arms mean beautiful
legs, they say.'

'Umberto . . . no, Umberto, not here. What is it you
wish to talk of?'

'I want you to say a word in my favour . . . to your
daughter.'

'My *daughter*?'

'Euphemia. Do not worry, Signora. My intentions . . .
there . . . are honourable. Ah . . . such a soft skin you have.
Like warm satin.'

'Umberto . . . oh, stop, Umberto. Come with me now.
Behind that screen—'

'—There is a little door. So you have already told me.
But first : you will talk to your daughter?'

'We do not know anything about you. Marriage in Italy
is a very serious matter.'

'In that case, I had better cease . . . to amuse myself like this . . . with a married woman.'

'No. No. Don't stop. I only meant that the making of a marriage for a young girl is a grave responsibility.'

'I shall use her well. Presently you may see how well I shall use her.'

'But money, family . . . who *are* you, Umberto?'

'I think I can satisfy your husband as to all that. Will you speak a word for me to your daughter?'

'You are well able to speak your own.'

'It will make her more trusting if her mother approves.'

'I am not sure I do approve. Oh, stop, Umberto, please stop. If anyone came in now—'

'—He would see your pretty bare thighs splayed all over the sofa. You *will* speak to Euphemia?'

'*Take me behind the screen.*'

'I will make you spend your pleasure like this, just on my hand, like a kitchen-slut here on this sofa, unless you promise to speak to Euphemia.'

'God, oh God . . . *Umberto*. Yes; I will speak to her.'

'Good. *Now* we will go behind the screen, Signora, and through your little door. . . .'

That same evening :

'How old are you, Euphemia?'

'I am sixteen, Signore.'

'You should call me "Umberto" as your brother does.'

'Umberto. Umberto.'

'In English, "Humbert". Try it.'

'Uh. . . . Uh. . . . 'Umburt.'

'Not bad, for a first attempt. Should you like to be able to speak English?'

'To whom would I speak it?'

'To me. Then the others would not know what we were saying. We would have a private language.'

'We are alone, Sign—Umberto. We do not need a private language.'

'We are not often alone.'

'We can be. My mother says I may be alone with you.'

'Does she now? Still, there are things that are better said in a private language, even when we are alone.'

'Teach me then.'

'Very well. Repeat after me: "What is love? 'Tis not hereafter".'

' "Wot ess luff? 'Teez nat 'ereefty".'

'Very good. "Present mirth hath present laughter".'

' "Preesent mith heth preesint lefty." Tell me what it means, Umberto.'

'It means that if we wish to love somebody we should not waste time, because soon we grow old.'

'Oh.'

'It is poetry. But there is other poetry, which tells us that we should not be in too much haste to have what we want, because when we have had it we no longer want it. It tells us to prolong the pleasure of waiting, of imagining.'

'Oh.'

'That is what I am going to do with you, Euphemia, and you with me. We are going to tempt one another; to tempt one another, but to remain covered and veiled, until we are almost frenzied. And then, after a long time of this delicious frustration, we shall marry and come to each other at last. We shall have guessed many things but seen and known nothing. We shall lust to compare what we have guessed at with what is really there.'

'I do not quite understand, Umberto. As for marrying, that is as my father may command me.'

'I will take care of your father.'

'But what is this . . . about tempting each other?'

'I will tell you another time. To begin with, you see, I am tempting you with the mere idea of temptation.'

And on fitzAvon's way downstairs, a quick visit to the nursery:

'Francesca. . . . Francesco. . . .'

'Rock me on my rocking horse.'

'You are big enough to rock yourself.'

'I want *you* to rock me. Francesca says you rocked her yesterday and made her feel nice. I want to feel nice.'

'Very well. Climb on to your horse and grip tightly with your knees.'

'I want to ride too.'

'Then get on to the other horse, Francesca, and sit as I showed you yesterday. Not sideways, but as your brother sits. That's right. Now, first I rock you both slowly . . . then a little quicker. See what your sister is doing, Francesca, sliding up and down along the saddle . . . faster and faster. . . . Push yourself up towards the head as it goes up, back towards the tail as the head goes down.'

'It tickles.'

'Now try to do it the other way. Back towards the tail as the head goes up, down towards the head as the head goes down. Is it nice, Francesca?'

'Yes, but help me as you helped me yesterday.'

'Help me too.'

'Ladies first. I will help your sister first, Francesca, and then I will help you.'

And so the weeks went on :

'Umberto . . . come with me to the tower.'

'Not today, Piero. I must see your mother.'

'What do you want with her?'

'We have matters to discuss.'

'Then promise you will come tomorrow.'

'Tomorrow, Piero, we will go in my gondola together. The one which your father has lent me. That will be much better than the tower.'

'Promise?'

'I promise, *caro*. Now I must go to your mother . . . .'

'. . . . . Euphemia is beginning to yearn for me, Maria, but I do not touch her.'

'You still wish to marry her?'

'Yes. She will not regret it.'

'You have spoken to my husband?'

'Not yet. I want you to prepare him.'

'He does not trust you.'

'He has lent me a gondola.'

'He does not trust you, Umberto.'

'The times are dangerous, Maria. Italy is threatened, Venice is threatened. Euphemia may need me by and by, and I Euphemia.'

'Fernando will never let his daughter marry a man of mystery.'

'I shall not be a mystery to him much longer. Meanwhile, prepare him, Maria.'

'I want you for myself.'

'For as long as possible you shall have me—if you do as I say.'

'Very well, I will speak with him. Now kiss me, Umberto. Have me. Take me. *Do it to me.*'

'I have already done it to you once.'

'Again.'

'But we have dressed ourselves and I must go.'

'*Again.*'

'Quickly then. Quick, Maria, down on your knees, Maria. Like the dogs do it, Maria. Up with your dress and . . . a nice, plump bottom you have, but getting slack and dimpled. Now Euphemia's, which I have never seen—'

'—Do not talk of her *now*—'

'—Euphemia's will be smooth and firm. And Euphemia will have a neat, tight virgin cleft. It will not be like ploughing in a muddy ditch.'

'*Umberto.*'

'Be grateful for what you can get, Maria, and next time do not ask for too much. Do not ask at all until you have talked as I told you with your husband.'

'But don't stop now please don't stop.'

'You have one minute to reach your pleasure, Maria, and then I am going down to the garden to talk with Euphemia . . . .

'. . . . . And so yesterday I tempted you, Euphemia, by telling you what little boys do, what I did and what my nurse did to me. Today you must tempt me. What do little girls do?'

'Once, when we were on a journey, I was put into the same bed as Piero. He was tired and fell asleep at once. When he undressed I had seen that thing of his. And now I was curious and put my arm round him to feel it.'

'Now you *are* tempting me, Euphemia. But I shall not touch you. What happened?'

'It went stiff under my hand . . . as you told me yours did under your nurse's. But he did not wake. So I took my hand away and felt myself in that place. I found a tiny piece of flesh, but it would not go stiff like Piero's.'

'Did you feel nothing?'

'Something began to stir inside me. But then our mother came in, and pulled back the bedclothes to rearrange them.

When she saw Piero's thing, sticking out under his shirt, she looked at me and said, "Have you been touching Piero?" I said, "No", and she said no more. But we were never put in the same bed again.'

'Did you wish to be?'

'Perhaps. But to make up there was a little black page, who used to let me play with him. I never let him touch me, but I would get him in the nursery cupboard and play with him and make stuff run out of him. When the stuff came out he used to whimper like a little dog. When I was in bed later, I would play with myself and think of him whimpering and the warm stuff running over my hand. Umberto, could we not . . . play together?'

'No, Euphemia. We can only talk and tempt. Now I must go. . . . . . .

'. . . . . . Good evening, Francesco. Where is your sister?'

'She is ill, Umberto.'

'Would you like a ride on one of the rocking horses?'

'No. On your knee, like last time.'

'Come here then. You shall have an especially nice ride, Francesco, if you will promise to help me.'

'All right.'

'Just tell your father and mother that I have been kind to you and how much you like me.'

'Shall I tell them about our rides?'

'No. I shouldn't tell them about those.'

'Why not? Are they wrong?'

'Of course not. How could it be wrong just to have a nice feeling? But mothers and fathers sometimes get jealous and angry if their little children have fun with somebody else. So just say that I have spoken kindly to you from time to time.'

'All right. Now give me my ride. Someone will come soon to take me to bed.'

And some days later Maria and Fernando together:

'The twins like him, Fernando. And we know what he has done for Piero.'

'Yes. I have a shrewd idea what he has done for Piero.'

'What do you mean?'

'Nothing. Go on, Maria.'

'Why should he not marry Euphemia?'

'We do not know anything about him.'

'But if he sets that right?'

'We will see what he has to say. If anything. I mistrust him, Maria. He has a way with him which makes me uneasy. I know we must be grateful, but I could wish my family saw less of him. I do not like his visits to the nursery. There is a funny look about Francesco when he speaks of him, and Francesca is very sly.'

'Do not forget, Fernando: a word from fitzAvon, and Piero would be in trouble with the Inquisition.'

'A word from Piero, and fitzAvon would be in trouble with the Inquisition.'

'No. fitzAvon is a foreigner. He has a post under the British Minister—that at least we know. The Inquisition would not make trouble for him.'

'The French would, if they came here.'

'The French would make trouble for us all. At least fitzAvon could take Euphemia to his own country.'

'If the French let him go. Anyway, the French will not come for a while yet.'

'We should be prepared.'

'I am not at all sure that fitzAvon can help us with our preparations. I am not at all sure that I want Euphemia to leave Venice—least of all if it is he that is taking her.'

'But at least talk to him, Fernando.'

'Yes. I have been meaning to talk to him for some time.......

'....... And so now, Mr fitzAvon, let us converse together. You have been making rather free of my household, I think.'

'At your invitation, Signore.'

'You have interpreted my invitation . . . somewhat loosely.'

'I do not think any member of your household is the less happy for it.'

'Perhaps our notions of happiness differ.'

'We are at least agreed that if Piero were . . . shown up . . . to the Inquisition, that would be most *un*happy for him.'

'They would deal leniently with Piero. He is only a boy.'

'Nevertheless, Signore, it is not what you would wish.

Another thing on which we could agree is that Euphemia has arrived at an age when she is not averse from being courted.'

'When, and by whom, my daughter is to be courted is for me to decide, Mr fitzAvon.'

'Would you reject me as a suitor?'

'We know nothing of you.'

'You know my name and my condition.'

'We have a name by which we can call you. We may accept that you are a gentleman. But beyond this we know nothing—not even why you are here in Venice.'

'To serve his Britannic Majesty's Minister here.'

'But in what capacity? It is not the kind of employment that most English gentlemen would choose at a time like the present. At times like the present, gentlemen take up arms. They do not lurk in foreign cities, or not without a clearly defined office to perform. What is your office, Mr fitzAvon?'

'I grant that I must be something of a mystery to you. Soon, very soon, I will make everything clear to you, for I shall owe this to you if I am to solicit your daughter's affection. I understand that.'

'Pray understand also that even when you do declare yourself you will not necessarily have my support in your approaches to my daughter.'

'When you know everything about me, I think you will be very happy that I should approach her. Although there is one . . . circumstance . . . which may displease you, it is more than outweighed by others.'

'Perhaps so. How soon can I expect your revelations?'

'In a few days.'

'Very well. In the meantime, though I can hardly object to your intimacy with my son Piero, I should prefer that you visit my two younger children only when others are present.'

At this stage, Fielding knocked off for lunch; it seemed a suitable place for an interval. The state of play was that fitzAvon, like the imported 'Greekling' in Juvenal's satire on Rome, had debauched an entire family—except Euphemia, whom he had enslaved but not yet seduced, and except, of course, for the paterfamilias himself, an omission

which, if Fielding remembered aright, had not been made
by the canny Greekling. So now the paterfamilias was
entering a mild protest, to meet which fitzAvon had promised to reveal himself very soon in his true colours—*i.e.*
to give Fernando Albani the information on which, Fielding supposed, Albani was later to base his fable of the Wolf-
Prince. Now, at last, both Fernando and Fielding in their
separate generations were about to learn who and what
fitzAvon really was.

Meanwhile, Fielding asked himself, was he sure that his
interpretation of this second MS was not too licentious?
Fernando had never said in so many words that his wife
and his elder son shared fitzAvon's favours, that his two
youngest children had been corrupted, and that his elder
daughter had been enticed in a fashion far more sinister
than outright seduction. The only conversations reported
verbatim were those in which Fernando himself had taken
part; all the others, and the activities which accompanied
or concluded them, had been imagined by Fielding. And
yet Fielding reckoned he had good warranty for his
imaginings. They might be due in part to prurience, or in
part to the lack of sexual exercise in his own recent life;
but nevertheless everything which he had pictured to himself was there in Fernando's MS; by implication, or between the lines, in metaphorical palimpsest, so to speak, it
was all there quite as surely as if Fernando had described
it word for word. The comparison which occurred to
Fielding was with Henry James's *Turn of the Screw* : there
was not a syllable, in that novel, which spoke directly of
physical acts, but the reader was none the less certain—as
certain as if James had spoken in the roundest terms—that
Miles and Flora had been sexually manipulated and, more
or less, how.

He would, in any case, ask Tom to adjudicate; if level-
minded Tom agreed with him, he must be right. Tom's
opinion would also be very useful in the area which
Fernando was just beginning to enter—the whole question
of fitzAvon's actual identity and provenance. If, as now
seemed the case, fitzAvon was about to be revealed as
someone whose standing corresponded with the splendid
title of Wolf-Prince, under which he had gone in the fable,

then Tom the historian's knowledge of eighteenth-century grandees and their families would be invaluable.

"I think," said Max de Freville to Lykiadopoulos in the Palazzo Albani, "that Fielding Gray may have found out something about that picture. He was very excited yesterday afternoon."

"Found out what about what picture?" said Lykiadopoulos indifferently.

"That stranger in the Albani family group. You remember he was interested. He may have a clue about him. Tom Llewyllyn says he'd almost given up, but now it seems he may have discovered something important after all."

"Discovered what?"

"I don't know. Tom has promised to let us in on it if it's anything to our purpose."

"How could it be to our purpose? Our purpose it to make money out of this Baccarat Bank."

"Well, we might be concerned," said Max. "After all, if Fielding found out something disagreeable about the family from whom we're renting this house—"

"—It would still make no difference whatever to the Baccarat Bank," said Lykiadopoulos sullenly.

"You . . . don't sound too happy about that."

"I'm not. Those Arabs have arrived here before they were expected. I haven't had time to prepare my defences."

"You mean your reserves aren't big enough?"

"Partly that, yes. Since I began, I've won a handsome sum which the Casino is holding for me as a liquid asset. But yesterday I lost at least half of it. It just isn't large enough, Max my friend. Another day like yesterday—with those Arabs betting in maximums—and it'll all be gone."

"The luck could change. Anyway, the Casino is funding your bank on the strength of the securities you've lodged. They're still sitting there intact."

"And must continue to do so. As we have said before, if the Casino demands the sale of any of those securities, we could be in trouble. So what I want is to be sitting on a nice healthy pile of ready money *over and above* any other surety."

"Of course that's what you want. But you're too old a

hand to think you can have your own way all the time."

"Indeed I am. What I'm really saying, Max, is that those Arabs are making things happen too quickly. They're forcing the pace. I had hoped to take precautions against that, but they are here too soon for me."

"Let's get this straight, Lyki. Do you just mean that you'd hoped to build up a large reserve of winnings before the Arabs arrived? Or had you . . . something else in mind?"

"Both. You see, I could never be sure of building a large reserve, let alone one large enough to protect me against really heavy betting. So as you may remember, Max, I went to see an acquaintance in Padua."

"I remember. A professor. An expert in metaphysics."

"A special branch of metaphysics."

"Like Diabolism?" said Max sarcastically. "I don't know of any other branch that could help you."

"You are very near. My friend has made a study of the Black Art. Being a sane man, he does not believe in sorcery but he is fascinated by the methods of sorcerers. Such men did produce remarkable illusions."

"Conjurors, Lyki. Shit," said Max dully, "you're not going to try to rig the game like that? They'll have you in prison."

"Don't be silly, Max. As we know, there are only two ways of rigging the game like that: to insert the cards into the shoe in a predetermined order, favourable to oneself; or to substitute a specially prepared shoe of cards in place of the one in proper use. With the surveillance they have here in Venice, either method would be far too risky, even with the cleverest of conjurors to operate it. A single slip—and one would indeed, as you say, be in prison."

"Thank God you've got that straight. So where does your tame Black Magician come in?"

"That is just the trouble. He can't come in yet, as he has not had enough time to make his preparations."

"For Christ's sake, Lyki. What is he going to do when he has made them?"

"For one thing, he is going to need your help. That is why I am telling you this."

"I don't like the sound of it."

"Nor do I, but I have no choice. It is these Arabs, Max.

So many of them, staking so high. Now, my academic friend has devised a method, not necessarily of ensuring that I win but at least of limiting those Arabs to stakes which I can reasonably afford to lose if the luck goes sour on me. It is quite indetectible, and even if it goes wrong there can in no case be discovery or accusation against him, or you, or me." Lykiadopoulos lowered his voice. "Listen, Max," he said: "you are aware that there are certain sounds which animals can hear but are either too high or too low in pitch for human ears?"

"I've heard something of the kind."

"It was early realised by sorcerers and Diabolists that the waves caused by noise had definite effects on the nervous system. If you wanted to alarm a crowd, or to soothe it, certain tunes and sounds could be a great help—and even more help, my friend, if they were the kind which could not actually be heard by the ear. If you hear a shrill noise, you start; if you don't expect it, you start even more; and if you do not even hear it but just receive an unpleasant shock on the nervous system for no reason you can discern, you will come near to panic. You follow?"

"I think so."

"My friend has investigated descriptions of instruments with which the old Magicians produced such influential but unheard vibrations. Very soon he hopes to have made and tested some of them. Then . . . he will come to the Casino and soothe or alarm the punters."

"It'll look pretty odd if he stands about blowing sub-sonic whistles or whatever."

"He need not—should not—be too close to the table. All his instruments will resemble such commonplace objects as cigarette-holders and so on. No one will be aware what he is doing; everyone will respond to the vibrations . . . or so we hope. When the gamblers are alarmed or uneasy, they will bet low; when they are soothed, they may bet high."

"Where do I come in?"

"I shall not be able to communicate with my friend, even by signs. It might be observed. You will be able to talk to him, quite naturally, whenever you wish. You will be able to tell him, at any time, whether in your judgement I am in for a good streak or a bad. If a bad—and you will of

course lean heavily on the side of pessimism—you will tell
him to alarm the punters and so keep their stakes low. But
if you feel really confident, you will tentatively try soothing
them and thus enticing them to increase their bets."

"Those instruments could affect my judgement too."

"No. You will know about them and so discount their
influence."

"What makes you think these Arabs will respond?"

"They are very much the kind of people that the old
Magicians had to cater for. Ignorant and impulsive."

"As to that, we shall see. When will your chap be ready?"

"He has had great difficulty in the manufacture of the
instruments. I hope he will be ready for his first serious
trial in three or four days. It is longer than I would wish,
and meanwhile one can only pray that the cards will be
kind."

". . . And so," said Fielding Gray to Tom Llewyllyn, "a few
days after his conversation with Fernando, fitzAvon kept
his promise and told him who he really was."

"And who was he?"

Fielding took a deep breath.

"He was Charles Humbert fitzAvon d'Azincourt Sarum,
called by courtesy of England Viscount Rollesden-in-Silvis,
only son and heir apparent of the Earl of Muscateer."

"He was what?"

"He was Charles Humbert fitz—"

"—Just the last bit."

"Viscount Rollesden-in-Silvis, only son and heir apparent of the Earl of Muscateer."

"Canteloupe's lot?"

"Yes, Canteloupe's lot. Come to think of it now, there
were signals right from the start. In the first MS, the
Wolf-Prince was also Lord of the Forest—Rollesden-in-
Silvis, Tom. The Mighty Wolf was κρατῶν λύκος in
Greek. KRATON is not far from an anagram of
CANTE, and λύκος—wolf—equals and resembles the
French loup. Put 'em together and you get something
pretty near Canteloupe—which was Muscateer's title by
the time Fernando got round to writing the fable. And
then the names Humbert and fitzAvon—both sometimes

used in the Sarum family as subsidiary Christian names. I should have spotted them."

"You seem very knowledgeable about the Sarums."

"I ought to be. I went through a lot of the family stuff with Detterling when old Canteloupe died last month. So here's a little more about them. Fernando is here relating the events of 1795. This Earl of Muscateer just referred to was made first Marquis Canteloupe in 1799. By that time his only son by his first wife—*i.e.* Viscount Rollesden-in-Silvis, alias Humbert fitzAvon—was dead. According to the family records, he had died abroad, in 1797."

"That fits. Does Fernando get round to telling us about his death?"

"He does. And more of that later. Meanwhile," said Fielding, "note this: the first Marquis Canteloupe, when so promoted in 1799, had no male heir. His wife was now mad (which may incidentally explain some of his dead son's behaviour) and was in any case too old for child-bearing. So he arranged for the new title to be passed on through the male issue of his daughter, the Lady Julia Sarum, who married a Detterling. Then his mad wife died and he managed a son by her successor, so in the event there was no need of the special arrangement about the issue of Lady Julia . . . or not until the other day, when the main line ended with poor old Canteloupe, and the Sarum/Detterling side of the family came up with our friend Captain Detterling, who has now inherited."

"Why are you telling me all this?"

"You'll see. Oh my paws and whiskers, Tom, *you'll see*. But first: what do you, as an historian, know of this Earl of Muscateer?"

Tom thought carefully. Then he gave a satisfied nod, as of one who has just fitted an awkward piece into a jigsaw puzzle.

"He was never a really big man," Tom said, "but he was clever at managing things behind the scenes. According to the gossip, he ingratiated himself with the Royal Family by having George III to stay down in Wiltshire and keeping a discreet eye on him when he first started having the funny spells which afterwards became lunacy. Muscateer was later made a marquis in return for his services, and these

being what they were the powers that be would doubtless
have been happy to oblige him in the matter of the special
remainder. He had also been previously granted another
and less official favour—again, according to the gossips. In
1794 his son had been involved in the Maids of Tyburn
Affray—a very nasty business in which a Roman Catholic
Priest interrupted some noblemen, who were amusing
themselves with some young Irish children in a brothel, and
was killed for his interference. There was a blazing scandal,
and young Lord Rollesden-in-Silvis was in the middle of it.
But before the affair could come to trial, he was spirited
away, with official connivance—and then never heard of
again until reported dead . . . in 1797. It was said that he
had been serving the Government under the rose in Europe,
and had been killed in a brawl with some French agents,
several of whom he took on single-handed. All this was
generally held to wipe out, to some extent, his guilt in the
Maids of Tyburn case, and to justify the Government men
who had smuggled him abroad when he should have been
standing trial."

"They must have been whitewashing him, Tom. According to Fernando, later in this memoir, he was certainly
killed in a brawl in 1797—but *not* with French agents.
Apart from that, what you say—"

"—What the contemporary gossips said—"

"—Seems to square pretty well with Fernando's account,
both in the fable of the Wolf-Prince and in the memoir."

Fielding patted the memoir with affection.

"Yes," said Tom. "I should have seen the resemblance—
between fitzAvon's activities and those of Rollesden-in-
Silvis—much earlier. It was a celebrated scandal in its
time."

"Anyway, we agree, now, that the mystery of the stranger
in that picture is solved. He was called Rollesden-in-Silvis;
he was son and heir to Lord Muscateer, who was later promoted Marquis Canteloupe—"

"—And he died in Italy, in some kind of fight, in 1797.
A very ingenious piece of minor research, Fielding, and a
very amusing conclusion."

"The only thing is," said Fielding, "that this isn't the
conclusion."

"You have discovered who the stranger in that picture was, and you know that he was killed in 1797. That sounds pretty final to me."

"But I haven't yet told you what Fernando says of fitzAvon's goings-on between the time when he revealed who he really was and the time of his death. There is a nasty little joke to come, Tom, which I hope you will enjoy as much as I do."

"You mean . . . he married Euphemia Albani before he died, perhaps?"

"Dear me, no. Nothing as wholesome as that. True, he went on trying, but it didn't come off."

"Then what did happen . . . which you find so funny?" Fielding turned the pages of the MS in front of him.

"As soon as fitzAvon had revealed his true identity to Fernando," Fielding said, "Fernando remembered the story of the scandal in England some while before, and was quite horrified to think whom his family had been entertaining. But fitzAvon—we may as well go on calling him that—told Fernando not to be a silly bourgeois prig, and then proposed a deal. . . ."

"Tom and Fielding are discussing that new MS again," said Daniel to Piero, when the latter joined him in the tower that afternoon. "Tom's been gone hours."

Piero shrugged crossly.

"It's too late to worry about that," he said.

"I know. But I still have the feeling that whatever they find out . . . may do none of us any good."

"Meanwhile, there is something actually happening, now, that may do none of us any good. Mr Lykiado-poulos is worried about his Baccarat Bank."

"If he should fail, you know by now where you can turn."

"To you? To a dying man," said Piero neutrally. "There is little comfort in that for either of us."

"There is some money you can have."

"Mr Lykiadopoulos will not fail . . . entirely. He will retain, somehow, much more than you could ever give me. But he will be unhappy. You see, Daniel, if this bank fails, he will have failed all those Greeks who depend on him.

It will not console him that he will still have enough for himself and me."

"Will it console you?"

"A little. But it will be miserable living with him."

"Then leave him and take what I can offer."

"He is . . . he is my career. He is my living and my parents' living. He is my master, in a way you do not understand, and he has bound me to him. I may be disobedient to him, even in quite important things, but I am still his to command, Daniel, and I cannot leave him, however disastrously he should fail here in Venice. Anyway," said Piero, picking up the kettle, "he may not fail at all."

"So the terms were drawn up," Fielding told Tom Llewyllyn. "Fernando took a good deal of persuading, and the bargaining went on for some months, but at last the thing was agreed. What Fernando would be getting was fitz-Avon's absolute oath of silence about Piero's presence in the brothel at the time of the raid by the Inquisition; an ancient and noble name, and eventually the title of an English Countess, for his daughter Euphemia; and a guarantee of financial aid (for fitzAvon already enjoyed a considerable fortune in his own right) in the event of the Albani fortunes' being wrecked by the troubles which were sweeping over Italy.

"What fitzAvon would receive in return was, first, Euphemia, whom in some way he seems to have coveted; and secondly, protection. He could not return to England for a long time—not until the Maids of Tyburn scandal had finally fizzled out; and he might have considerable difficulties, as things appeared in 1795, in establishing himself anywhere in Europe. But in Italy, he said, Albani could arrange for him to be adopted into the family of the Monteverdi on the occasion of his marriage to Euphemia, and once he was known as the adopted son of the influential Count Monteverdi, and went under the same name, he would probably be safe—even if Buonaparte conquered the entire country.

"But here, as Fernando told him, there was one nasty snag. The Count Monteverdi was an honourable and also a pious man, and he would never adopt fitzAvon if he knew him to be really Lord Rollesden-in-Silvis, the notorious debaucher of the Maids of Tyburn and the murderer of a priest. Therefore fitzAvon must be presented to the Count in the guise in which he had first presented himself to Fernando—as an orphaned English gentleman of means. And if that wasn't good enough for the Count, it would be just too bad for fitzAvon.

"Here, of course, we revert to that letter I had the other day from the Albani lawyers in Siena. As the letter related, in the autumn of 1796 Fernando took himself off to Siena to see Count Monteverdi, carrying with him a copy of the family group which had recently been painted and in which fitzAvon was portrayed in the family's company. When asked by Monteverdi to account for his prospective son-in-law, Fernando trotted out the orphaned-English-gentleman-of-means-and-education story—and was turned down flat. So back he came to Venice with news of his failure. And then the trouble really started. fitzAvon was furious at this rejection, and was by now a frightened man as well; for Buonaparte's forces were rapidly crossing the North of Italy, and it looked as if he might be trapped—without the benefit of Tuscan papers and passport, which adoption by the Count Monteverdi in Siena would probably have procured for him. As a mere English agent in Venice, dubiously employed and without official diplomatic standing, he knew he would get very short shrift from the French—a cell or even a firing squad."

"But surely," said Tom, "if we've interpreted the fable correctly, the Wolf-Prince, i.e. fitzAvon, had definite and official duties, should Venice be threatened with capture, in aid of the British Minister. Wouldn't this have given him some kind of diplomatic standing?"

"No. His instructions had always been secret. He had never been properly accredited. And according to this memoir no arrangements had been made for him. If things got dangerous, he was to help the Minister destroy certain records and papers—after which the Minister would be taken up by a British frigate and returned to England; but of course there was no such passage home available to the Maids of Tyburn murderer. Once the Minister left, fitzAvon was on his own."

"He hadn't even a special passport?"

"Not special enough for the Armies of the French Revolution. No doubt about it. In a very few months or even weeks, fitzAvon was going to be up against it. No adoption, so no Tuscan papers, and no Euphemia—for in the circumstances Fernando was certainly not going to marry her to a man, Viscount or no, who would confer on her the taint of British nationality without being able to take her off to safety in Britain. So the game was nearly up. But fitzAvon still had enough pull with Maria to persuade her to arrange a hiding place for him in the family villa in the Veneto; and there was enough time, before he would have to leave, for him to have a last little fling with other of his favourites in the family. He would seem to have devised it partly as a farewell pleasure, partly as an act of revenge for his disappointments. From what Fernando writes, I imagine something rather like this. . . ."

'. . . . . . But there is one thing we can do before I go, Piero. One final delight we can enjoy together. We . . . and another.'

'And another, Umberto?'

'Your sister, Euphemia.'

'I do not understand.'

'You have often said that there is nothing you would not do for me. Surely you will not go back on that, now that I must leave you?'

'No, but I still do not understand.'

'Then listen. Euphemia has told me that when you were both children you were put into the same bed, in an inn. Do you remember what happened?'

'I was tired and fell asleep.'

'But Euphemia was not tired. She can remember what happened. She will show you and me.'

'But she is grown now, Umberto, and so am I. We cannot . . . lie down together.'

'You will be children again, and so it will all be quite innocent. We shall be reverting to paradise, where all pleasures are the innocent pleasures of children. . . . . . .

. . . . So you see, Euphemia, you will simply do what you did that night in the inn, and leave the rest to me.'

'But what will happen?'

'We shall be playing. You have often urged me to play, but until now I have refused, so that we could have the more pleasure in tempting one another. Now that I must leave you, the time for temptation is over; at last, Euphemia, it is time to play.'

'It is only a game then?'

'Yes. A game of children, innocent. For you and Piero will again be children.'

'And you, Umberto? What will you be?'

'That you will see. It is my surprise. Now. Piero tells me your father will be out tomorrow afternoon. So at three o'clock you will meet us both in the tower. . . . . . .

. . . . Good afternoon, Signor Albani. I have come to say goodbye to you and your family. The French are very near, and tonight I must leave for your Villa at Oriago.'

'Rooms are prepared for you, my lord, and the servants are expecting you. Or rather, they are expecting Mr Humbert fitzAvon. You will be wise to keep to the humbler designation . . . though I do not think the French will worry you at Oriago. But you cannot stay there for ever. What shall you do? Where shall you go?'

'I shall hide at Oriago until things settle again. Then I shall make a plan to escape.'

'Where to?'

'Perhaps I shall be able to return to England sooner than I had thought. I hear my father gains daily in influence. What a pity, Signore, that you could not serve me with the Count Monteverdi. Think what a son-in-law you would have had.'

'Indeed.'

'You should have tried harder with the Count, Signore.'

'He is an obstinate old man. Perhaps it has turned out for the best. Although you would have made a rich and noble husband for my daughter, you might not have made a good one. But let us not part unkindly. I must go now. I have business, though what it will lead to in such times is hard to say. Allow me to wish you good fortune, my lord, and a safe journey to Oriago.'

'Goodbye, Signor Fernando, and thank you for your hospitality . . . .

. . . . Your father has gone. Your mother is resting. The

twins will not disturb us here. And so now, Piero and
Euphemia, let us remember. Let us remember that night
in the inn. First you undressed . . . Piero down to his shirt,
Euphemia down to her shift. And as you undressed,
Euphemia glimpsed Piero's childish maleness. Show her,
Piero.'

'Umberto. . . .'

'*Show her*, Piero. Briefly, as if by accident as you undress. . . . *Good*. Then you both lay down on the bed—this
rug will serve—and Piero was so tired that at once he fell
asleep. Euphemia, made curious by what she had seen,
was restless . . . and made investigation of her brother. Tell
us what you did. Show us, Euphemia.'

'I put my arm across him . . . like this . . . and played with
him . . . like this.'

'And then?'

'I felt his flesh grow under my hand, as it is growing now.
But he did not wake. So then I tried what I could do with
myself.'

'Show me.'

'Like this. And after a time I felt a warmth stir within
me . . . as it is stirring now, Umberto.'

'But then your mother came in?'

'Yes.'

'*I* shall be your mother. She lifted the bedclothes and saw
that Piero was roused. She lifted his shirt to look more
closely, and she felt him . . . like this . . . to make sure of what
she was seeing.'

'Yes.'

'Then she said: "Euphemia, have you been touching
Piero?"'

'And I said: "No, mama".'

'You *have* been touching Piero, Euphemia. Show me
how.'

'No, she did not say that.'

'But now, today, the story takes a different turn. Remember only that I am your mother and that you must obey me.
You have been touching Piero, Euphemia, and you have
been touching yourself. See there, I can tell. We must wake
Piero so that we can tell him. Wake up, Piero. . . . *Piero*.'

'What is it, mama?'

'Euphemia has found a new game, Piero. Show him, Euphemia. Show him how you played with him as he slept.'

'It was like this, Piero.'

'Oh, God. *Euphemia.*'

'And how you played with yourself, Euphemia . . . so that he may learn to do it for you. There. Go on, Piero.'

'But Umberto—'

'Not Umberto. Your mother, your mother in the inn, commanding you. Play with her, Piero. Kiss her and fondle her as you long to do. Kiss him, Euphemia. Love him. Open to his hand. Wide. Wider. Good children, pretty children. Obey your mother. Your mother will show you what to do.'

'Oh God, Piero, Piero. . . .'

'Oh God, *Euphemia.* . . .'

'No more like that, Euphemia, or you will pleasure him too much and too soon. Kneel to her, Piero. Open to him, Euphemia. This is the right true game of love. Open to your brother. Guide him. Do not hasten, Piero. Let her relish the passing of her maidenhood, for she can never have it back. Easily, easily, trying not to hurt her. . . .'

'*Piero.* It is hurting.'

'Yes, but not much. Open wider to him. Help him. There will be a little blood but there will also be ecstasy. Can you feel it, Euphemia, the ecstasy that is coming? Ah, how I love to watch you both. So pretty, so obedient. Pretty Piero, pretty Euphemia. How beautiful you are in your game of pleasure . . . .'

"And so this is the little joke you found so funny?" said Tom to Fielding Gray.

"No, as it happens. The real joke comes later."

"I see. Well, to confine ourselves to what has passed so far," said Tom, "aren't you reading rather a lot into that memoir? I grant I haven't looked at it as carefully as you have, but are you sure you can build . . . all *that* . . . on it?"

"The details are mine, I admit. But something like that must have been."

"Obviously fitzAvon/Rollesden had a hold on them. But to *that* extent?"

"Fernando writes: 'I know that what took place in the tower on the last afternoon before our accursed guest left us was shameful beyond imagining'."

"You seem to have imagined it all right," said Tom. "How can you be sure you are not imagining too much?"

"Because of what comes next. You see Tom, the events which followed, the *facts* which Fernando now goes on to give—and from here on he is explicit—make the whole thing clear beyond any possible doubt."

"Very well. Convince me, Fielding. *What* events followed that torrid afternoon in the tower?"

In the Casino, that same afternoon, Lykiadopoulos was facing up again to the white-robed princes of Araby. This time the edge of luck was paring the game narrowly in his favour; and by the time the afternoon session was nearing its close, he had recovered perhaps a quarter of what he had lost to the initial Arab attack the day before. So far, so good, he told himself : but there would be another session to face after dinner, and several more in the next few days before his friend from Padua would be ready to test his devices on the company; and at any or all of these sessions this high-playing mob might take ruinous sums from him, if the cards fell their way, in a matter of minutes. In normal circumstances, he would expect only one player at the table, at the most two, to be wagering the maximum stake; as it was, ten or twelve were doing so—at every coup which he dealt. No doubt about it : his reserves were not large enough to sustain an assault of this magnitude; if the Arabs were consistently successful, even at a margin as slight as four coups in seven, he would soon be in a very bad case.

The only thing to do (until the gentleman in Padua was ready) was to pray. Lykiadopoulos returned after the session to the Palazzo Albani, mounted to his private chapel in the penthouse, and prayed most heartily. Later, when he left the chapel and was walking along the corridor towards the stairs, he heard, through a half-open door, the voice of Max de Freville. He must be having one of his conversations with Angela, thought Lykiadopoulos, and paused to listen.

"It's all very well, Angie," said de Freville's voice, "to say that Fielding Gray ought to help me finance the survey of that palace; but he's earned his money the hard way and you can't expect him to be too lavish with it."

De Freville was silent for a while. Then he said,

"All right. Detterling has inherited a good deal, I grant you, but I don't think he can touch the capital. . . . . Yes, he did have quite a lot before he inherited, but he was always rather tight with it. Anyway, Detterling's in England, so that's no help for a start. . . . . What's that? You say that Fielding could help me make Detterling stump up? How, Angie? I just don't get it."

Nor do I, thought Lykiadopoulos, as he crept on along the corridor and started down the stairs; but one thing I do know : if anyone's in a position to tap Detterling/Canteloupe, there may well be a more urgent use for the money than any crazy scheme of Max's for restoring ruined palaces. And then, as he prepared for his bath, Lykiadopoulos began to think of the second of his troubles : quite apart from the precarious situation of his bank at the Casino, there were now signs that ugly pressures might start to threaten his interests in Corfu in the very near future. Although he had always expected trouble, he had hoped that the pressures would not become serious until the spring, by which time he would have the profits of his Baccarat Bank (God willing) to enable him to fight off the dangers. But the most recent news from Corfu made it clear that inflation and recession were working very much more quickly than he had anticipated; his supply of ready cash in Greece was running down fast, and most of the securities against which he might have borrowed were lodged with the management of the Casino in the Palazzo Vendramin to guarantee his bank. No, Max, thought Lykiadopoulos; if fresh money should become available, from Detterling or any other source, this is no time to spend it on gilding the decay of Venice.

". . . And so you see," Fielding Gray was saying to Tom Llewyllyn, "there can be absolutely no doubt. Listen :

" 'When Maria told me that Euphemia was with child, I at first assumed that the child must be fitzAvon's—that is, my Lord Rollesden's. Since his lordship was still hiding in my villa near Oriago, the misfortune was not beyond repair. Euphemia could be taken to Oriago and there married to Lord Rollesden-in-Silvis, and the haste and secrecy of the wedding could later be explained by the dangers and uncertainties of the times. I therefore sent word to Euphemia to attend me in my study in the tower, meaning to tell her, with what kindness I could muster, of my purpose. However, when I reached the tower myself, my daughter, and with her Piero, were there before me. Doubtless they knew it had been my intention (before Maria's communication put all else from my mind) to meet with friends in the Piazza that afternoon; and so they thought to have the tower to themselves.

" 'Their voices were raised in agitation, and, not expecting my intrusion, they did not hear me as I mounted the stairs . . . upon which, troubled by the tone of their exchanges, I halted to listen. Piero was beseeching his sister to yield to his judgement in some matter, though I could not at first make out in what. Finally, however, he spoke to this effect : we have sinned the sin already, he said, and sown the seed of our punishment; but meanwhile we may yet enjoy the pleasures for a season without further increase in the penalty. As I crossed the threshold of the room, his arm had already gone about her, and she, for all her tears, was making ready to receive more than fraternal comfort. "I wish that Umberto was here with us," said Piero, then looked up, at the sound of my step, and shrank away, both from her and from me, trying to hide and repair the disorders of his dress'."

"Poor Fernando," said Tom; "not his day."

"Nobody's day. But Fernando seems to have collected his wits pretty quickly. After all, he was a civilised and urbane man, not much given to antiquated superstitions and taboos. 'Shameful' all this certainly was—but not incurable. Let his original plan hold, he said to himself; let fitz-Avon be made to marry Euphemia—under pain of being kicked out of his refuge from the French at Oriago—and Euphemia's child would then be satisfactorily accounted for. So Fernando, all credit to him, simply proceeded to tidy up. He stopped the game that was afoot and forbade its resumption at any future time, but he eschewed moralising. He dried Euphemia's tears, told Piero to brace himself up, and then explained to them both what would happen. After which, he despatched a reliable servant to Oriago, with a message to fitzAvon/Rollesden to tell him that Euphemia

was in the club and that he, fitzAvon, must provide her with
respectable sponsorship. And all might have gone as merry
as a marriage bell, had it not been for recent events, of which
Fernando as yet knew nothing, in the villa near Oriago."

"Tom and Fielding are taking a long time with that manuscript," said Piero to Daniel in the tower. "I must go now
for dinner in the Palazzo."

"Please stay," said Daniel.

"Mr Lykiadopoulos will be angry if I am not at dinner.
He might find out I was here, and then he would be angrier
still."

"You need only stay for a moment. Piero . . . I have been
meaning to tell you all the afternoon. I shall not be able to
come with you to see the Carpaccios."

"But you promised—"

"—And events have overtaken my promise."

Piero considered this. At length he said,

"So it is to be sooner than you thought."

"I think so."

"But Daniel, there are doctors in Venice, For God's
sake—"

"—I am thinking of my own. No doubt there are doctors
in Venice—who could prolong the agony to me, and the inconvenience to my friends, for weeks or even months.
Common sense and common decency reject such a notion.
I shall simply do as Plato tells me to: remain in my station
until I am relieved of it."

Piero nodded and said nothing.

"Now you had better go," Daniel croaked at him. "There
is no point in upsetting Mr Lykiadopoulos or anybody else
on my account; that is specifically what I do not wish."

Piero nodded again, rose touched Daniel briefly on the
cheek, and went.

" 'Meanwhile'," Fielding was reading aloud to Tom, " 'my
messenger to Oriago was crossed by another who was coming thence to Venice. It was the local priest that had written
to me. My guest (whom he knew only as Humbert fitz-
Avon) had shamed my hospitality, he wrote. He had
seduced and got with child a peasant girl of thirteen years.

The peasants had been likely to kill him, but the priest had restrained them, urging that fitzAvon was under my protection and that in any case it was needful that he should marry the girl whom he had abused, to make the unborn child lawful and, so far as possible, keep disgrace from the girl's family. To this all had assented. FitzAvon, under constraint, had made some crude profession of submitting to the Catholic faith—enough to satisfy the priest that he could be married in the Roman Church—and the marriage ceremony would happen that very day, would indeed already have happened by the time the messenger reached me'."

"Back to square one," said Tom. "No husband for Euphemia."

"And a very grand husband, if she'd only know it, for a thirteen-year-old peasant girl. From then on events moved very fast. A few hours after Fernando received his letter from the priest, his own messenger returned from Oriago—having found fitzAvon both married and dead on the same day."

"Dead?"

"Yes. As soon as fitzAvon and the girl were safely pronounced man and wife, the peasants hung him from the nearest tree. 'They still wanted revenge for the violation of the girl—for such they said it was—and they were too foolish,' writes Fernando, 'to realise that fitzAvon, even only as fitzAvon, was a man of substance who might have done much for them if treated with respect. In him they saw only a fugitive from the French, and they were, among other things, afraid lest the French should discover they were harbouring him among them.' Fernando goes on to say some disagreeable things about the local peasantry, who were 'squalid creatures at best, made sullen and cretinous by the vapours which are exhaled from the marshes, and much given to inter-marriage'. Rather like the people who used to live in the Cambridgeshire fens, I suppose."

"Why did the Albani have a villa in such a district?"

"Lots of Venetians had their villas pretty much in that district."

"But not bang in the marshes, which is where he implies this one was."

"The Albani owned other villas as well. Apparently they'd picked this one up on the cheap, when the chap who built it died. He was notoriously eccentric in several ways, and that may explain his choice of site. Anyway, it seems it wasn't too bad there in the summer, which was when the Albani would want to use it."

"And what time of year was it now—when all these high jinks were going on?"

"The spring of 1797. But fitzAvon had been there for some time, remember, and it must have been horrid when he first arrived in the middle of winter. No wonder he needed diversion. The stupid thing about it was that he needn't have gone into hiding so soon. The French didn't get to Venice until the early summer of 1797, and he could have stayed on there months longer than he did."

"Thereby avoiding death at the hands of the peasantry."

"Yes. I expect he'd been panicked by rumours. Anyway, there it was. On top of all his other troubles, Fernando now knew that fitzAvon was decorating a tree near his own country villa. So off he went to sort *that* out. He saw the priest; he saw the little girl ('coarse and sturdy, eminently fit, and fit only, for the satisfaction of a brute and casual appetite'); and he saw the peasants. They were un-contrite, even quite pleased with themselves. Fernando, though angry with them for their mindless violence, and annoyed that by the enforced marriage and then the murder they had doubly deprived Euphemia of a possible saviour, had to admit that from most points of view they had done the world a favour. Together with the priest and a local apothecary, he fudged up what would pass for a death certificate, buried fitzAvon—under that name—in the local church, and returned to Venice to write an account 'to Lord Rollesden's noble father, the Earl of Muscateer, as at that time he was still titled'.

"But before he could get down to that, there was another job to be done. Piero, during his father's brief absence, had run amok. Whether it was grief at fitzAvon's death, or shame at being caught out with his sister by Fernando, or the realisation that Euphemia's predicament was now absolutely desperate—whatever it was, something had proved too much for Piero, never, one suspects, a well-balanced character even at his best. He had, quite simply, strangled Euphemia and then blown half his own head off with one of an elegant pair of duelling pistols which fitz-Avon had given him for his last birthday. There is some speculation, in Fernando's text, that perhaps Piero was trying to seduce Euphemia, despite his father's recent admonishment, that this time she refused him, and that he strangled her accidentally in the ensuing struggle. Equally, it seems possible that he did it to provide her with an infallible solution to her problem. In either case, guilt and/or misery must have given him quite sufficient motive to make away with himself as well.

"Once again, Fernando showed great talent for tidying up. It seems he was a substantial benefactor of an institution called the Vecchia Scuola della Misericordia—'

"—I know, that huge barn of a building up near the Madonna dell' Orto—"

"—Right. Then as now, there was a tiny plot of grass, covered with weeds and brambles, tucked between one wall of the Scuola and a minor canal. If you go past there these days, you'll see what looks like a white stone hidden inside the bramble bushes. If you're very sharp-eyed, you may spot two or three of them. Under one of these are the remains of Piero and Euphemia, who were hastily buried there by discreet courtesy of the Councillors of the Scuola, who were doubtless mindful of benefits both past and potential. As Fernando himself observed, 'Growing fear and conjecture in the city about the proximity of the French' (for now, Tom, they really were proximate) 'caused at this period such laxity in official deportment as made possible the disposal, without enquiry or formality, of the bodies of my two unhappy children'."

"Having seen to which, Fernando now had the job of writing to Lord Muscateer. What did he tell *him*?"

"He very nearly told him nothing at all, because he only just managed to get his letter on to the last British ship to leave Venice before the frogs arrived. However, despatch it he did, at a steep price which was to be borne by Lord Muscateer on its delivery, and here is the summary Fernando gives of the information which his lordship was to receive for his money.

"Fernando wrote, first, that he had the honour to inform the Earl of Muscateer that his son and heir, Lord Rollesden-in-Silvis, was dead. About the circumstances Fernando tells us he was tactful : Lord Rollesden had been friendly with himself and his family, he wrote, so friendly that he had eventually revealed the true identity which underlay the *alias* of fitzAvon; when the French threat to Venice had begun to appear serious, Fernando had offered Lord Rollesden a retreat, in his less conspicuous identity of Mr fitzAvon, in his villa near Oriago in the Veneto; and there. . . . 'Lord Rollesden, I wrote to the Earl, had been apprehended by those who wished him harm and, at the last, murdered by them, though honourable burial was later afforded him'. If one considers the nature of fitzAvon's employment, the formula was quite plausible."

"Yes—and also vague enough to account for the later rumour in England that he had been killed while fighting off French agents."

"Certainly. It had the merit of being truthful as far as it went and allowing those who wished to put a charitable construction on it. As we shall see, Fernando Albani was anxious to let Lord Muscateer and the Sarum family down very lightly. He followed the announcement and account of the death with details of where the body was buried—'in case his lordship should wish to visit that melancholy spot when the times were more favourable to travel'—and an assurance that the death had been officially notified and recorded . . . 'although I had of course to tell his lordship that in the situation which then obtained in Northern Italy and the Veneto there could be no question of bringing the malefactors to justice'."

"Just what did he mean by 'officially notified and recorded' ?"

"Presumably that the details of the dead man had been logged by the priest in the register of the church where he was buried. With civil conditions growing more chaotic every day, I doubt whether anything further could have been done in that line, even if anyone had wanted it done."

"But in fact we know from a little earlier in the memoir that the dead man was recorded as Humbert fitzAvon.

Would that have amounted to proper official proof of the death of Lord Rollesden-in-Silvis?"

"Yes, I think so, because a lot of people other than Fernando knew about the *alias*. For example, those that first smuggled young Rollesden/fitzAvon out of England."

"Fair enough," said Tom. "And of course one forgets that in those days people were not as fastidious in proving such matters as we are. The word of a *bona fide* gentleman-merchant like Fernando Albani would have been enough to satisfy even a court that fitzAvon-cum-Rollesden was dead. What else did Fernando write to the father?"

"A brief and formal commiseration, with which, he tells us, he concluded the letter."

"Nothing about fitzAvon's marriage? or the fact that the bride was pregnant?"

"Nothing. And so now, as you will appreciate, we are approaching the pith of the whole matter. Fernando states in this memoir that he did not inform Lord Muscateer of Rollesden's marriage, or of the child that was on the way, for the following reasons." Fielding picked up the MS. " 'The family was ancient and noble'," he read. " 'It was not, in my view, fitting that its line should continue through the coupling of such a vile man as I now knew Lord Rollesden to be and of such a woman (if woman she could be called) as the peasant hoyden whom he had been forced to make his wife; for the marsh peasantry, as I have already written, are brutish and sullen, and their stock degraded. By concealing the fact of Lord Rollesden's marriage, I should be leaving my Lord Muscateer free to assume that his heir was now dead without issue, and to make such arrangements as he could for the more proper inheritance of his Earldom and Estate. The bride, now the widow, knew only that she had married one Humbert fitzAvon, and neither she, nor her people, nor the priest, would ever be the wiser; there could be no chance, therefore, that she would claim or presume on the place that was now legally hers (and her child's) among the noble clan which her husband had dishonoured.' Fernando," said Fielding, "seems to have had a touching regard for the English nobility. Listen to this. 'Some time after I wrote to his lordship, I learned that he had been raised to the high dignity of an English Marquisate, as 1st Marquis Canteloupe of the Estuary of the Severn. This only confirmed me in thinking that I had been right to protect so illustrious a House against continuance through the get of a vicious criminal on a common country bawd.'"

"Ah," said Tom, "but *what* get? Did that girl at Oriago have a son?"

"Fernando doesn't tell us. All he says is that he took early opportunity to persuade the girl's family that her name should be changed from fitzAvon, as it now was, to the more Italian-sounding Filavoni, giving as his reason that she would be happier in their community if so called. His real motive, of course, must have been to stop the use in the area of the alien name of fitzAvon, which might later have attracted the attention of the curious. So the Signora fitz-Avon became the Signora Filavoni"—he lifted the MS and let if fall back on to the table before them—"and there the story ends."

He grinned savagely at Tom.

"Except that it doesn't," said Tom, returning the grin. "Because if the thirteen-year-old Widow Filavoni gave birth to a boy, that boy was entitled to be called Lord Rollesden-in-Silvis, and was from birth the lawful heir apparent to the Earldom of Muscateer and to the Marquisate of Cante-loupe when it was later conferred on his grandfather."

"Exactly so. And if he grew and had children of his own, as peasants tend to even when they *are* of degraded stock and live in a marsh, then there is at least a possibility that the line of Filavoni is still extant."

"And if *that* is the case," said Tom with relish, "then every single Marquis Canteloupe after the first has been bogus. Beginning with the son whom the first marquis got on his second wife, and ending with our good friend Detter-ling. They have all been standing in the shoes which should rightfully have been occupied by the rural descen-dants of Humbert fitzAvon and the barely pubescent slut with whom he was joined in holy wedlock."

"If," said Fielding, "and only if, that barely pubescent slut gave birth to fitzAvon's posthumous son. A miscarriage, or a daughter, and the thing ends there."

"Well," said Tom, "I think—don't you?—that we had

better go and find out what happened at this momentous birth in the marshes. In the interest of historical truth."

"And if there *is* still a family of Filavoni," said Fielding softly, "what duty do we have to that truth?"

"Let us consider that problem when and if it arises?"

"Very well," said Fielding. He consulted a page of the MS. "I have been talking loosely of Oriago," he said, "but in fact the Albani villa stood in a small village some way outside and called Samuele—after Moses Samuele, the architect and first owner of the villa, of which the village was a later accretion."

"Samuele?" said Tom. "He'd be the chap you were talking about just now—the notorious eccentric who liked marshy sites?"

"Yes. An interesting character—but that's another story. The point is, for us, that the church in which fitzAvon was married and buried is the village church, which was also built by Samuele, despite his being a Jew, in the eighteenth century. It was later named, for him or after him, the church of San Samuele—though God knows how he arranged that."

"So we look for an eighteenth-century church near the villa, and we ask the priest to see the records."

"That's about it," Fielding said.

"And we'd better take Piero. We may need an interpreter."

"That means letting Piero in on the story."

"What harm in that? It'll be nice to have an audience to see how clever we've been."

"Discretion?"

"We shall be telling Daniel in any case, and Daniel would certainly tell Piero, whether we wanted him to or not. They're thicker than ever, those two."

"Piero's been so hostile to our investigations," grumped Fielding, "that he doesn't deserve to be told."

"Don't be such a baby, Fielding. I'm not too keen on Piero myself, as you well know, but we're going to need an interpreter for an expedition like this, and he's the obvious choice."

Piero was told the story on the way to Oriago the next morning. To Fielding's irritation, he showed little interest in it and no surprise. The only stage at which he was moved to comment was when Fielding was telling him about the little plot, by the Scuola della Misericordia, where Euphemia and her brother were buried.

"I knew there were sad ghosts there," Piero said. "Miss Baby Llewyllyn told me."

"Baby told you?" said Tom.

"Yes. In a letter. So Daniel and I went by there in a boat one day to see the stones. Baby says that the ghosts rise up to go to the Casino degli Spiriti, where they mingle with the ghosts of the friends who once met there, and that with them they can be happy for a time. But now that you have found their secret," Piero said accusingly to Fielding, "they will stay alone by the Misericordia for very shame."

"Piero . . . you cannot believe in all that."

"Who are you, Major Gray, to say what I can believe? I believe it is better not to meddle with unhappy secrets."

"Until you know what the secret is," said Tom, "you cannot know that it is unhappy."

"You both knew . . . from that first manuscript which I found for you, just from looking at the picture on the front . . . that this secret must be horrible and unhappy. Why did you have to meddle?"

"There is another secret still to come," said Tom. "You'd better get on with the story, Fielding. Piero needs to know it all if he's to be efficient, and we're not far off Oriago."

"*Oriago—dieci minuti*," said the driver of the car which they had hired. Since the fellow did not know English, Fielding reflected, he had seized on the word 'Oriago' as an excuse to remind them, in the officiously democratic mode of modern Italy, that he too was of the party.

"*Grazia a voi*," Fielding said, deliberately choosing the brusquest form of the second person pronoun and bringing a scowl to the driver's face. And then to Piero, "Now for the rest of it."

"Today or very soon," interrupted Piero, "I should have been going with Daniel to see the Carpaccios in the Accademia. But now he says he is too weak. Yet we, his friends, are not sitting with him for company. We are going to Oriago. Why is this?"

"*Oriago nove minuti,*" interjected the driver.

"Daniel prefers that we do not make a fuss," said Tom. "Now listen to Fielding."

Piero shrugged, but now listened quite attentively as Fielding rehearsed the actions taken or omitted by Fernando Albani after the death of Lord Rollesden and started to draw the necessary deductions.

"You are going to say," said Piero, cutting Fielding short, "that perhaps your friend Lord Canteloupe is not Lord Canteloupe; that perhaps this Lord Rollesden left successors in Oriago."

"Yes," said Fielding.

"*Oriago cinque minuti,*" said the driver venomously.

"There you are, you see," said Piero, quietly triumphant: "that is what comes of meddling with such manuscripts."

"Please tell the driver," said Fielding, refusing to be baited, "to enquire for a village called Samuele."

Piero spoke quickly to the driver in Italian and received a gleeful answer.

"He says there is no such place," said Piero. "He hates me because I come from Sicily and speak English, and he hates you because you are paying him, and he will do his best to disoblige us. I shall have to enquire myself."

The driver reluctantly obeyed an order to stop. Piero limped from the car to a group of men who were standing in front of a tavern. There was much shaking of heads and one venerable old gentleman crossed himself.

"They say it is a difficult place to find," said Piero when he was back in the car, "and that it is better not to find it. But I think I now know the way."

Piero instructed the driver to turn left over a broad canal, shouted at him when he tried to turn right instead, and then directed him, when they were about a furlong beyond the canal, to drive down a minor road which forked away to the left across low, damp fields that were intersected by frequent willow-lined ditches. The driver started whining at Piero.

"He says the road is bad," Piero told Fielding and Tom, "and he must be given extra money."

"Tell him we'll settle all that with his boss when we get back to the Piazzale Roma."

On receiving this information, the driver stopped, got out, urinated at the side of the road, and then, after some leisurely stretching and scratching, lit a cigarette. At this point, Piero called to him through the window in a low voice, whereupon the driver reeled slightly, seemed to lose an inch or two in height, got back into the car, and drove on across the fields.

"What did you say to him, Piero?"

"That unless he drove on, I would put a spell on his pool of urine that would make him impotent."

"He can't have believed you."

"Probably not. But Sicilians have always been famous as witches, and since this man is a fool and a poltroon— poltroon means a coward, yes?—he will not care to risk it."

A few minutes later Piero told the driver to turn off down a cart-track which ran along the top of a dyke between two flooded fields. The man sniffed, blinked piteously, and obeyed. On the far side of the fields the dyke ran into a bank; the track continued through the bank in a small cutting, then passed through a copse. When the car emerged from this, it was forced to turn, with the track, and proceed alongside a high stone wall, behind which was a thick forest of pine trees. Eventually they came to a gateway without a gate, followed the track through it, drove on through about a hundred yards of pine forest, and came out into a meadow, at the edge of which the track abruptly ceased. On the far side of the meadow were a few small houses of dull red brick, beyond these a ridge perhaps fifty yards high, and on the spine of the ridge a handsome villa with a pillared portico.

"Samuele," Piero said.

"But where is the church?"

"We shall enquire."

Piero took the car keys out of the dashboard, climbed out, and started to limp across the meadow. The driver, torn between a desire to execrate the village for its remoteness and the need to preserve his *bella figura* by pretending the place did not exist, compromised by closing his eyes tightly and shaking both fists in the air, and so did not discern the sequestration of his keys for some minutes. When he did so, he hurtled out of the car, took three steps on to the meadow, and then realised that it was very damp and that Piero, followed by Tom and Fielding, had by now almost reached the far side of it; which being the case, he blubbered noisily for thirty seconds, went snivelling back to the car, and shortly afterwards fell childishly asleep.

"The church," said Tom to his companions, "will be more or less a private chapel to the house. I expect it's on the far side."

"There don't seem to be many people about," Fielding said. "But the villa appears to be cared for. I wonder whether the Albani still own it."

"No," said a sharp voice; "I do."

A trim man, in his late forties and a short fawn overcoat, walked from behind one of the little brick houses and came towards them. As he came, he picked violently at the skin round his left thumb.

"Shit," muttered Tom; "Jude Holbrook. We all wondered where you'd been, Jude," he said, "this many a year."

"Hong Kong, I heard," said Fielding, remembering, with a resentment much diluted by the passage of fourteen years, that the last time he'd seen Jude Holbrook Jude had threatened him with an open bottle of acid.

"Hong Kong for money," said Holbrook; "now here for peace and quiet. Not to mention obscurity. I do not like being disturbed. Why have you come, you two? And who's your little friend?"

"Our interpreter," said Fielding. "We didn't know, you see, that we'd find an English-speaking acquaintance here. How is that amiable mother of yours?"

"She lives here and reads books."

"What do *you* do, Jude?" said Tom. "You were never one for books."

"I mind my business. What do you want?"

"To look at the church of San Samuele; to inspect a tombstone which should be in or near it; and to examine the parish register."

"Why?"

"Tom is doing historical research."

"Yes," said Holbrook. "I remember he was always nosing into something or other." He wrinkled his mouth, like a bookmaker calculating a difficult shade of odds. "If I show you the church and the rest," he said, "will you go away and not come back?"

"Gladly."

"And will you promise to tell no one that you've seen me?"

"Yes, if that's what you want. But can you trust us?"

"Short of killing you, which would displease my mother, trust you is all that I can do."

"Who is this gentleman?" Piero asked.

"Never you mind," Holbrook said. "Come on to the church, all of you. The priest's away but it's open. And I know where he keeps the register."

He led the way up the gentle slope of the ridge. They skirted the villa itself, which stood in rough open grass, without garden or proximate adornment of any kind. Then they descended towards a grove of holm-oak, beyond which was a small building with a classical portico (a replica of the one in front of the villa) and without tower or transept.

"You don't realise it's a church," Holbrook explained, "until you get inside. When you do, there's all the usual Catholic paraphernalia, also two or three slabs in the floor carved with the names of the bodies buried underneath. Samuele—the chap who built the place—is one of them."

"Where are the villagers buried?"

"There's a cemetery out by the marshes for them. What's left of them. Most of them went away fifty years ago—or so the priest tells me."

They all walked up the steps into the portico and through a narrow wooden door into the church.

"Slabs," said Holbrook, and pointed to one: "there's Samuele's."

MOSES SAMUELE
Natus Kal. Jan. 1705 Obiit Kal. Jan. 1780

"Neat," said Holbrook. "Exactly seventy-five years old. Tidy number." He picked at the skin round his thumb.

"That one over there is worth looking at. Rum sort of name for a wop."

HUMBERTUS FITZAVON Armiger
Ob. 1797

"Only the year," murmured Fielding to Tom. "Discreet." And to Holbrook, "What about the register?"

"In a cupboard behind the altar. The priest is very proud of it because it's been kept up properly since 1745. Most of the registers in Italy—or in England, come to that—are unreliable any time before about 1830. But this one was taken special care of. And there's a very odd tale about why."

Holbrook led them behind the reredos (a rather chilly low-relief of the raising of Lazarus) and opened a cupboard.

"I have to dine the priest once in a way," Holbrook went on; "my mother likes it. Not that she's a Rom. Cat., far from it, but she thinks it's the thing to do. And when the priest comes to dine, he tells his stories—the same ones every time, but this one about the register isn't at all bad."

Jude's really being quite pleasant, Fielding thought; I wonder why. Making the best of a bad job? Wanting to send us away happy so that we'll keep our side of the bargain? Very possibly; he always had a sound sense of business.

"It seems," Holbrook was saying, "that this man Samuele moved into the villa after he'd built it and encouraged several peasant families to come and live nearby and form a new village—for the benefit of which he built this church. All this would have been around 1735, when Samuele was thirty. Well, in 1743, three small children disappeared out of the village, and another two in 1744. They vanished just like that—there one second and gone the next. But the funny thing was, the parents didn't seem to mind. When the priest of the time went round asking questions, the parents shrugged the whole thing off and muttered some excuse about how the children had gone to visit relations or the like. But since the children never came back, the priest at length knew that something was badly wrong, and eventually he got a notion of what was happening from an old woman on her death bed. Although her tale was very garbled and unclear, the gist seemed to be that Samuele, who had several commissions to build villas for rich clients in the Veneto, was buying children from their parents in the village and burying them alive under the foundations of his buildings, in order to recommend the buildings to the old gods and protect them against floods and so on—a common practice, I understand, in certain pagan eras. Apparently the clients knew all about it—or so the story went—and gladly payed a considerable extra sum to have these human sacrifices performed.

"Given the rather curious nature of Samuele's erudition and the reported contents of his library, the priest was disposed to believe the dying woman; but he had no proof—he hadn't even got official proof that the children had ever existed, because his predecessors, and up till then himself, had kept the register so slackly that most births and baptisms had simply gone unrecorded. So in order to make certain that from now on he had at least had a proper roll of his flock, the priest determined to keep an immaculate register, a determination of which he informed Samuele, with a quiet hint that any further unexplained disappearances would be reported to the Inquisitions both of Church and State. After which caution, I'm told, Samuele gave up his previous practice or went elsewhere for his victims. But the custom of keeping a precise register persisted up to his death in 1780 and by that time was too well-established a tradition to be discontinued. Any priest would have felt himself ashamed not to keep up the high standards of those before him. Hence we have a detailed record of birth, marriage, misdemeanour and death in the village of Samuele from around 1745 to this very day."

Holbrook produced a pile of leather-bound volumes and dumped them on top of the cupboard.

"But why," said Piero, "if Samuele was so wicked, did this church continue to be named for him?"

"For the same reason," said Tom, "as the Greeks called the Furies 'the Kindly ones'. Or so one may presume. It is prudent to flatter what you fear."

Holbrook gave a sour chuckle.

"Always the pedant, Tom," he said. "Even in the old days, when you were a cheque-bouncing, whore-grubbing drunk, you were full of sly classical precedents for your behaviour."

"Were you ever a cheque-bouncing, whore-grubbing drunk?" Piero asked Tom.

"Yes," said Tom. And to Fielding, "Where do we begin with this register?"

"With the wedding and the burial of our hero," said Fielding, "and then the widow's change of name—it should certainly be in here—from fitzAvon to Filavoni—"

In England, Detterling obtained special permission from the Headmistress of Radigund's School to take Baby out for two hours on a weekday.

"I don't mind telling you," Miss Wentworth Rex said to Baby, "that I'm breaking the rule simply and solely because he's the Marquess Canteloupe."

Baby smiled with polite scepticism.

"Don't grin at me like that, Tullia," said the Headmistress. "The truth is that I'm a colossal snob, and I may as well admit it."

In the end, Detterling did not take Baby out; they walked all round the school and its grounds instead, because Baby, who was proud of Radigund's, wanted to show it to her friend.

"You like it here, don't you?" Detterling said.

"Yes. And I like the things we do. I wouldn't want to miss what I'd be doing now—for anyone except you."

"What would you be doing now?"

"Statics."

"Sounds a bit dry."

"Yes," said Baby: "but it gives you such nice exact answers."

After a little while, as they walked round the cricket field, Detterling said:

"Bad news, sweetheart. That's why I'm here."

"Daniel?"

"Daniel. It can't be long."

"Did Poppa write to you?"

"Oddly enough, no. It was Piero. He thinks that Tom—

your father—doesn't quite realise how near it is for Daniel. He thinks that Daniel is deliberately misleading Tom, so that it can happen very suddenly, without a long and ghastly time for everyone to wait first."

"But Daniel must be showing—well—signs, however hard he's trying."

"Piero says not. Or rather, he says, there are signs, but only very slight ones, and everyone else, even Tom, is too busy and selfish to see them."

"Rather conceited of Piero to say that."

"Yes. But apparently he spends more time with Daniel than the rest—or has done just lately. Do you think he's telling the truth?"

"He has no reason not to."

"That's rather my view. So I'm going to Venice tomorrow. As good a day as any, and an old friend of mine is going there on business, so I can fly out with him."

"Be careful of Fielding Gray, my lord."

"What did you say?"

"Be careful of Fielding Gray," said Baby in a puzzled voice. "The poor ghosts say that he has learned their secret and that from this he will learn others."

"What ghosts, sweetheart?"

"I have heard them before. When I was in Venice."

"Their secrets can have nothing to do with me."

"Fielding Gray knows their secrets. Be careful of Fielding Gray." Baby paused for a mere second. "I'm glad you're flying out with a friend," she said, as though continuing the conversation from the point at which Detterling had mentioned this; "it will be more fun like that."

". . . So there it is," said Tom to Fielding, as he closed the last volume of the Register of the Church of San Samuele. "Paolo Filavoni, now aged ten years and odd months. Orphaned son and only issue of Giuseppe and Susanna Filavoni, who were drowned in the floods of sixty-six. Taken into care by a spinster sister of his mother's, one Anna Tomasino." He consulted the notes which he had taken while going through the register. "And so now, we gather, this Paolo is the sole surviving descendant, in the male line, of Umberto and Cara fitzAvon, who were married in this church on April 7, 1797: of which happy couple, Umberto died of 'violent misadventure' on the day of the wedding, while Cara, subsequently *per gratiam et officium Episcopi* called Cara Filavoni, was delivered, on November 10 of 1797, of a male child baptised as Nicolo. In the course of time, Nicolo begat in wedlock Giacomo, Serena and Giovanni, the last of whom died in infancy; Giacomo begat in wedlock Maria and Pietro; Pietro lawfully sired Giorgio, Teresa and Serafina . . . and so on and so forth. Small families, you notice, by peasant standards, and a high rate of early mortality, doubtless due to the unwholesome climate of these marshes, particularly in the winter. A curse to the Filavoni, perhaps, but a boon to us, because it simplifies the family tree and now reduces the field, beyond any question, to one. And so where," said Tom, turning to Jude Holbrook, "can we find the spinster, Anna Tomasino, to whom Paolo Filavoni is in ward?"

Holbrook smiled urbanely and gently picked at his thumb.

"What's your interest?" he said.

"As Fielding has already mentioned," said Tom, "I am doing historical research."

"Into peasant brats of the Veneto?"

"I am studying the decline and fall of the Serene Republic—which, as you will remember, Jude, finally fell in 1797, the same year as that in which Umberto fitzAvon, whose name you showed us on that stone over there, died here in Samuele. Now," said Tom, in the most plausible manner he could muster, "fitzAvon, before he came here, had been prominent in social affairs in Venice in the days when her collapse was imminent, and so he will figure in a chapter which I am preparing about the social scene of the Serenissima in its death throes. Out of sheer curiosity," he concluded smoothly, "I should like to see this Paolo Filavoni, who is fitzAvon's direct descendant. He might be good for a footnote."

"You're taking a lot of trouble for a footnote. Who was this fitzAvon anyhow? As I said earlier, it's an odd name for a wop."

"He was probably the son of an English tourist and a Venetian courtesan," Tom lied easily, "called La Rotella.

Hence his own name—the sort of fantasy name which an Italian tart might invent for her English bastard—and hence also the young man's need to take refuge here in 1797."

Holbrook looked very sharply at Tom, and then, to Tom's relief and Fielding's, lost interest in the whole matter. His face turned suddenly grey, he fumbled in his pocket and rapidly swallowed two tablets which he found there, and then he tottered away down the church.

"Jude . . . are you ill?"

"Yes. Go and see this child, if you must, and then leave here. My mother and I want to be left alone. It isn't much to ask."

"Why not sit down for a moment?"

"I must go to my mother."

With some difficulty, Holbrook negotiated the steps down from the portico and stumbled slowly away through the grove of holm-oak.

"He didn't tell us where to find the boy," said Fielding.

"Let us trouble him no more. I will find out for you," Piero said.

He led Tom and Fielding back on to the raised ground (where they overtook Holbrook, who curtly gestured them on their way), past the villa and down towards the brick houses. He knocked on the door of the first of these, talked briefly to a humped old woman in black, and then led on to a cottage which stood slightly apart by a small, black pool. A large and slovenly woman with long, grey, greasy hair eventually answered his knock. After arguing with her for some minutes, Piero beckoned to Fielding and Tom.

"She wants to know why you wish to see the boy," he said : "he is only one more orphan."

"Tell her," said Fielding, "that we are journalists who are investigating families that were broken up during the floods of sixty-six."

Piero argued further with the woman. At length he said,

"If you are journalists, she says it will cost you five thousand lire to see the child."

Fielding handed a new note to the woman, who examined it with a mixture of delight and suspicion, then yapped something at Piero.

"She wants the money in single thousands," Piero said: "round here they are not familiar with anything larger."

Fielding produced five crumpled and dirty notes of a thousand lire. The woman took them, reluctantly returned the larger note which Fielding had first given her, and then backed into the living-room-cum-bedroom-cum-kitchen which apparently comprised the entire interior of the cottage. Still walking backwards, she crossed the room to a window which overlooked a small allotment. She turned, opened the window, and signed to her three guests to come to it.

Quietly digging in the allotment was an exceedingly handsome little boy who had auburn hair, wide and strong shoulders for his age, and classically formed bare legs.

"There you are," said Piero indifferently: "Paolo Filavoni. If I have been understanding all your talk this morning correctly, the rightful Marquess Canteloupe of the Estuary of the Severn."

The boy stopped digging, stuck his spade into the mud, and smiled at them, pleasantly enough but rather slyly, Fielding thought. Then, with a quick movement of his left hand, he jerked his shorts down from his haunches, and with his right hand, skipping and cackling for glee, he began to waggle his penis at his audience.

"Paolo," called the woman sharply.

But Paolo merely cackled the louder, skipped and waggled the more heartily, until the woman rushed from the cottage and appeared in the allotment. As she approached him, Paolo flexed his knees gracefully, pointed his piece at her, and then, emitting a series of deep and imbecile grunts, began to piss fiercely up into her face.

"A chip off the old block," said Fielding; and the pinched little mouth began to throb and twist and gape like a fresh scar in his ruined face, issuing pipe after pipe of thin and self-gratulatory laughter.

PART FIVE

THE SURVIVORS

THE FRIEND with whom Detterling was flying out to Venice was Peter Morrison, who had succeeded the previous Lord Canteloupe as Minister of Commerce. Detterling had discovered that Morrison was going to Venice when he had called on him in London, some days before, to request his help in disposing of his man-servant. Since the corporal had now gone almost totally if quite harmlessly insane, and appeared to imagine that as Detterling's self-styled 'chamberlain' he was a high-ranking officer in the service of some semi-Royal prince palatine, it had occurred to Detterling that the man needed a change of scene along with some therapeutic occupation which would take his mind off his fantasies of court and castle. He had therefore proposed to Peter Morrison, who was an old and understanding ally, that the corporal should be sent down to Morrison's farm in Norfolk, where he could be employed on elementary tasks in the company of Morrison's once brilliant but now imbecile son, Nickie. Nickie and the corporal, he pointed out, had been on friendly terms since Nickie was a little boy, and they might now derive some solace from each other's companionship, if either of them could still remember who the other was. Furthermore, the corporal could make himself useful in tidying up after Nickie, who was apt to be rather messy in habit and in person.

Peter Morrison had seen the possibilities of this arrangement and agreed to a trial run of two months. It was after this that he had told Detterling he was going to Venice.

'You remember that tour you went on for your cousin Canteloupe just before he died?' Morrison had said.

'Very clearly. The idea was to check up whether anyone

had caught on to the old man's new methods of industrial swindling—the ones he'd worked out with Somerset Lloyd-James.'

Morrison winced.

'You mean, new methods of industrial diplomacy,' he said; 'and your conclusion was that these were still valid?'

'Right. No one had rumbled them, as far as I could make out.'

'Well, I'm sorry to tell you, Canteloupe, that now some-body has. Or so we think. There's a big deal afoot with an Italian corporation in Mestre, which is being negotiated under the aegis of my Ministry. We are using the Cante-loupe style of diplomacy aforesaid, and the whole thing seems to be turning sour on us. I'm going out to take a hand myself in a day or two.'

'To Mestre? Rotten luck.'

'Oh, I shall put up in Venice, of course.'

Whereupon Detterling had remembered that he too must go to Venice before long, and the two men had agreed to fly out together.

During the few days before the flight, Detterling had done three things. First, he had persuaded his 'chamber-lain' to undertake a 'delicate mission' to Norfolk, where he would be required to act as tutor and bodyguard to the eldest son of one of Her Majesty's Ministers of State. Secondly, he had gone to see Baby Llewyllyn, had told her of his fears for Daniel and had heard of hers for himself. Thirdly, he had rung up his friend, Leonard Percival:

'Can you take a few days away from Jermyn Street, Leonard?' he had said.

'What for, Detterling—sorry, Canteloupe?'

'I want you to meet me in Venice. I've had a . . . rather curiously based but very sincere warning that someone there might make trouble for me.'

'Who?'

'Fielding Gray.'

'Why should he? What's up?'

'That's just what I want you to find out.'

'This warning : what do you mean by "curiously based"?'

Detterling had swallowed and then come straight out with it.

'The person who gave it was relaying a message from ghosts.'

But Percival had been unexpectedly lenient.

'*Or* relaying a message from the sub-conscious,' he said. 'Bearing in mind all the help you gave me last year with the Lloyd-James business, I think they'll let me off to meet you. Time and place, Canteloupe?'

And so Leonard Percival would be joining him in Venice, Detterling reflected now, as he seated himself next to Peter Morrison for the journey. It would be pleasant to see Leonard again. They had dined together twice since getting to the bottom of the Lloyd-James affair, but somehow Leonard was not very good company unless there was some immediate problem or crisis to be discussed. Given such a problem, Leonard and he could not only wrangle at it, they could exchange, for hours on end, theories and instances and memories of which it put them in mind. But given no problem there was no catalyst to get them going; and the two occasions on which they'd met in the last year had been quite dismal. Now, however, thought Detterling, there will be a problem again: Baby's warning—that should set them up. For even if Fielding Gray was up to nothing at all and the warning therefore false, there would still be the problem of what had got into Baby (ghosts, as she said? a mistaken instinct? or sheer malice?) to make her give it.

"Very pensive, Canteloupe," said Carton Weir (who was accompanying Morrison as his PPS from the other side of the gangway.

"I'm going out to see a man die."

"A friend?"

"No. I hardly know him, beyond the odd meeting in Venice last month . . . and in Germany more than twenty years ago. I did him a bad turn that time, though I couldn't really help myself. So now I'm trying to make it up to him."

"By going to watch him die, my dear?" said Carton.

"I'm hoping I shall say the right thing before he does."

"What does one say to a dying man?" said Morrison.

This question brought the conversation to a stop. A little later, when the aeroplane had taken off and champagne had been served to them, Detterling raised a different subject.

"What shall you do," he said, "if this deal in Mestre goes wrong?"

Carton Weir fluttered his hands reproachfully; but Peter Morrison, having made sure that the three of them were alone in the first-class section, was prepared to talk of the matter.

"Your late cousin's diplomacy," he said to Detterling, "consisted in discrediting rival products by causing them to receive praise which was so obviously inflated that it was then assumed to emanate from the producers themselves, and so made them appear ridiculous and untrustworthy. It was a kind of anti-advertising, and he had several agencies who practised it very skilfully, most notably an important merchant bank—the Corcyran."

"That I knew. Ivan Blessington works for it."

"Correction. Used to work for it. Ivan has boobed. Or so we think."

"Unlike him."

"Ivan was too decent, dear," said Carton Weir, "and too clean. He should have spent the whole of his life at school playing footer and having showers."

"He did well in the Army," said Detterling. "He was Military Attaché in Washington and had some important appointments on the Staff. And I understood he was doing well with the Corcyran Bank."

"Too decent, dear," Carton insisted, "too wholesome—like bread and butter pudding. And like bread and butter pudding, too soft. He went and got religion the other day, rather late in life as his sort often do. And then of course he started thinking that dear old Canteloupe's tricks weren't frightfully Christian, and so he split."

"We *think* he did," said Morrison.

"We had enough evidence to get the Corcyran to sack him."

"To pension him off. You do no one a service by exaggerating, Carton."

"Anyway," said Detterling, "it appears that the code has been cracked. So what do you do now?"

"Think up a new diplomacy."

"You were always good at that. I shall never forget how you handled that business in India in forty-six."*

Morrison gave a look of mild distaste.

"I was lucky," he said, "and the circumstances permitted a certain licence."

"So do these. The old country's up against it. We *need* this deal at Mestre and many more like it."

"Indeed."

"So what are you going to do?"

"In general," said Morrison carefully, "I'm not yet quite certain. But over this affair at Mestre, there's a relatively easy solution. If this corporation there will let bygones be bygones, forget how we've tried to flannel them, and go ahead and clinch the deal, then we shall promise them, in return, the British Government's moral support at the next international conference about the future of Venice. As you know, there are some nasty rows brewing."

"But Peter. The industrialists on the mainland want to destroy Venice. You can't mean the British Government will support that?"

"You exaggerate as badly as Carton. The industrialists do not want to destroy Venice, only . . . to trim it a bit, so that they can have more room for their installations."

"*As well as* polluting the air, and wrecking the fabric of the city, *and* letting their horrible tankers wash away its foundations. You'll support them in all that?"

"We need this contract from Mestre to go to a British firm. As you say, the old country's up against it. Venice is a beautiful city, Canteloupe; but I think the tide of progress may be allowed to claim a few of her outlying churches in the popular interest. The people—both British and Italian—want a certain kind of wealth, and Venice is one of the things which stands in the way of their getting it."

"Venice is one of the richest parts of their inheritance."

"Only they don't think so, Canteloupe. They want cars and washing machines and fish fingers, not Venice. They don't understand it and they resent the pleasure it gives to those that do."

"But Peter . . . *you* can't sympathise with such attitudes?"

"If I don't, someone else will. And that someone else,"

*See *Sound The Retreat*, passim.

said Peter Morrison, "would very soon be Minister of Commerce."

The day after the visit to Samuele, Tom Llewyllyn went to see Max de Freville.

"You may remember," Tom said, "that as my host you asked me to let you know if anything came of Fielding's investigation into that picture in the gallery . . . anything that might make trouble for you and Lyki as tenants of this Palazzo."

"I remember. Has Fielding found anything?"

"Nothing that need obtrude on your convenience."

Tom had already given much thought to what should or should not be said about Fielding's discovery. The previous night, after the party had returned from Oriago, he had given Daniel a full account of their findings, and asked him what he thought should be done about them. Daniel, who had seemed feverish but alert, opined that nothing should be done about them. The scandal of Piero Albani and his sister, Daniel said, now had no consequence for anybody, save as an antiquarian freak; and as for the matter of the Canteloupe inheritance, what possible point could there be in revealing to the world that the real Marquess Canteloupe was an idiot Italian boy called Paolo Filavoni who lived with his aunt in the marshes? To present the proof in legally valid form would be difficult (albeit not impossible) and exceedingly expensive. Who would have the time and money (certainly not Tom) to undertake such a suit, on whose behalf, and in any case *cui bono*? The marquessate would be no good to poor Paolo, while the loss of it would seriously discommode Detterling.

'The probability,' Daniel had concluded, 'is that whichever of them has it, it will die with him. Detterling suits the place and the place suits Detterling. Let's just leave it at that.'

With this judgement Tom was in complete accord; indeed he had already decided on just such a course even before consulting Daniel, whose opinion he had sought only from academic interest. And so now, while talking with Max de Freville, Tom's sole concern was to keep his promise. He had promised Max, on the afternoon when they had gone together to the Ghetto, that if Fielding's enquiries brought anything to light, he would tell Max if it was something that he and Lykiadopoulos, as tenants of the Albani family, should know about. The answer now, in Tom's view, was 'no'. Fernando's manuscripts had been addressed to his two younger children and to anyone thereafter who might happen to come across them; it was no fault of Max or Lyki that someone had done so during their tenancy. If the Albani should subsequently find cause for complaint, let them blame their own ancestor.

In any case, unless the facts revealed by the manuscripts were subsequently published, the Albani need never know of the discovery, let alone complain of it. He himself intended to publish nothing, if only because the right to use the material was undoubtedly Fielding's. As to Fielding's intentions he was not altogether clear; but Fielding had said one thing on the way back from Oriago that was indicative.

'Pity Detterling and I were in the same regiment,' Fielding had said : 'otherwise one might have raised rather a stir.'

This Tom understood to mean that the prescribed loyalties of the British caste system forbade Fielding from using what he had learnt to embarrass an old companion in arms. So far, so good; both Fielding and himself were determined on silence or at least discretion. But what of Piero?

'Perhaps you are sorry I know of this?' Piero had said. 'But you needed an interpreter; any interpreter would by now have known more or less what I do; and better that I should know it than a stranger. And besides'—he echoed what Tom had previously told Fielding—'you will be telling Daniel and he would have told me. I was bound to know sooner or later.'

'What is your . . . opinion of it all?' Fielding had asked.

'A curious story which is none of my business. It could, I suppose, injure your friend who is now called Lord Canteloupe. It is no business of mine to do that.'

'So you will not repeat the story?'

'I cannot say quite that, Major Gray. In all things a man

must render account of himself . . . of himself and his
conduct . . . where that account is due. At one time or
another I shall be required to render account of myself,
from the time I found that first manuscript for you up to
the time of what we have done and seen today.'

After that he had been silent. Tom had supposed, and
now still supposed, that Piero was referring to the confes-
sional. As a Catholic, the boy would have to search his conscience to decide whether the part he had played was a
worthy one; and if he decided that in any respect it was
not (if, for example, he felt that he should not have ap-
propriated the first manuscript, an action which he clearly
regretted), then he would have to make confession and
some small part of the story might have to be told to his
confessor. This in itself could do but little harm; the
trouble was that Piero's language had been ambiguous;
Tom could not be sure exactly to whom Piero's account was
to be rendered, or how comprehensive it must be in its
scope.

But there was nothing to be done about that now. Now
Tom's task was to reassure Max, who was beginning to
press him.

"You say that nothing Fielding has discovered need concern Lyki or myself," Max was recapitulating, "as the
Albani's tenants here; but presumably it is of interest to
somebody?"

"To scholars."

"But amusing too?"

"You could call it that."

"Then let's hear it."

"I'm sorry, Max. Fielding has completed a very intricate piece of research, the results of which he will not want
generally known until he has decided what use he himself
will make of them. It's quite normal for writers to be
secretive in such circumstances."

"I hadn't thought of that," said Max. "But though I
quite see he wouldn't want anyone else cashing in, I'm not
exactly a rival. And it was in my house—mine and Lyki's—
that the whole hunt started. So I should have thought you
might tell me a bit more."

"I promised you, as your guest, to tell you anything

which you and Lyki ought to know. Well, you ought to know that the investigation is concluded and that what has come out of it poses no worries for you or Lyki. I've only raised the matter to set your minds at rest for once and for all. I knew you were bothered about what Fielding was up to, and I've come to tell you it's finished with."

"Very scrupulous, I'm sure. Scrupulous to the letter, Tom. So let's exercise a few more of your scruples: oughtn't Lyki and I to know what's happening to Daniel Mond? Whatever it is, it's happening in our garden."

"You need not worry about Daniel. He is living quietly in the tower and one day—quite soon—he will leave it. There will be no embarrassment."

Max considered this. At last,

"No," he said kindly, "I'm sure there won't be. But do you know where he will go? I suppose they'd have him at San Michele—I think they've got sections for all sorts—but San Michele's a dismal place. Not right for Daniel."

"Funny you should speak of him like that. You hardly know him."

"I saw him that night at dinner . . . and every now and then, when he still came over for baths. That's how I knew something was wrong, because he's stopped coming over any more. We used to have a word or two sometimes," said Max lightly. "I looked forward to it. Did you know that I too am a thwarted mathematician? In a different way of course: he was too good at it and I just wasn't good enough. But I knew enough to sympathise, and I liked—well—I like his spirit. I tell you, Tom: San Michele's no place for Daniel."

"He could go back to Lancaster."

"Would he want that?"

"He was . . . contented there."

"But now the yobs are beginning to break the place up, Tom. There was that business the other day when the chapel was savaged by hooligans—one of the tombs was pick-axed, Tom—and now they've found out that your own undergraduates did it."

"I know."

"Who wants to go back to a college chapel where that sort of thing can happen?"

"Does it really matter where he goes—when he leaves the casino in the garden?"

"I think so. Piero will too, if I am not mistaken."

"Then I shall be glad to know," said Tom crisply, "what you and Piero may decide between you."

In the Hotel Gabrielli Fielding Gray settled to work. It had become quite clear to him, after a little thought, what he should do with the secret which he had discovered. He was an entertainer by profession; he would therefore use the story—or rather, one very like it—in order to entertain. Although he had some pretensions as a literary critic, he was not a scholar as such, and to prepare a scholarly presentation of the facts, complete with proof and documentation, would have been exceedingly irksome to him. He had no wish to displace Detterling; and to initiate proceedings on behalf of Paolo Filavoni, in the courts or the College of Arms, he found quite unthinkable. Finally, he was not a busybody and cared very little about notions of justice, social or otherwise; and so to confront Detterling with the facts and urge that Detterling had a duty to set matters to right would have seemed to Fielding the grossest piece of impertinence. (Besides, as far as he knew Detterling was in England, which would have made confrontation a cumbrous affair at the best.) No, he told himself now, there could be no question of it: this tale was just what he needed to provide the substance of a new novel, which would be of a rather different kind from anything he had written heretofore. He would write of just such a search (but not the same) as he had lately been engaged in; he would gradually disclose just such mysteries (but not the same) as he himself, with Tom's help, had recently uncovered.

Fielding spent some hours drawing up a table of fictional equivalents. He decided, provisionally, on a narrative in the first person; the narrator should not be anyone like himself, he thought, but a young man who was in Venice for the first time and would therefore have to contend with the terrors and deceits of a strange city as well as with all the other obstacles that lay between him and the secret which he sought. His first inkling (that there *was* a secret) would not be given to him in a private gallery but in a public museum (the Correr); it would not come from an eighteenth-century picture but from a nineteenth-century ball dress, so displayed as to reveal some peculiarity in cut which in turn suggested some unusual (but not necessarily repellent) physical deformity. The dress, it would transpire, was that which had been worn by the wife of a prominent Austrian officer at a banquet in honour of a visiting Arch-duke. The lady, tormented by obsessive hankerings, had returned home early from the banquet, had mounted to her eldest son's quarters . . . and had there found, or herself committed, God knew what of horror or delight, which the son had subsequently committed to a secret diary. This diary Fielding's hero would track down, through libraries and dank palaces and murky chantries, creeping from one to the other along the treacherous passages of snow-bound Venice. . . .

Ah, thought Fielding, as he began to plot the outline of the early chapters, what it is to have work again, something to put my mind to day after day, something to wrestle with and curse at and be wholly possessed by, while the hours pass like minutes and the pile of written sheets slowly grows at my left hand.

The telephone rang in his room.

"Lord Canteloupe is in Venice," said Max de Freville; "at the Gritti."

"Oh?" said Fielding. "I'll call on him if I have time."

He put down the receiver without saying goodbye to Max and returned to the half-filled sheet before him.

"I have disobeyed you," said Piero to Lykiadopoulos in the Palazzo Albani . "I have spent many hours with Mr Mond in the casino in the garden while you were at the Casino Municipale."

"Why do you tell me now?" said Lykiadopoulos.

"Because I owe you a duty and must render my account."

"Then render it."

"You said I might go out with Mr Mond and Mr Llewyllyn, but that I must not be with them in the tower. But Daniel is dying and cannot leave the tower."

"At least he can do no harm by dying," Lykiadopoulos said. "I was afraid of something quite different. That is why I forbade you the tower."

"You were afraid that through me he might come at things which you would wish hidden."

"Yes."

"There is small danger of that now," said Piero. "Nevertheless, I have disobeyed you, and I must offer something in reparation."

"They have certainly taught you a lot of English in that tower. What is this . . . reparation?"

"Major Gray and Mr Llewyllyn have discovered that Lord Canteloupe is not Lord Canteloupe. There is a prior claimant whom nobody knew of—until now."

For almost the first time in his adult life Lykiadopoulos was wholly and genuinely surprised. He had often been partly surprised, as he was, just the other day, when the Arabs suddenly appeared in Venice some weeks before he had expected them; but since their arrival had always been a possibility, since talk of them had been in the air for some time, he had been merely startled rather than astounded. What Piero had now told him, however, would never have occurred to him in a thousand years. To fake noblemen of various nationalities and degrees he was altogether accustomed; but that Canteloupe should not be Canteloupe, that an English marquess, upheld as such by all the authority of the Heralds' College in London, should turn out to have inherited his dignity in error—this, to a man of Lykiadopoulos's conservative and anglophile disposition, was quite beyond his intellectual scope.

"Tell me more," he said hoarsely.

Piero told him.

"By telling you this," he said in conclusion, "I have done some good, to make up for my part in disturbing the ghosts; for I have done my duty, my service, to you who are my master. Captain Detterling, we hear, was a rich man, Lyki *mou*; the Marquess Canteloupe is even richer."

The day after Detterling arrived in Venice, Leonard Percival waited on him in his rooms at the Gritti.

"Here am I," said Percival; "what now?"

"You remember Tom Llewyllyn's girl, Baby? We met her briefly last year when we went to Cambridge."

"Vividly. A vicious little sex-trap."

"She's changed since then." Detterling gave Percival some account of the improved Baby and what had improved her. "It's she," he concluded, "who . . . listened to the ghosts and warned me. The threat, as I told you, appears to be Fielding Gray."

"Where's he staying?"

"The Gabrielli."

"I'd better start there, I suppose. You've no idea why Fielding Gray should spell trouble for you?"

"None."

"And incidentally, Canteloupe, why are you in Venice?"

Detterling told Percival about Daniel Mond and what he deemed to be his obligation to him. Percival was brusque.

"A long time ago, that business with Mond in Germany," he said. "I don't think you need hold yourself to much on that account."

"I like to say proper goodbyes."

"Fair enough. You attend to Mond and I'll try to sniff out whatever savoury little dish our friend Fielding Gray is cooking up."

Detterling, anxious to see Daniel but uneasy lest he should intrude at an awkward time, went to the Palazzo Albani and made enquiry, since Max, Lyki and Piero were all out, of the Major-Domo. The Major-Domo, sycophantic of marquesses but contemptuous of the tower and everyone in it, said that he knew of no reason why the *due professori* should not receive the *Excellenza* if the *Excellenza* was so gracious as to wish to be received by the *due professori*. Rather uncertainly, Detterling crossed the garden, and having knocked on the door of the casino found Tom, Piero and an animated Daniel within.

Daniel was examining, with evident interest, an object which looked like a detachable cigarette filter. This, as Piero explained to Detterling, had been left behind in the Palazzo earlier that afternoon by a gentleman who had now gone off to the Casino with Max and Lykiadopoulos.

It had excited Piero's idle curiosity because engraven on its metal rim were some symbols and figures which were far too elaborate to be a trade mark and appeared to be some kind of mathematical formula.

What Piero did not tell Detterling was that he had seized on this toy in the vague hope that it might amuse Daniel for a few minutes, since Daniel, who had altered much in the last two or three days, was now only to be entertained, and that intermittently, by trifles of this nature. What Piero *did* tell Detterling was that Daniel was finding the formula on the rim of unexpected interest and was busy trying to solve its meaning.

But after a little longer Daniel handed the object to Tom and sank back in his chair, clearly exhausted by his temporary show of energy.

"Something to do with friction and velocity," he muttered. "I could have done it properly once. God knows what it's doing on that thing."

Then Daniel fell asleep.

Detterling, who had so far not exchanged a single word with Daniel, asked Tom when it would be convenient for him to call again.

"Any time," said Tom. "Just take a chance. You're more likely to find him approximately himself if you come in the morning. It rather depends when he takes his powders . . . not that they work for very long now."

"Will he wake up this afternoon?" said Detterling. "I'd gladly wait."

"Please don't. You wouldn't like what you saw when he wakes from his afternoon sleep. Leave Piero and me to cope."

So Detterling, disconsolate and yet somehow relieved (for since he had said nothing to Daniel, at least he had not said the wrong thing), wandered away down the passages, came to a vaporetto stage, got on to the first boat that came by, and got off, without really thinking what he was doing or why, at the Palazzo Vendramin. Then his head cleared, and he remembered that the afternoon session of Lykiadopoulos's Baccarat Bank would now be in full swing. He asked for a ticket to the special rooms, winced as he paid for it (for the charge had gone up to fifty thousand lire soon after the arrival of the Arabs), and went up in the lift.

Standing some distance from the rails round the Table de Banque was Max de Freville. Detterling waved, as to an old friend whom he had not seen for some weeks, and was surprised at the perfunctory way in which his greeting was returned. Then he realised that Max was in close conversation with a man who was standing next to him in the crush, a man with a long, seedy face and wearing a long seedy suit. The man nodded, took a cigarette straight from his pocket, and inserted it into a holder which he was carrying in his other hand. He placed the holder between his lips but did not light the cigarette. Why he was bothering to watch these commonplace actions, Detterling did not know; if asked, he would have said that there was something nervous and rehearsed in the man's manner, as though he were taking part in an amateur play. He might have added that there was a look of strain in the man's long face, the kind of look Detterling had seen on the face of a ventriloquist somewhere (one of those Gyppo conjurers during the war, perhaps) who had been striving to keep a still countenance while throwing his voice through clenched teeth.

After a while, the man took the holder from his mouth (the cigarette being still unlit) with a more relaxed movement than any he had so far made. Detterling now turned his attention to the table. He noticed that the stakes for the coup about to come were fairly light, and that Lykiadopoulos had an indefinable air of satisfaction and relief. In the event, Lykiadopoulos lost the coup to both sides of the table but retained his air of content.

Detterling went over to Max.

"How's Lyki getting on?" he enquired.

"Rather well. These Arabs are being more cautious than usual, and on the few occasions they have been greedy Lyki has usually beaten 'em."

"Good. Who's your friend?"

"No one you'd want to meet," whispered Max. He turned and nodded twice, each time with two very distinct movements (down with his chin and then up), to the man with the holder.

The man nodded back and once more produced a cigarette. A prime neurotic, this one, Detterling thought. Once again the cigarette went into a holder—but a different holder, Detterling noticed, from the one he had used before. Once more the holder went to the man's mouth, once more the muscles of cheek and jaw tightened in strain.

"How are your plans to save Venice going?" said Detterling to Max.

"One good idea," said Max shortly, then craned forward to watch the table. The stakes for this coup were much higher, Detterling noticed, indeed many of the players must have wagered the maximum.

"What idea?" he asked Max.

But Max wasn't listening. He was absorbed in the cards which Lykiadopoulos flicked out of the shoe, gazing at them as though he hoped to see through their backs. A further card was called for on the right; a natural eight was displayed on the left; and then, as Max inhaled breath with a long hiss of his nostrils, Lykiadopoulos turned up a natural nine.

"What idea?" persisted Detterling.

"A palace that needs doing up. Fielding Gray found it. Look, Canteloupe," said Max, "will you excuse me? I'm rather tied up in Lyki's fortunes just now."

Detterling, who resented such incivility, hated crowds, and despised Arabs, went downstairs and rode home to the Gritti, where he had anchovy toast for tea and waited for Leonard Percival to come and report his day's findings.

Daniel was in the Forest near the Warlocks' Grotto, looking for Fielding Gray. If only he could find his way through all these trees. But of course! He needn't go forward, he could turn back, trace his path back, become a thread through space and time, threading back to where he last saw Fielding, so that he could speak to him just once more. Daniel was a particle reversing through space and time, tracing its path back—back and back and back—to find Fielding Gray. There were no trees now, only emptiness and, very far away, a dull red sun. In the sun was Fielding, but he would never reach him now, because the particle that was Daniel had gone as far back as it could go. There was a blinding flash which had once, aeons before, been its birth, and then Daniel was alone in no-space, before the universe and before time.

Funny, thought Detterling, as he drank his tea and waited for Leonard Percival, that cigarette holder which the chap with Max was using—it was very similar to the filter (or whatever) that Daniel was so interested in. There was the same oddity of line, the same kind of elaboration in the curve which led to the rim. But of course Piero had said that the filter had been left behind in the Palazzo by a man who had gone off to the Casino with Lyki and Max—so presumably this was the same man and he had a whole collection of the things. He'd used two different ones in the Casino just in the short time during which Detterling had been watching him there. What had Daniel said about the formula on the filter, before he went to sleep? 'Friction and velocity'—that was about it : 'Something to do with friction and velocity'. Well, thought Detterling vaguely, it might be interesting to find out what.

It was some time before Tom and Piero realised that Daniel was dead. When they did, Tom looked rather helpless and said :

"Where must he go now?"

"I shall arrange," Piero said.

Then Piero crossed the garden to the Palazzo and rung up Lykiadopoulos's doctor, who agreed to come to Daniel and see that he was taken where he must go first. But the more important question was where Daniel should go at the last, and to this question, which Piero had pondered for many days, he had, he believed, found the right answer . . . if only the necessary permission could now be obtained.

Piero left the Palazzo and went to a quay from which motor-boats plied for hire. It was beginning to rain, and there was only one boat waiting in the dusk. Piero gave his instructions. The driver gagged slightly and opened his mouth to refuse.

"Help me brother," Piero said, "for the love of God—and double the fare."

Piero stood by the driver as they drove slowly down the Grand Canal, more quickly along the Riva degli Schiavoni, and then slowly again as they turned left to cut through to the Fondamente Nuove; of which once clear, they sped past the island of San Michele (no, that was never for Daniel, Piero thought) and then skirted Murano. The rain was very heavy now and a strong wind blew from the East, but still Piero remained outside with the driver, not caring to sit in the comfortable cabin while the man who was serving him in his need must stand in the wet and the cold. They passed little islands, whose crumbling farm houses they could just make out in the darkness, they passed sand banks covered with low, creeping bush, they ran through dense, high beds of reed, and once they nearly struck an empty punt which was moored to one of the lantern-poles that marked their route. Then they turned off the marked route and edged carefully away to the right. After a time they approached a line of trees, which appeared, in the boat's headlight, to grow straight out of the water; but as they came close, the trees were seen to be growing from a low bank of mud, through which ran a gradually narrowing creek.

"We cannot go far up the creek," the driver said: "the tide is too low."

So Piero let himself down off the boat and struggled through mud and reeds, aided but little comforted by the headlight which the driver played ahead of him; and at last, wet through to the bone and cold to the marrow, plastered with stinking mud and throbbing with pain in his maimed leg, Piero came to wooden steps. He scrabbled his way up these and along a platform, and reached a door in a wall of stone. He pulled a bell rope.

"They must, they *shall*," he said between his chattering teeth as he waited.

At last the door opened. A large robed figure stood between Piero and a dully lit hall.

"Please bring me to Brother Hugh," Piero said.

"You may see only who is sent."

"Bring me to Brother Hugh," said Piero; "I have come here to him."

"What do you want with Brother Hugh?"

"I want . . . his intercession for a friend, that the Good Brothers of St Francis may receive him."

And now, overcome by pain and weariness and grief and chill frustration, Piero began to cry, in a fashion neither weak nor effete, but wild, savage and horrible.

"Hugh, Hugh, Hugh," he howled through his tears, "DANIEL IS DEAD."

As the last of his strength left him with his howls, he fell forward into the dark.

"You're late," said Detterling to Percival. "I expected you before dinner."

"Long day," said Percival; "one damn thing after another. Can you order me up a snack? Warm milk and digestive biscuits. That's about my mark these days."

A little later, when Percival was settled with his humble refection,

"Fielding Gray was most cooperative," he began. "Since *you* wished to know what was up, he said, he had no choice but to tell. I'm afraid, Detterling, I've got rather a surprise for you."

As he sipped his milk and nibbled a biscuit, Percival reported the facts which Fielding and Tom had discovered, just as Fielding had reported them to him that afternoon.

"I . . . don't quite understand," said Detterling unsteadily. "Can all this be proved?"

"With some difficulty and enormous expense . . . probably."

"But you say Fielding has no intention of making it public?"

"Fielding intends only to write a novel loosely based on the true story. No harm there. But others, I suppose, could take a more awkward line."

"Baby said the threat came from Fielding."

"Ultimately it does. I mean, even if he's not out to expose you, he was the chap who dug it all up."

Detterling went to the sideboard in his sitting-room and poured himself a quintuple whisky from a bottle labelled 'With the Compliments of the Management'.

"Who else knows?" he said after a long swallow.

"Tom Llewyllyn—who will do nothing, if Fielding is to be believed. And an Italian boy called Piero, property of one Lykiadopoulos. He might do anything, Fielding says, but should keep quiet if handled right."

"Jesus. I can't believe it, Leonard. It's just not possible. A potty boy of ten in a tiny village in the Veneto . . . *him* the real Marquess Canteloupe?"

"Some of the story is pretty shaky. But the bit about Lord Rollesden and his descendants by that Italian girl—that cetainly seemed to stand up."

"But whatever am I to do?"

"Nothing."

"I could have a word with Piero. The sooner the better. He seems to be the most likely to make trouble."

"You'll not be having a word with him just yet. He's gone."

"Gone?" said Detterling hopelessly.

"When I'd heard the full tale from Fielding, I went round to the Palazzo Albani to see Llewyllyn and Piero and get their line on it all." Percival paused, then said mildly: "Daniel Mond died this afternoon."

"But I was with him—"

"—And later on he died. Tom was off talking with doctors and policemen, I was told, and Piero had done a bunk. Then, just as I was leaving, a Franciscan Friar turned up. English, of all things—Brother Hugh, he called himself. He said he'd come from the Island of San Francisco del Deserto to tell Lykiadopoulos that the boy was there, suffering from exposure and concussion—he'd fallen down on arrival and hit his head on the offertory chest they keep just inside the door."

"What in God's name did Piero want with the Franciscans?"

"He wanted them to find room on their island for Daniel. He was raving about it, according to this Brother Hugh. When they promised him Daniel could come, he calmed down at bit, though they had to keep repeating the promise. They're rather afraid he may die on them."

The day of the funeral dawned with a low grey sky, a sharp north wind, and thin, spiteful rain. But at about ten o'clock the cloud rose, allowing a watery yellow sun to filter through, and the rain ceased.

Fielding Gray and Leonard Percival, both of whom disliked burials too much to attend this one, had nevertheless stationed themselves where they could see the procession pass, on a bridge just off the Canale della Misericordia. This was the bridge on which Daniel and Piero had first seen Brother Hugh, a stone's throw from the little plot in which Euphemia and Piero Albani lay buried. Fielding explained this latter curiosity to Percival, and then,

"Do you believe in ghosts, Leonard?" he said.

"No."

"Then where did Baby Llewyllyn's hunch come from— that I had discovered something which might injure Detterling? You *did* say that's what started your enquiry off?"

"Yes," said Percival. "I think Baby's instinct told her that your research might end up with something nasty."

"But why should she have guessed that the something nasty had to do with Detterling?"

"It seems she is very close to Detterling. When anything nasty is likely to turn up, one's first thought is, 'Will it affect me?', and one's second, 'Will it affect those I love?' From this it's a short step to an irrational fear that it will."

"But Baby's fear was amply justified. In slightly different circumstances, this information of mine could have been very dangerous to Detterling indeed. It might be even now. Baby was bang right."

"Pure chance," said Percival.

"At very long odds against."

"Anything that ever happens has very long odds against, if you think of all the other things that might have happened instead. If that bomb which got you in Cyprus all those years ago had been thrown a moment earlier or later, you might now be a corpse. Or you might have gone unwounded and become a poor general instead of a rich author. Or it might just have blown your balls off, in which case God knows what you'd have become. But it was thrown exactly when it was thrown, and things are as they are. One must accept everything, including Baby Llewyllyn's hunch, as having come about in the natural and logical continuation of prior events—any one of which might have been different, given a split second here or there, but wasn't. The most commonplace events are fantastically improbable," Percival said, "and the most improbable, if properly regarded, are entirely commonplace. Here he comes now."

Up the Canale della Misericordia came a tawdry, gilded barge. A black canopy was held aloft by barley-sugar shafts, and under it was a coffin draped with a Union Jack.

"Military Honours?" said Percival.

"Yes. We found he'd kept his badge—the one he wore when we hid him in my squadron. All these years he'd kept it, Leonard. He never let us down, though it cost him very dear later . . . as indeed you of all people must know.* Surely he qualified as an honorary soldier?"

"Then how to salute him as he passes, Fielding? No hats. . . ."

"Stand to attention, I think."

So Fielding and Percival stood to attention as Daniel went by, and then Fielding, absurdly, waved after him.

This was observed by Tom Llewyllyn, who was riding with Detterling, Max and Lykiadopoulos in the cabin of the first boat after the barge. Baby Llewyllyn (whom Detterling, somewhat to Tom's annoyance, had insisted should fly out for the funeral) was standing in the open at the rear of the boat, and waved to Fielding for Daniel. Lykiadopoulos nodded kindly approval of this little scene, then leaned forward and tapped Detterling on the knee.

"I need money, my friend," he said.

"Do you indeed? For your bank at the Casino?"

"No. My Baccarat Bank is now safe—"

"—How do you know?—"

"—Because the conditions are in my favour. But this bank will not bring in enough."

"Enough for what?"

"To keep things tidy in Corfu. There are difficulties there."

"There are difficulties everywhere."

"None of which cannot be solved by ready money."

"Good," said Detterling; "a simple solution."

*See *The Sabre Squadron*, passim.

"If the ready money is there," said Lykiadopoulos.

"And if it isn't?"

"In this case, it is. I want you, my good friend, my lord Canteloupe, to let me have half a million pounds."

"Out of what?"

"Out of what you have."

"Why should I?"

"Compassion. For my people will be thrown out of work if the money is not forthcoming."

"Including you?"

"*I* shall not be beggared," said Lykiadopoulos, quick to preserve face, "whatever happens."

"Then count yourself lucky and stop scrounging."

"I am not—scrounging. I have a basis for business."

"Ah. You are offering interest on this half-million pounds?"

"In a sense, yes, but not in money."

"Not very businesslike, Lykiadopoulos."

"Lord Canteloupe, can you find me half one million pounds?"

"Candidly, no."

"Then candidly . . . you will have to part with your new marquessdom. And the new estate that has come to you with it."

"Neither is saleable or transferable."

"You haven't understood me, my lord."

"Understand *what, Kyrie* Lykiadopoulo?"

"Either you pay me this money, or I tell the Heralds' College and your solicitors in London all I know about that boy in the marshes near Oriago."

The barge and the first attendant boat passed into the wide Sacca della Misericordia, heading for the lagoon.

In the second boat, Peter Morrison said to Lord Constable of Reculver Castle, Provost of Daniel's college:

"That's Fielding Gray up there on the bridge. Do you ever regret that you kept him out of Lancaster?"

"No. He was a shallow, treacherous boy."

Morrison, who did not know Daniel, had come to the funeral nominally to honour a faintly distinguished compatriot who had died far from home but in fact to give himself a trip round the islands and an excuse for spending twenty-four hours longer in Italy. He had concluded his business in Mestre, and had earned a brief period of holiday and celebration, for his terms had been accepted : the contract which he was so anxious to win for Britain would now go through as he had hoped—on condition that the British Government played its part, at the forthcomng international conference, in betraying Venice. And so Peter, who was pleased with himself this morning and expected (in this autumn of 1973) to have almost two more certain years of power and office ahead of him, did not want his agreeable mood to be spoiled by Constable's grating assessment (however accurate) of his old friend, Fielding. He therefore changed the subject :

"Tell me, Provost," he said to Lord Constable, "did the left-wing element in Lancaster make a fuss when you accepted your peerage?"

Jacquiz Helmutt and Balbo Blakeney listened from the other side of the cabin. As Fellows of Lancaster, they knew very well that Constable had done a deal with the left-wing element : there were to be no rows about his barony, provided he undertook to pardon and recall to the college, as soon as their prison sentences were done, the undergraduates who had been found guilty of robbing and desecrating the chapel. This being the case, Jacquiz and Balbo were very interested to hear how Constable would answer Morrison's question.

"There has been no fuss," Lord Constable now replied. "I made it quite plain that nobody, not even the college servants, need address me as 'my lord'."

Whether or not his audience might deem this explanation to be adequate, Lord Constable was clearly going to say no more on the topic. As a matter of fact, Balbo Blakeney reflected, most of the college servants did call the Provost 'my lord' and seemed very happy to do so. It made a change for them, Balbo supposed.

"I met Provost Constable once," said Percival to Fielding on the bridge. "Interesting man : an expert at transforming the plain into the devious. And now what have we here?"

The third boat contained Alfie Schroeder, the famous

columnist of the Billingsgate Press, who had been in
Venice to do his routine three-monthly article on the city's
decay and had heard of the funeral through an accidental
meeting with Tom Llewyllyn. Alfie, who had come a very
long way since his one and only encounter with Daniel in
1952, was following the coffin partly in a mood of humility,
as a journalist paying tribute to a scholar, and partly in one
of immense satisfaction, as a man whose professional
prestige had continuously mounted since that encounter in
1952 while Daniel's had done little but stagnate. Conscious
that this was an ungenerous and (if the gods were paying
attention) a perilous sentiment, Alfie tried to expel it from
his mind by speculating on the personalities of the three men
with whom he shared the cabin. Two of them, one fat and
one stringy, obviously were or had been soldiers : short hair,
the same regimental tie, well-pressed grey suits of indifferent
material and cut—all of this to Alfie spelt Warrant Officer.
The third man, however, was a mystery : a dapper man,
middle-aged yet smooth-faced, wearing highly polished
black leather slippers.

"Perhaps we should introduce ourselves," Alfie said.

"I know you," said one of the soldiers, the fat one :
"you're the journalist who came nosing round the squadron
in fifty-two, when we had Danny with us on the run."

"You broke my box Brownie," said Alfie, remembering
the grey afternoon and the rotting piles of bricks and the
sullen soldiers who were sweeping away rubble to make a
football pitch : "in Kassel."

"God, what a dump," said the second soldier.

"Not any more," said the dapper man in the polished
slippers. "Kassel is now rebuilt and very prosperous and
has been for years. This place . . . Venice . . . is the dump,"
he said, in a just detectible American accent. "I expect we
shall be doing away with Venice before very long."

"But there's this fund—" Alfie began.

"—Indeed there is," said the American, "if anyone can
find where the Italians have hidden it."

"What a funny little boat-load," said Percival to Fielding on the bridge. "That tittle-tattling Schroeder and the
two old muckers from your regiment. How did you dig them
up?"

"Through the Regimental Association. Tom Chead and Basil Bunce. I also tried to get hold of some of the officers who knew him."

"But none of them came, I see. A rotten lot, the officers in your regiment."

"Detterling came."

"Detterling's rich. Chead and Bunce have paid their fares out of Sergeant-Majors' pensions."

In fact Fielding had paid their fares, and put them up in the Gabrielli the previous night, but he let this pass.

"I see Earle Restarick's there," he said.

"Yes. *I* got hold of him, through Jermyn Street. We still have close contacts with the Yanks. It turned out that Restarick was working in Mestre. The wops there want to scrub out Venice, and the Yanks are helping with the dirty work—in return for future concessions."

The third and last boat passed on into the Sacca della Misericordia.

"Back to my book," said Fielding contentedly. "And you, Leonard?"

"Back to the Gritti, to wait for Detterling. Canteloupe, I suppose I'd better say. I don't think anyone's going to mess that up for him."

"Not me at any rate."

"He's going to make me his personal secretary. He reckons that he'll need someone like me about—just in case, Fielding."

"You're not giving up spying, Leonard? The Service won't be the same without your nose for turds."

"Jermyn Street and ulcers don't mix," Percival replied. "They'll be glad to be shot of me."

"And you of them?"

"It's time I settled. I'll miss it all." Leonard removed his wire-framed spectacles and wiped his red eyes with a grubby handkerchief. "Oh, I'll miss it, turds and all. But it's time I settled."

The two men turned to leave the bridge, then turned back to take a last look at the distant line of boats, as it veered slowly left and into the Laguna Morta.

In Lykiadopoulos's boat there had been silence ever since he had made his demand of Detterling. Only as they were passing San Michele did Detterling break that silence, quietly enquiring,

"Who told you about the boy in the marshes?"

"Piero," said Lykiadopoulos. "He is mine, you see."

"No one told me," said Max. "Tom said there was nothing I need know."

Max looked reproachfully at Tom Llewyllyn.

"Nor there was," said Tom. "What was it to you?"

"To *me* it is money," Lykiadopoulos persisted calmly.

"Blackmail," said Detterling.

"In a good cause. Like your Robin Hood. If I do not have this money, I shall have to close two-thirds of my hotels and there will be much misery on Corfu."

"I have no money for you, Lykiadopoulis. My new estate is tied up. The money I had before is not enough."

"If my affairs must come down," said Lykiadopoulos, "so must yours."

"That's mere spite," said Tom. "Especially as you've already told us that you personally will be safe." He shifted uneasily and took a small object from his pocket to fiddle with.

"Where did you get that?" said Max sharply.

"Piero found it and brought it over to amuse Daniel."

"I mean exactly what I say," said Lykiadopoulos to Detterling. "I know that somewhere you can find this money."

But Detterling hardly heard this. He was looking at the object in Tom's hand. What had Daniel said about the formula engraved on it? Friction and velocity. And the man in the Casino with Max had been . . . sucking . . . or mouthing . . . on something very similar.

"You're up to something in the Casino," Detterling said to Max, speaking on impulse, having no idea what if anything the accusation could mean. "I saw that man who was there with you the other day." He gestured at Tom's object. "He was using a thing like that. Put it to your lips, Tom. Blow."

He had no idea of where all this could lead, but he did know that both Max and Lykiadopoulos were disquieted.

"Go on, Tom. Blow," he said.

"No," said Max.

"Let him," said Lykiadopoulos. "What harm can he do here?"

Tom blew.

There was absolute silence while he did so—until, one second after he had begun, Baby Llewyllyn flung open the doors at the rear of the cabin. Her face was contorted.

"Did none of you feel it?" she cried. "What was it? That horrible jarring feeling."

The boat began to rock in the light wash made by the funeral barge ahead.

"Blow again, Tom," said Detterling.

Tom blew. Baby shuddered.

"Stop it," yelled Max at Tom. "You may upset the driver. He's already got too close to the hearse."

"So," said Tom; "I blow this thing, my daughter shivers with horror, and it upsets the judgement of the driver. What did you feel, Canteloupe?"

"A sort of pricking. I expect Baby is more sensitive than most of us. You remember what Daniel said, Tom? Something to do with velocity and friction."

Tom turned to Lykiadopoulos.

"You were always afraid that Daniel would find you out," Tom said. "I'm not quite sure *what* he found out, but since Canteloupe has seen an associate of yours using one of these things in the Casino, I fancy the directorate might care to investigate further."

"Only there will be no need," said Detterling. "We shall repay Lykiadopoulos's silence with our own. I shall continue to hold my title, and Lyki will continue with . . . whatever game he is playing in the Casino. Both of us undisgraced, and undisturbed by the other."

"Daniel Mond," said Lykiadopoulos in a soft, sick voice. He peered at the barge ahead. "I thought he was harmless once he was in his coffin."

"So he is. If *you* keep quiet, and *we* keep quiet. This trick of yours, Lyki . . . could it bring you in a profit?"

"It is a means of control, of influencing the players' nerves and thus their bets. If we take risks . . . if we make them bet high when we think they will lose . . . then it *could* bring profit."

"Enough to keep the hotels open," said Max. "We shall not try—shall we, Lyki?—to make enough to build more. Angela wouldn't like that."

"We shall need much luck even to make the bare minimum we need," said Lykiadopoulos, "the way things are now going on Corfu."

"But it could be done?" said Detterling.

"Yes."

"Then from one fraud to another," said Detterling, "let me wish you joy of it."

And now the procession had rounded Murano and was sailing straight ahead for San Francesco del Deserto. From the window of the friars' infirmary, Piero watched the boats as they approached. He was still too ill to go outside, the Brothers had told him, but they had arranged it all so that he could watch his friend complete his journey. Time and tide, he knew, were right : Daniel could come straight up the creek to the gate and need not flounder in the mud as Piero himself had done. Here he came now, under his Union Jack, while the Good Brothers stood to receive him. Four of them stepped forward, one of these being Brother Hugh, to bear him away; and after him followed those whom he had loved and some whom he had feared; those who had wounded and those who had cherished him.

Daniel's grave was near the caged bird sanctuary, under a tree which would bloom white next spring. Daniel would not see the blossom on this tree, but Piero would, for he too was to stay on the island with the Good Brothers. As he watched through the infirmary window, while Daniel's friends and enemies came forward one by one to scatter earth on Daniel, Piero considered the farewells that he must make after the burial was done. . . .

"Let me stay here, Lyki. Give some money to my family, and some to the Brothers, and then forget me."

"Why do you wish to stay?"

"All prostitutes must seek refuge from their trade in the end. It is better they do so before they are worn out. This will be my refuge . . . .

. . . . Your secret is safe here with me, Lord Canteloupe. I told it to Mr Lykiadopoulos, I admit, but I gather it is now safe with him too. So will you do one thing for me?"

"If I can."

"Give money, what you can afford, to Mr de Freville, so that he can make his restorations in Venice."

"I don't know . . . that it's worth it any more."

"Please, my lord. Do as Piero asks."

"If *you* ask, Tullia."

"Piero and I, we both ask.'

"Very well."

"Thank you, Lord Canteloupe. Thank you, Miss Baby. You will say goodbye to your father for me? He has never liked me, but he has tried hard not to show this. Take him my thanks."

"You know," said Baby to Detterling, as they walked from the infirmary to join the others by the boats , "I shouldn't mind if they did all find out and you were plain Captain Detterling again tomorrow. I think Miss Wentworth Rex at school would be rather sick—she only let me come out here because you asked—but I shouldn't mind one bit."

"I should. Keep it quiet, Baby, for my sake."

"I shall do whatever you wish, my lord, both now and later. You know that."

As Baby and Detterling came up to the landing stage, a curious thing occurred.

While Lord Constable of Reculver Castle, who had suddenly recognised Brother Hugh as the former Hugh Balliston of Lancaster, was reintroducing him, as it were, to Jacquiz Helmutt and Balbo Blakeney;

and while Tom Chead and Basil Bunce were talking of the brave days when Daniel had 'served' with them in the 10th Sabre Squadron;

and while Peter Morrison and Earle Restarick, having sensed what they had in common, were quietly discussing American plans for the erasure of Venice;

and while Max de Freville and Lykiadopoulos were planning the tactics which they would follow that evening in the Casino;

and while Alfie Schroeder of the Billingsgate Press was

asking Tom Llewyllyn about his plans for future books, hoping to get a free gobbet for his column;

while all this was going on :

a dark stain crept up the creek towards the landing stage, at first just a trickle of black, then spreading until it covered the entire width of the creek, coming fast and strong with the tide as more and more poured in behind it, lapping against the banks where the birds nested, lapping round the shining boats, finally coming right up to the steps of the landing stage and settling there, barely an inch below the bottom rung, silent, filthy and opaque.

And yet nobody noticed except Piero, who was staring down from the infirmary window and saw that the black stain was over all the lagoon, whichever way he turned his eyes.

THE HISTORY OF VINTAGE

The famous American publisher Alfred A. Knopf (1892–1984) founded Vintage Books in the United States in 1954 as a paperback home for the authors published by his company. Vintage was launched in the United Kingdom in 1990 and works independently from the American imprint although both are part of the international publishing group, Random House.

Vintage in the United Kingdom was initially created to publish paperback editions of books acquired by the prestigious hardback imprints in the Random House Group such as Jonathan Cape, Chatto & Windus, Hutchinson and later William Heinemann, Secker & Warburg and The Harvill Press. There are many Booker and Nobel Prize-winning authors on the Vintage list and the imprint publishes a huge variety of fiction and non-fiction. Over the years Vintage has expanded and the list now includes great authors of the past – who are published under the Vintage Classics imprint – as well as many of the most influential authors of the present.

For a full list of the books Vintage publishes, please visit our website
www.vintage-books.co.uk

For book details and other information about the classic authors we publish, please visit the Vintage Classics website
www.vintage-classics.info

www.vintage-classics.info